INTO THE MOONLIGHT

Enjoy the book

GBJerster

INTO THE MOONLIGHT

PART 1

G.S. FOSTER

Matador
Unit E2 Airfield Business Park,
Harrison Road, Market Harborough,
Leicestershire. LE16 7UL
Tel: 0116 2792299
Email: books@troubador.co.uk
Web: www.troubador.co.uk/matador
Twitter: @matadorbooks

ISBN 978 1803133 294

British Library Cataloguing in Publication Data.
A catalogue record for this book is available from the British Library.

Printed and bound by CPI Group (UK) Ltd, Croydon, CR0 4YY
Typeset in 11pt Minion Pro by Troubador Publishing Ltd, Leicester, UK

Matador is an imprint of Troubador Publishing Ltd

I would like to start dedicating this book,
with a famous saying:
"I have a dream," someone once said.
Well, I followed my dream, to write this book, one of a trilogy.
Motto: Never give up on your dreams, always keep
believing, even when others say you can't do it.
Also, without the support of my wife and children, none of
this would have been possible.

PROLOGUE

Paul Arnold and Sarah Waysmith, a couple who have been together around a year, live in a vibrant city called Barnwood, which has a population of around 250,000 people. She is a successful fashion designer, the owner of a global business; he is a company director of a financial company.

Sarah is a stunning thirty-three-year-old bisexual blonde woman whom Paul, thirty-four, met in a nightclub.

Everything appears to be perfect, but is it?

Beneath, there lies a secret in Sarah's past that Paul is unaware of, or so she thinks.

Things will eventually come to a head.

Things are about to turn sinister and dark.

There is something very dark about Paul's past, and things are about to happen that no-one was expecting...

MOONLIGHT

As the two lovers arrive home from the party, and after far too much to drink, he pulls Sarah close into him. She could feel the throbbing in his well-ironed trousers: he wanted her. He pawed at her silky green dress, with her breasts bulging out of it, breathing heavily, as if she had just run for miles.

She quivered and trembled, as she could feel the passion of wanting him inside her. The moistness between her legs; she was getting wetter and wetter; her nipples were hardening with anticipation.

He unzipped her dress from behind, slowly kissing her neck and nibbling her earlobes. She felt his hardening cock; she wanted him deep inside her. As the dress fell to the floor, her long, slender legs glistening in the moonlight shining through the window, her huge breasts were on show for all to see.

He unclipped her bra and her heaving breasts slid out majestically.

He cupped them in his hands, and, coming from behind her to face her, sweetly kissed them, swirling his dripping tongue around her now-erect nipples.

He sucked on each one, hardening them even more, as she gasped with pleasure. Her breathing became deeper, and she moaned louder, thrusting his head harder onto her waiting breast.

He sucked on them like he never had before, as if he was not wanting to come up for air.

As she pulled him up, her breasts now soaked with his saliva, she kissed him passionately, their tongues swirling together, almost becoming stuck like glue.

His cock was throbbing. She undid the belt on his trousers, slowly pulling his zip down; she proceeded to fondle his cock gently and cup his balls.

He unbuttoned his shirt and frantically pulled it out of his trousers, to reveal a perfectly toned, yet sweaty chest, droplets coming from his nipples like he had been out in the rain.

She unclipped his trousers and they fell gently to the floor, his bulging cock pulsing in his stylish underwear. It's a hive of activity; she wanted to feel it racing in her mouth.

She pulled his underwear down slowly, revealing his large, throbbing cock and full clean-shaved balls. She wanted him to explode his juices in her waiting mouth, but she also wanted to feel the explosion in her dripping wet pussy.

Could she have both? Would the feeling and intensity feel the same?

She felt him throbbing as she took his cock in her hand.

As she elegantly dropped to her knees, she slid her moist lips, still caked in lipstick, onto his waiting shaft, sliding it further and further into her widening mouth. It rolled around on her tongue and she gently caressed his balls with her left hand, making sure that she was guiding his huge cock into her mouth with the other hand.

Further into her mouth it went, as he let out a groan of pleasure. His legs started to tremble as he felt his juices rising up his huge shaft, but he wanted to explode his pleasure in her pussy.

She sucked harder on his throbbing cock; he didn't know how much longer he could hold off before he exploded in her mouth. She was getting wetter and wetter, just her panties holding her juices in, as she slid her hand inside her underwear to feel how wet she actually was.

"I MUST have him," she thought.

They glided across the floor to the bedroom, like two elegant ballroom dancers. As she slowly and seductively pulled her panties down, they quickly dropped to the floor.

He caressed her buttocks as she strode seductively in front of him, gently brushing his hand with her fingertips, before they entered the bedroom.

As they both gently laid on the bed, she saw the wanting of her, in his eyes and body. She felt him sliding up her body to her heaving breasts; she was breathing so heavily, after only just sucking so hard on his cock.

He began to suck again on her hard yet moist nipples, one by one; they were as red as strawberries. He sucked them so hard, even though he had already made them erect.

He flicked each one in turn with his tongue as she let out an almighty groan.

He gently slid his sweat-soaked body down hers, his tongue gliding down her sweaty body to her navel.

He swirled his tongue around it, and, as her legs slowly parted, her pussy was dripping wet, just waiting for his tongue to lap it up.

Her clit was out in anticipation, popped out, as if to see what was going on, but it was just waiting to be sucked.

She pushed his head towards her waiting hole, as he started to flick his tongue on her moist clit. He circled it, making her wetter still; was it even possible to be wetter than she already was?

She groaned with pleasure. He dived in again and sucked on her some more, like sucking on a straw, getting that last drop of juice from a glass.

Now he had all of her clit in his mouth, sucking it harder and harder. She let out a scream of pleasure, a scream that felt like it could be heard for miles around.

She didn't want him to stop, yet she also wanted to feel his throbbing cock inside her.

He carried on sucking her now-tender hole, before he started sliding his tongue in and out of her, exploring every part of it, like he never had before, but she could take no more: she wanted him inside her NOW.

He pulled her down to the edge of the bed, as he thrust his rock-hard erection deep inside her.

He thrust hard the first time, then slower movements, allowing her to catch her breath. He thrust hard again, and was so deep inside her, his balls slapping on her pert buttocks, as they both let out a groan of pleasure.

Her juices were dripping on the dark wooden flooring, as she grabbed hold of the bedsheets, as if her life depended on it, not wanting to let go, their sweaty bodies adding to her moistness on the floor.

He was trying to grip hard on the floor with his feet, so he can thrust harder inside her, but he keeps losing his grip, but he doesn't care, he is caught up in the passion.

He grabbed her breasts, so she could feel the fullness of him inside of her. She lifted up her left leg and pulled her knee up to her breasts, so he could push deeper inside her.

Harder and harder he went. The bed was creaking hard, the headboard banging on the wall, making dents, but they didn't care; the fucking was just way too good.

"Oh baby, I'm going to cum," he said, almost struggling to hold back.

"Don't cum yet, I want you to fuck me for hours," she demanded, almost instructing him to obey her.

He pulled her up from the bed and took her back into the lounge, where it all started. The moonlight was still shining brightly through the window, almost like a spotlight on the passionate couple, giving them lots of light to see what to do with each other.

As he pushed her against the wall, and she pulled him towards her, he nestled in between her legs, and, pulling her knee up, as he had done on the bed, slid his dripping cock back deep inside her.

They both ground against the wall, pulsating faster and faster; she could almost feel that he wasn't going to last much longer before he exploded inside her.

He kissed and sucked on her breasts again as he went.

Her legs were trembling, as she felt that her juices were about to explode all over his throbbing penis.

The feeling of him inside her was making her feel so alive, so fresh, she never wanted the feeling to end.

Her breath quickened and then, letting out the biggest

squeal, her juices exploded all over his shaft and down to his full balls.

He quickened his pace, as he felt her juices on him; he can hold back no more, and he exploded his juices deep inside her, filling every inch of her, leaving her fulfilled with the utmost ecstasy.

Their sweat-drenched bodies collapsed in a heap on the wet floor, as they tried desperately to catch their breaths. She curled up in his arms, finding it hard to put into words the feeling she had running through her mind and body.

He was also feeling the same, wanting more of her, not just sexually but also the togetherness he was feeling at that moment.

"Surely things cannot be this good forever, can they?" he thought.

They lay in each other's arms for what felt like an eternity. It was the early hours of the morning, and the day would soon be breaking, as the moon was slowly disappearing into the morning sky.

They both gingerly got up from the floor; they'd both summoned up the energy to do so and, despite it being how warm it had been lately, they were both starting to shiver in the morning coldness of daybreak.

"We must get a little bit of sleep," she said to him in a tired voice. "I'm not sure I can keep pace with your energy." She smiled.

He nodded and chuckled in agreement. They wandered back into the bedroom, remembering what exhausting, passionate sex they had just had.

They pulled their perfectly creased satin sheets back on their king-size bed. They didn't care how wet and stained the sheets might be with their bodily fluids; they were both just so tired, and the sheets could be cleaned later, they thought.

Once in bed, he lifted his arm up to invite her to come in closer to him and give her the sense of protection from the world, to make her feel safe and feel loved.

She gently lay her head on his muscular chest as she felt herself drifting off, so she could start to dream.

They were still both tingling with sexual energy and emotion as they closed their eyes and awaited a brand-new day, to see what adventures they had in store for them.

ENCOUNTER

The couple awoke hours later, and Paul decided to take a shower. Sarah got up too, took her laptop with her, and, partially dressed in a shirt that she had just grabbed from his wardrobe, went into the lounge and sat on the sofa. Being a warm morning, from having a hot night, Sarah fantasised about the passionate sex from the night before.

She could not get over the passion and energy he'd given her last night, and she felt hungry for more.

Though Sarah, having a bisexual side, decides to search for some lesbian porn, still feeling horny.

She found some porn that she had watched years previously, and started to touch herself.

It seemed like ages since she had been on the sofa, caressing areas of her body that Paul had explored earlier.

She began to once again feel very wet while watching the porn, and, as her pussy was about to explode with her juices again, Paul walked in from his shower, with just a towel covering his ripped, muscular body and clean-shaved chest, with his hair still dripping wet.

"Why are you watching that? Was I not enough for you last night?" he said, with a jokey yet puzzled tone in his voice.

"I was still feeling horny." Sarah smiled, with a seductiveness in her voice. "Want to watch it with me, and we can carry on where we left off?" she said, waiting for Paul's reaction.

She could see a fresh bulge in Paul's thick green towel, clearly aroused by his partner watching women having sex with each other.

He walked over to Sarah and, with the floor dripping wet, he straddled her, the towel clinging to every inch of his masculine body.

She put the laptop, still open and with the porn still playing, on the floor, the dampness of his hair dripping on the fresh-smelling shirt on Sarah's beautiful body, wetting it so much that her huge breasts become visible through it.

Sarah slowly pulled the towel down, off Paul's waist, to reveal his perfectly toned arse and stiff cock.

He seductively kissed Sarah's neck and, almost in an instant, as Sarah put one foot on the floor to open her legs, his cock gently slid into Sarah's wet pussy, as the porn carried on playing in the background.

Sarah could once again feel her toned man throbbing inside her. He fought to undo the shirt buttons on the shirt of his that Sarah was wearing, but he decided to rip it open anyway. He was yearning to devour her body; he simply could not resist her.

He frantically kissed her neck and nibbled on her ears.

Sarah was sighing with pleasure. She had never felt passion the way she felt it with him; none of her previous lovers had given her as much pleasure as this.

She was loving the attention that Paul was giving her; she could not get enough of him.

It was like something out of a porn movie, except both Sarah's and Paul's passions were real.

She wanted to cum all over her man, while Paul was just wanting to go deeper into her dripping wet pussy, his full balls slapping on her perfect arse.

Sarah was almost fighting to catch her breath; the passion was so intense.

"Ah, baby, I'm going to cum," squealed Sarah, as Paul built up momentum, and, in the blink of an eye, they both tensed up, and Paul burst inside her, as her own juices flowed out of her.

"I should watch lesbian porn more often in the morning," Sarah joked to Paul.

"Maybe I should have got out the shower sooner," replied Paul, with a chuckle in his voice.

After a slight rest, the pair decided to get dressed and make the most of the day; after all, it was a warm day, it was a Saturday, and Paul wanted to go and spend some time in the sun, especially as neither of them had to work today, and Paul wanted to take a look round the city, browse some shops, see what home improvements they could make.

He put on a favourite light-blue shirt of his, cream linen trousers and slip-on flat shoes.

He looked like something out of a fashion catalogue with his look.

Sarah, looking equally fashionable, as of course she would, due to her profession, decided to wear a silky short white skirt that showed off her long, slender legs, red polo-necked top and a thick black belt, covering her perfect waist.

She also put on some flat shoes, so her feet didn't get too warm.

After applying her make-up and spraying her favourite Chanel perfume, Sarah too was ready to venture out. She looked a million dollars, her flowing long blonde curly hair flowing halfway down her back.

"You look FANTASTIC, Sarah," Paul gushed.

"You look pretty sexy yourself, Paul," she replied sweetly. "Oh, meant to tell you. I'm going to go out with the girls tonight; will you be ok while I'm out?"

"Work colleagues, you mean?" he asked.

"No, my girlfriends, won't be home late, not seen them in a while."

"I'll be all home alone, I'm sure I'll find something to occupy myself with; you go and enjoy yourself," he replied.

Sarah had a close group of friends: Charlie, who was a married mother of two girls; Harriet, who had been dating for a couple of years; Amber, who was single but on the lookout for a nice man; Zoe, who was also married but had no children; and Constance, who was also married, with one boy, and who always appeared to be the one to go to if any of the needed advice, but Charlie was the one who Sarah had a closer friendship with.

All the girls were all around the same age, and had all been together when Sarah and Paul met at the nightclub, but were not overly keen on him, as they felt that he'd pulled her away from them.

As the couple left the house, Paul locked up, took Sarah by the hand and strolled down the street. There were lots of happy people out and about, enjoying the sunshine, lots of couples holding hands, including two handsome gay men, walking towards them.

"Lovely day, isn't it?" said one of the gay men, with a big smile on his face, as they walked past Paul and Sarah.

"Certainly is," replied Paul, not quite knowing whether the gay couple had heard him, as they appeared to be so wrapped up in each other.

"Have you ever thought about fucking another guy, Paul? I mean, surely you've thought about it."

"Growing up I messed about with mates," he said, nervously, not quite sure how to answer the question. "It's what you did growing up, isn't it? But no, why would I, when I have you?"

As they carried on walking down the street, there were lots of families out with their children, the children with excitement in their voices. The sun was shining and they were happy to feel warm, excited about being out with their families. Paul looked across the street and noticed an attractive lesbian couple, walking hand in hand, sharing a kiss.

"Look over there, then, Sarah, right up your street, those two." He waited to see how Sarah would respond. "Would you fuck one of those?"

"What do you mean one?" She laughed. "I'd want to fuck them both, at the same time," she whispered, being wary of families and children around.

Neither she nor Paul had any children, though there had been occasions in their past when they had both thought about having a family.

Sarah smiled at Paul and, catching him glancing in a few shop windows as they walked by, Sarah could not help but wonder what it would be like to be have fun with the beautiful lesbian girls that they had just seen.

It started to make her think about the lesbian porn she had been watching earlier, and she wondered if maybe she could run over to the two girls and ask if they'd like to be in an amateur lesbian porn movie with her.

Sarah's mind was wandering, but she had Paul, who fucked her pussy so good, made her cum so hard.

'Yes, I like girls too,' she thought, 'but I have Paul, and he meets all my needs. I do love to fuck a good pussy, love the taste of another woman, but I'm enjoying Paul's hard cock too much and BOY, does he get hard quick.'

"Are you ok, Sarah? You seem to be in a world of your own. Have those two lesbian girls turned your head?" He was unaware of the thoughts she had just had running through her head, especially as one of the girls had particularly caught Sarah's eye.

"Don't be silly." She laughed. "I'm just enjoying the moment with you," she replied.

"Isn't that how you want me to be?"

They continued walking down the street, Paul pointing at things in windows that he liked the look of, that he thought would go lovely in the house, and Sarah was just agreeing, but she could not help her mind wander to the two sexy lesbian girls she had clasped her eyes on moments earlier.

"Can we stop for a coffee, Paul? I'm parched," said a weary Sarah. She felt like she had been walking for hours, and shopping wasn't her favourite pastime.

"Yeah, of course we can. Carl's Café is here," said Paul. "We'll stop for a drink here."

The café was busy, lots of families with their weary children, the children eating ice cream and having their soft drinks, and lots of bustling assistants, clearing tables and helping customers with their orders.

"Will you go and order, Sarah?" He appeared to be in a hurry to go somewhere. "I'll just have a coffee and maybe some cake. I'm just popping to the toilet; I won't be long," he called across the bustling crowd.

Sarah went up to the service till, and there stood one of the beautiful girls she'd seen earlier.

Sarah's heart started to race.

The girl was tall, about six foot tall, leggy with long curly blonde, shiny hair, almost gloss like. The girl was wearing a short black skirt and a low-cut pink blouse, with huge breasts. The girl, waiting in front of Sarah, dropped the ten-pound note she had been holding to pay for her and her girlfriend's order.

Sarah bent down with the girl at the same time to pick it up, Sarah's eyes locking onto the girl's bulging chest. The girls' eyes met, the girl giving Sarah a momentary glance and a smile.

Sarah wanted Paul to take an eternity in the men's toilets, as she was having far too much fun and so much to feast her eyes on. As Sarah and the girl started to stand up, smelling just how good the girl smelt, Sarah was hoping that the leggy lesbian girl would notice her now-erect nipples on her own ample chest.

"Thank you for getting that for me." The girl smiled. "It was very kind of you."

Sarah and the girl's eyes met once again momentarily, and, with a sweet smile to Sarah, the girl paid for her order and took her tray to sit down with her girlfriend, who was just giving Sarah a stare of slight anger and jealousy. Just then, Paul reappeared from the bathroom.

"Have you managed to order yet, Sarah?" he asked.

"I'm next." She hoped that her nipples were less erect.

Paul didn't notice the girlfriends sitting in the café, and he managed to find a spare table by the door.

Sarah ordered Paul a milky latte, his favourite drink, and a Belgian bun to eat, also a favourite of his. Sarah, in full view of the two lesbian girls, ordered a hot chocolate and a warm scone, and waited for it to be prepared. While she waited, she turned round to see the two girls holding hands and laughing together. She was hoping to get the attention of the leggy beauty that she had stood next to moments earlier.

'I would just love to get my tongue in her pussy, and fuck her too,' she thought, her nipples starting to become erect again.

She was starting to get very wet, but she'd not felt this way about another woman for some time, but she could feel a moistness in her knickers.

The tall, leggy lesbian girl who Sarah was attracted to, glanced across at Sarah briefly, allowing herself a genuine smile, and a small wave, as if to thank Sarah once again for picking the money up at the till earlier, but it was all Sarah's pleasure; she just wished that the café was empty, just her and this beauty whom she almost couldn't take her eyes off, so Sarah could get the girl up on the counter, pull the blinds in the café down, lift the girls skirt up, pull her knickers to one side, and bury her tongue deep into her pussy and caress her tits too, squirting her juices into Sarah's waiting mouth.

Sarah, coming back to reality, got the order for her and Paul, and sat down at the table by the door that he had found moments before.

Paul started chatting to Sarah, but she was in another world, thinking about work, her life and incredible sex life, the girl and the things that could lie in store for her.

"Have you been listening to a word I have been saying, Sarah? You appear to be miles away; are you ok?" He was slightly worried about her, squeezing her arm in a loving and gentle way.

"Yes, I'm ok," she said, to reassure him. "I've just got so many things happening. Work is stressful, as you know, and Mum and Dad aren't in the best of health; they worry me a lot too."

"We can go and see them anytime you want to, you know? I enjoy seeing them too," he said, in a show of support.

"I know, they like you too, especially my dad, thinks the world of you, always has," said Sarah lovingly.

"Then we'll make a special trip to see them next weekend then, and I'll have a beer with your dad."

Sarah couldn't help but keep looking across at the two girls, sitting a few tables away, dirty thoughts still running through her mind.

Just then, the two girls got up from their table to leave, having finished what they had. They both walked over to the serving area, and thanked the staff for their order, and started heading towards the door. The girl who Sarah was particularly keen on glanced over to Sarah, and their eyes once again locked. She flashed Sarah a smile; her teeth were bright white, and the sun coming through the window appeared to glisten on them.

Sarah could not take her eyes off her perfect body and long legs.

"Oh my God, what a body," Sarah thought, with thoughts of fucking her again running through her mind. "If only," she dreamt.

Paul was starting to tell Sarah of the plans he had for the house, waiting for Sarah's approval, but her eyes were still fixed on the beauty still going out the café door.

"Yes, yes, whatever you say, Paul." She did not want to be distracted with what she was really thinking.

"Let's finish our drinks, and let us go for a walk, Sarah, shall we? After all, the sun is shining, and I want to catch some rays." Like a big kid, as if he had not seen the sun in such a long time.

"Good idea," said Sarah, hoping that she might get a glimpse of the sexy lesbian girl again. She was becoming almost obsessed with her, but Barnwood was such a big city, so many people, so it might be difficult to see her again.

'I've not seen her around before,' she thought. 'Maybe they're not even from round here.' She sighed to herself.

Paul and Sarah headed out of the door, while the sun was still shining, and it was still so warm. Both had brought their sunglasses with them, and they put them on. Paul took Sarah by the hand and walked on the roadside edge of the pavement, again, to shield Sarah from oncoming traffic. Barnwood was such a busy city, lots of vehicles. As they strolled down the street, there were still lots of happy children out, carrying ice creams and cold drinks, to keep them cool.

Sarah noticed lots of scantily clad girls walking around, and she seemed to notice so many not wearing bras. Sarah was a very highly sexed woman, but she was with Paul, and only had eyes for him – well, she had until she saw this girl who she could not get out of her head.

They were enjoying the warmth of the sun hitting their faces and bodies. Paul was still browsing the shop windows for home improvements, while Sarah's mind just wandered, thinking about how perfect things were for her; after all, she had a successful fashion business that was doing well in both the UK and abroad; she was also working on new fashion designs, and also might be looking to expand and take on more staff.

Paul, on the other hand, was more of a stressed man, with his employers giving him constant targets to meet, and pressure from his bosses to meet them. Sarah was paying particular attention to the sexy girls, who were wearing next to nothing, and this was starting to make her feel horny, especially the busty girls, as this is what she preferred in a woman.

"Let's go home, Paul," she mumbled. "I'm in the mood for you."

"In a while. I want to go and take a look at a nice rug I spotted for our bedroom that I saw," he said, feeling excited. Probably also thinking about the extra grip it would give him when he fucked Sarah standing up again.

She decided to go to the shop with Paul, to take a look at some of the rugs.

They walked into the shop. It was very large, smelling fresh and new, carpets and rugs everywhere, with lots of people mingling, looking at various carpets. There were shop staff walking around, looking smart in their navy-blue suits, asking customers if their help was needed in any way.

"What about this one, Sarah?" he said, with a keenness in his voice. He was looking at a thick, grey rug, about four feet by two, with gold sparkles.

"Sorry?" Sarah said blankly, almost totally disinterested.

"This one," he stated again.

Suddenly, Sarah spotted a familiar person, among the crowd of people in the shop. It was the sexy lesbian girl she had spoken to in the café.

Suddenly, Sarah perked up, probably wishing she could have her on a rug, licking each other out.

'I MUST go and talk to that girl, if only to find out her name, find out more about her. Hopefully her girlfriend isn't here,' she wished, but, unfortunately for Sarah, her girlfriend had just gone to speak to the shop assistant about a carpet they had both shown interest in.

In a flash, the lesbian girls were back together, and Sarah had missed her chance, after having agreed to purchase a carpet they liked and had just paid for.

The couple were just about to head towards the door. Sarah found an excuse to seem like she was browsing near the exit door.

"Oh, hello again," a nervous Sarah said. "Fancy seeing you both in here. I promise I'm not stalking you," she joked, with a slight chuckle in her voice. "Found anything you like?" Sarah fantasised that the girl she had picked up the money for in the café, and the one she particularly fancied, would say, 'Yes… YOU.'

"We've just paid for one," said the girl who Sarah liked. "We've just bought a new house, have just moved here from Anderson, and we're just buying bits for it; it's a work-in-progress house," the girl joked, with a smile and laugh.

The girl's smile and laugh melted Sarah's heart even more for her.

Anderson was a stone's throw away from Barnwood, a small town.

"That's nice." Sarah smiled. "Maybe I'll be seeing you around a lot more then," though only wishing she would only see the girl who had turned her on in the café.

The couple once again started heading towards the door, Sarah not able to take her eyes off the girl's shapely body and amazing long legs, once again fantasising about fucking her with her strap-on, and licking her out.

"I didn't catch your names," Sarah called.

"I'm Alice," said the girl who Sarah fancied, and "I'm Stacey," the other girl called back, probably realising that Sarah only had eyes for her girlfriend.

Alice looked back at Sarah, with a sexy wave and a flash of her bright white smile, while Stacey looked a bit disgruntled with the unwanted glances that Sarah was giving her girlfriend.

Paul continued to look at other rugs in the shop, but he really liked the grey gold-speckled thick rug he had seen.

"I've had a look round, and I keep coming back to the grey one. What do you think, Sarah?"

But she was in another world, fantasising about sex with Alice, and she couldn't stop thinking about it.

"If that's the one you like, Paul, then… then… let's get that one," she muttered.

Paul went over to the service till to pay for it, and asked if he could also pay the delivery fee on his card, for it to be delivered later that day.

The rug was ninety pounds, with an extra ten pounds for delivery. Paul paid for the rug and delivery charge, and arranged a delivery slot.

Time was ticking on. It was four in the afternoon, and they had been in the shop for about an hour, and Sarah was getting sick of the sight of rugs and carpets.

"Let's head home, Paul, I'm getting tired."

"I was about to suggest the same thing, Sarah. Think we've had enough rug excitement for one day," he joked.

The couple left the shop and started to stroll home. Sarah was hoping that she'd see Alice again on the way, even if she was with her girlfriend, Stacey. Paul and Sarah didn't live too far from the main centre of Barnwood, and were home in the blink of an eye.

"My feet are killing me, Paul, I'm going to go for a soak in the bath."

"Ok. I'll rustle us up something to eat, a stir-fry, perhaps? Pour you a nice glass of wine too."

She looked back at him with a tired smile, as she headed towards the bathroom. The bathroom was huge, painted sky blue, with quaint little pictures on the wall, a big walk-in double shower, bidet and roll-top bath.

She turned on the gold-coloured taps, poured some crème bath liquid in, and as the bath slowly started to fill she started to wearily get undressed. As she removed her top and undid her bra, her huge breasts fell out, and she started to slowly caress them, and slowly pulled her green skirt down, to reveal her lacy underwear, she put her hand down the front to caress her pussy, fantasising that Alice's hand was touching her instead.

"Everything ok in there?"

"Yes, I'm just about to get in." Just wanting some 'her' time.

She was suddenly naked, and about to step into the now-full, nearly overflowing bath.

'Ah, that feels better,' she thought, as she slipped elegantly in, the water going gently over her curvaceous body, wishing that a certain woman would join her.

Sarah started to fantasise about Alice again, fucking her; as she did, she started to caress herself, sliding her fingers into her pussy, while cupping her breasts with her other hand.

She loved to masturbate, and she had someone else, as well as Paul, to fantasise over now.

She finished her bath and emptied the water. She wrapped the towel around her dripping wet body, and walked into the lounge, near to the very large kitchen where Paul was dishing up the delicious-smelling stir-fry. The house was open plan, one of the things that attracted Paul to it. Its lay-out was perfect; he liked that style.

"That smells delicious, Paul, looking forward to eating that, then eating you." She looked up at Paul in a seductive and sexy way, with a slight smile on her face, as if to invite him in.

He liked the sound of that.

Sarah strolled elegantly towards the bedroom, to get a robe out of her walk-in wardrobe. She wanted to put one on before dinner. The robe was a thick, light-grey robe, that she didn't wear very often, didn't even realise she still had it.

Sarah also had a towel wrapped around her head, to stop her hair from dripping.

She then walked back into the lounge, and towards the seating area. The lounge was big enough to have in the middle a large six-seater thick pine table that could be extended if needed, if they had any guests.

Sarah sat down at the table, her breasts peeking through her robe, sitting in such a way as to tease Paul.

Paul brought the food over to her, as he also sat down to eat.

"This stir-fry is delicious, Paul, but not quite as delicious as your meat in my mouth," she teased again, raising her eyebrows to him, hoping it might turn him on.

Sarah was still feeling horny after her fantasises about Alice.

She sat slightly away from the table, purposely, allowing her to open her legs towards Paul, so he could see her moist pussy.

She put her cutlery down and loosened her robe a little more, as if still feeling hot from her bath.

Paul's eyes reverted from his delicious meal to her sexy body. She started to caress her inner thigh and she glanced up at him as she did it, giving him a seductive smile, and again, raising her eyebrows towards him, wondering how long it would take him to wander over in her direction.

She started to see a bulge in his trousers and they both stood up and away from the table, not having eaten much; they had something more physical in mind.

She walked over to him seductively, like an elegant peacock, and did not take her eyes off him, giving him a sexy look all the way to him, letting him know just what she has in mind for them both.

But he DID know, as he had the same thoughts running through his mind.

As Sarah's and Paul's bodies met, her hands could only start exploring his masculine body.

She gently started to unbutton his shirt, and slid her left hand onto Paul's heaving chest and nipple.

His erection was getting larger, and she could feel it throbbing on her robe.

Sarah opened her robe a bit more, so she could feel his intensity between her legs.

Paul could take no more, as Sarah's right hand slid down to his large erection.

"Maybe you need to do something with that," she whispered into Paul's ear.

She started to caress her pussy, wanting to feel if she was still wet.

Paul was getting so turned on. He started to kiss Sarah gently around her neck, and bulging breasts, pulling her robe open to lick her nipples.

Just then the doorbell rang; the couple had forgotten about the delivery of the rug.

Sarah covered up.

"Just a second," Paul shouted towards the door, as he raced to grab a T-shirt from his bedroom drawers.

He opened the door wide to see a strapping man standing there, with the rug that the couple had purchased from the shop earlier. Sarah, watching on a few feet away, her arms crossed to keep her robe intact, not baring all for the stranger at the door to see, started to recollect being in the shop, and seeing Alice.

Sarah had a smile to herself.

Paul took the rug from the man – his erection thankfully having gone down sufficiently, though not completely – thanked the man, before closing the door.

He then took the wrapped rug into the bedroom, and laid it by his side of the bed to sort later.

"Now, where were we?" he said, wanting to hurry back to their previous activity.

Paul started to open her robe again, her breasts waiting for his attention.

His erection again started to grow and, as she had before, she started to fondle him through his trousers.

He started to kiss Sarah passionately, slowly working his way down her neck, licking and sucking it, making sure he had covered every inch, before he moved down to her now-erect nipples.

He loved Sarah's breasts, and he started to suck on her right one, before he moved over to her left. Sarah started to moan with pleasure; her pussy was starting to get very wet.

He removed the white T-shirt he had grabbed to answer the door to the man; his muscly chest and arms were a big turn-on for her.

She seductively kissed his chest and licked his nipples. Paul loved her doing this, just as much as Sarah loved doing it, to see the ecstasy in his face.

Paul's nipples were soon erect too, as Sarah brushed her nipples across his, sliding them left and right, as if she were wanting to make them harder.

Sarah's hand then lowered down towards Paul's now-erect cock; it was throbbing so hard.

Sarah wanted to suck him, as she knew just how much he loved it.

She unbuttoned his trousers, slid her robe off gently, to reveal her beautiful, almost hourglass-like figure, got down on her knees in front of him, and pulled his trousers down, making sure that his stylish Calvin Klein underwear stayed up.

Paul then stepped out of his trousers. Sarah wanted to tease Paul, and started to caress him through his underwear.

"You need to pull them down before I cum," he said sexily.

Sarah did as he had asked, and pulled them down to reveal his massive shaft, one that gave her so much pleasure.

She took him gently into her mouth and opened her mouth wide, before sliding more and more of his cock in, gently gliding her mouth forwards and backwards onto him, with slow movements.

His pace of breathing got faster and faster, and he wasn't sure that he was going to last much longer.

Sarah was so good at oral sex. Suddenly, he pulled away, picking her up, like a warrior carrying his queen, and took her into the bedroom.

He wanted to get some of her pussy too, so he laid her down into a position where they could go head to toe and suck each other at the same time, pleasuring each other.

Deeper into her pussy his tongue went, exploring every inch of her, swirling his tongue around her waiting clit.

He then slid his tongue deep inside her, like feeling the taste of ice cream on it.

As he did this, her legs started to shake; she let out a little cry of ecstasy, as did he, as she was swirling her tongue around his stiff shaft, feeling the intensity of his throbbing cock.

She teased it again, not wanting to let Paul go of his sexual highs, swirling her tongue around the tip, before pulling him, throbbing, into her mouth.

Up and down onto his shaft she went, first slowly, then fast. She could feel his juices rising, as were hers, and she thought that he was going to explode into her mouth.

Paul's legs also started to shake with ecstasy, and he knew that he was about to explode. He sucked her clit harder and harder, as she let out little groans of pleasure; she too sensed she would cum.

Suddenly, he let out a groan and spurted into her mouth, then, almost in an instant, she too climaxed, a sudden release of sexual emotion colliding into each other's.

She didn't think she was going to stop cumming, and neither did Paul.

As their bodies came to a shuddering halt, they both lay still, almost motionless in the same position.

They stayed like that for a few minutes, to draw breath, before they wrapped their arms around each other's thighs. They lay still, happy with the energy and passion they had just given each other.

Paul then sat up, pulled the bedsheets back, and invited Sarah to come and lie beside him.

"I love you, Paul." She waited for Paul's response.

"I love that you do, Sarah, I really do, but I'm just enjoying the moments that we share. I'm not saying that I don't, but you're more expressive that way, aren't you? Always have been. Love is such a strong, emotional word, isn't it?" he added. "I still think we are getting to know each other, and I don't want to ruin the great things we have going on."

"What, like buying rugs?" groaned Sarah, with a slight annoyance in her voice, thinking that Paul cared more about the house than her.

"No, of course not, don't be silly, it's just, you're happy, I'm happy, and I don't want to ruin things. Everything is great as it is, isn't it?" he said nervously.

After catching their breaths, Sarah started to think about getting ready, to go out with the girls.

"What time are you planning on going out? It's already six."

"I wanted you first, before I went out; now I've had you, it's time to go and get ready."

Paul watched as she got up from the bed, her perfect body in full view of him, and he watched her go over to the walk-in wardrobe.

"What are you planning on wearing?"

"Don't know. Maybe this little black number, what do you think?"

She showed him a tight-fitting black sequined dress that she had worn the night they met.

"Hmm… I remember that VERY WELL," he reminisced.

"Then this black one it is."

Paul loved to watch Sarah get dressed. Despite their lovemaking just now, and watching her slowly put her stockings on, followed by the dress, she was starting to make him feel horny again.

Paul sat up quickly, and pulled his naked body over to the front of the bed, where she was sitting.

"MAYBE you should come back to bed instead, get all sweaty again."

"As much as that sounds like a GREAT IDEA, I've made a date with my friends," she laughed.

Paul pulled himself back to where he was in bed, and watched as Sarah went to the bathroom, before spraying some deodorant and one of her favourite perfumes.

She came back into the bedroom to get her black heels, before sitting back down on the bed to slip them on.

Sarah had also readjusted her hair after her lovemaking to him, and was all set to go.

"Where are you meeting them?" he asked, wanting to show interest.

"Just going down to Shakers wine bar, it's where they wanted to meet."

The wine bar was THE place to go. It was the city's most well-known bar, and it was always vibrant, even during the week.

"Well, have fun, but not TOO MUCH fun." He chuckled.

"Oh, DON'T YOU WORRY. YOU won't be there so I'll PROMISE NOT to have TOO MUCH FUN while I'm out," she joked.

Sarah went over to the bed, to give him a kiss, just as outside the horn of the taxi that she had booked earlier beeped.

She left the bedroom, and was soon out of the door, closing it behind her.

Sarah arrived at Shakers around seven-fifteen, and her girlfriends were already inside.

"AAAAAAAAA… here she is," shrieked Zoe, as she flung her arms open to embrace Sarah.

"Finally let you out, then?"

"He's cool with me coming out tonight, he knows how much I've been looking forward to it; besides, he didn't have much say in the matter," Sarah joked.

All the girls were dressed to impress, and they had found some seating in a cosy booth before Sarah arrived.

"Let me go and get you a drink," said Charlie, so pleased to see her best friend.

"Glass of medium white wine please, make it a large one." Sarah laughed.

Charlie came back with the wine while Sarah chatted with the others.

All the girls had grown up together, and their bond was strong.

Charlie had always been Sarah's best friend, and they had messed around with each other sexually growing up.

Sarah had missed all her friends.

"So, what's going on with Paul, then?" teased Zoe. "Still all going well?"

"OH MY GOD… the sex is mind-blowing; I couldn't be happier. I DO miss my girlies, though, and we REALLY SHOULD do this more often."

"Is it just the sex that's good?" Constance asked, wanting to know if everything else in the relationship was good.

"It's not just the sex; we seem to have a connection with each other. He always makes me laugh, he's a good cook, AMAZING between the sheets, like I say, it's just…"

"Just what?" asked Charlie.

"Well, I told him earlier that I loved him, but he wouldn't say it back."

"Give it a chance, girlie, you've not really long met, have you?" said Amber.

All the girls chatted and laughed for a while, and the drinks were flowing.

"So, seen any nice men around, then, Amber?" asked Sarah.

"No, they're all idiots around here, I'm fed up with being leered at. There was one guy who I took a shine to at work, he'd only just started, but he turned out to be gay… story of my life." She frowned, as the other girls laughed, Charlie putting a consoling hand on her shoulder.

"Anyway, come on… LET'S DANCE," screamed an excited Charlie, as all the girls put their drinks down, and took their handbags with them to the dance floor, before putting them all in the middle of their dancing group.

The girls were all having a whale of a time, laughing and joking with each other, as Charlie began to dance behind Sarah, grabbing her by the hips and thrusting into her, in a sexual motion.

All the girls started to laugh. Sarah found this hilarious, although the others didn't know of Charlie and Sarah's secret sexual experience as teens.

They were even joined by a group of young men, who wanted to dance around them, but the girls only had time for each other, and they started to move away from them and go and dance somewhere else.

They were soon back in their booth, their feet killing them from all the dancing, and they were getting their belongings together, ready to go.

It was getting late, and all the girls were a little worse for wear, and they'd all had an amazing time.

The end of the night came for them. It was nearly midnight, but the girls had had so much fun.

"We really MUST do this again soon; it's been far too long," Amber enthused. "Not had this much fun in AGES."

"You're RIGHT," slurred Charlie, "we MUST do it again soon."

The girls all made their way out of Shakers, and into waiting taxis outside.

They all lived in and around the vicinity of Barnwood, so it was hard to understand why they hadn't made arrangements to see each other sooner, though they all had busy lives, with work and children.

Sarah arrived home, and, with the lights all off, crept out of the taxi and paid the driver, before he pulled off.

She decided to take her shoes off, as they made such a noise, and quietly opened the door.

Even though she had not been out for so long, Sarah was good at holding her drink, and was appearing fairly sober, though she had had a lot to drink, and her head was starting to hurt.

After closing the door and locking up, she put her shoes down and crept towards the bedroom.

She could see that Paul was fast asleep, and didn't want to wake him.

She went and gently sat on the bed, and this stirred him slightly.

"What happened to 'I won't be late'?" he joked. "What time is it?"

"Shh… go back to sleep, it's about midnight. So, do you love me?"

Paul dropped back off to sleep, unaware of what she had said.

'Hmm,' she huffed, still a little aggrieved that she hadn't heard him mention the word "love" earlier, but, knowing that that was just how he was, she just had to accept it.

She undressed, put a nightshirt on, got into bed and lay down to sleep, just getting comfy with her man. As she cuddled up to him, Paul fell back asleep almost immediately, while Sarah stayed awake for a few more minutes, probably thinking about her amazing night out with the girls, and of course Alice, no doubt.

NO-ONE CAN KNOW

They awoke the next day, all refreshed for a Sunday.

"I'm heading for a shower. Fancy joining me?" Sarah asks.

"I will. Give me a few minutes, though, just want to quickly check that I have some documents together for a meeting at work tomorrow, then I'm all yours."

Sarah strode elegantly towards the bathroom, and turned the walk-in power shower head on. The spray of the hot water covered her body, as she squeezed lots of body wash into her hands and started to wash her body, using a large yellow sponge they had.

She slowly started to wash her breasts and neck, as the suds started to stroll down to her legs. She washed the body wash off under the power shower, then started to wash her legs and arms. She poured a little more body wash in her hands to wash her pussy, as if to give herself an excuse to touch herself, while waiting for Paul to join her.

Just then, Paul walked in, having organised what he needed to for his meeting at work.

"You look very inviting," said Paul.

"I'm missing you in here." She moved over so he could get in. "You need to get in and wash my back, and maybe some other important areas," she teased.

He undressed and got in the shower.

Paul was erect, and his cock was pressing against Sarah's peachy arse, as she pressed back onto it.

"Mmm… you've not fucked me from behind for a while, Paul, now's your chance," Sarah said sexily.

Paul loved Sarah's peachy bum, and could not resist getting an almost instant erection.

Sarah pressed back onto Paul's hard cock again and, almost instantly, Paul was penetrating Sarah anally.

He slowly started to slide his cock in and out of her, trying to be as gentle as he could, having not used any lubricant.

She didn't mind, as it had been a while and she had missed it.

He gently pushed his throbbing cock deeper in, again, not wanting to hurt her.

Sarah started to pant with sexual energy as she started to ride his cock, her huge breasts pressing on the shower wall.

Paul grabbed her breasts as he started to ride her faster and harder.

He was somewhat surprised with just how much energy he had, from the night before, and, again, he didn't feel it was going to be long before he ejaculated again.

"Ah, come on, baby, let me feel you explode inside me."

Sarah was pushing hard onto Paul's throbbing cock, and, in an instant, he came inside her, letting out a groan as he did, as his cock slowly starting to slide out of her, giving her almost every drop that he had left from the night of passion.

"Now for my back?" Sarah joked.

After the shower, the couple got dressed. It's another really warm day in Barnwood.

Sarah put on a beautiful white, flowery, flowing knee-length skirt, and a revealing sky-blue polo-necked jumper and flat shoes, with Paul deciding to wear a thin, stylish, casual V-necked green jumper with white cotton trousers, also with a flat pair of slip-on casual canvas shoes and no socks, with it being so warm.

The pair looked like they had just stepped out of a catalogue.

After having their bowls of muesli for breakfast, Paul took their empty bowls, put them in the dishwasher and went to prepare the picnic that they were going to have for lunch, while Sarah grabbed her laptop to check out the latest fashion trends, wanting to keep one step ahead of the game, for her to carry on being as successful as she was.

"I might need to take a trip to Paris in the week, Paul, meet some potential new clients." She did this every so often, so it was no surprise to him, and she had travelled extensively across Europe the previous few years, meeting wealthy clients.

"Ok, I understand, it's your work, cannot get in the way of progress."

Sarah started to ponder. She usually spent a few days away at a time, and she started to have an idea.

'I wonder if I could persuade a certain lady to come away with me; those nights away can feel terribly lonely on your own,' she fantasised, wondering if she could entice Alice in any way.

Paul had packed quite a bit of food for them both, putting it into his rucksack.

They were both ready to go, and went and grabbed their mountain bikes that they had stored under the stairs. They grabbed their cycle helmets and sunglasses, and headed out of the door, Paul locking up behind them.

They decided that they would head over to the large park, about fifteen minutes' ride away, where many people went when it was nice. There was a large lake in the park, full of ducks, swans and canoeists sometimes.

There you can also find little pockets of the park that are discreet, if people want some privacy.

Paul and Sarah ride into the park, full of parents, and their children playing.

There are many children with their families down by the lake, feeding the ducks with bread that they had brought with them.

There was also an ice cream van near the lake, and it appeared to be quite busy with it being a warm day, and there wasn't a cloud in the sky.

"Let's camp down here, seems a good spot to be," Paul said. "Seems like a nice spot to be to have our lunch," he continued.

"Just perfect, Paul."

Sarah had brought along a blanket that she had packed in her own rucksack. They got off their bikes, laid them gently down in front of them, and Sarah began to unfold the blanket to lay out, nicely overlooking the lake, and just a stone's throw from the ice cream van.

He removed his rucksack, with the picnic in, along with a bottle of wine and two glasses that he'd packed, and set the food out onto the blanket.

There were brown-breaded cheese sandwiches, some ham sandwiches in white bread, a few slices of pork pie, crisps and some farmhouse cake.

The grass that they sat on smelt very fresh, as if it had just been mown.

"Glass of wine, Sarah?" as if in his element for it being such a nice day.

"Thought you'd never ask."

Paul poured Sarah's wine, then his own.

"Oh, look over there, Sarah." He pointed out. "Aren't they the two girls we saw the other day?"

Her heart started to race and, sure enough, twenty feet away are Stacey, and Sarah's love interest, Alice.

Stacey had her back up against a tree, shielding from the heat of the sun, facing the lake.

Alice was lying down across her, her head on Stacey's lap. Stacey was stroking Alice's hair, with Sarah looking on, wishing it was Alice on her own lap instead.

Sarah couldn't help but stare at Alice's beautiful body, slight beads of sweat dripping from Alice's arms.

She was checking out every inch of her.

Alice was wearing a low-cut, sleeveless V-necked T-shirt and black shorts, while Stacey was wearing a sleeveless black T-shirt and cut-off jeans.

She could not take her eyes off Alice's beautiful body.

"Oh yes, so it is." She made Paul think that she hadn't noticed.

"Fancy an ice cream?" he asks, jumping up.

'Only if I can put some on Alice's nipples and slowly lick it off,' she fantasised.

"Yes please, a ninety-nine with all the trimmings."

There was a queue for the ice cream van, as there had been all day, but Paul got up to join the queue anyway.

Suddenly, Sarah saw Alice's girlfriend also get up, to go to the van too, leaving Alice alone, lying by the tree.

'This is my chance,' she thought.

Sarah looked over to the ice cream van, to check to make sure that both Paul and Stacey were still embedded in the queue.

She decided to seize her chance, so she got up and wandered over to where Alice was lying, soaking up the day.

Alice had her eyes closed, taking in the warm sun, with the cooling breeze in the shade. Sarah stood gazing over her body for a few moments. Alice then awoke.

"Saw you lying over by the tree, so I thought I'd come over and say hi again," muttered a nervous Sarah.

"Hello again." Alice smiled, squinting slightly with it being so bright. "We must stop meeting: people will talk," she joked, as her and Sarah's eyes met again.

'If only,' Sarah thought.

"Been thinking: with you being new in town, could maybe meet up for a drink, welcome you to Barnwood?" asked Sarah, with a nervous smile.

"That would be lovely," said Alice.

"Here's my card with my number on, free anytime," a slightly nervous Sarah said, hoping that Alice might want them to go somewhere to fuck now.

"Thank you, Sarah, I'll text you later. I'd better not

tell Stacey: she can be a bit jealous like that sometimes," exclaimed Alice.

"You remembered my name!" a surprised Sarah said.

"I couldn't forget a pretty face like yours," teased Alice, with a glint in her eye and a smile for Sarah.

Sarah smiled, as wide as the River Thames. They gazed at each other for a few moments, not taking their eyes from each other.

"What is it you do work-wise, Sarah?" Alice wanted to know more about her.

"I own a successful fashion business," she said proudly. "It's a global business, can take me all around Europe, and sometimes the world, looking to go into the Asian market. It sounds very glam but, believe me, it's exhausting. I've got to go to Paris next week, meet some potential clients."

"I bet your partner doesn't get to see much of you then," an interested Alice asked.

"I do travel a lot; he's just about getting used to it now. What of you, Alice, what is it you do?"

"You remembered my name too." She chuckled.

"I never forget a pretty face," joked Sarah, laughing.

This also made Alice chuckle, and this turned Sarah on about Alice even more, thinking that they had chemistry.

"I'm a part-time model. I sometimes do some nude modelling, but mainly clothes modelling, but, between you and me, I have done some porn, not much, wasn't really my thing, only did a couple of shoots, as I needed the money at the time, but I don't do that now," she said, hoping that Sarah wouldn't think any less of her.

"I wouldn't judge you, maybe I'll have to search for those shoots you did," laughed Sarah.

"If you are on the lookout anytime for any models," joked Alice, though hoping that Sarah might need her for work. She did want Alice, but not just for work.

"I'm sure I could find you something, discuss it over that drink, maybe?" Sarah was feeling that she might finally be able to get Alice on her own.

"Ok, I'll text you later, when the coast is clear."

"Ok. I'll look forward to it. I'd better head back: I think my partner is being served now," said Sarah, though wishing she could spend more time talking to Alice.

As Sarah headed back, she gave Alice a fashion-shoot walk, and a wiggle of her bum, hoping that Alice was watching.

Alice WAS watching, looking Sarah up and down the same way Sarah had looked Alice up and down earlier.

Paul returned with the ice creams. There were a group of children playing happily by the lake.

Suddenly, there was a commotion, as one of the children, a boy around five years old had accidentally fallen into the lake.

Paul noticed this happen, as he had been glancing over at the lake at the time, like a concerned parent.

"Hold this for me!" he asked as, without hesitation, he dashed over to the child's aid.

None of the parents appeared to have noticed the child, and no-one else appeared to be reacting to the danger.

The child had ducks and swans flapping around him, in a state of panic, as the child was frantically trying to keep his head above water, but he was going further into the deep lake.

Suddenly, the boys' parents heard the commotion and rushed down to the lakeside.

Paul, without thinking, waded out to the stricken boy.

Deeper and deeper into the lake Paul went. The parents stood helplessly by as Paul reached the boy, grabbed him and carried him out to the edge of the lake, and into the arms of the grateful parents.

"Thank you so much," they said to Paul.

"That's ok," said Paul. "Just glad I saw what had happened," he stated, as if to say that they should have been keeping a closer eye on him.

A sodden Paul walked back over to Sarah, with onlookers watching him as he went; some were clapping as he walked by.

"My hero," said Sarah proudly.

"It's what any decent human being would have done," he said, slightly smug, taking a side swipe at the parents.

The warm sun was starting to dry Paul off slightly.

"I'm afraid your ice cream melted, so I thew the cone in the bin."

"That's ok. Anyway, I'd better head back, I'm drenched and I'd better get out of these wet clothes. Stay here, if you like." He smiled, knowing how much Sarah enjoyed the sun.

"It's ok," said Sarah. "I'll head back with you, help you out of those wet clothes, maybe even reward you for your heroics," she continued, raising her eyebrows to him in a provocative way.

They packed up what they hadn't eaten, along with the blanket that Sarah had brought for them, and got on their bikes.

Paul started to ride off first, with Sarah about to follow.

Sarah, glancing over at Alice, got Alice's attention briefly, as Stacey's eyes were closed, taking in the warm day.

Sarah pointed her finger into her hand, gesturing for Alice to text her later. Alice nodded across in agreement that she would do just that.

Sarah, without thinking and with no-one looking, and Paul riding off, blew her a kiss, as Alice smiled. Sarah then got on her bike, and rode off after her hero.

They soon arrived home.

"Think I need a shower," said Paul, wanting to get out of his lake-infested clothes. "I won't be long."

Paul undressed in the bathroom, turned the shower on, and got in.

He'd only been in there a few moments when a naked Sarah walked in.

He looked at her with a beaming smile on his face.

"I've come to reward my hero," she said, with a glint in her eye.

"How can I resist?" he replied.

Paul then took Sarah in his arms, and started to caress her body.

He slowly started to kiss Sarah around her neck and caress her breasts.

Paul was starting to get erect once again, as they passionately kissed, and Sarah was starting to feel very horny.

Paul twisted Sarah around and, with her back to him, pulled her hips towards him and thrust his throbbing cock deep into her waiting pussy.

He thrust harder and harder inside her, groping her breasts as he did.

Sarah was moaning with pleasure.

Both he and Sarah were about to climax and, almost in an instant, their bodies came to a shuddering halt; they had both cum.

His now-softening cock slides out of her, and she turns around to face him, carrying on showering.

"I'll have to save people more often, get myself a cape," he joked.

"You don't need a cape with me," said Sarah proudly.

Paul turned the shower off, grabbed some towels to dry off and passed one to Sarah; they proceeded to wrap them around themselves and walk, refreshed, into the lounge.

Suddenly, Sarah's phone bleeped with a message.

'*Hi Sarah, it's Alice. This is my number. Wondered if you were free for a drink later? Could meet you down at the Mary Rose Inn around eight o'clock tonight? Let me know xx*,' the text read.

Sarah's face lit up, and her body quivered slightly.

"Who was that?" said Paul quizzingly.

"Oh, just a bunch of the girls from work, wanting to cover some work stuff regarding tomorrow, wanting me to go over a few bits with them at one of the pubs later. Want to come along?" As if to cover herself, by asking Paul to join her, knowing he would probably decline the invitation.

"No, it's ok, it's work-related, I'll leave you girls to talk shop," he said. "Besides, I've got work stuff to sort too for tomorrow, gives me a chance to concentrate."

This was the chance Sarah had been waiting for, wanting to get her hands on Alice's beautiful body.

'Now, what to wear later,' pondered Sarah excitedly, knowing she wanted to look as sexy as possible for Alice, yet not so sexy as to make Paul suspicious.

She found a tight-fitting white dress that clung to every curve of her body, making her breasts bulge out even more. The dress was cut just above the knee.

Time had ticked on; it was seven in the evening.

Both Paul and Sarah had just snacked on their leftover picnic from earlier.

Besides, Sarah was too excited to eat, even with a few butterflies in her stomach, with the thought of seeing Alice.

"WOW… you look a MILLION DOLLARS," said Paul proudly. "Are you going out clubbing afterwards or possibly meeting someone?"

"Of course not," said Sarah. "It's my job to look glam. I've a reputation to uphold as the boss, got to remind the girls who's in charge, look the part." She shot a wry grin in Paul's direction.

"I guess so," he acknowledged Sarah. "I only said it in jest."

"I won't be late." But she was really hoping she would be, so she could spend as much time as possible with Alice.

Sarah's taxi was booked for seven-forty-five, and the pub was just ten minutes from where they lived.

Seven-forty-five arrived and, sure enough, there was a car beep from outside the house.

"That must be your taxi. Have fun."

'Hopefully,' an excited Sarah thought, as she came over to give Paul a quick kiss, not wanting to smudge her lipstick, as she was wanting to save it for Alice instead.

She opened the front door and got in the passenger seat of the taxi. The taxi arrived at the pub in a flash. Sarah stepped elegantly out of the car, like a movie star stepping onto the red carpet.

She paid the driver five pounds – the journey was three pounds-eighty, and she told him to keep the change – and the driver drove off, leaving Sarah to go into the pub.

Despite the Mary Rose Inn being a city pub, it was still an old-style pub, which was only really used by regulars, but tonight it was particularly quiet.

There were lots of old-fashioned wooden beams overhead, and pictures of the *Mary Rose* ship scattered around.

The pub had a warm and cosy feel to it, with an old log fire in the corner, which wasn't lit, as the days had been warm and sunny for some time.

Despite it being a Sunday night, the pub was virtually empty.

Sarah excitedly looked around for Alice, though she was slightly early.

"Over here," muttered a familiar voice and there, in a quiet little corner, sat Alice, wearing a low-cut strapless black dress, also showing off her ample chest, and also cut short, above the knee.

"You look STUNNING," Sarah said to her, with her mouth dropping with just how beautiful and sexy Alice looked.

"You don't look bad yourself, Sarah," said a smiling Alice.

Sarah momentarily looked Alice up and down, and Alice caught Sarah looking.

"Like what you see?" she teased, in Sarah's direction.

Sarah smiled and started to blush. "I'll get you a drink; what would you like?" she asked.

"A gin and tonic, please, ice and lemon."

Sarah went up to the bar, opposite to wear the girls were sitting. She leant across the bar slightly, wanting her dress to ride up a little, so Alice could have a better look, as if to tease her. As Sarah was waiting to be served, Alice's eyes looked her body up and down, admiring her own shapely long legs. It turned Alice on a little, looking at her.

Sarah came back with the drinks, and the girls got chatting.

"Tell me more about your business, Sarah, what got you into fashion?"

"Well, it's been a childhood dream, really, to get into that line of work, be my own boss, own my own company, travel the world, have no money worries, that kind of thing really. I see some AMAZING countries, and, like I think I said earlier when I saw you, got to make arrangements to travel to Paris next week, meet up with some stuffy old men." She laughed.

They were having a great time, the drinks were flowing, and they were laughing together. The subject then turned to love.

"How long have you been a lesbian – sorry, erm, I meant, with Stacey?" blushed Sarah, realising what she had said.

"Haha, it's ok."

"I've been with Stacey a few years, about four I think."

"She can be stressful. I like my own space sometimes but we had a row tonight, so I came out to meet you. She knew I was coming out anyway, and I never tell her where I go," she said, tearfully.

Their eyes met across the table they were sitting at, but it didn't matter how long they looked at each other now, as their partners weren't around to check up on them.

Alice began to cry, slowly smearing her mascara.

"Don't cry, Alice." Sarah leant across the table to wipe the tears from her reddening cheeks with her thumb. "Come to the ladies with me, and I'll fix you back up." She was more concerned by her sadness than her own intentions.

She took Alice by the hand and led her to the bathroom.

There was no-one else in there, just the two of them.

They stood in front of the slightly smeared pub mirror, which had a slight crack in the top-left hand, and they faced each other, as Sarah then wandered over to the ladies' cubicle to grab a handful of tissues from the toilet roll.

She then came back over to face Alice, and proceeded to wipe her face.

Alice put both of her hands on Sarah's hips, as if to steady herself, while Sarah was wiping her tears from her face.

They both started to gaze lovingly into each other's eyes.

Suddenly, Sarah leant forward and kissed Alice full on her bright red lips.

She kissed her for a few seconds, before withdrawing.

"Why have you stopped?" asked Alice confusedly. "You can do that again if you like," she continued.

Sarah smiled at her and, with a sexy tone in her voice, she replied, "I can think of a more discreet place to do it." Once again taking Alice by the hand, she led her to the cubicle where Sarah had grabbed the toilet tissue from to wipe Alice's face.

It was a fairly tight cubicle for one, let alone two, but they both squeezed in, and locked the door behind them.

Sarah started to kiss Alice passionately, their hands all over each other's curvy bodies.

They unzipped each other's dresses, and pulled the tops of them down, just enough for their breasts to be out, and pulled each other's bra straps down, to reveal their breasts to each other. Alice then started to kiss and lick Sarah around her neck and ears, before moving down to her hardening nipples, swirling her tongue around them.

Sarah was starting to feel very horny, wanting this moment so much, and she started to pant heavily, loving the attention Alice was giving her breasts, as she pulled Alice's head onto them.

Sarah pulled Alice's head up and, once again, kissed her passionately, her breasts now covered in Alice's saliva.

Sarah, too, wanted to suck on her breasts and nipples. She went to work on Alice's neck and ears, swirling her tongue around them, before moving down to her chest; at the same time, Sarah put her hand up Alice's tight dress, and into the lacy black panties that she was wearing.

She started to finger her while she was sucking her nipple.

Alice was as good as riding Sarah's finger, and was getting VERY WET.

"OH MY GOD, SARAH, DON'T STOP," she moaned, in a height of ecstasy.

She was really enjoying Sarah touching her, but she wanted to return the compliment.

She pulled Sarah's head from her breasts, and also put her hand up Sarah's tight dress and into the white panties that Sarah was wearing, and fingered Sarah.

"OH MY GOD, BABY," cried Sarah, she was so turned on.

They stopped fingering each other for a few moments, as they started to kiss each other passionately again.

Sarah then directed her nipples onto Alice's and proceeded to brush them together for a few minutes, getting them harder still, while they carried on kissing.

They then put their hands back up each other's dresses, and back down their panties, to carry on fingering each other.

They were trying not to moan too loudly, just in case anyone else came into the bathroom.

"OH MY GOD, I'M GOING TO CUM," cried Sarah.

"ME TOO, BABY."

Almost in an instant, all of their legs quivered in ecstasy, before suddenly climaxing, almost collapsing into each other.

They then started to catch their breaths.

"I didn't know you liked girls," Alice said, quizzingly.

"I'm bisexual," replied Sarah.

"You caught my eye as soon as I saw you," she continued.

"No-one can know about this, not even Stacey, or my partner, Paul."

"Don't worry, my lips are sealed. Well, the ones on my face are." Alice chuckled curtly, and they both laughed at Alice's response.

Before leaving the cubicle, they adjusted their dresses, and pulled their bra straps back up, making sure that everything was back to where it should be.

"Let me check that the coast is clear," said Sarah, popping her head out, before they then both walked out of the cubicle together.

She once again took Alice by the hand, went back over to the mirror, and checked to make sure that she was, once again, looking the picture of beauty.

"How do I look?" Sarah asked Alice, hoping that she still looked as sexy as she did from the moment she arrived.

"You look AMAZING," said Alice, with a huge smile.

"Let's go and finish our drinks, shall we?" said Sarah.

They casually strolled out of the ladies' bathroom; they must have been in there at least half an hour.

Their drinks were still sitting just where they had left them.

"I'm looking for someone to come and help out at my office, if you fancy it, Alice?"

"You could start tomorrow. You've got my card with the business address on; you might need to stay back the odd evening, though, help me 'clear up', shall we say?" She raised her eyebrows towards Alice, in a provocative way.

"What time do you want me?" asked Alice keenly.

"Well, NOW! Work-wise, though, shall we say nine?" Sarah grinned.

Leaning forward, so no-one else could hear, Alice replied to Sarah, "But you've just had me!" with a slight chuckle. "Great," continued Alice, "nine it is. I know where it is, too. I live just round the corner from your company."

The company was called Sarah's Fashion House and it was a fairly new building, modern-looking both on the inside and out, and Sarah employed around a dozen staff.

She had known her staff around eighteen months not long before she met Paul.

"Shall I walk you home?" Sarah asked.

"No, it's ok, just in case Stacey or anyone who knows us sees me with you, she can be a bit jealous, like I say."

"Can I walk you part of the way?"

"Don't see why not." She still felt slightly uneasy with the partial walk.

They were both still trying to catch their breaths from their lovemaking at the pub.

As they stood just outside the pub, Sarah rang for a taxi.

"Hi, yes, can I order a taxi? Portland Street? Five minutes? That's great. My name is Sarah," she said to the taxi operator.

They started to walk away from the pub, and walked onto Portland Street.

Alice lived just a stone's throw from there; it was dark, and pretty quiet, with no-one around.

They were just about to walk under an overhanging tree branch, where it was dark and discreet.

"But let me leave you with this," said Sarah, as she pulled Alice into her, and kissed her passionately, making sure that there was no-one else around, their tongues colliding.

"Until tomorrow then!" said an excited Alice.

"I'll have to tell Stacey that I have work, so she knows and doesn't get suspicious."

"I understand. As long as she won't mind you being stuck behind for the odd 'late meeting'," replied Sarah sexily.

Alice smiled. "I'll make sure she won't." She laughed.

Just then the taxi arrived to pick Sarah up.

"You sure I can't give you a lift back?"

"No, honestly, it's ok. It's literally up there, over the bridge, and I'm practically home, but, thank you anyway. Besides, if Stacey spots us together…" she added.

"I get that," said Sarah.

It was around eleven at night, not too late, and she fantasised about her erotic evening, looking forward at more to come, as she watched Alice disappear into the night.

CHANGING

Monday morning arrived, and Sarah, fresh from her rendezvous with Alice the night before, was up at seven.

She showered, alone this time, as she didn't have time to make love to Paul this morning.

As a fashion business owner, she looked glamorous, in her bright yellow dress, with a thick black shiny belt tied around her slender waistline.

She smelt amazing, wearing her favourite perfume, 'Seductive', the one that she had worn last night.

She paused for a moment, while getting her things together; besides, she was not going in until just before nine, and she was excited at the thought of seeing her lover Alice from last night.

She fantasised about just how hot last night was.

"What time are you due in, Paul?"

"I'm in at eight-thirty this morning. Got a boring meeting to attend."

"What did you do with yourself last night, while I was out with the work girls?" she asked so as he wouldn't quiz her about her "meeting" with her employees.

"Not much. Just had the TV on, and sorting out paperwork for today. I got into bed just before you got home."

Suddenly, there was a knock at the door.

"Who could that be this early?" muttered Sarah.

She opened the door, and there stood two burly police officers.

"Good morning," said the tall, blond male officer. "Sorry to disturb you so early in the morning. We're just making some door-to-door enquiries, as there was an incident nearby last night, and wondered if you'd heard or seen anyone around, acting suspicious," continued the officer.

"No," replied Sarah. "I was out with some work colleagues so not seen anything. Did you, Paul?"

"No, I was watching TV and catching up with some paperwork, while Sarah was out." He held the paperwork aloft so the officers could see.

"A woman was killed last night, murdered we think, and we're just making some enquiries at the moment," said the officer.

"We may need to speak to you again at some point," said the other male officer.

"Of course," said Sarah, having shuddering thoughts of Alice walking home alone last night.

"We'll bid you a good day; sorry to disturb you," said the blond officer, as Sarah closed the door, as the officers walked away and back into their police car.

Sarah had gone pale.

"Are you ok?" said a worried Paul.

"Erm, yes, I've, erm… just remembered I've… erm… got some paperwork I need to catch up on, back at the office," she said, nervously, hoping the girl in question wasn't Alice.

"I'd better go."

She walked quickly over to him, kissed him gently on the lips, and scurried off, quickly opening the door and, just as quickly, closing it behind her.

Sarah's office was just a quick drive away for her, ten minutes. She got in the driver's seat in a hurry, after stumbling nervously to find her car keys. She was so worried about Alice.

After getting in the car and closing the door, she turned on her Bluetooth on her phone and linked it to her in-car phone.

'I'll call her on my way in. I'm sure she's ok,' Sarah thought, trying to calm herself down.

"Search Alice," she said to her in-car phone.

"Dialling Alice," came the reply from the car phone.

Ring… ring… ring… ring… ring. "Hi, this is Alice. Sorry I can't come to the phone right—" said the voicemail.

Sarah cut off.

"Search Alice," a slightly frantic and concerned Sarah asked her car phone once again.

"Dialling Alice," said the car phone.

Ring… ring… ring… ring… "Hi, this is Alice. Sorry I can't—" again, a concerned and hurried Sarah rang off.

She had already put her foot down, racing to work; a few people along the way crossing over roads slowly, with Sarah in a state, wasn't helping her mood.

"Oh, COME ON, HURRY UP," she shouted, waving at the pedestrians to get a move on, crossing the road.

She was normally a calm woman but she had more pressing matters to think about.

She arrived at her company building in a flash, undid her seatbelt after screeching to a halt in her parking space, grabbed her Gucci bag and phone, and jumped out of her car, before locking it behind her.

Suddenly, her phone rang; she had a sudden feeling of relief.

It was Alice.

"Oh my God, Alice, are you ok?" said Sarah, with relief running right through her body.

Worryingly, though, she could hear Alice sobbing down the phone.

"Oh my God, darling, what's wrong?" she said, concerned.

"Sarah. I… I… I… I've been arrested," she cried, stumbling to get any words out that would make sense to Sarah.

"Oh my God, darling, for what?"

Alice still continued to sob.

"Don't cry. Try and take deep breaths, and tell me what's happened," Sarah continued, trying to remain calm herself, hoping it would settle Alice's nerves somewhat.

"Ok, I'll try. I've been arrested on suspicion of murder." Still sniffling, and also not quite believing herself what had happened. "Stacey was murdered last night," she said sobbingly, suddenly bursting back into tears.

Sarah stood motionless, her mobile phone clasped tightly to her ear. She was stunned, not quite knowing what to say.

She had gone pale.

"OH MY GOD... wh... wh... wh... when?" She was hoping that Alice was ok but didn't give her a chance to answer. "How long are they holding you for?" She had a million questions she wants to ask, but knew that she wanted to just be with her lover. "I'm coming down to the station!"

"I'd lo... lo... love you to," cried Alice, "but you've got work."

"Work can wait. Besides, this is far more important. I'm on my way," she said meaningfully, hoping that a familiar and happy face to support Alice would comfort her.

Barnwood Police Station was a relatively small station, of around sixty officers, including desk staff. It was both clean and modern.

Despite it being a city, Barnwood had little major crime take place, apart from some robberies, shoplifting and petty crimes.

Crime rates were very low for a city.

A few of the staff had started to arrive at Sarah's Fashion House to start their day.

Sarah rushed into her building briefly, to speak to her staff, before rushing to the police station.

"Morning, boss," said one of her cheery staff. "Shall we just—"

Sarah stopped her in mid-sentence.

"I'm going to be out for the day," she exclaimed. "You've all got work to do. My phone will be off, too so, if anyone asks, I'm at a meeting; take any messages, and I'll answer them when I get back."

The staff noticed that Sarah didn't quite seem herself, but knew she could be a little stressed sometimes when she had important meetings to attend.

"So, crack on, everyone, and I'll see you all tomorrow," she called, as she was stumbling out of the building door, quickly closing it shut.

Sarah quickly scurried to her car door, opened it, threw her phone on the passenger seat, hurriedly got in the car, put her seatbelt on, and slammed the car door shut, before starting her engine.

She quickly pulled out of the car park to race to the police station. The station was approximately fifteen minutes' drive from her workplace.

She pulled into Barnwood Police Station, found a parking space and hurriedly got out of her car, before locking it.

She quickly walked into the station and approached the front desk. "I'm here to see Alice— oh, God, I don't know her surname. She's just been brought in: tall, long blonde curly hair," she muttered. Just then, she peered around the corner; she could see someone who resembled Alice. It was her.

"Madam?" said the officer at the from desk, but Sarah wasn't listening; she just wanted to be with Alice and quickly walked over to be with her.

Alice was in handcuffs, sitting next to another female officer, who was keeping a close eye on her. She looked a little dishevelled, with dried tears on her cheeks.

"What the hell is going on?"

Sarah went to hold Alice's hand. "Madam, no touching," came the commanding voice of the officer sitting with Alice.

"Stacey was murdered last night, and… and… they've

arrested me on suspicion," a teary Alice said, with fresh tears rolling down her cheeks.

Sarah went to wipe Alice's tears away.

"Madam, no touching please," the officer said again, sternly.

"I'm just wiping her tears," she snapped at the officer. "Can I get you a drink, Alice?"

"Don't suppose they serve gin and tonic here, do they?" chuckled Alice gently, trying to raise her own spirits.

"I'll grab you a coffee."

Sarah got up from the seat where she'd been sitting next to her, and quickly saw the vending machine.

She was still shaken at the news of Alice's arrest, and was still trying to take it all in herself.

She bought two cups of coffee, and went back over to where Alice sat.

"Drink this. It'll make you feel a bit better."

"What happened after I left you last night?" Sarah asked. "By the way, I'm going to stay with you the whole day if I have to." Sarah wanted to support her, in every way she could.

"You don't have to do that. You've got work."

"I'm the boss, I can take leave when I want. Besides, they think I'm in a meeting." Sarah chuckled, hoping it would make Alice smile, and it did.

Alice started to tell her what had happened.

"I got home, maybe five minutes after leaving you, I don't know, and when I arrived at the house the lights were all on and the door was slightly open, like she hadn't closed it properly, or she was expecting me back or something. I called out to her, 'I'm home... I'm home,' I think, and... and... I... I... I went upstairs, as she wasn't downstairs, but she didn't reply. While I was upstairs, I could see that the bathroom light was on, with the door open a little. I think I asked if she was ok, so I went to open the door, and there she…"

Alice couldn't finish her sentence, bursting into tears again. She went on.

"I called the police, I think straight away, and when they arrived they arrested me," she said, still sobbing.

"But you've no need to worry; you were with me last night, weren't you, so you're in the clear," said Sarah, trying to calm Alice down.

"But they still arrested me, want to interview me in a few minutes." She sniffled, trying to hold back the tears.

"We're ready for you now," shouted an officer from down the corridor of the station.

"Do you have a solicitor with you, or would you like an independent station-appointed one?" he hollers.

Alice's head bowed, tears rolling down her cheeks once again, in a state of shock, feeling confused, not quite knowing what was happening, almost in a blur. She remained silent.

"Ok, we'll get you a station one," bellowed the officer.

"I'm coming in with her, as she was with me last night," Sarah defiantly shouted down to the officer.

The officer walked up the corridor and faced Sarah.

"And you are?" asked the officer sternly.

"My name is Sarah, and Alice was with me most of the night," she said angrily.

"You'll get your chance to have your say," said the officer, nonchalantly walking away and back down the corridor.

"We'll have to speak to you too, in that case, so don't go away," he shouted, with his back facing Sarah.

The officer, now outside the interview room, shouted down to the officer sitting with Alice.

"If you would bring Alice down with you, officer," called the man.

Just then, the holding officer picked Alice up by her arm, with her still in handcuffs, and led her down the hall, as she was led into the interview room, Alice glancing tearily back at Sarah.

Just then, a female officer appeared from behind the front desk. "Are you Sarah?"

"Yes, I am." Sarah wondered why the officer was asking.

"I've been informed that you were with the accused last night, is that correct?" asked the petite officer.

"Yes, I was, so she couldn't have done it, could she?" said a slightly aggrieved Sarah.

"We just want to gather some facts. Do you have a solicitor?" asked the officer, trying to keep Sarah as calm as she could.

"Or can we get you an independent appointed—" The officer was interrupted.

"Get me the station solicitor if you must," she said, still feeling angry.

"Come with me, then, please," said the officer, as she got up from her seat and walked towards the officer, and away down a different corridor to another waiting interview room.

A few hours ticked by, and Sarah finished her interview and waited in the seating area, just where she had been before.

Alice was still being interviewed.

"Do you know how much longer she is going to be in there for? She's not even done anything," Sarah said to a different officer at the front desk.

The officer momentarily looked up at her, gave her

an empty look, then turned his eyes back down to what he was doing.

Just then, the door to the interview room where Alice was being questioned opened, and the interviewing officer and Alice came out together.

She was out of her handcuffs.

Both Alice and the officer approached the desk.

"Will you release this lady, please?" said the interviewing officer to the officer at the desk.

Alice looked completely drained and very tired.

"Will you sign this, please?" the desk officer said to Alice. She had obviously been crying in the interview room; her face was all red and blotchy.

"So, we'll be making further enquiries, so we'll be requiring you to come back in to see us when we've investigated further. We'll be wanting you to surrender your passport, which we'd like you to drop into us today," the interviewing officer said to her.

"You're free to leave."

Sarah took Alice by the arm and led her out of the station.

"I'll book you into an hotel for a while, just while the dust settles, but feel free to come into work if you feel up to it. You don't need to do anything, apart from keep me company," joked Sarah, trying to raise a sniffly Alice's spirits.

Alice gave Sarah a little grin, and nodded in agreement.

Sarah knew a quaint hotel in the city, not cheap but comfortable enough for her. Plus, Sarah could go and see Alice whenever she wanted, thinking briefly of her own sexual desires.

They arrived at the hotel, called 'The Beaufell Hotel', a hotel Sarah knew well.

She would sometimes book in there, if she had important work to concentrate on and needed some peace and quiet.

The hotel was a four-star hotel, and she knew that Alice would feel very comfortable there, at least for the time being.

They both approached the front desk.

"You really don't have to do this," a calmer Alice said.

"Nonsense. It's the least you deserve, with what you've been through, just wish you could come and stay with me instead."

"Now, I definitely wouldn't impose there, two's company and all that," Alice replied.

"Can I book an en suite room for one, please, ongoing, and just charge it to my account?" Sarah was a regular guest.

"Yes, of course," said the lady. "Would the guest like to eat here this evening?" she continued.

"Whatever she wants." Sarah's mind wandered elsewhere.

Sarah booked Alice into room 117, on the first floor, a room that she had used before.

It was a large and very plush room, with a king-sized bed and a pretty dressing table. The room smelt fresh and airy, with large open windows overlooking the city.

"I'll go to yours, grab you some—" Sarah said, before being interrupted by Alice.

"Please don't go there." Tears started to roll down her cheeks again.

"In hindsight, I probably wouldn't be allowed in, probably surrounded by tape and…" Sarah stopped in mid-flow, not wanting to upset her any more.

She probably didn't hear her anyway, with her crying.

"Just want to get you some fresh things: clothes, deodorant, perfume and bits. I'll just pop into the city, I won't be long. You stay here and relax. Put the TV on, take your mind off it all. What size are you? A ten, I'm guessing."

"You really don't have to do all this for me." Alice was reluctant to get Sarah running around after her. "You really are too kind," she continued, as she sat contemplating on the bed.

"I'll be back before you know it. You just call for any room service you want; I'll soon be back."

Sarah stopped, about to open the door to leave, but instead walked over to Alice and planted a reassuring kiss on her forehead.

She knew Barnwood like the back of her hand, going into all the fashionable clothes stores, some that took some of her orders in, though not as much as the big spenders abroad, and spent over one thousand pounds, buying underwear and clothes that she thought would suit Alice.

She also had other things in mind, and wandered into a local erotic shop that she bought stuff herself from when she wanted to buy something for her and Paul.

There she spent another hundred pounds.

She also then went into chemists, to buy her some perfumes, deodorants and sanitary wear.

Sarah arrived back at the hotel a few hours later, and

up to the room where Alice was. She tapped on the door lightly. "Only me."

When Sarah walked in, she found Alice sitting up in the bed, naked, with her breasts on show.

"I've been touching myself thinking about you," teased Alice. "I want you now," she whispered.

Alice slowly pulled the bedsheets back to reveal her toned body and smooth skin.

This really turned Sarah on.

"Are you sure?" She almost threw the shopping bags full of clothes and accessories on the floor. "I mean, you've just been through an ordeal."

"What do you think?" smiled Alice seductively in Sarah's direction.

Despite what had happened, Sarah wanted Alice, so she slowly walked over to where Alice lay and ran her fingers through Alice's hair, as Alice began to run her hand up and down Sarah's inner thigh.

Sarah pulled away, but only to lock the hotel room door and to get out of her dress and shoes.

Sarah was wearing a matching set of silky purple underwear, and was bulging out of her bra.

She then slowly climbed into bed with Alice, before pulling the bedsheets back over them both.

She started to kiss Alice passionately, kissing her neck and licking her ears.

She made her way down Alice's body, slowly kissing and licking her breasts, before sliding her tongue down to her navel.

Alice was panting with ecstasy.

Soon, Sarah's head was buried between Alice's legs, tasting every inch of her waiting pussy.

She was swirling her tongue around Alice's clit, as Alice's legs began to quiver with built-up sexual emotion.

Alice needed this feeling, after everything that had happened.

Alice pulled at her head, summoning her to come up for air.

Sarah duly obliged.

Alice was struggling to get Sarah's bra off but it was soon off, and their bodies were pressed together; they couldn't get any closer.

Alice started to try to pull Sarah's knickers down but Sarah helped, pulling them down as far as she could, before finally wiggling out of them.

She was lying naked on top of Alice, their hourglass bodies pressed together.

Sarah felt in dreamland with what she had fantasised about since meeting Alice.

"I bought a few things," teased Sarah. She got out of bed, and sexily walked over to where she had thrown the bags down.

Alice began to touch herself, wondering what Sarah could have bought. Sarah pulled out a vibrator, and a strap-on, and hid them behind her back, teasingly putting the tip of her finger of her other hand in her mouth, giving Alice a sexy smile.

"You tease," Alice said gleefully, also putting the tip of her finger in her mouth, having stopped touching herself.

Sarah then revealed what she had been hiding behind her back.

"Oh WOW." Her face lit up, clearly starting to feel happier. "I cannot wait for you to use them on me," she whispered.

Sarah chucked the strap-on on the bed, and turned the vibrator on, and started to tease Alice's clit with it.

Alice was moaning with ecstasy.

She felt so sexually charged; she knew she wanted Sarah there and then.

"I want you," Alice whispered in anticipation.

Sarah stopped the vibrator, put it on the bed, and grabbed the strap-on.

She put it on, while Alice started to touch herself again, knowing what was about to happen.

"Want to fuck you with this."

"Oh, baby, yes please," said Alice.

She was already very wet, so she shouldn't have any trouble with what Sarah was about to give her.

Sarah got on the bed, and knelt between Alice's open legs.

Sarah teased Alice's clit with it momentarily, before sliding it gently into Alice's waiting pussy.

Sarah started to gently push it deeper inside her, sliding it in and out of her.

Alice pulled Sarah's head towards her, wanting to kiss her, while Sarah was fucking her.

Alice moaned louder with pleasure.

"Oh, baby, you're so good," she cried.

Sarah started to thrust harder and deeper inside her, knowing how much pleasure they were both getting from it.

"Oh, baby, I want you," moaned Sarah, almost feeling the same pleasure as Alice.

She was thrusting harder and deeper into Alice, wanting her to explode her pent-up emotions.

"St… st… stop," said Alice. "You need some enjoyment too."

Sarah sat up, undid the strap-on and took it off.

Alice laid her flat on the bed and smiled at her, before lying reverse to her, so that they could bury their heads between each other's legs to lick each other.

Alice started to swirl her tongue around Sarah's pussy, while she did the same to Alice, their tongues exploring each other intensely, as all of their legs began to shake.

"Oh, baby, don't stop," cried Sarah, as she felt that she was going to explode.

But Alice didn't appear to be listening; she was having far too much fun.

"Oh my God, I'm going to cum," cried Sarah.

Their legs started to shake once again, frantically, and, both letting out a charge of sexual emotion, came to a shuddering halt.

They both lay motionless for a few moments, before Alice got off and pulled Sarah across and back into bed with her.

They pulled the bedsheets over them, although they both felt slightly sweaty with the sex they had just had.

Sarah lay slightly higher up in the bed, so she could wrap her arms around Alice. Alice curled up in Sarah's heavily breathing chest, as they both pondered what was in store for the future, and also where things may lead between them.

LONG ROAD AHEAD

After lying in bed for a few hours, drifting in and out of sleep together, both started to awaken.

"Tell me more about you, Sarah, where you're from, where you met Paul, your friends, family… everything."

"Well, I met Paul in a nightclub. He was with a group of his friends, and he took my eye straight away. I'll be honest, he isn't the kind of guy I'd go for. He's AMAZING, don't get me wrong, and FIT, gives me AMAZING SEX, as you do, but I don't know, I didn't think he'd be my type really. Family-wise, my mum and dad are still with us, don't live too far away actually, in Churchfield, have you heard of it?"

"Yes, I have, that's not too far away, is it?"

"I have two brothers, Simon and Jonathan, and a sister called Liz. I have quite a few friends – well, acquaintances, really, but I do have five REALLY CLOSE friends: Zoe, Amber, Harriet, Charlie and Constance, and, I guess, I can add YOU to that list too, can't I?"

Sarah laughed. "You'll have to come out and meet my other friends, maybe have a night out together, what do you think?"

"I'd like that. I don't really have any friends around here; it's so hard when Stacey kept me on a tight leash." Alice started to cry again.

"Why did she keep you on a tight leash, if you don't mind talking about it?"

"She just wasn't keen on me having friends, I guess. She was a bit of a control freak, never let me out of her sight. I felt imprisoned sometimes and, no, I don't mind talking about it with you; you're so easy to talk to."

"Anyway, I'm going to go for a shower. Fancy joining me?" Sarah whispered seductively.

"That sounds like a good idea." Alice smiled.

Sarah casually walked naked towards the bathroom, and turned the shower on.

As she opened the door and stepped in, she was soon joined by Alice.

It was a double-sized shower, so more than enough room for the two of them.

Sarah put some body wash in her hands and began to lather Alice's body.

She slowly washed her breasts, as her nipples began to harden once again.

Alice then put some body wash in her hands and also began to seductively and slowly wash Sarah. Her nipples also started to harden, as they moved in close together, and once again started to seductively kiss, their tongues entwined, and soapy bodies pressing together, as they had their hands all over each other.

Alice went down and slowly started to tease Sarah's waiting nipples with her tongue.

Sarah felt in dreamland, wondering what sex with Alice would feel like.

After a few moments, Alice came back up, to erotically kiss Sarah again, exploring every inch of her mouth with her tongue.

Sarah then began to go down, to kiss and lick Alice's breasts.

Alice was enjoying the feeling of being touched again, and it was turning her on.

Sarah started to caress Alice's pussy, sliding her fingers between her lips.

Alice started to moan once again with pleasure.

"Oh God, baby, that feels so good," she cried.

Sarah carried on, while coming up to kiss her. Alice's hand then went down to touch Sarah, as they both started to kiss each other passionately.

They both began to move with the touch from each other, adrenaline running through their bodies.

"Oh my God, I'm going to cum again," whispered Sarah.

Just then, both girls exploded their emotions on each other's hands; they then held each other close, as the water splashed down on them.

They then started to wash each other once again, Alice turning round so Sarah could wash her back and pert bum, as Alice then did the same for Sarah.

Alice then stepped out, grabbing a towel to wrap around herself, as Sarah turned the shower off and also stepped out, grabbing the one big towel left to wrap around herself.

"We must get dressed," proclaimed Sarah.

The time was approaching four-thirty, and neither of them had eaten.

"I'm going to head back when I'm dressed, Alice. Order as much room service as you want, and I'll text you when the coast is clear, ok?"

"Ok. I'll be lonely here without you." Alice hoped it would make Sarah want to stay with her, at least for the night. "Can I come into work with you tomorrow?" enquired Alice, knowing that she would probably start to feel a little bored on her own.

"Give it a little bit of time, darling. You've just been through a tough experience." Sarah didn't quite know what to say. "It'll be a long road ahead. I know you won't feel it right now but things will turn out ok in the end; they always do." She smiled sweetly towards Alice.

"I know. But I don't want to feel stuffed up in here."

"You won't," said Sarah, reassuringly.

"Get some rest, order whatever you like from room service, and I'll text you later, ok? Besides, what are you going to do about a funeral for her? You should arrange one."

"Yeah, I know. We didn't know too many people round here but I guess I'll have to sort one out."

"I'll sit down with you and discuss what you want to do, ok?"

Sarah opened the door, looked back at Alice for a few moments, and walked out the door, before closing it behind her.

Alice was feeling all alone, contemplating life without Stacey but having found someone in Sarah.

Sarah had been home for around half an hour before Paul returned, looking exhausted. He didn't seem himself.

"Hi, darling." Sarah glanced over in his direction.

Paul just glanced at her and grinned, without saying a word. He walked towards the bedroom, taking his suit jacket off in the process, before going to hang it up in the walk-in bedroom wardrobe.

"Are you ok?" She was concerned that he hadn't given her a response since coming home.

"Fine," he snapped, as if he were in a mood with her. "Sorry," he apologised. "Just work stress. Maybe I just need a holiday."

"I know how to help you relax," she teased, while massaging his shoulders.

"Hmmm, not tonight, so much going on at work," he huffed, as he pulled away from her sensual massaging.

"Want to talk about it?" She tried to offer her support to him.

"No, I just want to switch off and relax."

She knew that it was time for less talk and more relaxation. She also wanted to give him a bit of space, though it was a side of him that she didn't see very often, but felt that she should give him the space he needed.

Besides, she had Alice on her mind, but also realised that she had a trip to Paris to sort out.

She wondered if she should take Alice with her, maybe do her some good.

Sarah decided to text her.

Hi honey. I've got to go on that business trip to Paris on Friday that I mentioned to you. Fancy coming with me? Might do you the world of good! X

Sarah didn't wait long for a reply.

I can't leave the country, can I, until the police have completed all of their investigations. X

DAMN, of course you can't. I'm sorry, I totally forgot that you had to hand in your passport. Listen, I won't be gone for long, just a couple of days. I'll text and call you when I can, and, you never know, I might even bring you a little something back!

That would be lovely but you don't have to.

I'd like to though. I'll be thinking of you and, like I say, I'll call you when I can.

Don't you get falling in love with any French women over there, you've got ME to come back to.

Oh, don't you worry, you're more than enough for me!

Paul noticed her texting so much on her phone, and, being in a bad mood, asked the question.

"Who do you keep texting?"

"It's just work colleagues, just telling them about my business trip to Paris on Friday, just telling them what they need to be doing while I'm gone."

Friday came, and Sarah's flight to Paris was at eight that morning, but, as she was normally up early anyway for work, she was up before Paul, and arose at five.

She had a large portfolio of work that she kept at the house, of all of her successful outfits and all the latest trends, and the night before had packed her suitcase with a few days' clothes.

She decided to leave at five-thirty, having got up at four, showered, dressed and breakfasted.

She was dressed in an elegant two-piece bright yellow dress and matching-coloured heels. She looked just like she's just stepped out of a catalogue, she looked so glamorous.

Having checked the weather for Paris, and seen that it is warm, she made sure that she took her sunglasses with her.

She went into the bedroom to say goodbye to Paul.

He was just starting to awaken, and started to sit up in bed, although the room was still dark.

"Darling, don't worry too much about work; it will sort itself out. These things always do. Plus, remember, you've got ME to come home to," said Sarah sweetly.

"Huh, that's easy for you to say," he huffed.

Sarah kissed him as he tried to pull her back on the bed.

"I can't, I'll miss my flight."

"Then just book another one." He kissed her amorously, trying to arouse her.

"When I get back, we can do it as much as you want, IF I can keep up, that is." She smiled, pulling away from his advances.

She walked away, brushing his face with her hand, as he collapsed back into bed.

She grabbed her things, ordered a taxi, which arrives soon after, and left the house, locking it up behind her.

She was soon at Barnwood City Airport, and it was bustling with people.

Lots of children were running around, probably excited at the thought of going on holiday with their parents.

Sarah checked in and went for a coffee.

She was constantly thinking about Alice, and hoping she was ok.

'Is it too early to text?' she thought. 'Yeah, I'll leave it for a bit; she might be sleeping.'

"Flight F2289 to Paris will soon be boarding," came the message over the tannoy.

She hadn't realised she'd been sitting with her coffee so long, thinking about the fun she'd had with Alice, but also the troubles Paul had with his work.

She got up from her table in the coffee shop, and wandered elegantly towards the departure lounge, having already put her labelled-up portfolio and luggage on the conveyor belt to be loaded onto the plane.

She had arranged a meeting with Mr Moniet and Mr Dumont, as well as a few of their colleagues at the offices of Mr Moniet's business, M&D Fashion Paris.

Sarah had booked into a hotel called Le Parisis Paris Tour Eiffel, which overlooked the famous tower, and, with her meeting at eleven that morning, she arrived at the hotel by ten, after her smooth and relaxing flight.

"Good morning. I'm Sarah Waysmith, and I have booked room 117," she said to the receptionist.

"Bonjour, Ms Waysmith, please can you sign in the book? Here are your keys to your room, have a pleasant stay."

Sarah went up to her room, and put her luggage and portfolio on the bed.

'I must text Alice, let her know I've arrived ok,' she thought. 'Actually, I'll call her.'

Ring… ring… ring…

Alice picks up.

"Hey, Sarah, you have arrived ok, I take it."

"Hey, darling, yes, I have, are you ok?"

"Yes, I'm ok. Just having a late breakfast, and watching some TV, also trying on some of the clothes you bought me; you didn't have to spend so much, you know. You've bought me loads, lots of sexy underwear too, thank you."

"I wanted to treat you, seeing that you cannot get back to the house, and you didn't really have anything."

"I'm just going to put all the bits on the bed that you got me, and try them on one by one, maybe even send you a few sexy pics of me in my underwear," Alice teased.

"Now THAT would be lovely, making me want to jump back on the plane to be with you, but I'll soon be home."

"What time is your meeting again?"

"Eleven. I don't really have much to do, just lots of meetings with these slimeballs, take in a bit of Paris, and look for something nice for you."

"Well, hurry home, maybe show you the underwear in person."

"Mmm… now, there's an image I'll find hard to get out of my head during my stay here," Sarah replied.

"Right, got to go. I'll give you a call later, ok?"

"Ok… thinking of you."

Alice blew a kiss down the phone, and Sarah blew one back, before hanging up.

"Right, off for my meeting."

Sarah arrived at M&D Fashion with time to spare.

She went up to the receptionist.

Bonjour, I'm here for a meeting with Messieurs Moniet and Dumont. I'm Sarah Waysmith.

"One moment, please, take a seat."

Sarah sat down and patiently waited for their arrival.

Mr Moniet appeared.

"Ah, bonjour, Mademoiselle Waysmith, did you have a pleasant flight?"

Monsieur Moniet kissed her hand.

Sarah didn't really like this. She knew it was customary but she found it all a bit creepy.

"Yes, I did, Monsieur Moniet, it was a pleasant flight."

"… and you've brought glorious sunshine with you too! Come and join us in the meeting room, let me introduce you to the others."

Sarah walked in, and Messieurs Moniet and Dumont had ordered a big buffet, as there were other directors in the meeting room, eager to see what designs Sarah had brought them.

The meeting went on for a few hours, and it proved to be very lucrative for Sarah, as the company put in a large order.

"Thank you, Mademoiselle Waysmith, we are very impressed with your designs, and we'd like to continue to do business with you in the future, and we look forward to receiving our order. Let me see you out." Monsieur Dumont smiled.

"Thank you very much for your order; it has been a pleasure, and thank you for laying on such a delightful spread. It was delicious. I'll look forward to doing more business with you in the future, and I'll keep you up to date with the progress of your shipment in due course," replied Sarah.

"Au revoir, Mademoiselle Waysmith, speak again soon."

Sarah said her goodbyes, and she was out of the building.

She arrived back at her hotel, and went straight up to her room.

'Right, time for a shower, then explore this AMAZING city, just wish Alice was with me right now,' she thought.

She got undressed and was soon in the shower. It was approaching three-thirty in the afternoon and she wanted to see a little bit of Paris before she headed home on the Sunday.

After Sarah fantasised about being in the shower with Alice, she was washing herself, and touching herself, thinking of the shower she had been sharing with her, as much as she had with Paul.

Sarah had brought some light cream trousers, and stylish blouse; she got dressed into them, and put some comfortable flat shoes on that she had brought with her.

She got out of her hotel and looked around for somewhere to eat.

She was not a big lover of the French cuisine, and wanted to try to stick to the kind of foods that she knew.

While walking around the city, she was leered at by some French men who were standing on one of the street corners.

"Yes… can I help you?" she shouted at them.

She turned her back to the leering men, to look for somewhere to grab some food.

She had eaten a lot at the buffet, but she wanted something else.

She suddenly turned round, as she felt her body being groped; it was the men who had been looking at her from across the street.

"GET YOUR FILTHY HANDS OFF ME," she yelled at them.

"*Elle est anglaise*" (she is English) as they laughed with each other.

Sarah was feeling a bit unsafe, and quickly walked away, as they watched her go quickly into a different direction, close to where some French police were standing.

"You need to keep a close eye on those sleazeballs over there; they've just tried groping me," she declared to one officer standing nearby, but the officer just looked at her blankly, muttering something in his language that she couldn't quite get her head around, even though her understanding of French was quite good.

"Oh… never mind," she angrily declared, before scurrying off.

She came across somewhere to eat, called *L'Entente Le British Brasserie*, which was a quaint bar, where she could just grab a quick bite to eat and a coffee.

She ordered herself a ham and cheese sandwich in brown bread, and a coffee.

She sat in the bar for an hour. There were plenty of people in the bar, and she looked around at the wonderful décor, thinking of Alice, and hoping she was ok.

A dark-haired man approached her table, and Sarah looked up.

"You look like you could do with some company," said the handsome stranger.

"No, it's ok. I'm here on business, and I'm seeing someone, sorry, and I'm just about to leave anyway."

She still felt flattered, though, that someone else found her attractive but she had Paul and Sarah and didn't want to get involved with anyone else.

She duly got up to leave, as the man pulled away, so she could walk away, giving her the space to do so.

"He's one lucky guy," he said, as she walked past him and out of the bar.

Sarah arrived back at her hotel just before six, and decided to call Alice.

Ring… ring… ring… ring…

"Hi, darling, how are you?"

"Are you missing me?"

"Yes, of course I'm missing you. Can't you catch an earlier flight? He won't find out, will he?"

"I want to look round Paris some more. Besides, I haven't bought you anything yet."

"Don't worry about that; you're 'present' enough," Alice replied.

"What have you been doing with yourself since I've been gone?"

"Just bored, watching some TV, thinking about how I go about organising Stacey's funeral, and fantasising about YOU, obviously."

"I'll soon be back, though. My flight from here is at eleven on Sunday so I'll soon be home, and I can show you what I've got you, and sit down with you, and go through what you want to do about the funeral."

"I'll look forward to that, apart from the funeral bit, I mean," Alice replied.

"Right, I'd better ring off, give Paul a call, see if he's ok. Chat later."

As both girls rang off, they blew a kiss to each other down the phone.

Sarah rang Paul.

"Hi, darling, are you ok? Thought I'd give you a call, see how work was, and if you were ok and not missing me too much."

"Hi. Work was work, I guess. How did your business meeting go?"

"I got a MASSIVE order in, I'm delighted, AND they want to do more business with me in the future, how good is that?"

"That's great news… well done."

"When are you flying home?"

"I've got my return flight at two on Sunday afternoon, so I'll be home soon after."

She knew that she had lied to Paul about the time of her flight back but she wanted to go and spend some time with Alice before she went home to him.

Paul still sounded a bit dejected over the phone but she knew ways of cheering him up.

She put her phone down until later, and went through the orders that she had received from her visit.

She was over the moon that she got such a large order, and thought about passing on some of the extra money to her staff, as she liked to look after them; they were doing such an amazing job for her.

Sarah had brought her laptop with her, so she could look at other possible companies in Paris that she could do business with, and expand her clientele.

The night drew in, and it was time for sleep.

The next day came, and she was wide awake, the bright Parisian sun shining through her window.

She awoke at six-thirty, ready for her day ahead, remembering that she wanted to buy something nice for Alice.

After having her shower and getting dressed, wearing a thin light-blue turtle-necked jumper, lime-green trousers and flat shoes, she grabbed her handbag and sunglasses, knowing that she'd need her sunglasses to protect her eyes from the piercing sun.

After locking her room door and walking out of the hotel, she once again looked every inch a model, even a Parisian model; she looked the sight of beauty.

Sarah strolled down into the city, and towards the Eiffel Tower, something she'd been wanting to see.

She stood in a queue and waited to purchase a ticket to go up, when she was approached by a ticket master.

"*Bonjour, madame, billet Tour Eiffel?*" (Hello, madam, Eiffel Tower ticket?)

"*Oui, s'il vous plait*" (Yes please) replied Sarah. "*Juste un*" (just one).

She paid for her ticket, twenty euros, and waited her turn.

"We must stop meeting like this," came a voice from behind her, and there stood the man who had wanted to join her at her table in the bar the day before.

He was a strapping man, handsome, around six feet tall, very smartly dressed, with silky side-parted hair and smelling of expensive cologne.

"Hello again," said Sarah, not wanting to appear rude.

"Did your person turn up yesterday?" he said.

"I wasn't waiting for anyone; I just said that I was with someone."

"Oh, I don't doubt you are, just wanting to be friendly. I'm Neil."

"Nice to meet you." Sarah did not want to give him any encouragement.

"… and you are?" he asked.

"I'm not trying to be rude but I'm fixed up, and not the slightest bit interested, I'm afraid," she said, with her back still turned to him.

"Like I say, only trying to be friendly."

"Ok, but maybe go and be friendly with someone else."

Sarah was starting to smile to herself that the man was showing interest in her, although she always got both male and female attention anyway.

"I'm Sarah," she said finally, still with her back turned, before turning round, and giving him a tiny smile.

This lit Neil's eyes up as the queue started to lessen.

"Are you going all the way? To the top, I mean?" She chuckled, still with her back turned.

"Yes, I want to get the full experience. Are you pleased that we're going all the way together?" he said, raising a wry smile for her, as she turned round to face him.

Sarah smiled, and chuckled. "I'm only here for the day; like I said yesterday, I'm here on business."

"I've just come away alone. I've just split from my fiancée, so here to clear my head a bit. What is it you do?" he asked, quizzing her some more.

"I own a fashion business back home. I had a meeting with some potential clients, and it was all wrapped up early, so I thought I'd take in the sights."

Sarah was gradually starting to warm to Neil, but was also glad that neither Paul nor Alice was there, as they'd be furious, but she was only being polite, despite her lapping up the attention she was getting.

"Where's home?" he asked.

"England," she replied, not wanting to divulge exactly where she lived.

"What a coincidence, I live in England too, we'll maybe have to catch up when we're both back there." He chuckled.

"I don't think so," came the stern response. "I don't think my partner would be very happy."

Sarah and Neil both got to the front of the queue, and made their way up in the lift.

The view of Paris was breathtaking, as they stood close to one another.

Sarah could smell the waft of Neil's cologne, and she quietly sniffed it up, not wanting to let him know how good she thought he smelt.

"What plans do you have for the rest of your day? I thought we could tour Paris together."

"You're very persistent, aren't you." She smiled.

"Just you're very interesting, and I'd like to share my time here, with a beautiful lady." He smiled. "Perhaps a drink later too?"

Sarah and Neil came back down from the tower, after taking lots of snaps on their mobile phones, the breathtaking scenery blowing them both away.

Sarah relented, and allowed him to accompany her around this beautiful city.

"What does your partner do? Kids?"

"He works in finance, has done a few years, and no, no kids yet. What is it you do? You've not said."

"I'm a private detective, so no getting into any trouble now," he joked.

"That must be exciting. Challenging, though, I guess too?"

"It pays the bills but is also very tiring, hard work."

"What happened between you and your partner, if you don't mind me asking?"

"Perhaps I should tell you another time. Still too painful. Maybe talk to you some more over that drink later? I'll be in the bar, around seven."

Sarah smiled sweetly to him. "I'll see," she said as they both parted, going in opposite directions, Sarah smiling to herself as Neil stopped to look back at her as she walked calmly back to her hotel.

Sarah was actually looking forward to seeing him later; he smelt so good, though she realised that she needed to stay faithful to both Paul and Alice, as she wasn't the type to go cheating on either of them, even though she was technically cheating on Paul, being with Alice.

It was four in the afternoon, and Sarah suddenly realised that she still hadn't bought Alice's present.

'I must go back out, browse the shops for a while, though they're open until late here, but I'm looking forward to having that drink with Neil,' she thought. 'I guess I should get some nice aftershave or something for Paul too.'

She left her room and went back out.

She came across a shop called Maitre Parfumeur et Gantier and purchased a bottle of Garrigue for one hundred and sixty euros for Alice, which had a fresh water smell, combined with lemon, mint, bergamot and lavender.

She also needed to hunt around for something for Paul, but was thinking something more for him to wear, so she carried on walking around Paris, before she came across a men's fashion store called Faconnable, and purchased a pineapple-printed cotton shirt, costing one hundred and sixty-five euros, for him.

She took her purchases back to her hotel room, and she was back by five-thirty.

'Time for a shower, before I head to that bar,' she thought.

Sarah had a tinge of excitement running through her body, but why?

She didn't even really know this guy, she was very much in love with Paul and Alice but she was enjoying being chased by a handsome stranger.

Seven o'clock came, and the bar was a five-minute walk from her hotel.

She put on a stylish low-cut green dress, tying her long blonde hair up in a ponytail, looking every inch a fashion model, putting on matching-coloured green heels, red lipstick and her favourite Chanel perfume.

She was dressed to kill, and looked a million dollars.

It was a Saturday night, after all, and she wanted to let her hair down, after a gruelling meeting earlier with men she would not want to associate herself with.

She arrived at the bar around ten past seven, and strolled elegantly in.

Neil was waiting for her, looking very suave in his casual jeans, blue jacket and a light-blue V-necked shirt that had a few buttons open at the top, and smelling of the best cologne money could buy, Sarah found him very tempting.

"WOW, you look AMAZING, Sarah."

"Thank you. You scrub up well too."

Neil and Sarah both stand at the bar.

"What's your poison?" asked Neil.

"I'll have a glass of sweet white wine please."

A barman approached the pair.

"*Bonjour. Puis-je avoir un verre de vin blanc doux, s'il vous plaît?*" (Hello. Can I have a glass of sweet white wine please). "*Faire que deux*" (Make that two).

"You're very fluent in your French," she remarked.

"It's part of my job. I get all kinds of nationalities in my line of work, though I don't know them all."

"How long have you been doing that?"

"Coming up to ten years; there is quite a lot involved. Like I said, can be stressful, and tiring, but rewarding when your work leads to a result."

"I can relate to that," she joked.

They talked long into the night, laughing and joking with each other, telling each other their stories, like two lovebirds sharing their love of one another.

"Can I ask what happened between you and your partner, if you want to, of course?" asked Sarah.

"She died, recently, was murdered." His head bowed, looking lost and upset.

"OH MY GOD… I'm SO SORRY." Sarah thought back to Alice's ordeal. "Why aren't you there, investigating?"

"I've been told to stay out of the case; it's too close to home, so I've been advised to take a break, have some time out, so here I am."

"I'm sure they'll get to the bottom of it; they always do."

"Yeah, I guess." Neil still felt upset with what has happened to him.

They carried on chatting about themselves, and it was time to leave the bar.

"Thank you, I've had a fabulous evening, been lovely to meet you."

"Thank you, Sarah, I've had a lovely time too. Fancy a nightcap back at mine? I'm just about five minutes further away."

"I shouldn't, but just a drink, ok?"

They stroll to where Neil was staying, at *Hotel La Bourdonnais Paris*, a posh hotel, and Sarah was quite impressed as she walked in.

"This is very plush; they must be paying you a small fortune for what you do."

"Like I say, pays the bills," he joked.

They went to the bar, and ordered some drinks.

They talked longer into the night, and they were the last to leave the bar in Neil's hotel.

"Fancy carrying on with drinks in my room?"

"No, I'm sorry, I really must be going. My flight back is in the morning, and I still haven't packed or anything yet."

"Can I maybe take your number, in that case?"

"I shouldn't but I have enjoyed your company and, who knows, if I'm back in Paris again, as I'm sure I'll need to be, because of the nature of my job…"

Sarah exchanged numbers with him, and he walked her out, ready to get in a taxi, parked outside.

"I really have had a lovely time, thank you."

"No, thank YOU. I needed someone to talk to."

They stared at each other momentarily before Sarah planted a kiss on his cheek.

"Look after yourself, Neil. Hope whoever did that to your partner is caught very soon. I'm sure they will be. Keep your chin up."

Neil smiled as she got into the taxi to go the short distance to her hotel.

Paris can be dangerous at night, and they wanted to take no chances.

He waved her off as the taxi pulled away.

She arrived back at her hotel, realising just what a wonderful day she has had, going up the tower, buying the gifts for Paul and Alice, and running into a handsome stranger, though she'd better not tell either of them of her meeting with him.

Sarah felt absolutely shattered, and was ready for her bed, just a shame it was going to be alone, despite the advances of Neil, but she wouldn't have slept with another man; she was too in love with Paul to even contemplate it.

Sarah arrived at Paris airport, ready for her flight home.

She was looking forward to seeing Paul and Alice again, especially with the gifts she had bought them, and was looking forward to smelling the perfume on Alice and seeing the stylish shirt on Paul, before seeing it off him, and on the floor, but she couldn't help but think of the man who she had met in Paris, and thinking how she might have been tempted to sleep with him; after all, he did both look and smell good, but she wasn't that type of girl.

She had his number, anyway; she could always keep in contact with him, to see if they'd managed to catch his partner's killer.

Her flight arrived on time, and she was back on Barnwood soil just after eleven, due to the time difference.

She grabbed her belongings from the conveyor belt, before taking herself, and her goodies, to a waiting taxi outside the airport.

"The Beaufell Hotel, please, driver," she asked.

The taxi soon pulled up outside the hotel; Sarah, paying the driver, grabbed her belongings before walking into the hotel foyer.

She went up to the room that Alice was staying in, and knocked on the door.

"Guess who?"

Sarah opens the door, which is unlocked, and finds Alice jumping up from the bed, with the television on, and into Sarah's arms.

"OH MY GOD... have I missed YOU." Alice cries.

"I've only been gone a couple of days; have you been ok?"

"Well, apart from missing you, being bored out of my skull, I've been ok."

"I've got something for you," teased Sarah, smiling away to herself.

"Didn't get attracted to any of those sexy French women, then?"

"No, I didn't, why would I, when I have YOU?" She tried not to think or say anything about meeting Neil.

Sarah opened her bag and pulled out the perfume that she'd got her.

Alice sprayed some on her inner wrist, and had a smell.

"Oh my God, that smells AMAZING... THANK YOU. I'll only wear it just for YOU."

"You're welcome." Sarah smiled, glad that Alice was happy with what she had got for her.

"How I've missed that body of yours. Come and get into the shower with me, and let's make love," suggested Alice, seductively. "I've been fantasising about you since you've been gone, worried you might have met some sexy maid out there and you'd have gone off me."

"No chance of that. I've missed you loads too."

Both Sarah and Alice got naked and headed to the shower, before drying off and making love on Alice's bed.

They lay in each other's arms for a while, talking about Sarah's trip away.

"Did your meeting go well? What else did you do while you were there? Miss me, I hope."

Sarah didn't want to tell her about meeting Neil, but she went about showing Alice the pics she took while up the Eiffel Tower.

"WOW… the views look INCREDIBLE. I've been to Paris on a modelling shoot but never got the chance to go up the tower." Alice sighed.

"Well, maybe we could find time to go ourselves, and we could take in the views together."

"That'd be lovely. I'd be worried that I'd want to hide away up at the top, though, and we could make love up there."

Sarah had the same thoughts running through her mind, and, giving Alice a sexy smile, rolled on top of her, as they made love again.

It was two in the afternoon, and it was time for Sarah to get dressed and head back to see Paul.

"Do you REALLY have to go? Can't you just stay here with me, tell him that your flight was delayed?"

"I can't. He's the type to check the flights back to the UK, so I don't want to chance it."

Sarah got dressed and left a naked Alice, her blonde locks flowing after their shower and lovemaking together, sitting alone on the bed.

"We really must start to think about the funeral. I know you don't want to but you can't leave it." Sarah was worried that Alice no longer wanted to think about Stacey, that the ordeal was still too painful.

"Yes, I know. I'm dreading it, if I'm honest. I'm not putting it off; I've even got to go and identify her body too, haven't I?" Alice's eyes started to well up with tears again, thinking about her late partner.

"Don't worry, I'll go with you; you won't be alone there." Sarah tried to reassure Alice that she'd have her for support.

"Ok, well, I guess I could make a few phone calls. Thank you for agreeing to come with me; it means a lot." Alice briefly grinned at Sarah, as a show of gratitude.

"I'll text you later, darling. Will I see you at work in the morning?"

"Yes, I'll be there, take my mind off things, will do me good."

"That's good; I'm sure I can show you the ropes."

Sarah was ready to leave, grabbing her bits and making ready to leave.

She walked over to Alice and gave her a passionate kiss, still trying to catch her breath from their sex.

"Let's arrange to go out with my friends. They'll all like you; they're lovely." Sarah smiled. "I'll text you later." And, with that, she was gone, and out of the hotel, before she flagged down a taxi to take her home.

Sarah arrived home and walked in with her belongings.

"Hi, darling, I'm home," she shouted, as she walked in the door.

Sarah could hear the shower going, and realised that he must be in it.

'I know… I'll surprise him and join him,' she thought.

She put her bits down, pulled the blinds shut, and got undressed quickly.

She wandered into the bathroom, where he was washing his hair, not even hearing her open the bathroom door.

She opened the shower door and climbed in with him, almost startling him.

"I didn't hear you come in."

"Well, I'm here now, so, move over, and give me some of that body that I've been missing," she teased.

Paul wrapped his arms around her and started to kiss her frantically, kissing her neck and licking her ears. He is getting very aroused, pushing her against the shower wall, before driving his erection deep inside her, thrusting as hard as he ever had.

"Ah, God, baby, I've been so wanting you like you wouldn't believe," he said.

"I've missed you just as much, missing you doing this to me. Oh, God, baby, keep giving it to me, I want to feel you explode deep inside me."

Paul was riding her up against the shower wall hard, kissing her neck and breasts as he did so, as the water burst down onto them.

Faster and faster they both went.

Being made love to by him in this way, she hadn't felt like this for what seemed like an eternity.

Suddenly, he stopped thrusting inside her, as he let out an almighty groan.

His breath slowly started to become normal, and his cock started to slip out of her.

"You've missed me, then?" She chuckled.

"What do you think?" He laughed.

"Tell me all about your trip, what you did, sightseeing, did you take any photos? I want to know EVERYTHING."

"… and you WILL, as soon as I'm dry, relaxed and sorted out my luggage, and shown you what I've bought you."

"Oh, presents, the best part of you coming home from your business trips."

Sarah made sure not to mention Neil, who she had met in Paris, as she knew this would anger him.

The couple got dried off, and casually dressed, in loungers and a T-shirt each.

"That's a nice shirt. I'll wear that the next time we go out. Thank you."

"You're very welcome."

Sarah filled him in on her trip away, remembering not to mention the handsome man that she met, but showed him the pics she took at the top of the tower.

"That looks AMAZING," he said as he looked through the pictures she'd taken.

"It WAS. Maybe WE could go there sometime," as he gave her a wry smile.

The next morning came, and it was time for work.

'I must call the girls, organise another night out with the girls, and take Alice with me this time; they'd like her,' she thought.

Paul, looking as smart as ever in his light-grey suit and grey shoes, got his belongings together, kissed Sarah, and left.

Sarah was thinking about Alice, as well as her girlfriends, and was excited at the thought of the girls meeting her.

She looked the picture of beauty, before leaving the house, and driving to work.

Sarah walked into her company building, just after nine, and was greeted, as always, by her employees.

"Morning, boss," came their collective voices.

Alice was already at her desk.

"Good morning, you." Alice smiled.

"Good morning back to you." Sarah winked.

She sat down at her desk and turned her monitor on, wanting to catch up with any e-mails she might have missed.

"How has it been here while I've been away?"

"Pretty quiet, in truth. The girls have missed you and, me, well…" Alice smiled, putting the end of a pencil in her mouth and sexily looking over to Sarah.

"I've been thinking. Why don't I arrange a night out with my girlfriends this weekend? Thought we could go to Shakers, that wine bar, what do you think?"

"That would be AMAZING. Do you think they'd like me?"

"LIKE YOU? They'll LOVE YOU! I'll text them all tonight, see what they are doing this weekend, I'm sure they'll be up for another night out. I'll tell them that I'm bringing you with me too."

"It'll be lovely to meet your friends. Maybe we could arrange a few nights out with them. I need to let my hair down."

Alice smiled away to herself, putting the end of the pencil back in her mouth, excited that she was going to meet some new people, especially that they were friends of Sarah's.

"Do you know what else I'm thinking?" said Sarah again. "I'm thinking we could join that new gym that's just opened up in the city."

"Oh, Finesse Fitness, you mean?" quizzed Alice.

"Yes, that one, and don't worry about the cost of joining. I'll sort all of that out." Sarah smiled to herself, thinking that it'd be a fun thing to do.

"Are you sure you want to pay for our membership?"

"Yes, I do. It was my suggestion in the first place." Sarah did not want to burden Alice with any additional expense, despite her paying her a good salary for working for her.

"Ok, yeah… why not? I'm up for it." Alice smiled, thinking it would help get her out and meet different people.

"GREAT. How are you fixed for maybe us going for an induction next weekend, burn off some energy?"

"Not too much, I'd want you to save some of your energy for me too," Alice joked.

It was Wednesday morning, around ten, and Alice's mobile phone rang.

"Hello, is that Alice Johnson?" came the voice down the phone, sounding very professional.

"Erm, yes, can I ask who this is?" Alice glanced over at Sarah, as Alice stood up to go somewhere quieter to take the call.

"Yes, my name is Alan Attwood, and I'm at Barnwood Mortuary. Are you the partner of a Stacey Miller?"

Alice's voice started to break; it was the phone call she had been dreading. She tried to quickly compose herself, knowing it was something that she needed to address.

"Erm, yes, I'm her partner, I mean, was, I mean… you know." Tears started to roll down her cheek, knowing what was about to face her, but also knowing that she was going to have the support of Sarah.

"We need you to come down and identify the body please, Miss Johnson, as soon as you can. When are you free?" This was something that the mortuary people did on a regular basis, but was all very new to Alice, and she knew that, even with Sarah with her, it wasn't going to be an easy visit.

"I'm at work at the minute, can you give me a second?"

Alice, stone-faced, walked over to where Sarah's desk was, as Alice covered the speaker on her mobile with her hand, so she could speak to Sarah.

"Are you ok, Alice?" quizzed Sarah, looking a little worried as Alice had gone so pale.

"It's the mortuary, asking if I can go and identify her body. Can you still come with me?"

"When do they want you to go?"

"I thought I'd ask you first, but they said as soon as possible."

"Do you want to go now, get it over with?"

Alice couldn't put it off any longer; she knew that, and spoke to the mortuary assistant once more.

"Yes, I'll come down with my boss, this afternoon, one o'clock?"

Sarah nodded in her direction; that that was fine with her.

One o'clock was booked, and the time came for the girls to leave the office, though the mortuary was just a five-minute walk from Sarah's company.

They arrived at the mortuary. Alice paused at the entrance, almost reluctant to go inside. She looked at Sarah, to almost get her sense of support, even though she knew she was with her.

"It's ok," Sarah whispered to her, with a slight smile, before motioning Alice to go inside.

A gentleman approached them both.

"Good afternoon, can I help you?"

"Yes, my name is Alice, Alice Johnson, this is my boss. I'm here to see…" Alice couldn't bring herself to mention her late partner's name, for fear of getting too upset, even though she knew she was going to be in a few moments.

"Yes, if you'd like to follow me, please. You spoke to me on the phone, I'm Alan Attwood."

The girls and Mr Attwood walked down a dark and lonely corridor. It was cold, as expected, yet almost peaceful at the same time.

They arrived at a window, and stopped, and Sarah grasped Alice's hand.

"Just a moment, please," said Mr Attwood. "I need to go into this room, and make arrangements, and then I'll pull the curtains open, ok? I won't be long."

Mr Attwood's attitude appeared to be cold and a bit heartless but this was something that he had obviously done for many years, and was used to doing what he did.

He walked through the side door of the mortuary room, as the girls waited patiently by the window, not knowing what emotions were going to come pouring out of them.

The wait seemed like an eternity. Alice's hand was shaking in Sarah's, tears already started to run down her cheeks, at the very thought of what she was about to face.

There were noises coming from the room, and sounds of Mr Attwood near the other side of the curtain.

"I'm just about to pull the curtains open now, ok?" came the voice.

Just then the red velvet curtains opened, and there lay Stacey, looking asleep, and also very pale.

Emotion overcame Alice, and she turned to Sarah, bursting into tears, burying her head into Sarah's right shoulder, wetting her blouse as she did so.

Mr Attwood looked solemnly at both girls, keeping the curtains open for a few short moments, before closing them, and walking out of the room.

"I'm sorry to have to ask you but I need you to confirm that that is Ms Stacey Miller." Mr Attwood felt almost guilty at the very question.

"Yes," sobbed Alice, still trying to recompose herself, "that's her."

"Let me walk you back to the exit, please, ladies. Can I ask, have you made funeral arrangements, can I ask? I can sort it from here for you if you haven't, take all the stress away." Mr Attwood was trying to be as gentle-voiced as he could, understanding the emotion of the moment.

"No, I've not planned anything yet, I've had so much going on, and, erm." Alice burst into tears once more. "Can we just go, please, Sarah?"

"Thank you, Mr Attwood, for your time today; we'll be in touch." Sarah gave the mortuary assistant a nod and a slight grin, before wrapping her arms around Alice's shoulders, and ushering her out of the building, Alice still very overcome with tears and sadness.

Sarah was unsure if Alice was going to be in any kind of state to handle going out on the Friday, but she'd see.

Friday came, and Sarah had told Paul in the week of her going out with her girlfriends, not that she was taking her new sexy assistant, though; it wasn't really anything to do with him who she went with, anyway.

The girls had arranged to go out on the Friday night again, instead of the weekend, as it was much easier for all the others, as they had plans with their families over the weekend, and Friday was better, so they could forget about the stresses and strains with work and life in general.

They once again had all arranged to be at Shakers wine bar around seven, so Sarah booked a taxi from hers at six-forty-five, so she could go and pick Alice up.

This time, Sarah put on a tight pea-green dress, and matching heels.

She had a vast array of shoes, to match every outfit that she owned.

She was still in the bathroom as a car horn beeped outside.

"Think your taxi is here," Paul shouted to her, as she came racing out, not even having put her heels on yet.

She grabbed a jacket, went and gave Paul a quick kiss goodbye, and headed out of the door.

Sarah asked the taxi driver to be taken to Beaufell Hotel, where Alice was staying, and he was soon pulling up outside.

It was seven in the evening, and Sarah waited patiently in the taxi for Alice to come out, having arranged a time with her earlier.

In the corner of her eye, she spotted Alice coming out of the hotel lobby, and she stepped out, wearing a boob-tube and ski-pants but still looking super-hot.

Alice went and sat in the back with Sarah, as they looked each other up and down, seeing how amazing the other looked.

"WOW, you look FANTASTIC," said Sarah, her smile as wide as the River Thames.

"You look pretty special yourself," Alice said, excited at the thought of meeting Sarah's friends. "I'm really excited about tonight, it's going to be AMAZING."

"Are you ok for tonight?" Sarah wanted to make sure that Alice was ok coming out, especially after Wednesday.

"Yes, I'm fine, besides, I need a night out." She smiled at Sarah.

Sarah held Alice's hand, the taxi driver checking them both out in his rear-view mirror.

"Eyes on the road, please, driver." Sarah laughed.

The girls arrived at Shakers bar just after seven-fifteen, as Sarah had previously agreed, and they both stepped out, as Sarah paid the driver.

Shakers was again buzzing with revellers, people laughing and joking as they came in and out of the building, clearly some the very worse for wear.

Charlie, Amber and Constance were all inside and, once again, Charlie greeted Sarah with a massive hug, much to the slight displeasure of Alice, before saying hi to the other two.

"I've brought my assistant out with me. She's not been with me overly long, so be gentle with her." Sarah smiled, as Alice looked around, feeling slightly out of place and pulling away from Sarah slightly. "This is Alice, guys."

Charlie, Amber and Constance all greeted her by shaking her hand.

"Nice to meet you, Alice." Charlie smiled. "Sarah's not really mentioned you, well, not at all, really, but I bet she's a nightmare to work for, isn't she?"

"She has her moments." Alice smiled, as the other girls laughed.

"Where are Harriet and Zoe?" quizzed Sarah, worried that they wouldn't be coming.

"Ah, they're on their way, you know what those two are like." Amber laughed. "They'd be late for their own funeral."

The doors of Shakers swing open and, almost right on cue, the latecomers arrived.

"I was worried you weren't coming," sighed Sarah. "Been looking forward to us all getting together again."

"I'm still not sure I've recovered from our last night out," joked Harriet.

Sarah pulled them over to where her sexy assistant was standing, still feeling slightly out of place.

"Girls, this is my new assistant, Alice."

"Nice to meet you, Alice. Have I not seen you somewhere before?" Zoe smiled.

"I don't think so; I've not lived here overly long."

The girls wandered over to the booth they had sat at the previous time they'd been in Shakers.

"So, what is it you do at Sarah's, Alice? I bet she's got you running around all over for her, hasn't she?" Charlie laughed, waiting for her response.

"I sort some invoices, check e-mails, and just go over what needs going over really," she replied with a smile, thinking of the late-night "meetings" they had every so often.

"How long have you all been friends?" Alice slowly started to relax, knowing she was in the company of nice friends of Sarah's.

"Oh, it's been an ETERNITY. Can you not see the wrinkle lines on our faces? Being friends with your boss, she's stressed us all out down the years, we're just hiding our battle scars well." Harriet laughed.

"We can tell you a few stories about her." Amber smiled. "She's not as clean-cut as you think she is; she has plenty of skeletons in her closet."

Alice chuckled, as she knew that Sarah had a past, as did she.

Alice became chattier as the evening wore on, and the wine was flowing, and she started to have a laugh and joke with Sarah's friends.

"So, are you dating?" smiled Charlie. "A beautiful girl like you, you must have lots of men queuing at your door."

"Actually, I'm gay." Alice smiled, as Sarah's friends all fell silent, wondering if she was joking or not. "It's ok, though, I don't fancy any of you." She laughed.

Amber started laughing, before the others all joined in.

This put Alice even more at ease, now they knew of her sexuality.

"I was in a relationship but she died." Alice tried to hold back the tears.

"I'm so sorry," said Charlie, grabbing hold of Alice's hand briefly. "You're with us now, though, you're lovely, and it's time to PARTYYYYYYYY."

The girls all got up from the booth, and started to dance in the middle of the busy dance floor, taking their handbags with them, with Alice making sure that she was as close to Sarah as she could be, still needing her reassurance.

The music was in full swing, and the girls were having a great time. Alice was loving the feeling of freedom, and being with some lovely new-found friends.

They carried on chatting in the booth, talking about their work lives and home lives.

Sarah, Alice, Harriet, Zoe and Constance all got up to dance some more sometime later, leaving Charlie and Amber to chat in the booth.

"I don't seem to have much luck with men," sighed Amber. "MAYBE I should give girls a go instead, what do you think? I'd certainly give her a go." She nodded over in Alice's direction.

"I don't think you have that in you." Charlie laughed. "Besides, you love cock too much."

"I guess you're right, but where is my elusive man? It's getting really frustrating; I need some cock soon."

"He'll turn up when you least expect; don't try so hard."

"It's HARD I need," Amber joked. "Vibrators get a bit boring after a while."

The other girls were still dancing, and being eyed up by a lot of men, especially Alice.

"Do you think Alice is dancing a bit close to Sarah?" Charlie asked Amber. "I mean, look at her, how close they seem, you don't think…?"

"No, don't be silly. She's got Paul; they are in love. It's only because they work together so, no… I don't think so."

"Yeah, I guess so, just my imagination running a bit wild, that's all."

All of Sarah's girlfriends worked.

Charlie worked in a nursery in Barnwood, where she had been for eight years, and loved her job. She was married to a nice guy called Gary, and had been married for the last five years.

Zoe worked in busy restaurant in the city, and loved doing what she did. She had been there for six and a half years.

Amber, who was the youngest of the friends, but only by one year, also worked in a nursery in the city, but a different one to Charlie.

Being single, Amber would look out for men who came into the nursery who showed signs of being single, and she would make a point of going to chat to them, but none of the dads who came in were single, or they were gay.

Amber had even joined a few dating sites, without much luck, so she was getting really fed up with being single.

Harriet worked for a major fashion company, just outside of Barnwood, but they concentrated more on other types of fashion: children's clothing, shoes, boots and coats, so they were not in direct competition with Sarah. She had worked for the company for around four years, and was in the process of thinking about engagement to her boyfriend.

Constance, who was the more level-headed one of the group, was a psychiatrist, and was the same age as Sarah.

The rest of the girls came off the dance floor, exhausted from their hard moves and all the dancing to the music.

"I need a sit down and a drink; I can't pull the shapes that I was able to before," chuckled Sarah.

"You are older now, though, don't give yourself such a hard time," laughed Charlie, "though I was getting tired just watching you, and I think your new assistant was pretty much keeping up with you too."

'She does in more ways than one,' Sarah thought.

The friends had been out for a few hours and again, it was time to leave.

"I've had the BEST TIME, and it's been SO LOVELY to meet you all. We MUST do it again soon." Alice smiled, with an enthusiasm in her voice.

"That would be lovely." They all agreed; Alice smiled, as the girls all drank up, got their shoes back on, grabbed their handbags and left the bar.

There were still lots of people going in and out of the bar, as it was open until the early hours, but the girls couldn't really take early mornings much anymore.

They all gave each other a hug, and a kiss on the cheek; even Alice got one from them all, and said they were looking forward to meeting up again soon.

The friends watched as Alice and Sarah shared the same taxi, Charlie feeling slightly suspicious that there was more going on between the pair than Sarah was letting on.

The friends waved Sarah's taxi off and, before the others got in theirs, Charlie gathered them all together.

"Do you think that Sarah and Alice are more than just…?"

"Friends?" replied Constance. "I watched them on the dance floor tonight, and they did seem pretty close."

"Do you think we should ask her?" said Alice.

"Is it really any of our business anyway?" replied Harriet. "Let's be honest, NONE OF US really like Paul, do we? So, IF they are together, or having some kind of a fling, fair play to them, let them enjoy themselves."

"I guess you're right, just don't want to see Sarah get hurt, that's all. Besides, she's a grown woman, she knows her own mind and body, doesn't she?" Zoe mentioned.

They all give each other a hug, and get in different taxis, all going different directions in and out of the city.

Sarah and Alice were soon back at the Beaufell Hotel, and they wearily got out of the taxi, as Sarah paid the driver.

"Coming up for a nightcap?" Alice asked, trying to tease Sarah to join her in her room.

"I'm shattered, far too tired for what you've got in mind," joked Sarah.

"Haha, don't worry, I'm shattered too for anything like that. A quick kiss and cuddle before you headed off would be nice, though, just to round the night off."

"Ok, not for long, though."

They got to the room where Alice was staying, and almost immediately collapsed on the bed together.

"I've had the BEST NIGHT, THANK YOU," said Alice. "And your friends are all LOVELY. You don't think that suspected anything was going on between us, do you?"

"Don't worry, I don't think we gave them any indication that there was; they were all enjoying themselves too much."

"Anyway, I'm thinking, let's go for that induction next Friday, shall we?" Sarah asked.

"If you're sure you really don't mind paying, though I'm sure I could try and find the money."

"Don't be silly. It was my offer in the first place, so membership is on me; it gives us a chance to get out of the office too."

"Ok, that sounds like fun." Alice beamed.

The girls were having a kiss and cuddle up on the bed, when Sarah sat up.

"Right, time to go, I think."

"Do you have to? I was just getting comfy on you," Alice sighed.

"Yes, I must, going to head home before he starts to wonder where I am. I'll text you, though, and call when I can."

There were always plenty of taxis outside the Beaufell, as it was one of the city's most popular hotels.

Sarah got off the bed, grabbed her bag and leant over to give Alice a kiss goodnight, though it was more like the early hours.

Sarah left the hotel, and straight into a waiting taxi, and arrived home.

It was eerily quiet.

Just as before, Sarah took her shoes off and walked into the house.

She was careful not to disturb Paul, who was probably fast off.

She crept into the bedroom, and there was no sound from him.

He was a deep sleeper, and nothing would normally disturb him, apart from the last time that she was out with her girlfriends.

She gently put her heels on the floor and grabbed a fresh nightshirt out of her drawer, before removing her sweaty dress from all the dancing that night, before putting it on the chair in the room and putting her nightshirt on.

She gently pulled part of the duvet back, before climbing into bed, and cuddling up to him.

Again, he hardly moved a muscle, and she fell asleep easily.

Saturday morning broke, and it was seven.

Sarah briefly opened her eyes to see sunlight shining through the window.

She turned over, to notice that Paul was already up, and she could hear the shower running.

"Morning, sleepyhead, how was your night out with the girls? I didn't even hear you come in," he said, coming back from his shower, towel wrapped around his waist and, using a different towel, drying his hair.

Sarah looked bleary-eyed at him, wondering what time of day it was.

"It was a really good night. What time is it?"

"It's just gone seven. I thought I'd leave you in bed longer, seeing as you'd had a late night, you dirty stop-out. Thought, with the sun shining this morning, and seeing that it looks like it's going to be a warm day, I thought we could use it to maybe go out somewhere for the day."

"That'd be nice, but I need to go through some files, as I need to plan my next trip away," she said, regretfully.

Paul gave her a sorrowful look.

Sarah looked up at him, thinking that she should spend some time with him.

"I'm sure I could put my files down, at least until later. Yes, a day out sounds lovely, maybe take a picnic out. Did you have somewhere in mind?"

"Not really; thought I'd leave that to you."

"Let's go to Maplefield, because we've not been there yet, have we?" said Sarah, sitting up, wiping her eyes.

"Right. I'm going to get some bits together, sandwiches and some nibbles; why don't you go and grab yourself a shower?"

"Why didn't you call me when you went for your shower?"

"I wanted to leave you to sleep in, with you partying with the girls."

Sarah got up and walked gingerly towards the bathroom. She took her nightshirt off and turned the shower on.

Paul walked in the bathroom just as Sarah was getting in.

Paul stood there, smiling, leaning against the bathroom doorframe, admiring her beautiful body.

Sarah stood showering, while Paul just watched her.

"Are you liking what you are seeing?" Sarah smiled, as she started to lather her body. "Want to come back in the shower and wash my back?"

"I'd love to, but we'd never get out." He laughed.

Paul walked away from the bathroom and back into the lounge, shuffling a few work papers.

Sarah was soon out the shower, a big thick green towel covering her wet body, and another big towel wrapping her long blonde hair.

She walked into their bedroom and over to the big walk-in wardrobe.

She was rummaging through, trying to decide which outfit would keep her the coolest.

She found a thin yellow cotton sleeveless blouse that she'd not worn for a while, and decided to wear a pair of lime-green shorts with it.

Sarah put the blouse on the bed and closed the wardrobe doors, before drying herself off.

She put the towels on the floor and pulled out some lacy underwear from her drawers, before putting her bra and knickers on and then her shorts and blouse.

She went over to her shoe collection, searching for the nicest pair of flat shoes.

Paul was already dressed, wearing stylish light beige shorts, a light-blue T-shirt and flat canvas shoes.

The couple were ready to leave out, looking like the glamorous couple that they were.

Maplefield was an hour's drive from Barnwood, and Paul decided to take his car, instead of Sarah taking hers.

It was a lovely little country town, full of quaint little shops and little side streets with cafes, and the locals were very friendly.

They got in the car, and pulled off.

They loved to see the scenery as they drove, and the roads leading to Maplefield were very picturesque.

They arrived around an hour later, and Paul looked around to find a parking spot.

Maplefield seemed like an old town that time had almost forgotten.

"This looks nice; can't wait to explore. Let's leave the picnic basket in the car for now, Paul; want to go and explore some shops."

Sarah walked off, looking in some of the shop windows, browsing at all the local pottery, and seeing one of the shops where the pottery was actually being made.

She was awestruck at their artistry, and couldn't help but watch for a while.

'I'm going to buy something in here; it's all so beautiful,' she thought.

Maplefield wasn't the cheapest place to buy goods, but Sarah was someone who liked to help local communities.

She spotted a large vase that was exquisitely painted.

"Hello," she said to the assistant sitting at the till. "How much is this vase?" She pointed over to the vase she liked.

"That's three hundred pounds," said the assistant.

"Ok, can I take that, please?"

The assistant came from behind her desk where the till sat, and carefully grabbed the heavy vase from the shelf, struggling to reach it, as the assistant was quite small.

"Shall I grab it for you?" Sarah chuckled.

"Yes, please," replied the assistant.

Sarah reached up and took the pot from the shelf, being careful not to drop it, with it being so heavy.

She looked around the shop, mainly to look at other pottery, but also to check to see where Paul was.

She looked outside, and he was wandering around, looking in shop windows, obviously waiting for her to finish what she had been doing.

Sarah thanked the assistant, and left the shop.

Paul looked round, and saw her holding a bulging bag.

"What HAVE you been buying?" he quizzed.

"Just a little something for the house."

"It doesn't LOOK little; it's HUGE, whatever it is," he replied.

"Ah, but not as HUGE as YOU," she laughed quietly, so as the locals didn't hear what she said to him.

"Let's go and put that in the car, and go for our picnic," he said.

The couple walked towards the car and put the vase in the boot, laying it flat.

Paul grabbed the hamper basket from the boot and closed it, before locking the car back up.

They leisurely strolled towards some signs that were pointing in different park directions, informing them where certain places were.

"Ah, the park is this way." He pointed, and they strolled leisurely in that direction.

They were in the park within five minutes, and, being a warm day, the park was full of people catching the rays, lying down sunbathing, in larger groups just chatting, with lots of children running around and playing.

The park was about as big as the one in Barnwood, but this time there was no lake, just lots of green for people to sit on, with some swings a lot further on for children to go and play on.

"This seems like a good place to sit," said Paul, turning around like a pet marking its territory.

Paul had also packed a blanket for them to sit on, and he laid it flat, before the couple sat down and put the hamper down on it.

"I've even packed some wine and glasses," he smiled, much to the delight of Sarah.

Paul took the glasses out and unscrewed the wine bottle top, before pouring the wine into one glass and passing it to Sarah, then pouring his own.

"I do enjoy days out like this," declared Sarah.

"It makes a welcome change, doesn't it?" he replied.

"Did you see anything you liked while you were waiting for me?" she asked him.

"One or two bits, yes. I'll go and take another look once we're done here."

This was a perfect day for Paul. He loved the sun and, after finishing his wine and having one or two sandwiches, he lay down and closed his eyes, his sunglasses protecting him from the sun's glare.

Sarah stayed sitting up, just enjoying the sounds of

children playing, and groups chatting, also wondering what Alice was up to today.

'I'll have to text her later,' she thought.

A few hours went by and the couple had finished their picnic.

Paul only had the one glass of wine, with him driving, while Sarah had practically finished off the rest of the bottle.

"Guess you'll be sleeping on the journey back, then?" He smiled to her, still lying down.

"Hmm, maybe." She chuckled, in a relaxed voice.

He sat up, and they decided to gather all of their things together and take them back to the car, and finish looking around the shops before heading home.

Paul put the blanket and basket back in the boot, where the vase was, closed it again, and headed back to a few shops where he'd seen a few things that he liked.

"Want me to come in with you?" she asked.

"I'm a big boy now, I'm sure I'll manage." He laughed, walking away, holding his hand in the air to her. "And I PROMISE… it's NOT a rug."

Sarah carried on browsing round other shops, while Paul went off to look at things he'd seen.

Half an hour passed, and Paul was still shopping.

Sarah was just wanting to head home now, the wine starting to kick in.

Paul finally arrived out of one particular shop with, what appeared to be paintings under his arm.

"Paintings?"

"Yes. There were two particular paintings I liked the look of, and I couldn't decide which of the two I liked the most, so I bought them both."

"I never really took you as a paintings kind of man, but, if you like them, why not!" she said.

"I'll show you them when we get home."

"I'll look forward to it." She smiled.

Paul put the paintings down on the floor of the back seat, so as not to damage them.

They got in the car and slowly pulled away.

"We'll definitely have to come back here; it's lovely." She smiled.

"Yes, it is, and I'm sure we will."

They arrived home an hour later and got all of the things out of the car.

Paul was careful getting the paintings out, as he didn't want to mark or scratch them in any way, even though they were well wrapped up, including bubble wrap.

"I'm intrigued to see these paintings now. Any idea where you're going to hang them?"

"Thought I'd get your expert opinion on that." He chuckled.

Paul went and grabbed some scissors from the kitchen drawer, before coming back into the lounge, where they sat down and grabbed one of the paintings, and carefully cut open the packaging.

The first painting depicted a river scene, with tiny boats sailing on it, with the moon glimmering on the surface of the water.

He then cut open the second painting, and this was a painting of an old man, sitting on a wall in what appeared to be an old village, smoking his pipe.

The man looked slightly bedraggled, with people wandering around him, but minding their own business.

"WOW, I like these, Paul. Didn't realise you had such an artistic eye. How much did you pay for these?"

"A thousand pounds for the two. There was a bigger one I really liked but they wanted five thousand for that."

"You should have come out and told me; I'd have paid the extra for the bigger one, if you'd really set your heart on it."

"No, thank you, but I wanted to pay for these with my own money, but I appreciate the thought. Anyway, where shall we…?"

"Why not put the painting with the old man just on the wall there?" Sarah pointed to a wall space in the lounge. "And the other painting in our bedroom?"

"Yeah, ok. We can always move it around a bit, can't we? I'll hang them up tomorrow, not now, I'm too tired. I'm feeling a bit sweaty so I'm heading for a shower. Fancy joining me?"

"Maybe tomorrow. I've got some paperwork I want to take a look at for work on Monday. You go and freshen up," she said. "Anything you fancy to eat tonight?"

"I'm not too fussed tonight, I'm still a bit full from the picnic, so shall we just nibble tonight?"

"What about food, though?" she teased.

"Now there's a thought." He smiled back at her, before heading to the bathroom and closing the door to have his shower.

Sarah got her portfolio out, unzipped it and pulled out a few drawings, pulling them out on the dining table, as if she'd been looking through them, but instead so she could text Alice.

Hi darling, are you ok? First chance I've had to text.

The text reply came:

Yes, I'm ok. Been watching a bit of tv, thinking of you and me obviously, cannot wait for another crazy night out with you and your friends again, and cannot wait to see you at work on Monday. Have you done anything exciting today?

Sarah texted back:

We've been to Maplefield, not sure if you've ever been there yet. It was lovely. Maybe I should take me and you sometime.

Alice replied:

Yes, I'd like that, very much.

Sarah could hear Paul's shower turning off.

Gotta go. Love you.

Love you too. See you Monday.

Sarah wished she could just go and see who she pleased, and when, and that Paul would be ok them having an open relationship, but she knew he wouldn't be, as that wasn't the type of man he was.

Sarah put her phone down and buried her head, looking through her drawings, as Paul came out of the bathroom, a towel wrapped round his waist, drying his hair with a smaller towel.

"What is it you're needing to do?" he asked, peering over her shoulder.

"Oh, I've erm… got to maybe… make some adjustments to some of these designs, nothing major," she replied, trying to think of a reason to be looking at them.

Paul walked away and into the bedroom, pulling the towel from his waist as he did, leaving him completely naked.

Sarah sat, looking at his perfect body, starting to feel very turned on, and got up from her chair, before seductively walking into the bedroom.

She walked up to him and started to slowly kiss his lips, sliding her hand slowly down his chest, to his cock.

He started to respond to her movements, and he started to undress her.

Soon, they were both naked, and Paul pinned Sarah up against the wall, as she felt the throbbing of his penis pressing against her moist pussy.

He kissed her neck passionately, grabbing her breasts as he did so, rubbing himself harder and harder up against her, before pausing and pushing his now-erect penis deep inside her.

He started to thrust harder, as the couple's breaths became heavier.

She then wrapped her legs around his firm arse, so he could try to go deeper still.

He pulled away, grabbed her, twisted her round and bent her down, her hands hitting the back of the bed with a thud, before he entered her pussy from behind.

Again, he was thrusting hard, the rug on the floor keeping his grip firm.

He was going deeper and faster, their groans becoming more and more intense, pulling her blonde hair so he could thrust deep.

Suddenly, the pair both came, and they collapsed on the bed together, Paul wrapping his burly arms around her.

"I've been thinking. Let's try for a family!" he said, with purpose and meaning in his voice.

"Wha… wha… say that again?" a startled Sarah replied.

"Let's try for a baby."

"Haha, I thought for a second then that you mentioned us trying to start a family."

"Why not?" he asked.

"No reason, just wondered where this has come from, that's all. Does that mean that you actually love me, then?"

"I care about you; I'm just not as up front about it as you are."

"Well, Paul, if you want us to start a family, you've got to start saying the word love."

"Oh, so you don't want to start a family?"

"I didn't say that, did I? I'm just saying…"

"Ok, I won't bring it up again."

"I didn't say no, did I? I'm just saying… oh… I don't know what I'm saying. If you'd like to, then, let's try. If you really want to."

"Do YOU want to, though?" he asked her.

"Yes, I do… it's just… Let's see what happens, shall we?" And the conversation about babies ended there.

Sunday came, and they just wanted to chill today.

"Think I might put those paintings up where you said," an excited Paul declared.

"That's a good idea. They are lovely; just wish you'd have let me get you that bigger one you like."

"I'm sure I'll find some money to get it. If not, there'll be plenty more."

Sarah looked across at him, as he started to hunt around for nails to hang the drawings up with, feeling a little guilty that she didn't know about the other, bigger painting that he liked.

"There… what do you think?"

"That looks LOVELY up there, I liked it."

"Right… now for the other one."

Sunday came and went.

The other painting was proudly up on the bedroom wall.

Sarah had been looking through her portfolio, and also on her laptop for the morning, while Paul had been looking through some files he needed for work in the morning.

Paul was dreading work, as he was slowly starting to hate it there.

He was being put under so much pressure to drum up new business, and it was slowly taking its toll on him.

Monday came, and both were at work.

The day seemed to go by quickly for the two of them.

Sarah had made lots of phone calls to previous clients, to try to arrange meetings for new business of her own, something that she then passed over to Alice to sort out for her.

Alice had become quite proficient with her new job, and was loving working with Sarah, giving her little sexy glances across the office.

"You're not bored with what you do, are you?" Sarah asked. "As opposed to modelling, I mean? I wouldn't want to hold you back if a big modelling job came about."

"No, I'm LOVING doing what I do. Besides, I have a sexy boss to work with." Alice smiled, holding the top of a pencil sexily between her teeth as she smiled, winking at Sarah.

Sarah smiled back at her.

"Got any 'paperwork' you want me to go over tonight, boss?"

"Hmm, I might have. See me after you've finished later."

The day finished, and Sarah called Paul on his mobile.

"Hi, Paul. I've got a few things to go over in the office; I'll only be another hour. You eat if you like, and I'll do myself something when I get in."

Paul acknowledged her, and said he'd see her later.

Sarah walked out of the office to check that the building door was locked.

As she did, Alice started to unbutton her blouse, pulled it out of her skirt and took it off, to reveal a lacy lilac-coloured bra.

Sarah walked back into the office and closed the door.

"My GOD, I want you," teased Alice. "You need to bring that sexy body over here now."

Sarah slowly walked over to her, herself undoing the buttons on her blouse, before pulling it open, then off.

Sarah was wearing a black see-through bra that Alice loved.

The girls pulled each other in close, kissing passionately.

Their hands were all over each other, Sarah undoing Alice's bra with ease.

She pushed Alice towards the desk she worked on, laid her down, and carried on kissing her, as Alice started to undo Sarah's bra.

They carried on making love on the desk for about an hour.

After their lovemaking ended, they began getting dressed.

"Paul has asked if I want to start a family," Sarah piped up.

"What? When?" said a stunned Alice.

"Last night. It was out of the blue, took me by surprise a little bit."

"What did you say?"

"Said I'd think about it. I was a bit shocked but we've not been together long."

"WOW, there's a statement. I wonder what brought that on."

"You never thought about kids, Alice?"

"Not really, I'm not too fussed by them, never been very maternal."

The girls dressed and made sure their desks were tidy and their laptops off.

"We still on for the gym induction on Friday?"

"We sure are. I'm going to ring and pay for our membership tomorrow; will you remind me, Alice, please?"

"Yes, I will."

The girls left the office, Sarah locking it behind her before leaving the building.

Sarah and Alice got in Sarah's car so she could drop Alice off back at the hotel.

"Oh, there's something I meant to tell you, Alice. I've paid for Stacey's funeral. Barnwood funeral are going to contact you to arrange with you when it'll be. I hope you don't mind."

"What made you do that? You didn't have to; I'm sure I'd have come up with the money." Alice was shocked that Sarah had even given it any thought.

"You've enough going on, so I thought I'd take the stress away from you sorting it. I'm sorry if that's offended you."

"OH MY GOD, no, that's SO AMAZING that you've done that for me. Thank you SO MUCH, you AMAZING AND SEXY WOMAN OF MINE."

"I think they mentioned this Saturday for her burial to me, or cremation, if you'd prefer. Are there any family of Stacey's you need to contact, and any family your side, for support, I mean?"

"They all kind of disowned her when she got with me, didn't like her being gay. She comes from a very Christian family, who don't believe in 'that kind of thing', as they put it. Did you know she was married before she met me?"

"OH MY GOD, no I didn't. How did her husband take to her getting together with you? Did he know about you?"

"No, thankfully he didn't, but she just ended it with him pretty much."

"WOW, that was VERY BRAVE of her to 'come out' like that."

"It's one of the things I loved about her: she knew what she wanted, and was determined to get it, that's why she was a bit controlling at times, I think."

"What about your side at the funeral? Would anyone come any give you some moral support?"

"Again, not really, I kind of moved away from family when me and Stacey met; disapproved of her, they did. I STILL cannot believe what you did, paying for her funeral."

"Just seemed the right thing to do." Sarah didn't want Alice to have the stress of paying for Stacey's funeral and needing to attend it.

"Well, I'll pay you back, how much was it?"

"Don't be silly, it's the least I could do; you've been through a lot, and I wanted to, so no more talk of paying me back, please. You've still got one more big hurdle to get over." Sarah was a generous woman, and she'd grown fond of Alice.

Alice held Sarah's hand in Sarah's car and gazed into her eyes, before giving her a deep, meaningful kiss goodnight.

Wednesday came; Paul had not mentioned any more baby talk, and Sarah had not thought any more about it.

The girls were busy in the office, arranging meetings for potential new clients, and lunchtime had approached.

"Come on, Alice, let's go to the Mary Rose for lunch, shall we?"

"Just what I was thinking."

The girls sat down to eat, at the table that they usually sat at.

Sarah went up to the bar to order the food and drinks.

She looked further into the bar, and a familiar-looking face stared straight back at her.

"Neil?" She smiled.

The man who she met in France smiled and waved at her, and made his way across to them.

"What are you doing in here?" She smiled.

"I was just passing. I live in a place called Maplefield, not sure if you've heard of it."

"What a coincidence, I was only in Maplefield last weekend." She smiled.

"Come and join us over here, I'm here with my girl— assistant." She corrected herself.

Neil went over to where the girls were sitting, and sat next to Sarah.

"This is my assistant, Alice."

"Nice to meet you, Sarah's assistant Alice." He smiled. "Have I seen you somewhere before?"

"I seem to get asked that a lot." She laughed. "I've not lived here long, so I don't think so. How do you two know each other, anyway?"

"Oh, I met Neil on a business trip, wasn't expecting him to be in here." Sarah stopped short of telling her it was Paris.

The girls chatted to him briefly, before their food came out.

"Listen, I don't want to be rude but I'm actually in here with some colleagues, so I must go. Enjoy your food. Good to see you again, Sarah, and you, Alice."

Neil walked off, and grinned at both girls, waving to Sarah, before walking back over to where his colleagues were.

"He seemed nice." Alice smiled to Sarah, feeling a little jealous.

"He was ok, only met him briefly." Sarah tried to brush their rendezvous in Paris off.

The girls finished their meals and trundled back to the office.

Friday was soon upon them, and today was their induction day at the new gym, Finesse Fitness.

Sarah had got her gym kit together, and had also brought a new one for Alice to work out in: white shorts, trainers, a couple of tops, leggings, a water bottle each, and a few towels.

Sarah had organised for the staff in the main room, who did most of the drawings and designs, to finish at noon, and they'd be paid for the full day.

She did this for her staff occasionally, in gratitude for all their hard work, as she liked to recognise their efforts.

Her staff left at noon, as asked, and the two girls then

got their gym kit together and walked the four hundred yards to the swanky new gym.

It was buzzing with people working out: muscle-bound men lifting weights, ladies running on the treadmill, and both men and women on the rowing machines and bikes.

It was alive with funky music playing in the background, and there was still plenty of equipment for the girls to go on.

They walked up to the desk, and Sarah signed in for them both and they were given their memberships.

They wandered off to the ladies' changing rooms, to change into the gym clothing that they had both brought.

They found lockers and put their changing bags and clothes in, locked them up, and walked back into the main gym.

There, they were greeted by Justin, who would take them both through the induction.

He had been an instructor at various gyms, but had only just joined this one, not long after it had opened a month previously.

Both girls had been to gyms in the past, but they thought it'd be a good idea to go over the equipment again, just in case.

The girls decided to go on the treadmills, next to each other, and the instructor showed them how they worked.

After the induction had finished, and the instructor felt confident that they knew how to operate the machinery, he left them both to it.

Just like their sex sessions, they started off slowly, before getting into their stride.

They ran on the treadmill for about an hour, sweat pouring from their bodies, not being able to take their eyes off each other, while at the same time, making sure that they were not coming off the treadmill belt.

The two stepped off the treadmills and, wiping the sweat off themselves, went to go on the bikes.

"I didn't think I was this unfit," puffed Sarah.

"I think you're pretty fit," chuckled Alice under her heavy breath.

They rode on the bikes for another hour, before transferring over to the rowing machines.

They rowed for about thirty minutes, before they both came to a stop.

"Let's jump in the Jacuzzi," a worn-out Sarah puffed.

"Now THAT sounds like a good idea," agreed a weary-looking Alice.

They wandered into a different room, where there was a large pool, saunas and Jacuzzis, and got into one where no-one else was.

"I'm just starting to catch my breath from that workout." Alice smiled and puffed.

"Me too but it will do us both good if we keep going. Sauna?" Sarah asked.

Both girls had been in the Jacuzzi for around thirty minutes, and decided to head for a sauna.

They managed to find one that was empty, and they stepped in.

"Ah, this is the life, I could get used to this." Sarah smiled, with her eyes half open, breathing in the steam.

"I'd like to make this a regular thing, if you do?" Alice replied.

Both girls nudged up to each other, gently caressing each other's hands.

Alice kissed Sarah, and Sarah responded.

They didn't care if anyone walked in on them; they were both still feeling horny.

They started to kiss passionately, Alice's hand going into Sarah's now-soaked T-shirt, cupping her breast, and Sarah doing the same.

Suddenly, another middle-aged woman opened the sauna door and walked in, pausing briefly, seeing what the girls were doing, before both Alice and Sarah pulled away from each other, slightly embarrassed, so the lady could have her sauna and not feel awkward, although she gave a wry smile at the girls, knowing what she had just seen.

They had been at the gym some hours, and decided to head for a shower in the changing room.

Deciding they were going to shower together, they came out of the sauna and straight to the changing rooms.

They took off their gym wear and walked naked into the shower together.

They didn't care if anyone saw or even heard them; it was an adult gym, so no children would be in.

Alice turned the shower on and they began to wash each other's bodies, as they had done before.

They were still feeling slightly horny, and began to kiss and touch each other, their hands feeling every inch of each other, as they began to kiss passionately, getting more and more turned on as they did.

They still wanted to be as quiet as they could, as not to upset any of the other gym-goers, or indeed have any complaints made.

Their hands were sliding between each other's legs, riding on them as they did; they wanted each other.

"Shh…" Sarah laughed quietly. "People will hear us." Alice covered her mouth up with her hand.

"Mmm… I just can't resist you," whispered Alice.

The girls finished washing each other, with soaps provided by the gym, and washed their hair.

They finished up and grabbed their towels, before they stepped out of the shower.

Luckily, there was no-one else where the showers were, so they walked over to their lockers and began to get dressed.

Once they were dressed, they put their wet gym clothes in their gym bags and headed out.

They walked the four hundred yards back to work, so Sarah could drive Alice back to the hotel.

"Want to come and join me in my room for a bit?" Alice asked, hoping Sarah would come in to spend some more time with her.

"As much as I'd like to, I'm going to head back, I think. I'm worn out, partly down to you," Sarah joked.

The girls reached Alice's room, and Sarah kissed her goodbye.

"Sure I can't tempt you? We can just relax on the bed if you like?"

"No, it's ok. I've got some of my portfolio to go through, want to check and make sure it's in order. I'll text you over the weekend, though."

"Ok, that sounds good. That gym was great; when did you want to go again?" Alice enquired.

"Soon. We'll arrange to go again maybe next week, if you're free?"

"How can I say no?"

Alice and Sarah kissed in the doorway, before Alice opened her hotel door and closed it behind her.

Sarah left the hotel and drove home.

She arrived home, and aromas were drifting out of the kitchen window.

She walked in and Paul was in the kitchen, rustling up a delicious-smelling meal.

"WOW, I'm loving the smells. What is it?"

"I've cooked us chicken in white wine sauce, baby potatoes and broccoli, and I've also just poured you a nice glass of wine, so you can relax," he said, feeling proud that he'd done such a nice meal.

"What's the occasion?"

"Does there have to be one? Just thought I'd cook us a really nice meal, talk about each other's day."

"I know but…"

"But NOTHING. I'm just about to dish up and serve, so get changed, as it'll be on the table in a few moments."

Paul seemed to be in a better mood than usual, and this made Sarah happy.

Sarah came out wearing some joggers and a T-shirt, though still looking stylish, even though she was very dressed down.

She sat down at the table and waited for him to bring their meals over.

"I just LOVE coming home to you, especially when you make delicious meals like this." She smiled.

Paul had also got out of his work suit and was also dressed casually, in jeans and a smart hoodie.

Paul brought their meals over and put hers down in front of her.

"WOW, that smells delicious, and so do you. Is that still the same aftershave from this morning?"

"I might have added a bit more," he chuckled. "I always like to smell good for you."

"I'm not sure I'm going to be able to resist you after this meal, with you smelling so good." She smiled.

"Only AFTER the meal?" he chuckled.

The couple started eating and chatted about each other's day.

"So, you had a better day at work, then, I take it?" quizzed Sarah, seeing that he seemed far more relaxed.

"Not really. That grumpy old boss of mine is still putting lots of pressure on us; it's just that I've just tried having positive thoughts to get me through my day."

They finished their meals and Paul took the empty plates over to the kitchen and put them in the dishwasher.

"That was rather delicious; let's have that again."

"You go and make yourself comfy with your wine, put your feet up, and relax."

She really felt like she was being spoilt by him, and this was a side of him that she loved.

Paul finished loading the dishwasher and went and sat next to her.

She curled up next to him, feeling very fulfilled.

They looked at each other and slowly started to kiss.

Sarah put her wine on the table, sat back down on the sofa, and put her arms around him, as they sensually started to kiss again.

This then got more and more passionate, as the aroma of his aftershave had just got too much; she could no longer resist him.

Sarah got up from the sofa and took him by the hand, leading him to the bedroom.

She took his hoodie off, revealing his bronzed muscly chest, while he slipped his hands inside her lounger bottoms to feel her peachy arse.

He was starting to feel more and more aroused, and she could feel him pressing on her, as he pulled her loungers down, allowing her to step out of them.

She was getting more and more wet with the anticipation of what they were about to do.

She knelt down in front of him and slowly unbuttoned his jeans.

Pulling them down, she could see his bulging shaft pulsating in from of her, as she slowly caressed it through his designer pants.

She pulled his underwear down and took him in her mouth, sliding gently forwards and backwards onto him, making sure that he controlled his excitement.

After a few minutes of sucking him, he pulled her to come up, and took her T-shirt off and threw her on the bed.

They rolled around on the bed, kissing passionately before she rolled on top of him, undoing her bra as he pulled her lacy blue knickers off.

They were both naked.

Paul rolled her back over, kissing her lips and neck, before going down her body, to kiss her breasts and nipples.

He carried on kissing his way down her body, slowly licking his way around her navel, before going further down, finally nestling between her legs to taste her sweet, moist pussy.

He swirled his tongue deep inside her, and she was in the height of ecstasy, not sure how long it would be before she came.

She pulled for him to come back up, and he paused to slide his hard erection inside her, covering every inch of her.

He began thrusting harder and harder, the bed-frame hitting the wall as the new picture shuddered, almost falling off, their passion was that intense.

Sarah was panting fast, as was he, as he carried on kissing her around her neck as he thrust into her.

His pace quickened; he was close to climaxing, as was she, and, almost in an instant, they came, shuddering to a halt almost immediately.

He pulled himself off her and dropped down next to her on the bed, both trying to catch their breaths.

"WOW, a delicious dinner, and YOU for dessert." She laughed. "What more could any girl ask for?"

He looked at her and chuckled at her comment.

"Have you thought any more about what we have discussed?" he asked. "Though I know I said that I wouldn't bring it up again."

"A baby, you mean?"

"Yes, a baby. I know we've not been together overly long but I think a baby would bring us even closer together. What do you think?"

"I don't know, Paul. I've not really given it much more thought, if I'm honest. I'm not saying no; like I said before, just want to see how things pan out, work-wise and stuff, I mean."

"Have you never wanted a family of your own?" he muttered.

"Yes, of course I have, but there is so much going on. Maybe when things settle down for us both, with work and getting to know each other more, then maybe."

She turned her head to look at him, and he had disappointment in his face.

She stroked his cheek, trying to comfort him, as he got up from the bed and got dressed, even though it wasn't too long before bed.

He wandered off into the lounge, leaving Sarah to get up, put some clothes on and come back into the lounge.

"I'm still worn out from that," Sarah joked, hoping to raise a smile from him.

"Sex with you is always so good," he replied. "I'm never disappointed."

She came and sat with him on the sofa, nestling back up to him.

"Fancy doing anything this weekend?" she asked, hoping that they could find some time for each other.

"What about another trip out? Maybe just go for a drive."

"That sounds like a good idea; we could maybe take another picnic, wherever we end up."

"That sounds like a plan." She had totally forgotten that she would be joining Alice at Stacey's funeral.

She decided to text Alice.

Hey honey, do you know what's happening with the funeral yet?

Alice – *I was just about to text you. I've rearranged her funeral for the following Saturday, at eleven in*

*the morning, going to have her cremated. It's what
she would have wanted. Are you still able to come?*

Sarah – *And miss offering you my support? I don't think
so, I'll be there. Do you need any more money for that?*

Alice – *No, thank you. it's cost the same, I don't want
to know what you paid but thank you again.*
    I love you, Sarah.

Sarah smiled, reading the text from Alice, and she knew
how she felt about Alice too, but she also felt guilty that she
had feelings for a woman who had not long lost her partner.

"I love you too," she sneakily replied, smiling to herself
once more as she texted it, knowing that Paul was still
hovering around somewhere.

The Saturday of the funeral soon came around, and
Paul asked why Sarah was dressed up all in black.

"You look like you're going to a funeral," he joked.

"Maybe it's because I am." She angrily scowled back, but
not wanting him to know that it was for her lover.

"Oh, well, I wasn't to know, was I? Who is it for, someone
at work?"

"Yeah, one of the girls. Someone close has passed away,
and they've asked me to go." She did not want to give him
any more information; as little as he needed to hear.

"Ah, that's a shame, pass them on my deepest sympathy."
He immersed himself back in paperwork and sat down in
his favourite chair, almost going into his own little world.

Sarah had agreed to meet Alice at Barnwood city
church, in the centre of the city, for the funeral service: a

lovely tall-spired church, lots of stained-glass windows, letting through lots of light; it was beautiful when the sun shone, beaming through the church, lighting it up with lots of colour hitting the windows.

The church would hold around three hundred, and its priest was a Father Hopewell.

Sarah left the house and turned up at the church a short while after.

As she pulled into the car park, she saw Alice, wearing a very elegant black outfit and hat.

Alice started to walk over to Sarah's car, Sarah winding her window down.

"How you feeling, honey?"

"I'm ok," declared Alice. "Just want the day to be over, though. Some of the regular congregation of the church have turned up too, and I've agreed that they can share the service with us, though she was never a people person really, pretty much kept herself to herself."

Sarah stepped out of the car, locked up and started to walk over to the church entrance.

"Thank you for being with me today; it means a lot."

"It's the least I could do. I said I'd be here to support you, and I keep my promises."

"You do look lovely, honey, just wish it was better circumstances really." Alice smiled to Sarah.

"You look pretty good too. Let's just through today, but remember, I'm here, ok?" Sarah whispered to Alice, showing her support.

"I know, thank you, just want the day to be over."

They wandered down to the front of the church, as the pallbearers outside slowly carried Stacey's coffin inside.

The church had a very sparse congregation, as solemn music started to reverberate around the church, bellowing out from the organ.

Everyone inside the church all sat down, as the priest started saying a few words for Alice's late partner.

Sarah grabbed hold of Alice's hand, as tears rolled down Alice's cheeks as she held a handkerchief in the other hand, wiping away dribbles of tears running down her nose.

"It's ok," Sarah whispered to her, giving her a reassuring grin. "It'll all soon be over."

Alice glanced at Sarah briefly, and gave a polite grin back, Alice's face grief-stricken.

The service was over in just over thirty minutes, as the congregation slowly started to pile out of the church.

Parishioners came over to Alice, to offer her their condolences, and Alice thanked them all individually.

Even though Alice never went to the church, she was grateful to them for being so kind, and also for wanting to stay for the service.

Sarah stood slightly back from Alice, as this was her moment, her time to think about her former partner, and to spend the time to thank those of the congregation who were consoling her.

Alice went over to that the priest to thank him for giving Stacey such a wonderful send-off.

Again, Sarah stood slightly back from her as, again, this wasn't about the two of them today, but for Alice, so she could reflect on what had happened between her and Stacey, and remember the good times they'd had.

"So, what happens now?" Alice turned to Sarah, not knowing what to do.

"Well, it's normally a wake, isn't it, but, seeing as it's just the two of us, do you want to maybe go for a meal or something, talk about the times you spent with Stacey, tell me about all your funny stories? You must have plenty to tell me." Sarah was intrigued about Alice's previous life with her, wanted to know everything there was to know.

"Not really much to say but is it ok if we just go for a meal? Don't really want to talk about Stacey; it's still too raw," Alice's eyes began to well up with tears once again, and Sarah didn't want to push any further.

"Yes, of course, we can talk about whatever you like. Come on, you decide where you'd like to go, and I'm paying, my treat," Sarah wanted to be a pillar of strength for Alice, knowing that she was going to be needed from here on in, and didn't want to let her down.

… and Sarah wasn't about to let her down.

Six months later

The trail of Stacey's murder had gone cold; the police had no new leads or fingerprints, although the case was still ongoing.

All suspects had also been questioned, and there was nothing new to go on.

Alice had moved back to the house that she shared with Stacey before her murder, and, with Alice working at Sarah's company, practically as her PA, where she had been for the last seven months, running errands for her, she seemed to get on really well with Sarah's other employees, and had settled in well.

Sarah and Paul, meanwhile, had bought a two-year-old red setter dog named Henry, who was a calm and well-groomed dog, and the couple had also hired a dog-walker while they both worked.

Paul still appeared troubled with his work life, while Sarah's business was flourishing. She had also managed to tap into the Asian market, with great success.

The time had just gone two in the afternoon, and Alice and Sarah had had a few late-night meetings at work, so they could spend some time alone, making love in Sarah's office.

"Any paperwork you'd like me to do tonight, Sarah?" She glanced across at her with a suggestive smile and wink.

"I'm going to head back tonight, I think; you're wearing me out," Sarah whispered, so that the other employees wouldn't overhear their conversation.

"Besides, Paul is being a bit off, stress with work, I think, but definitely tomorrow."

Both girls smiled at each other for a few moments, with their imaginations running wild.

"Anyway, been thinking. Let's go to the gym again later in the week, what do you think?" asked Sarah. "Maybe after pumping some iron, maybe we could pump each other after." She smiled, whispering so others wouldn't overhear.

A few hours had ticked by; it was six in the evening, and time for everyone to go home.

The other employees started to leave, just leaving Sarah and Alice.

"Goodnight, boss, goodnight, Alice, see you both tomorrow," came their collective voices.

"Goodnight, everyone. Thank you all for your hard work as always," shouted Sarah.

"Goodnight, all," shouted Alice, not wanting to miss out saying goodbye.

Just Alice and Sarah were left.

"Sure I can't tempt you?" teased Alice, as she undid a few buttons on her blouse and leant across Sarah's desk.

"As tempting as you are, I really must head back, but I'll make my excuses for tomorrow for sure."

As Sarah said that, she got together a few papers on her desk, before putting them in a folder, closing it shut and putting it away in the metal filing cabinet in the corner of the office.

She grabbed their coats from the large coat stand in the other corner of the office, before she casually walked over to Alice and planted a lingering kiss on her lips.

"Until tomorrow, then," whispered Alice invitingly.

Both girls walked out of the office, as Sarah locked the door behind her.

"Fancy a lift home?" said Sarah. "It is a cold night."

"No, it's ok. I'm only up the hill, aren't I?"

The girls said goodnight to each other.

Sarah got in her car and watched Alice in her rear-view mirror, walking out of the company car park, heading home.

She paused to watch her for a few moments, before starting her car to head home.

Sarah pulled up outside the house to find the lights were on.

He would occasionally get home before her, so this wasn't unusual.

He had already cooked, as this was their normal routine, and had started to eat already.

Again, this was normal for them.

"Good day, darling?" she asked, just after walking in the door and hanging her coat up.

"Hmm. I don't know why you ask such STUPID QUESTIONS sometimes," he snapped.

Sarah suddenly stopped in her tracks, not quite believing the way he'd just spoken to her.

"Well, I was only—" she said, before he rudely interrupted.

"Well DON'T," he angrily snapped back at her. "I'm going out with some friends down the local, don't know what time I'll be back," he growled.

Sarah decided to remain quiet, feeling quite angry and upset at the same time with his attitude.

He had obviously had another bad day at work, and she didn't want to antagonise the situation.

The atmosphere in the house was very frosty; you could cut it with a knife.

He got up, after he finished his food, and put the plate and cutlery in the dishwasher, walking around Sarah as he did. He went to grab his coat from the coat stand in the lounge, and walked back to the kitchen, to give a stunned Sarah a kiss on the cheek, before putting his coat on and walking out the door, slamming it shut.

It was a side that she had not seen of him before.

He did get frustrated occasionally but nothing like this.

Things must have been bad at work.

Paul arrived at his local, the Adlington Arms, soon after. His old friends from his schooldays, Gary, John, Charlie and Steve, were already there, waiting for him.

This was a livelier pub than the Mary Rose, which Sarah and Alice had been drinking in before, but it was a cold

Tuesday evening, and not many people were out, so the pub was half empty, however inviting the pub was, with a cosy real log fire crackling by the bar.

Paul had booked a taxi from the house; it was about a fifteen-minute journey from where they lived.

He got out of the taxi, paid the driver and walked in.

"Here he is," shouted John with a cheer, raising his pint of bitter as he did.

The others cheered too.

Paul had stayed in touch with his friends growing up, and had stayed friends ever since, though Paul was particularly closer to John than the others.

"Barman, a pint for this fine gentleman," called John towards the bar.

The friends were sitting a few tables away from the fire, so as not to get too warm.

Paul too liked a pint of bitter; the pub's own brew, "The Killer Whale", was particularly strong.

The friends didn't get together as often as they used to, not since Sarah had appeared on the scene.

"Out on good behaviour?" laughed John.

"I'm sorry we've not met up for a while but, what with work and…" said Paul.

"You don't have to explain to us," said Gary, cutting into Paul's explanation, to reassure him.

"Life just gets in the way, mate, you don't have to explain," muttered Charlie.

"So, what's been happening with you, then, Paul?" asked Steve.

The friends had been drinking for around three hours, and were all pretty worse for wear.

They'd been chatting about life, love and work, as well as reminiscing about their lives growing up, as well as their schooldays together.

"We should… hic… do this… hic… again," mumbled a drunken John.

"I… hic… agree," slurred Charlie.

"Not tomorrow," slurred Paul, smiling at his friends.

Paul then gingerly raised his hand towards the bar, as if he were back in class at school.

Paul's eyes were glazed.

"Will you call… will you call… me," stumbled Paul, turning round towards the barman, not being able to get his words out.

"A taxi?" laughed the barman.

With that, he nodded towards the barman; that is what he was needing.

The bar staff knew Paul, and within five minutes the taxi had arrived.

"Your taxi is here; get yourself home," said the barman.

Paul got up from his chair, almost falling over it before stumbling towards the pub door and the waiting taxi. He was just about to head out of the door when the barman appeared next to him.

"Your coat?" said the bemused barman.

With that, Paul grabbed his coat from the barman, waved over to his friends in a drunken fashion, almost struggling to stand up before stumbling towards the waiting taxi.

He was soon home. He fumbled around for his wallet before pulling out a ten-pound note from his pocket, and gave it to the driver.

"Keep the change," he mumbled.

He stumbled out of the taxi, hunting around for his keys.

A glazed-looking Paul looked back to see the taxi driver pull off.

"Shh," he hushed, putting his finger to his lips, to a ginger cat going across the driveway. The lights were all off, so Sarah must be asleep.

He felt all of his pockets for his keys, before finding them in his coat pocket.

He took an age to find the right house key.

Paul had a few keys on his keyring: front door, back, car and office keys.

He finally found the right key, before eventually putting it in the slot and opening the door, stumbling into it as it opened.

He was finally inside.

"Shh," he went once again to the cat, but the cat had gone; he was seeing things, being drunk.

He clumsily stumbled into the door once again, as he was closing it.

Again, he tried to find the right key to lock the door behind him, but he eventually did.

He then carefully, and gradually, walked towards the bedroom, swaying as he did.

He tried opening the bedroom door as quietly as he could, trying not to disturb Sarah, who was asleep.

She briefly opened her tired eyes and lifted her head slightly to look at him, even though the room was dark.

"You're drunk," she whispered to him, half asleep.

"Shh, go back to sleep," he slurred.

With that, she laid her head back down on her puffed-up pillow, and drifted back off to sleep.

Paul walked over to the chair that they had in the corner of the room, and sat down, as he was struggling to steady himself standing up, to remove his clothes.

He undid his shirt slowly, struggling to find his buttons, before undoing the buttons on his trousers, and tried to pull them down.

He stood up from the chair, as he was struggling to get them off sitting down.

Almost in the same motion, he collapsed in a heap on the floor, as he was trying to get one of his legs out of his tight trousers.

THUD!

This woke Sarah.

"What ARE you doing?" she snapped.

"Go back to sleep."

He finally managed to get out of his trousers, and got safely into bed, pulling most of the quilt from her before Sarah yanked some back.

They were soon both fast asleep.

He realised that he had work in the morning, but first he needed to sleep it off.

THERE'S SOMEONE OUT THERE

The next morning came, and Sarah woke around six-thirty.

Paul was already up.

She sat up and put her feet on the floor, before stretching and yawning.

She got up out of bed and walked towards the bathroom.

She walked towards the door, still feeling half asleep from her broken night, with him stumbling in from his lads' night out.

Paul was just getting out of the shower.

"Good morning," he said, in a slight grovelling voice.

"Is it?" a cross Sarah said, with her disturbed sleep.

Sarah took her nightshirt off that she had worn to bed, and stepped into the shower, alone.

Even if they had the time, she was in no mood to make love to him this morning.

Paul grabbed a big towel from the airing cupboard in the bathroom, and wrapped it around his waist, before walking out, leaving Sarah to shower.

She was looking forward to tonight, having her late night with Alice, to go over her "particulars".

Sarah was fantasising what they might get up to, remembering how they made love back at the hotel where Alice was.

She started touching and caressing herself at the thought.

She also realised that she needed to get out of the shower, have breakfast and a coffee, before getting dressed, before she headed off to work.

She stepped out, turning the shower off.

She grabbed another thick towel out, wrapping it under her armpits, and also one for her long blonde hair.

She walked out of the bathroom, and into the open-plan living area and kitchen, where Paul was already dressed, wearing a well-pressed pink shirt, a thin silk pink tie and perfectly creased light-blue trousers, and very shiny smart black shoes.

"How's your head this morning?" she snapped.

"I'm recovering," he sighed. "I've just had some strong, black coffee. I'm sorry I…" said Paul apologetically.

"Save it," she interrupted, too angry for an apology.

The atmosphere was again slightly frosty; she was still angry with him, especially from his mood earlier, speaking to her the way he did.

She made herself some brown toast and a milky latte from the coffee machine.

She sat at the breakfast bar in the kitchen, staring into

space, while munching on her toast, not saying a word to him; she was too angry.

Paul walked into the lounge to sit down, and get his documents together ready to take into work with him; it was going to be a busy day ahead.

He worked for a local finance company called Miller & Chamberlain Finance, where he had worked for the past five years.

Business was a little slower than usual, and he, and a few of the other directors, were tasked with putting that right.

"I need to go into work; I've got quite a lot to sort out." He fleetingly glanced across to Sarah as he spoke, still feeling a bit awkward about last night.

"I'm going to walk into work today. Don't want pulling over. Thought I might even go and pay my brothers and parents a visit this weekend too; not seen then for a while."

She just looked up at him, drinking her coffee, giving him a slight grin.

"Maybe you should," she snapped, still upset with his behaviour from the day before.

Paul had three brothers: Chris, who was married, a father of two boys and who was a bricklayer; Anthony, the eldest of the brothers, who was also married, with two boys and a girl, and worked at a local restaurant in Austin as a head chef; and Dean, who was the black sheep of the family, was always getting into trouble and getting arrested. He also took drugs with his equally wayward girlfriend, despite Paul's protests with him.

Dean and Paul rarely saw eye to eye now, and Paul often left him to his own devices, despite the fact that they had been the closest growing up, always going out together, and sharing girlfriends.

Paul's parents, Joan and Harold, also lived in Churchfield, where Alice's parents were, and were both very frail.

He grabbed his matching suit jacket, and walked towards the kitchen, to give Sarah a kiss goodbye.

But she was having none of it; she didn't want a kiss goodbye from him, so she pulled away as he tried to kiss her.

"Erm, ok, I'll see you later then," he mumbled.

He walked towards the door, opened and closed it soon after, without saying another word.

He arrived at work around eight-thirty, just getting into his office on time, as that was when he was meant to start.

His boss, Mr McGee, was an overweight, grumpy man, with receding hair and bad teeth, and smelly breath: no-one really liked to talk to him at close quarters.

Mr McGee had been with the company nearly thirty years, and was very stuck in his ways; he liked things being done a certain way.

Even though it was a local firm, it was one of the city's biggest finance companies, employing just over three hundred staff.

Just as Paul had sat down and put his file of documents on his desk, and turned his monitor on, Mr McGee appeared in the doorway.

"Now then, Paul, don't forget. We need to start looking at ways of generating new business. Get together with some of the other directors, put your ideas across to each other, as we can't allow things to start slipping, there's a good fellow," he said, in a gravelly voice.

"Right on it, Mr McGee." The overweight boss walked away and down the corridor.

Paul would rather be somewhere else today, though, as his head was still sore from the night before.

His mobile received a text message.

BEEP BEEP…

It was his friend John.

Last night was great. Is your head as sore as ours? Don't leave it so long next time.

Paul knew that he had to get on with his work, as he started to type away, arranging meetings with the other directors.

A few hours had gone by, and it was midday.

He was about to head to an early lunch.

He had arranged a meeting with the other directors for just after lunch, and it left him in a positive mood.

'I'm going to order Sarah a big bunch of flowers,' he thought, "have them deliver, send to her work."

He rang Barnwood Florists.

"Yes, hello. Can I order a big bunch of flowers, some red roses, about eighty pounds?"

He finished ordering the flowers before paying by card, and asked for them to be delivered to Sarah's work, and gave them the address.

He knew that he needed to make it up to her somehow.

It was two in the afternoon, and a van pulled into Sarah's work car park.

The driver of the van got out, went to the back of the van and pulled out a big bouquet of bright red roses.

Most of Sarah's employees gazed out of the window, wondering who the lucky recipient was.

The van driver walked into the building.

"Delivery for a Sarah Waysmith," he shouts.

Just then, Sarah appeared from her office, her eyes lighting up, and a big gleaming smile appearing on her face, seeing the beautiful arrangement, and knowing that they were probably from Paul.

Alice looked on, feeling slightly jealous.

"Someone is trying to apologise," said one of Sarah's employees.

Sarah casually walked over to the driver, took the bouquet from him, and strode confidently back into her office.

Alice continued to look on, with a slight hint of envy.

"They look nice, expensive-looking, too."

"I think someone is trying to apologise to me somehow; he was in a foul mood last night, and he was trying to grovel a bit this morning, I think. Listen, darling, I know we said about having a late-night meeting tonight, but would you mind if we did it another night instead? I am feeling a bit bushed," said a sad-looking Sarah, her bottom lip protruding, showing Alice that she was sorry about not having their late-night rendezvous as planned.

"That's ok. I could probably do with sorting out some modelling bits anyway. My portfolio is back at the house, and I can look online for extra hints and tips that may help me get more work. I can't stay here forever."

"As long as you save some 'hints and tips' for me too," teased Sarah, brushing her fingers along Alice's hand.

"But of course, darling, that goes without saying."

Time ticked on, and it was five o'clock.

It was an early finish today at Sarah's Fashion House.

And the employees were starting to grab their coats to leave for the day.

Sarah and Alice started to shut down their computers and tidy their desks, while putting their files away in the cabinet.

They waited for the other girls to leave for the evening, after they had all said their customary goodbyes, as the company door closed behind them.

Sarah approached Alice, who moments before had sadly buttoned her blouse back up, before being pulled in for a clinch.

"It's only because he's down, Alice, you understand, don't you?"

"Of course I do, now are you going to kiss me or not?" Alice laughed.

Sarah slowly started to kiss her, as their fingers ran through each other's golden hair.

Suddenly, the company door was flung open.

"Sorry, I just forgot my…"

Sarah's employee Helen stood motionless with shock, as she spotted Sarah and Alice in a clinch, coming back for her handbag that she forgot to pick up before she left.

"Oh, erm, I'll just, erm… go," said Helen, as Sarah and Alice pulled apart as quickly as they could, both blushing at the prospect of being caught.

"Goodnight, Helen, see you tomorrow," said a sheepish Sarah.

Helen rushed quickly back out of the door, not turning back round to see them.

"Do you think she spotted us?" said a nervous Alice.

"Hopefully not but I'll have a word with her in the morning, don't worry, I'll smooth it out."

Just then the girls got their belongings together, Sarah grabbing her flowers that had been delivered earlier, before walking out of the office together, Sarah locking it behind her.

"Lift home, Alice?"

"No, it's ok. I still enjoy my walk, plus it's not far."

Sarah was struggling to hold her big bouquet, as well as her bag and coat, before shuffling out of the building.

"See you tomorrow, then, Alice."

Alice started to walk away from Sarah's car, and glanced back at her with a grin.

Sarah's lips moved to the words "I love you" as she was looking back.

Alice stopped to glance at Sarah for a few moments, raising a bigger smile at what Sarah had said, before turning back round to head home.

Sarah opened the back door of her car, putting the flowers on the back seat, taking up so much room, before closing it. She then opened the passenger door, putting her bag on the floor. She then got in the car to drive home, wondering how she could make it up to Alice.

It was a dark, starry night, cold but the full moon was visible.

Sarah arrived home soon after, to find the lights on, and some nice aromas coming from the slightly ajar windows.

As she walked in, clutching her flowers and bag, all she could smell was steak being cooked in the kitchen.

"Hi, darling, good day?" said a happy Paul.

"That smells good; you been home long?"

"Half an hour. I stopped by the supermarket, and picked up a couple of sirloin steaks for us. Go and relax; it won't be long."

"Thank you for the flowers, by the way. Pleasant surprise: they're beautiful."

"Thought I needed to make it up to you for last night."

"It's ok. It's not often that you get a chance to see your friends, is it?"

Sarah put the flowers on the sofa, kicked off her shoes and lay upright on the sofa.

"Here you go. A nice glass of wine before dinner."

"You're spoiling me now. You should go out and see your friends more often," joked Sarah.

She went and sat at the dining table as he brought dinner over.

He had cooked them both an eight-ounce sirloin steak, medium, how they both liked it, with chunky chips, mushrooms and peas, and with a rich sauce for the steak.

"This looks amazing; what made you think of cooking us this?"

"Just fancied cooking us a steak tonight. Is that ok? Just know that it's your favourite."

"Good choice!" She smiled.

As the couple started to eat, the conversation turned to his work.

"How are things at work, Paul?"

"We're all under so much pressure to bring in new business," he sighed. "Mr McGee is cracking the whip a bit; it's really getting quite stressful."

"I know how to help relieve your stress," she teased.

Paul looked her up and down, with a broad smile on his face.

Sarah finished her meal in quick time, obviously feeling very hungry.

"That was delicious, darling, now then, maybe I need to leave you a little tip."

She got up from the table, her chair pushing away as she did.

She seductively leant across the table towards him, so he could get a good view of her heaving chest.

"Anything I can get you, sir?" she teased.

Paul was trying hard to finish his meal, but he knew that he wanted her.

Sarah slowly walked over behind him, sliding her hand down his shirt to his chest, unbuttoning a few buttons as she did, and caressed his muscly chest.

"You don't really want those last few chips and mushrooms on your plate, do you?"

With that, Paul let go of his cutlery, as he could resist her no longer.

He stood up from his chair, thrusting it back, and grabbed her, before pushing her towards the lounge wall.

Sarah started to frantically undo the belt on his trousers, like loved-up teenagers, as he started to grasp for the zip on the back of her dress.

Before long, the couple were naked, and as the moonlight was shining through the back window Sarah reached for the light switch to turn it off, as she liked to make love with the moonlight shining through.

Paul was starting to thrust hard inside her; she felt a passion from him that she hadn't felt for a while.

Their legs were trembling at the sheer passion of the moment.

Suddenly, there was a rustling noise outside their front window.

"What was that?" she gasped.

"Probably nothing, just enjoy the moment."

She felt that she also saw a shadow go across the window.

"Paul, stop. There's someone out there; I feel like someone is watching us. Please go and see."

Paul put his trousers and shirt back on, as Sarah shakily turned the lights back on before pulling her dress back up, covering herself up as quickly as she could, in case they were still watching.

Paul went over, opened the front door, calling their dog, Henry, to go out with him, and, in the still of the night, wandered outside and looked around.

"Can you see anyone?" muttered a frightened Sarah.

"No, there's no-one out here; don't you think Henry would have barked if there was? Maybe you just saw a cat or something."

"No… no, it was definitely someone. I saw movement."

"Well, there is no-one around now."

Paul came back inside, with Henry striding elegantly and majestically behind him, as Paul closed and locked the door.

"I'll pour us a nice glass of wine and watch some TV," he said, hoping that'd calm her.

Sarah turned the electric fire on, and curled up next to Paul on the sofa, as Henry lay down near the fire.

Time had passed and it was around eleven, and they both had to be up early for work.

They put Henry back into his dog bed under the stairs, a spacious room where he could roam freely, and they bid him a goodnight.

The couple, feeling tired after a long day, and their broken sex, decided to curl up in bed to sleep.

Sarah still felt anxious about what she thought she had seen outside, and it was stopping her from sleeping that night.

She was worried in case they were still lurking outside.

'Who was watching us?' she thought, before drifting off to sleep.

DEPTHS OF DESPAIR

Morning broke; it was six, and the couple arose to start their next working day.

Paul was still feeling pressured into finding new business at work. He knew how much he needed to please Mr McGee, and he woke up in a very quiet mood.

Sarah, on the other hand, although still feeling edgy from the previous night, was full of the joys of the day ahead. After all, business was booming, she had met Alice, where things were going well, and everything felt rosy.

"Are you SURE you didn't see anyone outside last night, Paul?"

"I said I hadn't, didn't I?" he snapped.

"Are you ok, darling, what's wrong?"

"Just got work stuff on my mind, lots going on, I'm going for a shower... ALONE."

Sarah watched as he walked towards the bathroom. She was starting to notice him in a slightly different light: not the same man that she had got used to. He seemed very withdrawn from her, apart from last night, and it was starting to put a strain on their relationship.

At least she had Alice to confide in, and to make love to.

Paul came out of the bathroom, having had his shower, water still dripping from his muscly body.

Sarah had sat on the bed, contemplating the day ahead and thinking about planning a trip to Asia to discuss business, and to have Alice with her.

Sarah patiently waited for him to come back into the bedroom, wanting a shower herself.

She got up and brushed past him, heading to the bathroom.

"Guess I'll just have to have a shower on my own, then."

Paul gave her a frosty look.

She was in the shower around twenty minutes, around the same time as Paul had been.

"I'm SURE I saw someone outside last night. There was DEFINITELY no-one outside?" she muttered, drying her hair, as she left the bathroom.

"Did I not just tell you that there wasn't!" he snapped.

"My God… I was only asking."

Paul made himself a bit of toast and a coffee, and sat at the breakfast bar, staring blankly into space.

Sarah made herself some muesli and went and sat away from him, at the dining table.

She didn't want to sit with him if he was going to be in a mood.

After their breakfast, they both quietly went into the bedroom to get dressed, not saying a word to each other. The atmosphere was very frosty.

Once both were fully dressed, Sarah in a stylish bright purple suit and Paul in a smart black shirt (to match his mood), white tie and light-grey trousers, he gathered his belongings together and, quick as a flash, he was out the door, without even so much as giving Sarah a kiss goodbye, or to see her later.

His mood was troubling her. She'd never seen him in such a mood but, knowing the pressures he had from work, was thinking of ways of relaxing him later. She had to try something; maybe they could carry on where they had left off last night. This was very out of character for him.

Sarah was almost ready to leave.

She went to check on Henry, as she did every morning before she left.

The dog-walker, Monika, had access to the house with a spare key, and she always let herself in after the pair had left off for work.

Sarah checked that she had got everything that she needed, and left the house ten minutes before nine, making sure that the house was locked up behind her, still feeling slightly unnerved from last night.

It was a normal routine day for her, lots of phone calls to discuss more orders, something that she generally passed over to Alice to sort for her, as Sarah had shown her previously what she had to do, how to sort the invoices, and she had become very adept at it.

Sarah had cleared things up with her employee Helen about what she saw, and told her not to discuss it with anyone. She told Helen that Alice was having some personal issues, and that she was comforting her.

Helen accepted this, apologised for barging in on them, and went about her normal day.

Sarah was particularly quiet this day. Paul was on her mind, with how moody he had become, but knowing he was feeling pressure from work.

"You're very quiet today," whispered Alice.

"Just got so many things on with work, and HIM being in a mood."

"Still?" quizzed Alice.

"Yeah. Think he just needs a holiday, recharge his batteries, he'll be fine then."

"I've missed you," whispered a sad Alice.

"I know, I have you, and I will make it up to you, I promise."

Time had moved on, and it was time for lunch.

"Come on Alice. Let's go to the Mary Rose for lunch, shall we? Do us both a bit of good."

"Liking the sound of that."

They closed their laptops and almost darted out of the office, like whippets from traps.

"Off out for lunch, girls, won't be long," said Sarah. "If anyone needs me or calls, just take a message for me please, if you're here of course."

The girls set off to the pub for lunch. It brought back memories for them, as this is where they first made love.

The girls normally brought lunch in to work, so this was a rare treat for the two of them.

"What would you like to drink, darling? The usual?" asked Sarah.

"Just a Diet Coke would be lovely, please."

"You can have something alcoholic, you know. I won't mind just this once," joked Sarah.

"No, it's ok. A Diet Coke is fine, thank you. I prefer a clear head when I'm working."

The girls then sat down at a table to order some food, Sarah having ordered herself a glass of white wine.

Sarah started to browse the food menu that was propped up against the wall by the table.

"What do you fancy to eat, Alice?"

"YOU!" she whispered, while glancing across at Sarah, with a glint in her eyes, giving her the biggest and sexiest smile, raising her eyebrows at her.

Sarah shuffled uneasily in her seat, knowing Alice was trying to arouse her.

"While you're browsing the menu, Alice, with what you REALLY want to eat, I need the ladies."

"That's ok, I need the ladies too, well, one particular lady," she joked.

The girls left their drinks at the table, as they had done before, before shuffling off, into a direction they were both familiar with.

Sarah entered the bathroom first, with Alice close behind, caressing Sarah's peachy bum.

"I want you, Sarah, I want you NOW."

Alice pushed her against the toilet wall, and started to passionately kiss her, and caress her breasts through her dress.

"No… no… not now, Alice. I want you too, but there is so much going on with Paul, and I need to try and get to the bottom of what's happening, we will soon… I PROMISE."

Alice, feeling slightly rejected and sexually frustrated, although she understood, grabbed Sarah's hand and kissed her lips.

Sarah did feel guilty, and she would make it up to her as soon as things were better at home.

Alice walked out of the bathroom first, and back to the table, and started to browse the menu.

Sarah came out, not long after.

"Decided what you're having yet?" Sarah asked, sheepishly.

"Hmmm, maybe a nice six-ounce steak, chips and salad for me, I think."

"Maybe the same for me too," Sarah replied. "Sorry," she whispered.

"It's ok. I understand."

The girls' lunches arrived in quick time, and they both devoured it.

The girls chatted generally, mostly about work but also about each other.

"I thought we could arrange to meet up again with my friends one of these nights, maybe one Friday night. What do you think?"

"Yes, that'd be AMAZING; where were you thinking of meeting up with them?"

"I was thinking that nice bar called Shakers again, the nice wine bar. It's always busy, and it's just a great place to meet up, maybe have a dance while we're there," Sarah said gleefully.

"That sounds great to me."

"Anyway, I'm going to need to ask you if you'd like to travel with me to Hong Kong. I've a business meeting," asked Sarah.

"WOW… I'd love to. I've never been there before, not even in my modelling days; it's somewhere I've always fancied going. Thank you."

"I need to make a few phone calls, organise a date with a businessman called Mr Yang. It'll only be for a few days; you sure that's ok with you?"

"That's more than ok. I'm already starting to look forward to it," said an excited Alice.

The girls had eaten their lunch, and drunk their drinks, before walking back to the office.

Once back at their desks, Sarah picked the phone up and asked to speak to Mr Yang, at Yang's clothes store.

Dialling tone…

Sarah gets through to the receptionist.

"Yes, hello, can I speak to Mr Yang, please? It's Sarah Waysmith from Sarah's Fashion House."

"One moment, please," said the receptionist.

"Ah, Sarah, I've been waiting for you to call. I hope you are well," said a chirpy Mr Yang.

"I am very well, Mr Yang. I hope you, your wife and children are also keeping well."

"Yes, thank you. How can I help you, Sarah? More orders for me to look over, I hope."

"Yes, Mr Yang, you know I don't like to disappoint you. I was hoping to come and pay you another visit, take a look at some new designs we've been working on. I was hoping I could arrange an appointment with you."

"Ok, let me check my diary. How about… a week on Friday, how does that suit you?"

Sarah looked over at Alice, whispering the date of travel, while covering the telephone mouthpiece.

Alice nodded with excitement, her face beaming with delight.

"Yes, a week Friday will be fine. I'll be bringing my assistant with me. Can we say about one in the afternoon, Mr Yang?"

"Yes. My diary is clear that afternoon, so will be fine. See you then."

Both Sarah and Mr Yang put their phones down, almost simultaneously.

"All sorted. You sure you'd like to come along, Alice?"

"I've been looking forward to it, plus we get to spend some time together too."

"Maybe being away from Paul, will do him some good, see what he's missing," said a defiant Sarah.

The day had ticked on, it was six in the evening, and Sarah's employees all started to leave for the evening, waving to the girls as they left.

The girls tidied away their files, and turned off their laptops.

"I thought we could maybe make a weekend of Hong Kong, Alice, what do you think?"

"That sounds like an awesome idea," Alice said, excitedly. "I really cannot wait."

"I wonder what sort of mood HE's going to be in tonight," said a disgruntled Sarah.

"You sure you don't want to take Paul away to Hong Kong instead? You said he needed a holiday."

"He's been away with me before and he hated it, so no. Besides, I'd rather take you."

The girls met in the middle of the office. Sarah walked off to check that the building door was locked; she didn't want to be caught out again. She wandered back over to Alice, still standing in the middle of the office, and they pulled each other in close, before slowly kissing and holding each other for a few moments.

They then parted and walked out of the office, Sarah locking the door behind them, before leaving the building, and locking up the building door.

"See you tomorrow, darling," said Alice, romantically holding Sarah's fingers, before letting go so Sarah could go to her car.

"Goodnight, Alice, see you in the morning."

Sarah looked back at Alice in her rear-view mirror, watching her walk home.

It was a cold night, and Sarah hated the thought of her walking home alone, especially because she had kept offering her a lift, but she preferred to walk, and it was only a short walk.

Sarah was soon home, the lights were on, and food smells were coming from the windows.

She walked in, and saw that Paul had been cooking.

"Hi. Mmm… that smells lovely." She smiled.

"It's just a Bolognese. I've had mine already," he said grumpily. "There's plenty there for you. I'm going for a shower, as I'm going out tonight, meeting up with the boys."

"Please tell me what's wrong. I cannot stand this atmosphere at the minute with you, plus you haven't really come near me in weeks."

"Like I keep saying, it's just work stuff, so many things going on; you know I'm under a lot of pressure, that's all."

"Well, I'm arranging a business trip to Hong Kong with an assistant at work. I know you don't like these business trips of mine, so, I'm taking someone else. We're going next Friday, and I won't be back until the Sunday," said Sarah, hoping to get a reaction from him.

"You do that," he said sternly. "I'm going for my shower. Oh, and I'm going to go and see my parents and brothers this weekend too."

He headed to the bathroom, before slamming the door shut.

Sarah could not be doing with his mood, and went to fix up her own meal that Paul had left her.

Sarah plated up the Bolognese that he had cooked, sat down to eat, and started to text Alice.

He's still in a mood, cannot be doing with his attitude at the minute. Maybe I should come and stay with you for a little while, might help him snap out of this.

Alice texted back.

Just stay strong. We're going away soon anyway.

Sarah put her phone down to finish eating, just as he came out of the shower.

There was a frosty silence between the couple, and this was making Sarah feel very down.

She carried on eating as he went to the bedroom to get changed, with him going out.

She picked her phone back up, to text Alice once more.

Alice, I won't be in tomorrow. I've decided that I'm going to go and see my parents, spend some time with them. You carry on with the paperwork that you have. Keep an eye on the girls for me, make sure they don't slack in my absence, and I'll pop in before you leave at six, to see you, and to lock up. Take any messages as well for me please.

Alice replied.

Ok, have a good day. See you tomorrow night.

Paul came out of the bedroom, wearing smart pressed jeans and a turquoise turtle-neck jumper, and shiny brown shoes, before putting his leather jacket on.

"Will you be late?" she asked. "Oh, and I've decided to take the day off tomorrow, go and see my folks, George and Jeanette."

"Don't know yet, maybe… don't wait up," came the stern response, as if he hadn't heard her say about her going to see her parents.

There was a beep outside – he had booked a taxi – and, without even saying goodbye to Sarah, pulled the front door open before slamming it shut.

She was starting to feel very alone in her relationship with him, but knew that her business trip with Alice to Hong Kong the following Friday would probably do them all good, plus she was excited at the thought of seeing her parents in the morning; she realised that she didn't spend enough time with them.

Time had ticked on, it was midnight and Paul still wasn't home.

Sarah was in bed, clock-watching, tossing and turning. Despite their relationship not going too well lately, she still worried.

She suddenly heard the front door open, startling her slightly.

"Paul, is that you?" she called.

"Go back to sleep," came the slurred response.

She drifted back off to sleep, as she felt him clumsily get into his side of the bed, his back turned to her.

She too had her back turned away from him, wanting to give him some space.

Morning came, and Sarah awoke. It was six-thirty.

Paul was already up, and she could hear the shower going. She lay in bed, wondering what had got into the man she loves, how much he had changed.

He returned from the bathroom, a towel wrapped around his muscly body, water dripping down from his finely tuned chest.

"Let's do something this weekend, Paul. It's the last day of the week. We could maybe go out for a meal somewhere, or even have a weekend away. What do you think?"

She was wanting to try anything to snap him out of his mood.

"I'm going to see my parents and brothers this weekend, aren't I, so that's out of the question, isn't it?" he snapped. "What time are you going to your parents', anyway?"

"Not sure yet… why?"

"Just wondered," he growled.

He was obviously still in a mood.

'Maybe I could get some sexy underwear to show off to him later,' she thought.

Paul got his well-pressed pink shirt out of the wardrobe, along with his designer light-grey trousers.

Sarah watched as he got dressed.

"You look good. Maybe you should be coming back to bed with me; you're turning me on."

She sat up, as he sat at the front of the bed to put his shoes on, ignoring what she had just remarked.

She sexily crawled over towards him, and tried to wrap her naked body around him, her arms wrapping around his neck to hold him.

Paul brushed her off.

"I don't have time for this; I've got to go into work early," he snapped.

Sarah was starting to feel very unwanted.

"Have I done something wrong?" she asked.

"As I keep saying…"

"I know… I know… it's work stuff." She clumped rejectedly back on the bed.

Paul walked out of the bedroom and headed towards the kitchen.

He put some bread into the toaster before heading into the lounge to make sure that his paperwork was in order in his work file.

The toast popped up and he buttered it, eating it as he moved around.

Sarah put her robe on and looked forlornly through her wardrobe, planning what to wear today.

"Say hello to your parents," came the shout from the kitchen as Sarah heard the front door open, before it slammed shut.

She was not going to worry about him now; she was looking forward to seeing her parents.

Sarah texted Alice.

Morning darling. He's still in a mood. Looking forward to seeing my parents today. I'll miss you, but I'll see you later. I'll text after I've left them, and on my way to you. Love you.

Sarah got a reply.

Ok, darling, have a good day. Yes, let me know when you've left out, and on your way back here. I love you too.

At least Sarah felt love from someone, even if it wasn't Paul.

She headed for a shower before she quickly got dressed; she wanted to make the most of the day.

She put on a knee-length beige skirt and light purple polo-neck jumper, and red flat shoes.

She looked very elegant, even though she was not working that day.

She headed to the kitchen and made herself a bowl of muesli.

She sat at the breakfast bar and wondered why Paul was being the way he was, but she had her business trip to Hong Kong with Alice to look forward to, plus time away from him might lighten the mood he was in.

'Absence makes the heart grow fonder,' she thought.

She left the house, before locking up.

Just as she was about to get into her car, she looked across the road and saw a car that she was not familiar with, and someone sitting in the driver's seat, wearing a baseball cap, with their head bowed, as if not wanting to be seen.

She frowned slightly but thought nothing of it; after all, it was just someone sitting in their car, but Sarah was familiar with all the cars that came around their way, as well as visitors.

She put her bag and mobile phone on her passenger seat, putting her seatbelt on, closing the door before pulling out of her driveway.

It was around an hour's drive to her parents, and they lived in a small village called Churchfield, a quaint little village, mainly full of elderly people who all seemed to know each other, and each other's business.

Sarah arrived at her parents', and pulled up outside.

As she got out of her car, she noticed the same car that she saw near home, parked on a road not far from her parents, but this time there was no-one in the driver's seat.

She felt slightly unnerved by this, and stared at the car for a few moments, frowning, before knocking at her parents' door and letting herself in.

"Only me," she shouted excitedly.

"Oh, hello, love, are you ok?" Jeanette shouted from her kitchen, peeling some cooking apples from their big garden tree.

"I'm doing you your favourite apple pie. You used to love this as a kid." Jeanette smiled, reminiscing about times gone by.

Sarah went over to give her mum a kiss on the cheek.

"Where's Dad?"

"Oh, where he always is, in the shed, either planting seeds in his pots, or having a crafty bottle of beer, knowing him. I don't know why he has to hide it away; it's not as if I mind, is it?"

Sarah chuckled to herself as she made her way outside to see him.

"Are you hiding in there, Dad?"

"Oh, hello, my darling daughter, didn't hear you come in. Are you ok?"

Neither George nor Jeanette was in the best of health, but George's gardening was his way of coping with the heart issues he'd had down the years.

"You wouldn't hear me come in, would you? You're in your shed, and you're deaf as a post anyway," she joked. "Mum was right, you ARE having a crafty beer, aren't you?" she laughed as she entered his "man cave".

"What has your mother been saying? It's the only pleasure I get these days, plus I'm out of her hair, let her get on with whatever she's up to."

Sarah went up to him and planted a kiss on his cheek.

Some hours ticked by, and it was time for Sarah to leave.

She had spent a lovely time with them, and realised just how dearly she missed them, especially with how things were going in her relationship.

She had not heard a thing from Paul, and she didn't divulge to her parents the problems they were starting to have, as she didn't wish to worry them.

'I must text Alice, as I promised,' she thought.

Sarah texted.

Just about to leave now darling, so I shouldn't be too long. Has everything been ok?

Alice replied.

Yes, everything ok here. Hope your parents were ok. See you in a while.

Sarah had almost forgotten about the car that was parked a little down the road, but it was no longer there, so maybe she had imagined that it was the same car.

Sarah got into her car, put her bag and phone on the

passenger seat, and pulled away as her parents waved from the window.

She was about to drive onto the main road before it joined the motorway that she had driven on to get to her parents.

As she pulled onto the main road, she looked in her rear-view mirror and noticed that same car again, about two hundred yards further away.

She was starting to feel a bit nervous that maybe it was the same car from home.

The main road was a long road before the motorway, and it was just her and this car following on the road.

She put her foot down, driving faster than she should have done to try to escape this car behind, but they also put their foot down, and they were gaining on her.

Sarah was starting to get scared, with tears rolling down her cheeks; she hadn't felt so frightened, as she looked in her mirror again to see if she recognised them.

The car behind was right up behind her, pushing and grinding on her bumper.

Sarah was breathing heavily, not knowing what to do.

Suddenly, the car was right beside her and, in an instant, collided into the side of her car, and pushed her off the road and into the side of a ditch.

"AAAAARGH," Sarah screamed, as she came to a grinding halt.

She was shaking, as she saw the car speed off down the road.

She sat in shock for a few moments, wondering what to do.

She sat waiting for what seemed like hours, before shakily calling Alice.

"Alice, I've been involved in erm… an… erm… accident. I'm feeling a bit shaky but I'll still be with you soon."

"Oh my God. Are you ok?"

"Yes, I'll be fine. This moron decided to run me off the road as I left my parents, the lunatic, but, yeah, I'll be ok."

"Take your time driving here. I'll wait."

"I will. I love you, Alice."

"I love you too."

Sarah felt ok to start back up and to drive.

She thought about calling the police to record it but it all happened in a flash; she was in too much shock to make a note of anything, so felt that it would be a waste of time, though she was still feeling slightly shaken by it all.

'What if they are still waiting for me further on?' she thought, nervously.

She started the car back up and gradually pulled out of the ditch and back onto the road, shakily looking around just in case the car was still hovering around.

She got to the junction where it joined the motorway, but, as she joined the stream of cars coming by, she kept looking left and right, fearing that the driver who had not long run her off the road might still be about.

Sarah had always been a confident driver, but this had shaken her world, and tears started rolling down her cheeks once again.

She was still in a slight state of shock.

She hadn't been on the motorway for long when she saw a service station close by, and decided to pull in, and have a coffee to help calm her down.

She pulled in and stopped, grabbed her bag and phone, and locked her car.

She looked around her car for damage, as she remembered that the driver from earlier had caught her bumper. It was slightly dented and scratched from the driver colliding into it.

She walked nervously towards the services, constantly looking around her.

A man walked towards her, wearing a baseball cap, head slightly bowed; she stopped and took a sharp intake of breath as the man brushed past her.

She scurried inside and reached the restaurant, ordering a coffee and a Belgian bun from the coffee desk.

She paid for them and sat down, still shaken from what had happened.

She kept looking around, watching a few people walking by, wearing baseball caps, but she just wanted to try to calm herself before she got back on the road.

She finished her coffee, and had only taken a bite from her bun, before leaving the table and chucking her bun in the bin.

She walked towards her car, putting her bits on the passenger seat, before pulling out.

She was soon back on the motorway, still feeling slightly edgy, but was back in Barnwood in no time.

It was just gone five in the afternoon.

She knew that all of her employees would have gone for the evening, but the building lights were all on.

She shakily got out of her car, locked it and walked into her work building.

Alice, as promised, was waiting for her.

Sarah, stone-faced, walked into her office, and into Alice's arms, before bursting into tears.

"I can't believe what's happened, Alice, I feel a wreck." Her make-up came streaming down her face; it had all got too much.

"Shh, it's all going to be ok. You come and stay at mine tonight, I'll take care of you."

"Are you sure that's ok?"

"Yes. I'm not going to leave you like this."

Alice held Sarah close as Sarah continued to cry; the shock was coming away from her.

"Leave your car here tonight, Sarah, I'll get us a taxi."

The taxi arrived soon after and whisked the girls off to Alice's home.

"Give me Paul's number; I'll tell him you're here and explain what happened."

Alice poured them both a glass of wine, telling Sarah to relax while she went into the kitchen to call Paul.

As Alice returned from the kitchen, Sarah was asleep on the sofa, her wine untouched.

Alice grabbed a blanket and laid it over her.

She sat next to where Sarah's head lay, and put her head on her lap, stroking her hair gently.

Alice sat contemplating what would happen between them, as the night drew in.

OK... I'LL DO IT

I t was the next morning, Saturday, and Sarah's eyes began to gradually open.

She remembered the night before, and the terror of being run off the road.

She awoke fully to find herself in Alice's bed, and she was wearing one of her nightshirts.

She began to wonder how she got there.

Alice walked into the room, also wearing a nightshirt.

"Good morning, sleepyhead, did you sleep well? I've brought you some breakfast, only scrambled egg on toast, not sure what you'd fancy."

"God, what time is it?" a startled Sarah asked.

"It's eight-thirty. Don't worry, I rang Paul last night, told him what had happened, and that you stayed here. It's fine."

"I've got to get up. He is planning to go and see his family this weekend; he'll be wanting to see me before he goes."

"I'm sure he'll be fine. Why don't you stay in bed, relax and eat your breakfast? You've had an ordeal."

"No… no… I must get up and go. Thank you for looking after me last night, Alice, and the breakfast, but I must go."

Sarah hurriedly shot up out of bed, taking her nightshirt off, revealing her curvy body, as she started to get dressed.

Alice casually walked up to her.

"You could always climb back into bed with me, and erm… we could have some fun," she said teasingly, with a big grin on her face, biting her bottom lip slightly, while brushing Sarah's face with her finger, before slowly sliding it down towards her breasts.

"I'd love to, you know that, and maybe we could make it a dirty weekend away next week, when we go on the business trip. I promise I'll make it up to you."

Sarah continued to get dressed, while Alice sat on the bed, watching her.

"How did I make it into your bed last night, anyway? I remember being on the couch. Did we…?"

"No, we didn't," Alice laughed. "You were too tired, and I was too worried about you to even think about it. Don't you remember us getting up to get into bed?"

"No, I don't, I must have been tired."

"What are you going to do about that idiot who ran you off the road?"

"What can I do? I have no information to give to the police. It'll just be a waste of time. Right, darling, I'm going. Thank you for last night, and I promise we'll have a great time away next Friday."

With that, Sarah scurried over to Alice, and quickly kissed her on the lips.

"I'll text you later."

Sarah grabbed her bag and phone, and was soon out the door.

She also remembered that she had left her car at work, and started to hurriedly walk in that direction.

She reached her car and she immediately started to text Paul.

Sorry, Paul. I hear my assistant text you last night. Some idiot ran me off the road. I've just left my assistant's house, where I stayed. I'll be home shortly, if you haven't left out already X.

Sarah was soon home, and there was no reply to her text message.

She parked up, grabbed her things and rushed to the house.

After finding her keys, and unlocking the door, she called out to him.

"Paul… Paul… are you home?"

There was a deafening silence.

She decided to text him again.

I'm home, where are you?

Sarah decided to text Alice.

I'm home, and there's no sign of him. I've text him, with no response. I don't know what to do, and if he is ok. I'm worried.

Alice replied.

You could always come back here, maybe spend the day together... in bed X.

I'm going to wait to see if he shows, I'll text you again later X.

Sarah decided to wait to see if she heard back from Paul or if he showed up.

She grabbed some work files and drawings, and decided to go through them, putting things together for her trip to Hong Kong next Friday, to try to take her mind off him.

Hours ticked by and there was still no reply from him.

She was getting worried, despite their problems.

Paul had decided not to text her, and was on his way to see his brothers and parents, who had all congregated at their parents' house.

Joan and Harold owned a very large detached property, also in Churchfield, and it was worth quite a lot of money.

He had been driving since the morning, after hearing from Sarah's assistant about the day before.

After pulling up on Greenwoods Drive, number 26, Paul was out of his car.

He rang his parents' doorbell.

"Hello, son, good to see you," said Harold. "Everyone else is here."

Both Chris's and Anthony's wives and children were there, but Dean was there alone, as their parents didn't approve of Dean's girlfriend and her ways.

Joan and Harold had got some caterers in, and prepared a big buffet for them all.

"Ah, you didn't need to go to all this trouble, but it looks amazing," Paul declared.

"We don't get to see you all together very often, though, do we?" Joan smiled, looking round at all of them, but only fleeting at Dean.

Both Harold and Joan were aware of Dean's troubles.

But, despite numerous attempts to get him on the straight and narrow, he just seemed to enjoy the lifestyle he was leading.

Chris's and Anthony's children were well-behaved children and were very respectful of their grandparents, and just loved going round to see them.

The detached property that Joan and Harold owned had a very large garden, and, being a nice day, it was too sunny to be stuck inside.

"We've got you some things to play with outside, some activities. Why don't you all grab some things from the buffet, and some cartons of drink there, and go and play in the garden, while us adults have some grown-up talk?" said Harold to the children.

"It's far too warm for you to be stuck inside with all of us, when we're sure you've all got lots of energy to burn." Joan smiled to them sweetly.

The children, all under ten, did as they were asked, and grabbed some food and drink, as the adults all watched on.

Dean was standing slightly away from the others, almost as if he didn't belong there, yet, he still loved his parents, despite him being wayward.

They all waited, as the children went into the garden to go and play, before talking.

"We thought it'd be nice to get you all together, seeing

as we don't get to see you very often, with all of your busy lives." Joan smiled.

"This is just a waste of time," moaned Dean.

"Oh, I'm sorry… are we keeping you from meeting up with your DEALER, so you and your LOVELY GIRLFRIEND can go and shoot up again?" groaned Paul angrily.

Dean was two years younger than Paul, but always used to look up to him.

Anthony, at forty-three, was the oldest of the boys, with Chris slightly younger than Paul, at twenty-nine.

"Why don't you BUTTON IT, Paul, or else I'll come over there and…"

"And what?" an angry Paul shouted back.

"STOP IT!" shouted Harold, with sadness in his voice. "We've got you all here today to have some quality family time. Like we say, we don't see you very often; we haven't asked you all here today to bicker."

"It really is time you sorted yourself out, brother," Anthony said calmly. "Do you really want to spend your life getting high all the time? Why don't you get yourself sorted, find yourself a good job, someone nice who you can maybe start a family with, and settle down? You're not getting any younger. If you carry on the way you are, you'll be dead before you know it."

"I don't need to carry on listening to THIS!" Dean stormed out of the house.

"LEAVE HIM if he wants to be that way," sighed Joan, getting a little upset. "We've done all we can for him; he's making his own life choices, so just leave him to it."

Paul looked around at everyone, before deciding to go out and hunt his brother down.

He got outside and saw Dean still walking up the driveway, on his cheap mobile phone.

Paul caught up with him.

"On the phone to your DEALER?" he snarled, as he swiped the phone out of his brother's hand, in an angry fashion.

"You've got your life all sewn up, haven't you? Since meeting your bit of stuff, you have had NOTHING to do with me, so just go back to your POSH lifestyle, and fancy things, and just leave me in the gutter, where you wanted me in the first place," Dean growled.

Paul lashed out and… PUNCH… flattened him, leaving him sprawled out on the floor.

"How DARE YOU talk to me like that! I've protected you all your life, but you've just wanted to chuck your life away on getting stoned. GO ON… THROW YOUR LIFE AWAY, leave Mum and Dad to pick up the pieces after you've gone, leave them in fear of being chased for money from your dealers. You're not worth it." Paul walked back into the house, leaving Dean to feel his face for any damage, before getting up and brushing himself down, before storming away.

"You didn't hurt him, did you?" Chris asks.

"He got what he deserved. MAYBE he'll take a good look at himself in the mirror," said Paul, defiantly.

"Always been a hot-head brother. When are you going to learn to control that temper of yours?" said Anthony angrily.

"Why, do you want some as well? You may be the oldest but—"

"STOP IT… ALL OF YOU!" Harold shouted, annoyed that his sons were behaving in such a way. "Stop acting like

CHILDREN! Those kids out there are more grown up than you are right now… GROW UP!"

"Sorry, Dad, Mum. Dean just makes me SO ANGRY."

"We know he does, son, but he's made his bed; he's got to go and sleep in it," said Joan, with a tinge of regret in her voice.

"The thing is, he's been inside for so many things: robbery, assault, drugs, obviously, burglary, and he was even accused of murder. Remember that?" said Paul. "Acquitted, obviously, but it's just the road he goes down, makes me so mad. I had high hopes for him growing up, but now look at him."

"Let's just forget it, and talk about nicer things," said Anthony, wanting to change the subject.

"How are things going between you and Sarah?" asked Chris.

"Ok," he replied. "How are things going for you at work? And what about you, Anthony? How are things going at the restaurant? Are you just as busy as before?" He wanted to change the subject between him and Sarah.

"Yes, thank you, brother, things at the restaurant are going great, there are even plans to expand it, and have a wider range of foods, and we're always busy, as you know."

"And what of you, Chris? How's the bricklaying going? Building many new homes?"

"Yes, Paul, thank you. The building trade has never been so busy around here. I'm working all the hours God sends, as I'm sure you're aware. Need to keep the wife happy, and accustomed to her lifestyle," Chris joked.

"You've not said how things are between you and Sarah; are you both going well still?" asked Joan.

"We're fine but I'm here with my family; don't really want to talk about anything else. Anyway, let's eat."

Paul's phone rang half an hour later. It was Dean.

"Just need to take this outside; won't be long," he told everyone.

Paul went out the front door, so that no-one could hear.

"What do YOU want?" snapped Paul angrily.

"I just need to see you. I've got myself into a bit of trouble, and... I owe someone some money, and I don't know what to do."

"Let me guess... your DEALER?"

"I owe him two thousand, and he's threatening to send the heavy boys round and, if they do come, and they aren't the type to be messed with, then I might lose a few limbs, shall we say, until I pay up. PLEASE HELP ME."

"Two thousand, you say? Ok, I'll get you the money. Meet me at the end of the street. Better still, I'll go and pay them off for you myself. GOD KNOWS what you'd do with the money if I gave it to you. Where can I find these lowlives? This REALLY HAS TO STOP, though, Dean. You're putting our parents through HELL. They're old and stressed with your behaviour, as we all are. You've REALLY GOT TO CHANGE YOUR WAYS, otherwise this is going to KILL YOU... and probably our PARENTS TOO... CAN'T YOU SEE THAT?"

"Yes, I know. I'm SORRY I've let you down. I will..."

Paul interrupted.

"You've not let ME down, Dean, but YOURSELF and our PARENTS. I'll go and get that two grand out, but this REALLY IS the LAST TIME, ok?"

Dean agreed.

"You need to see a Mr Barnes. He lives in Austin, on Highton Road, number 12."

"I'll find him," said Paul.

He hung up from Dean and went back into the house.

Paul made an excuse up to everyone for needing to leave early.

"Sorry, guys, I've got to run. Sarah is wanting to go over some work stuff with me, get my thoughts. It's for… you know."

"That's ok, son. Take some food with you; you've not really touched any. Maybe take some back for Sarah too," said Harold. "We won't get though all of this, and there's plenty here."

"It's ok, Dad, think Sarah is cooking soon so… I'd best run."

Anthony and Chris came over to shake his hand, and say their goodbyes to him, before he went out to the back garden to say goodbye to the children, who were all still playing happily.

Paul came back into the lounge, where everyone had congregated earlier, and gave his mum and dad a kiss each on the cheek.

"Don't leave it so long, son, and bring Sarah with you too next time," said Joan.

He looked at them, gave them a grin and small wave, and left the house.

Before driving to Austin, he stopped at a service station along the way, to fill up his car with diesel and to withdraw the two thousand that he needed to pay the dealer.

He paid for his diesel, got the money out of the cashpoint and drove to Austin, finding Highton Road quite quickly, before slowly looking around for number 12.

He soon found the right house.

Highton Road was known as a drug street, where criminal activity happened on a frequent basis and gangs would often meet up to discuss their next drop-offs.

The police were often seen on the street, patrolling in their cars, but not today.

Paul got out of his car, with youths circling around him on their bikes.

"Nice car, mister," said one of them.

Paul just gave them a stern look as he walked towards the house.

He went to knock, but the door just creaked open.

"Mr Barnes, are you here?"

Paul walked towards what appeared to be a front room that smelt of weed and stale odour.

As he walked in, there was an older gentleman, sitting on a leather sofa, just wearing boxer-shorts, a T-shirt and a robe, flanked by two naked girls either side of him, their arms wrapped around his pot-bellied waist.

The man looked as if he hadn't washed for a week, and was smoking the biggest cigar.

He was also flanked by two of his heavy mob, who you wouldn't want to mess with; they were like doorman on a nightclub doorway.

"I'm here to pay my brother's debt, Dean, Dean Arnold, I hear he owes you some money, so I'm here to pay it, two thousand pounds." He chucked it on the table in front of the dealer.

The man took one look at Paul and laughed.

"That doesn't include the interest," he chuckled. "But I'll tell you what. Let's forget the interest, if you'll do a drop-off for me," said the dealer, menacingly. "You look like a strapping boy; I could do with someone like you in my ranks. What do you say? I'll even give you one of these girls for free too."

"NO WAY, I'm not getting involved in your activity. It's not my style."

"Your parents are elderly, aren't they, and Dean seems like a good boy, brings lots of business my way. Just a shame he gets caught up with forever owing me money, and it'd be a shame to see anything happen to your parents, wouldn't it?" said Mr Barnes menacingly, with a wide grin on his face.

"You go anywhere NEAR my parents, and I'll—"

Just then, a heavy approached Paul, bald head, studded ears, and much taller and larger built than him, and grabbed him by the throat, giving him a menacing look and applying some pressure.

"Now, why not be sensible, take these bags of heroin with you, go and put them in your car, which my boys are looking after for you outside, and go and do some drop-offs for me, there's a good boy," Mr Barnes said, smugly. "Then we'll forget all about the extra wad of money that your PRECIOUS BROTHER owes me, and he and your folks will all be safe and sound."

Paul looked at Mr Barnes, with a wild look in his eyes.

"There is PLENTY OF MONEY and women in this for you, boy." One of the dealer's ladies, looking drugged up herself, suggestively walked over to Paul, before he shrugged her off.

Mr Barnes looked over to the other heavy, and nodded to him.

He went over to a drawer and pulled out a package, before chucking it at Paul.

"What's this?"

"Call it a little something for your journey," said the dealer.

Paul opened the package and saw a bundle of money.

"There's five grand. Plenty more where that came from."

"I don't want your DIRTY MONEY; it doesn't interest me."

"TAKE IT, you're doing me a MASSIVE FAVOUR. As you can see, I'm a bit tied up at the minute, and they've not even started on me yet." He chuckled away to himself. "Do the drop-offs, collect the money I'm owed… they know you're coming… and bring the money back to me, and, who knows… I MIGHT throw another wad of cash your way."

Thinking of Dean and his parents, fearing for their safety, he did as he was told and took the money, putting it in his pocket before picking up the holdall of heroin and taking it outside to his car.

Before he left, Mr Barnes shouted him back.

"Don't try anything STUPID, by the way. You're going to be tracked, to make sure you're going. Plus, remember what I said about Dean and your DEAR FOLKS."

Paul gave the dealer a sharp stare, saying nothing, before leaving the house with the holdall of drugs, making sure he was not seen.

He put the drugs in the back seat of his car and slammed it angrily shut, before walking to his car door as one of the youths rides up next to him, as he struggles to get in, with the youth being right by him on his bike.

"GET OUT OF MY WAY," he snapped at the youth, as the boy laughed, riding away towards the others circling the car.

Just as Paul was about to put his seatbelt on, his mobile rang; it was Dean.

"What the HELL are you involved with, Dean?"

"Did you find it ok? Were you able to pay him the money?"

"YES YES, I found it, AND I paid him the money, what a SHADY lowlife he is. Don't you EVER go back there again, or they WILL KILL YOU. You owe me BIG TIME," Paul snapped, angrily.

"What would I do without you?" Dean replied, with a slight chuckle, trying to make light of the situation. "They didn't ask you for any more money, did they? I know what these people can be like."

Paul paused for a moment, still angry with his brother.

"No, no… they didn't ask me for any more money; they were ok with it." He said it so as not to worry Dean about what they had asked Paul to do instead, as he rummaged in the holdall that he'd not long put behind him.

Paul found a burner phone and a list of properties that he needed to do the drop-offs to, and started to go down the list briefly.

On the list appeared just the one address where they needed to pay money or they would not get their drugs: specific instructions on the list from the drugs baron.

All but one of the drop-offs were in Austin, so he was going to use his satnav to locate each address.

Paul drove away, not wanting to be in the vicinity any longer than he had to.

As he pulled away, he saw a black Range Rover, with blacked out windows, pulling off not far behind him.

Paul soon arrived at the first address, 55 Blackheath Way.

He felt less on edge about this address – he just had to

hand the drugs over, according to the list – but still kept an eye out, so as not to be seen by any nearby police.

He pulled up, got out of the car and handed the drugs over, after approaching the house.

This continued for seven more houses, and, even though he wasn't enjoying what he was being asked to do, it was a simple drop-off each time.

The black Range Rover had followed him to each of the addresses as he went.

'They are obviously my tracker,' he thought.

He sighed slightly, as, after looking on the list, this was to be his final drop-off in Austin, 22 Masters Way, but this customer owed money.

Paul got out of his car, looked around for any sign of police, opened his back seat and took out a package, smothering it under his jacket so as not to arouse suspicion.

He went up to the door and knocked at it loudly.

A middle-aged man answered: scruffy, thin, with dark-ringed eyes, unshaven, scraggy hair and pale-looking.

"Who are you?" asked the man, nervously.

Paul sheepishly pulled his jacket to one side, to show the man the heroin bag.

"I haven't got any money," said the man, shaking, as Paul waited at the door, just wanting to drop the drugs off, collect the money and go.

"You need to pay, or you don't get this bag."

"Wait there," said the man, as Paul stood in the doorway, nervously, just wanting to go.

The man came back, holding something behind him.

He suddenly pulled out from behind his back a revolver.

"You'd better come inside with that bag, or you're going to eat metal," said the jittery man.

Paul, feeling both shocked and scared, did as the man said, and stepped inside, as the man ushered Paul into the lounge and closed the door behind them, standing away from Paul in case he decided to jump him.

The heavy in the Range Rover called Mr Barnes.

"They've both gone inside of Masters Way, boss, what shall I do?"

"Just give them a bit of time. He does owe me two grand; maybe he's wondering where he's put it."

Meanwhile, the twitchy man holding the gun, looking all bedraggled, directed Paul further into the lounge with the gun, Paul doing as he's told, not wanting anything drastic to happen, not knowing what the man might do.

"You really don't want to use that; there are other ways, you know," said a scared Paul.

"SHUT UP, I'M saying what's what here. Put the drugs on the table there. Do it SLOWLY."

Paul held the heroin bag, watching the scruffy man as he did, but did as he was asked.

The man edged over to the front window and pulled the curtains shut, keeping an eye on any false move by Paul as he does so.

The heavy in the Range Rover outside saw the curtains close, and again called Mr Barnes.

"Boss, the curtains have just been drawn. I'm going in."

"Just go and check it out; see what's happening," said the baron.

The big, burly man got out of the car and towards the house that Paul had gone into, what seemed like AGES AGO.

He approached the front door and tried to peer through the window, to see if he could see what was going on.

He was only able to catch sight of Paul, standing up, but just the edge of the other man.

Mr Barnes's minder knocked on the door.

"Oh, look, company for you," said the man to Paul, as he went towards the door, the gun still pointed at Paul, as the man pulled the door open, pointing the gun at each of them in turn, ushering the burly man inside to join Paul.

The man stood well away from the from door, so he was not charged by the burly minder.

The minder was soon standing near Paul.

"Well, isn't this interesting?" said the shaky man, "I've got two hostages, isn't this exciting?" The man with the gun walked over to his dining table and pushed out a chair for one of them to sit on.

"Well, isn't this cosy?" said the man.

He walked over to some chest of drawers and pulled out some thick rope, and chucked it in their direction.

"YOU!" – he waved the gun in the burly man's direction – "Tie your friend up."

Mr Barnes's minder, giving the man an angry look, promptly did as he was asked, sat Paul down and tied him up as tight as he could.

The shaky man chuckled nervously to them.

"This gun is all loaded, I could shoot you both right now, and, no-one would know, what do you think?" He laughed, nervously.

"My boss knows we're here, and he'll soon have others round, so you'd never get away with it," the angry minder shouted back.

"Just… just… SHUT UP. All I wanted was the heroin, you just HAD to make things complicated."

The man started to shake and cry, wiping his tears with his spare hand, making sure that the gun was pointed at the two men at all times.

"Why don't you just put the gun down? I'm sure you can come to some arrangement with Mr Barnes, I'm sure he'll be reasonable with you, he's a businessman at the end of the day; I'm sure he'll give you some slack."

Paul looked at the minder for reassurance, but the burly minder just gave Paul a disgruntled look.

"Mr Barnes doesn't give chances to people like me. I've begged and begged him for more time to pay him, but he's just sent heavies round like your friend here, broken bone here, broken bone there, broken legs; I've been in and out of hospital more times than I lived here," said the man, still with tears rolling down his cheeks from his earlier cry.

Just then the minder's phone started to ring.

"ANSWER IT, it's probably your PRECIOUS BOSS. Tell him that I'm still looking round for the money, and that everything is fine."

The minder answered his phone.

"Alright, boss. Yeah, everything is ok. We're still at Masters Way but he's just hunting around for the cash, shouldn't be too long now. I'll let you know when we've left."

The minder rang off and put his phone slowly back in his pocket, watching the man with the gun as he did.

"There… that wasn't so hard, was it?" said the man, still shakily pointing the gun in their direction.

"So, what are your plans now? I mean, we can only

stay here so long, before Mr Barnes and our families start getting worried," Paul said, nervously.

"I'm THINKING, I'm THINKING, DON'T MAKE ME PULL THE TRIGGER."

The burly minder decided to sit on the floor, next to where Paul is sitting, struggling to hold his bulky frame up any longer.

"I WANT MONEY... GIVE ME MONEY... EITHER OF YOU... I DON'T CARE WHICH... GIVE ME MONEY... NOW. I know, whichever of you who gives me money, the other will DIE," the crazy man said, laughing.

"You must have collected money along the way. GIVE ME IT."

There was a sudden screech of car tyres outside and the man looked away from Paul and the burly minder, and towards the drawn curtains.

Quick as a flash, the minder jumped up and hurtled towards him, pushing him to the ground as Paul tried to wrestle free from the rope.

Suddenly, there is a loud... BANG!

Both the crazed man and Mr Barnes's bodyguard are momentarily still, before the minder got up, blood pouring from the gunman, soaking the carpet bit by bit.

"We should call an ambulance; we can't leave him here to die," said Paul, as the burly man got him free from being tied up.

"Just LEAVE HIM... come on, LET'S GO... NOW," said the minder. "My boss will be expecting you."

The gunman was heaped in the corner of his lounge, blood pouring from his stomach, unable to move.

Most of the properties around were derelict, and beyond repair, with no-one inhabiting them from a lot further down the way, so no-one would know the gunman was there, or would have even heard the gun go off.

The minder managed to free Paul from the rope, as they both left the house in a hurry, where they had just been held at gunpoint, as he and Mr Barnes's minder sped off, knowing he still had to do the last drop-off, this time the final one, just on the edge of Churchfield, in a town called Thornbury.

Paul was still shaken by the events of what had just happened but, seeing that he was still being followed by the minder, decided to do this one last drop.

He looked at his last one on the list. It was indeed in Thornbury, to his BROTHER… DEAN.

'How can I drop drugs off to him? I just don't know how I can!' he thought.

Knowing that he was being tracked, and for fear of all of their lives, he reluctantly pulled up outside his brother's house and got the last drug bag from out of the holdall.

The house was like a squat, very run-down, and he got out of his car and walked up the pathway.

The pathway was barely visible, covered by rubbish and overgrown grass.

He hesitated before knocking on the door.

He was met by his brother's girlfriend, Heather, looking like she'd just got out of bed.

"Your brother isn't here, so you'll have to…"

"I'm not here to see HIM, just give him THIS," snapped Paul, as he looked around for any sign of police, before shoving the last of the heroin into her chest. "You've not got this from ME… ok?"

He walked away from the house and back into his waiting car, seeing the Range Rover still waiting behind him.

He turned around to head back to Austin and drop the empty holdall off to Mr Barnes.

Both Paul and the minder pulled up outside Mr Barnes's and went into the house.

"Ah, here they come," said the drugs baron, still sitting where Paul had last seen him. "I hear you had a bit of commotion. All in a day's work though, hey?" he said, smugly.

"That's the LAST THING I do for YOU; get someone else to do your dirty work, because I'm DONE."

Mr Barnes nodded towards the other burly minder, who again walked over to the drawer and pushed a package of money into Paul's chest.

"There's another five big ones there, and there's PLENTY MORE in store for you, probably the easiest ten grand you'll make today." Mr Barnes laughed, still flanked by the two girls. "You'll be back for more, easy money."

Just as Paul left, his mobile phone rang. It was his older brother, Anthony.

"To what do I owe this pleasure, brother?" He tried to calm himself.

"Where are you?" a frantic sounding Anthony asked him, hoping that he was nearby.

"Why, what's wrong?"

"Dad has been rushed into Barnwood City Hospital. He's had a heart attack; they're operating on him now."

"OH MY GOD, I'm on my way," said a shocked Paul, not quite believing what he'd just heard.

Paul left Austin and raced towards Barnwood, getting to the hospital in next to no time.

He managed to find a parking spot in the grounds, paid

for a ticket for his car for two hours, and raced to the main hospital reception.

There he was met by two of his brothers, Anthony and Chris.

"When did all this happen? Where is he now?" a frantic Paul asked them.

"Dad is in surgery as we speak," Anthony said. "He collapsed late this morning, Mum said. It's all we know at the minute."

Paul wandered around the reception area, not quite knowing what to do with himself, he was so worried.

"This is all Dean's doing, this," an angry Paul said. "I'll KILL HIM when I get my hands on him."

"Just calm down, brother," said Chris, trying to defuse the tension. "Let's just wait and see what the doctors say, ok?"

"I'll go and get us some coffee. Who wants some?" asked Anthony. "I'll get us something to eat too, God knows how long we're going to be here."

Both Chris and Paul both nodded to him.

Chris and Paul sat down momentarily, but Paul was too frantic with worry, and was soon back on his feet, pacing the floor.

"Why doesn't someone come out and tell us something?" he moaned, hating the silence from the hospital staff. "I need to go and make a phone call; I won't be long."

Anthony comes back with the coffee, along with a sandwich each, crisps and chocolate.

"Where's mister hot-head gone?" Anthony asked Chris. "He's not changed, has he?"

"He just said that he had to go and make a phone call; said he wouldn't be long."

Anthony sat down with Chris just as Paul was coming back.

"Anything yet?" he asked, unsure if he'd missed any news on their dad.

"No news is good news, brother, just try and relax, and eat this." Anthony went to pass him a sandwich.

"I don't WANT IT." Paul angrily pushed the sandwich back at his brother, in a fit of agitation.

Anthony, enraged with his brother's reaction, went to square up to him, but Chris stood up between them, trying to act as peacemaker.

"Let's all draw breath, and calm down. Dad wouldn't have wanted us fighting, now, would he?" Chris calmly said to them both.

They all sit back down, as Anthony again gingerly reached out to his fiery brother with the food again, Paul this time pausing before taking it from him.

"I'm not in the mood to eat. I just want to know about Dad," he said, as they anxiously waited for news.

"We all do," said Anthony, "but we'll know when we know."

Just then a doctor appeared, walking towards them.

"Are you all related to a Mr Harold Arnold?" said Doctor Thomas, a tall, mature man who looked like he'd been a surgeon for some time.

"Yes, doctor, we're his sons," said Paul nervously. "How is he?"

"Well, he's had a massive heart attack. We managed to fix some of the faulty electronics around his heart. It was touch and go at first but he's stable at the minute."

"Can we go and see him?" asked Chris, patiently waiting his turn to speak.

"Yes, you can, but he is heavily sedated at the minute; he won't really know you're there but, of course, you can go in," said Doctor Thomas. "Can I ask that it is just you three, though?"

"How long before he's conscious, doctor?" asked Anthony, worried that their dad won't wake up.

"It's been major surgery, so you need to give him time to recover, plenty of rest is what is needed right now."

The sons all thanked the doctor as he walked away from them down the corridor.

They all approached the room where their dad was lying, and closed the door as they entered, as Paul and Anthony pulled up chairs, either side of him, Anthony cradling his hand.

"We're here, Dad, you're going to be ok." Tears started to roll down Anthony's cheeks, not even sure if his dad could hear his sons.

Chris stood at the base of the bed, looking solemnly at his ill father lying in front of him.

"We've ALL brought this on him, in one way or another," mentioned Chris, looking at each of his brothers in turn.

They all stayed together with him for an hour, before deciding to go and check on their mum.

"We should go and see how mum is; she'll be in bits," Chris said, turning to each of his brothers. "We can't do much here right now, so let's come back later."

The three of them all took turns, and gave their dad a kiss on the forehead.

"See you later, Dad," said Paul. "You rest, and we'll be back before you know it."

They shuffled out of the room, each looking back at their ill father in turn, before closing the door behind them.

They got in their cars, and drove off to be with their distraught mother.

They were soon in Churchfield, and parked up behind each other.

They walked into the house, and Dean was sitting with his mum.

"You SON OF A…" Anthony had to restrain Paul from taking a swipe at his wayward brother.

"What are you so mad at ME about?" yelled Dean. "What am I supposed to have done?"

"What PLANET are you on?" exclaimed Paul. "Do you KNOW where our dad is right now?"

"This is neither the time nor the place," sniffled Joan. "It's time all of you boys learnt to get along. As for YOU, Paul, you need to get a grip of that temper of yours; it's getting seriously out of hand."

"We've been to see Dad, Mum." Chris tried to calm the situation. "He's in good hands. We're going to go and see him again later, if you'd like to come with us."

"I'd better stay here," she said, head bowed. "Anyway, I'd find it all a bit much for me; you know I don't like hospitals. Oh God, I need to go and get the shopping, I've been meaning to go but, with your dad…" she said in a panic, not knowing what to do with herself.

"We'll sort your shopping, Mum, you just look after yourself, don't worry," said Anthony. "I'll have a look in your fridge, freezer and cupboards, we'll sort all of that, see what you need."

Anthony walked off, heading to the kitchen.

Paul stared angrily in Dean's direction, not taking his eyes off him, thinking that this was all his fault.

Dean could feel Paul's stare, as if they were burning a hole in his head, but not wanting to look at his angry brother.

"I'm going, before I end up doing something I regret." Paul stormed off, and headed out of the front door.

"I'm going for a pint at the local, might give John a shout," he thought.

Paul arrived at the Adlington Arms, and rang his friend.

"Hi, mate, could do with some company. Got a lot of shit going on. I'm at the Adlington, if you fancy a pint."

"Thought you'd never ask," came the reply.

Paul was already on his second pint when John walked in.

"Fancy seeing YOU in here," he joked.

"I've put one in for you," huffed Paul. "Grab something to snack on while you're at the bar, mate."

John was poured his pint and sat next to Paul.

"What's going on, then, buddy?" John asked, eager to know his mate's news. "Bend my ear."

"Dad's in hospital, his heart, and I've got other shit going down," said a beleaguered and tired Paul.

"OH MY GOD, MATE, is he ok?" John muttered, concerned for Paul's state of mind.

"I hope so, but I'm worried."

"He's in the best place, don't worry." John tried to reassure him.

"I've also got something else going on, some DEEP SHIT." Paul leant in to whisper to him. "I've had to do a few drug runs for a baron my SHIT of a wayward brother has got mixed up in it, and now I'M involved. Got a gun pulled on me earlier too."

"WHAT? A GUN? SHIT, MATE, that AIN'T GOOD, you need to get the HELL out of that, inform the police."

"And tell them what? They're probably all involved in it too. Besides, these lowlives know where my folks live, and, there's Dean. I'm scared, John."

"What you going to do?"

"I've GOT to protect my family, John, and as long as I'm not hurting anyone..."

"But, Paul, a GUN! It's a DANGEROUS GAME you're playing."

"Can't see what choice I have, really," said Paul, as the pair carried on drinking and talking long into the day.

After far too many pints, Paul decided to get a taxi home.

Sarah was piecing her work portfolio together, ready for her trip, when the front door flung open... it was Paul... VERY DRUNK.

"Where have you been? I've been texting you, I've been worried sick."

"I've been out," he slurred.

"I can see that."

"Why didn't you just reply to my texts? I didn't have a clue where you were."

"GOD... NOT NOW. I'm going to have a nap, sleep this off."

She watched as he stumbled past her, as he headed to the bedroom before collapsing on the bed, face first.

Sarah was not amused.

'Some lunatic has run me off the road, yet all he could think about was getting drunk, no regard for my welfare at all,' she thought.

She knew that things were tough for him at work, but he seemed to be getting more and more distant from her.

Sarah thought that this was maybe the right time to break some bad news to him, with him being so distant.

"Paul, I need to talk to you, can we sit down?"

Both sat down, at either ends of the sofa, after he'd gingerly got off the bed and into the lounge, still feeling worse for wear.

"I've been to the doctors today, wanted to check a few things. I went for a check-up at Barnwood Hospital a few weeks ago, and I had to go back to the doctors for the results earlier," she said, waiting to see what kind of reaction she was going to get. "I'm SO SORRY... I... can't have children!"

Paul just stared blankly at her, not knowing what to do or say.

He had always wanted children, but his stare was so cold.

He got up, without saying a word, and walked calmly back towards the bedroom, not giving her a second look.

"Are you not going to say something?" She got up from the sofa and walked towards the bedroom door.

Paul was lying on the bed, his hands behind his head, staring up at the ceiling.

'I might as well have stayed with Alice,' she thought, as she walked away, sitting back down where she had just got up from.

She was upset that she couldn't have any children of her own, but she had always been a career woman, and children might have been an obstacle for her.

It was Thursday evening, and the atmosphere between

the couple was as strained as ever, maybe not helped by her just telling him that she couldn't have children.

They missed their weekend away, but she hoped that they could maybe organise another, to get over their disappointing news.

She had agreed with Alice that they would travel that Thursday night, with it being a near-twelve-hour flight.

Sarah had packed her suitcase for her trip away, and, even though it was a business trip, she always looked forward to getting away and catching up with Mr Yang and his family.

Especially that she was taking a new, sexy assistant too.

"Remember I'm going to Hong Kong tonight," she said to Paul.

"I hadn't forgotten. Have a lovely time. I'll miss you; call me after you've landed."

Paul's behaviour had suddenly changed, and this was a side to him that she had missed.

"Yes, I'll call you, I promise. I love you."

Paul paused.

"I love you too, Sarah." He grinned.

She scurried over to him, to plant a kiss on his lips, but he hardly responded.

His kiss back appeared cold.

She was somewhat shocked, however, as it was the first time that she'd heard the word "love" come from his lips.

She pulled away, looking sullen at him, before grabbing her bag, phone, suitcase and the case containing the design drawings, and left the house, but not before turning briefly back at him to see him motionless, looking at her, with the same grin he had had moments before.

Her flight from Barnwood City Airport was in three hours' time, and she had to go and pick Alice up.

Their flight was at eleven that night, and it was already eight, though the city's airport wasn't too far away, about a twenty-minute drive.

Sarah decided to leave her car at home and book a local taxi for them both.

The taxi pulled up at Sarah's house, and she asked to be taken to Applewood Road, where Alice lived, as she was getting in the car.

The taxi pulled onto Applewood Road, just as Alice was stepping out of her house, in tight stone-washed jeans, a designer top and baseball cap, looking every inch the model that she was, pulling her light-blue suitcase behind her.

Sarah stared, to see how sexy she looked.

Alice put her suitcase in the boot and got in the back seat, where Sarah was sitting.

Alice grabbed hold of her hand, with a broad smile in Sarah's direction.

"I'm so excited. Thank you for asking me."

"You're welcome. Time away from him should do us both good. Anyway, this is OUR TIME, and I intend to enjoy it."

They reached the airport by eight-thirty and checked in, before deciding to go to the bar for a few drinks.

They ordered a large glass of wine each, and sat down, while waiting for their flight.

"How was HE when you left tonight?"

"Hmm… rather strange, I couldn't make it out. He wished me a good time, and said that he'd miss me, even told me that he loved me, and that's the first time I've EVER heard him say that."

"Well, that's good, isn't it?"

"Well… I guess, but, when I went to kiss him, something didn't feel right, probably not helped with the news I gave him yesterday."

"What news is that? Fill me in."

"I can't have children, Alice." Sarah's eyes glazed over, with a tinge of sadness.

"OH MY GOD, I'm SO SORRY, DARLING, why haven't you told me this earlier?"

"I've been meaning to but, what with everything… I've only just got my head around it myself, but he was as cold as ice, said nothing, no reaction… nothing."

"Well, don't worry about him now, this is time for US."

"Exactly," Sarah replied enthusiastically. "I'm far too busy for children anyway," she joked.

"Flight BA7164 to Hong Kong is now boarding," came the message over the tannoy. "Please make your way to the departure lounge, and have your boarding passes and passports ready."

The girls finished their third glass of wine, and got up to board. They had earlier tagged their luggage and Sarah's drawings, and were soon aboard.

Sarah always booked first class, and this was no exception.

They found their seats, and settled in for the long flight.

"You ok, darling?" asked Sarah, turning to Alice.

"I couldn't be better; this is going to be AMAZING."

The plane lands at Chek Lap Kok International Airport at ten-thirty the next morning, and Mr Yang was based thirty minutes' drive away in the city of Victoria in Hong Kong, which had a population of around ten million people.

Sarah had pre-booked them into a hotel in the city, called the Four Seasons Hotel, which was a luxurious hotel, with a large outdoor pool, one that she had used regularly when visiting Mr Yang.

The girls were exiting the airport, and there was a car to pick them up, as there always had been, to drive them to their hotel.

A tall man was holding a board up, with 'Sarah Waysmith' on it.

"This is all very posh, Sarah," gasped Alice.

The man led the girls to the expensive-looking car, and they were soon at their hotel.

The girls walked in, and Alice was looking around, not quite believing how luxurious the Four Seasons was, and couldn't wait to spend time with her lover at last.

"Ah, hello, Ms Waysmith, good to see you again. Are you well?" said the receptionist.

"Yes, I'm well, thank you, Suki, how are you and the family?"

"All well, thank you. Same room as always, I see." Suki smiled.

"Yes, that'll be lovely." Sarah beamed.

The girls went up to their room, the suitcases carried by a porter. They reached their room, took the suitcases from the porter; Sarah tipped him, as she always did, and put the cases on the stunning king-size bed.

It was eleven-thirty, but Mr Yang's office was just a short walk from the hotel.

"Let's take a shower together, Alice, save a bit of time."

"Sounds good to me."

They first opened their suitcases, and Alice pulled out a stunning purple one-piece dress, with purple high-heeled shoes, while Sarah got out her favourite one-piece white dress, and black heels.

Sarah had seen Alice wear this before. It was short, and showed off her amazing figure, which turned Sarah on.

They hung their dresses up, pulled the blinds down, and stripped off naked.

Sarah grabbed Alice's hand, and pulled her towards the bathroom, both laughing as they did.

Sarah turned that large double shower on, and pulled Alice in.

They began to lather each other's bodies, sensuously kissing as they did so.

This felt like heaven to Alice. She had missed Sarah's touch, yet Sarah felt the same, especially with her troubles with Paul.

"We can't get too carried away; we've got to be prompt," Sarah chuckled.

"I know but I've missed this, I've missed you."

They pulled each other in close, their lathered bodies pressed together, their kissing continuing, before Sarah pulled slightly away.

"I have missed you too, Alice, and I've missed the feeling of being loved. Anyway, let's rinse off and get dressed. After our meeting, we can go exploring a bit, if you like."

"That'll be lovely, I'd like that."

The girls were dressed, and ready by twelve-thirty, and they both looked stunning.

"WOW... I DO love that dress on you, Alice, highlights your figure."

"Hope you prefer it better OFF." She chuckled.

Fifteen minutes later and they were ready to leave.

Sarah grabbed her fashion portfolio case and was ready to go.

"Ready?" asked Sarah.

"Whenever you are."

The girls strode elegantly out of their room and into the hotel foyer, like they were in a fashion shoot of their own.

It was a five-minute walk to Mr Yang's office, and they arrived with time to spare.

Meanwhile, Paul was getting ready for work, and not in the best of moods.

He got to his desk by eight-thirty; he hated being late. He sat down and turned his equipment on, ready to start his day.

Mr McGee then appeared in his doorway.

"Need to have a meeting in my office in five minutes, old chap, you, Brian and Gary. I'll see you in a minute."

Mr McGee then walked off, down the corridor.

'Wonder what HE wants,' he thought.

Paul was in no mood to take any more orders from Mr McGee; he'd had a tough time of it lately as it was, with his dad, and being held at gunpoint.

He left his office and walked the short distance to Mr McGee's, before knocking on the door.

"Come in," came the shout.

Brian and Gary were already sitting down, also wondering what the meeting was about.

"Where are all the other directors?" Paul asked, curious as to what was happening, "Why is it just us in here?"

"As you know, we've been needing to pull in some more business, as things have been very slow." Mr McGee got up from his chair and paced almost every inch of his smelly office. "I've been looking through office files, and I'm afraid we're needing to make some cutbacks."

Brian, Gary and Paul all looked at each other, in total shock.

"Does this mean...?" said a disgruntled Brian, unable to hide his anger. "I've been here seven years, with a family to support, what the HELL am I expected to do now?"

"Yes, I'm afraid we're going to have to let the three of you go, you'll all get a redundancy pay-off, and I'm sure you'll all find something else really soon," said Mr McGee, with head bowed, not wanting to let go of any of his staff. "It's not been an easy decision."

Paul thumped the meeting table in the office, in a fit of anger, jumping up from his chair, flinging it backwards and almost hitting the back wall of the office.

He stormed towards the office door and forced it open, briefly giving Mr McGee an evil stare before slamming it shut.

Brian followed suit, thrusting his chair backwards before leaving the office for the last time, before Gary casually got up and walked out of the office, closing it gently behind him, not quite believing what had just happened.

Some of the other directors and colleagues had heard the commotion in the meeting, and pretty much what had been said to the three of them.

Paul and the other two men went to their desks, grabbed a box for all of their personal belongings and filled it up, before walking out of their respective offices and towards the exit door.

"We're so sorry, guys," came the collective voices of the remaining staff, with their heads bowed. "Look after yourselves."

The three men carried on walking out, and towards their cars.

"What you going to do now?" Gary asked the others, unsure of his own future.

"I've got a LOT of shit going on, guys, so, not being rude, but I'm just going to dash." Paul was more concerned with what was going on with his dad in hospital, and family matters, to even care.

Paul drove away from his work for the last time, feeling slightly happier that he didn't have so much pressure, but still worried about his ill dad.

Just then, his mobile rang… it was his brother Anthony.

Paul put his phone on the passenger seat and put it on loud speaker.

"You need to get here… QUICK, Dad has had another heart attack."

Paul raced back to the hospital, worried that things had taken a turn for the worse.

He pulled into the hospital car park, got out and locked up.

He hadn't even thought about getting a ticket for his car, and he'd just pay the fine if he was caught; his dad was far more important.

Again, both Anthony and Chris were waiting for him.

"Dad's back in theatre now," said a worried Anthony. "He's been responding well to the drugs they've been prescribing him, before he had another attack, about thirty minutes ago."

"Have you had to dash from work?" asked Chris, trying to change the subject slightly.

"Yeah, yeah, but, it's ok, Dad takes priority."

The brothers had been anxiously waiting on news for what seemed like hours, each of them checking their watches and looking up at the clock on the wall.

Doctor Thomas, who had been the surgeon throughout their dad's ordeal, came out, his head slightly bowed.

"Can I speak to you all privately?" He turned to them all, with sadness in his face.

Anthony buried his face in his hands, Paul and Chris not knowing what to do or say, apart from follow the surgeon into a private room that he'd located.

"Just tell us, is he...?" Paul was starting to feel more and more distraught.

The silence from the surgeon told a thousand words; he didn't have to say any more.

"We did all we could... I'm so sorry, he passed away just a short while ago." Doctor Thomas, not quite knowing what to say or do, never found it easy telling loved ones of someone's death. "Of course, you may go and see him if you so wish. He looks peaceful; I can take you to him if you'd like me to."

Paul felt his world caving in, but there was nothing he could do about it.

He sat down, motionless, trying to take in the shock of the news they'd just been given.

Anthony sat down, his face still in his hands, sobbing, not quite knowing how to deal with his own sadness and shock.

Chris sat motionless, not saying a word to either of the brothers, himself still not believing what he'd just heard.

"Can… can… we go and… see him?" a distraught Anthony said, tears still streaming from his eyes, rolling down his cheeks, his face red with emotion.

"Come this way, I'll take you to him now," said a solemn Doctor Thomas, leading the brothers down the corridor and into a room where their father lay. "Take as much time as you need."

The surgeon then closed the door, leaving the grieving brothers alone with their father.

"Who's going to tell Mum?" asked Chris, looking at each of them in turn, "and we really should tell Dean too."

"I don't want to hear that useless piece of SHIT's name," Paul angrily responded to the very mention of his wayward brother. "HE'S THE ONE who's put our dad here, wait until I see him, I'm going to…"

"Would our dad REALLY have wanted you talking like this, Paul?" Chris interrupted, with a slight irritation in his voice.

Paul stared blankly at each of his two brothers, still trying to get his head around the fact that he wouldn't be seeing his dad anymore.

He then walked over to his father, who was lying on a table, covered over with a white sheet, and planted a kiss on his forehead.

"You rest now, Dad, you're not suffering any pain anymore." Tears streamed down his face. "I'm so sorry that we've done this to you; we're going to miss you so much."

He paused for a moment, looking at his dad one last time, before opening the door and walking out of the room, leaving just Anthony and Chris to say their final goodbyes.

Paul went and sat down in the waiting room, still crying from the events of the day, and waited for his other two brothers to appear.

After a short while, both an emotional Anthony and Chris came out, tears also rolling down their cheeks.

"We need to go back and talk to Mum," said Anthony, trying to hold back more tears. "We need to keep an eye on her; this is going to hit her pretty hard."

"Brother, we know how you're feeling about him right now but we need to tell Dean," Chris mentioned. "He was his son too."

"One of you can fucking call him," snapped Paul. "He's probably too drugged up with his girlfriend to care right now anyway. I'll see you at Mum and... Mum and Dad's."

He walked off, leaving Chris and Anthony to make their way back.

Paul was reflecting on how his world was falling apart.

He took a slow drive back to his mum and dad's house, dreading the news they were needing to break.

Anthony and Chris were pulling up just behind him, and the three of them got out of their cars almost simultaneously.

They walked up the path and opened the door, before walking into the lounge, seeing their mum sitting down, doing some knitting.

"What news on Dad?" she asked.

But she could see the looks on their faces, and the tears that they'd had.

"Mum?" sniffled Anthony. "He's gone." Tears started to roll down his cheeks again, before he burst into tears.

"OH MY GOD, NO," gasped Joan, putting her hands to her face before starting to cry aloud.

"Let us make you a cup of tea," said Anthony, still trying to hold back more tears. "It was peaceful."

Joan cried for what seemed like hours, but they stayed with her.

Chris had tried calling Dean, but had been unable to reach him.

They had all sat talking about their dad, and the wonderful memories of him, including when he first proposed to Joan, in an old caravan, which was practically falling to bits, when they were courting.

"I'll try calling Dean again," Chris said, to anyone who was listening. "He needs to know."

"Don't know why you're bothering," Paul snapped. "I told you, he's probably shooting up with his druggie of a girlfriend. Just leave him to it. Mum, I'm going to come and stay with you for a while, just so you've got one of us around; besides, Sarah's away, and I want to keep an eye on you."

"I'm not an invalid, son, I can look after myself," said Joan, "but would you mind going and grabbing me a bit of shopping? I've not got much in, and have been meaning to do it. I'll give you a list."

"Consider it done," said Paul.

Joan, in a state of bewilderment at her husband's death, passed Paul a sheet of paper, with a list of groceries and other items she needed.

"I'll grab these bits for you, Mum, and I'll be back before you know it."

"There's no rush, is there?" said Joan. "Besides, I've got Anthony and Chris here to keep me company."

Paul left his mum and dad's house, still reeling from everything that had happened today.

Just as he was heading towards his car, his mobile rang; it was Mr Barnes.

'How the HELL has he got my number? DEAN,' he thought.

At first, he thought about disconnecting the call, but then he thought about his now-fragile family, and the additional agony of being in danger from this drugs baron, let alone Dean.

Paul stayed silent as he answered the phone.

"Mr Arnold, what a pleasure it is to speak to you again," said the smug baron. "I've got another job for you, and more cash to come your way."

"I've told you before, I'm NOT INTERESTED in your shady dealings." Paul was not in the mood to deal with Mr Barnes, after everything that had happened. "I'm NOT one of your cronies that you can just push around, so get someone else to do your dirty work. Besides, how did you get my number?"

"Now, now, Mr Arnold, there no need to be like that." Paul could hear him arrogantly puffing away on a cigar. "It would be SUCH A SHAME for any harm to come to you and your family, just think of that extra bundle of cash that could come your way. Pop by at eleven tomorrow morning, so we can discuss business. Oh, and, your number? Your brother can be PERSUADED VERY EASILY."

Mr Barnes then promptly hung up.

All Paul could think about was losing his dad earlier in the day.

He was not concerned about losing his job at the finance

firm, as he was slowly starting to hate it there more and more anyway.

He put his phone in his pocket, got in his car and pulled away, to get the grocery bits that his mum had asked for.

Driving to the supermarket, he was starting to think about the drug baron's offer, as he knew that he'd need money to live, now that he was out of work, and of course he thought about his family's welfare too, and the dangers they'd be in if he didn't accept.

Besides, it didn't have to be for long, while he looked for something legal.

'I don't have to do it for long, and I'm sure I can discuss with him what kind of work I do,' he thought.

He wandered around the supermarket, almost in a daze, not quite knowing what to make of this day that he'd had, and also knowing that he had to keep an eye on his mum, and also contemplate what he was going to do about this offer he'd just had.

He managed to find all of the groceries that his mum had asked for, paid, and took the bags to his car.

Just as he was loading his boot, he looked across the car park, and saw who he thought was his brother Dean and his girlfriend.

He quickly put the rest of the groceries in the boot, before slamming it shut, and racing over to the couple.

"Oi, YOU… get yourself the FUCK over here," he yelled.

As he drew nearer, he was met by a couple looking blankly at him. It WASN'T them.

"I'm sorry, I thought you were…" The couple looked angrily back at him, quickly walking away.

Paul walked back to his car, slightly agitated that it wasn't them.

He arrived back with his mums shopping, and started to unload the car.

Chris saw him through the window, and decided to go out to help.

"You ok, brother? It's good of you that you have offered to stay with Mum," said Chris. "Let me give you some money, just in case—"

"Keep your money. I've got plenty of my own to keep Mum topped up if she needs it," interrupted Paul, snapping back in his now usual manner. "But… thanks anyway." Paul glanced across at Chris, giving him a slight grin, knowing that he was the calmest one out of all of them.

The two of them carried their mum's shopping in, and put it in the kitchen.

"Thank you, boys, so good of you," said Joan, still in a state of bewilderment with the day's events. "Will you be ok, Paul, getting to and from work, if you're going to stay here?"

He paused for a few moments.

"Yes, Mum, I'll… erm… I'll be fine, yes, don't worry about me," he said, wanting to change the subject about work, not wanting to worry his mum any further. "Besides, it's YOU we have to worry about now."

"I'm old enough and daft enough to look after myself, you know," said Joan proudly. "I had all of you to bring up, remember, well, me and…"

Tears started rolling down her cheeks, her eyes becoming red and very moist.

Anthony went and put his arm around their mum's shoulder.

"It's all going to be ok, Mum," he said. "We're all here, night and day, whenever you need us."

"You've all got your own lives to lead now, though, I will only get in the way," she sobbed.

"Don't be silly, Mum," Chris reassured her. "What kind of sons would walk away from their parents?"

"I can think of one," murmured Paul, in reference to his wayward brother.

Just then, Chris's mobile rang, right on cue; it was Dean.

Paul snatched the phone from his brother and went to yell down the phone to him.

"Where the f—" quickly stopping himself from swearing, suddenly remembering that he was in close proximity to his mum. "Where have you been?"

"I've been chilling with my girlfriend, why?" asked Dean casually, unaware of the earlier events.

"Well, while you've probably been shooting up, without a fucking care in the world." Paul was not able to hold back his anger any longer, before walking out of the house, and into the garden. "OUR FATHER has passed away today, not that you FUCKING CARE."

"OH MY GOD, when?" Dean was getting upset, and stressed that he was not there for his mum and brothers.

"Why do you care?"

"Of COURSE I care." Dean began to cry. "WH… WHAT happened?"

"You DON'T care so you just carry on with your drug lifestyle, with your LOSER of a girlfriend," he snapped angrily. "Two losers together." Paul hung up.

Dean tried calling back, but Paul just ignored the mobile ringing.

He walked back into the house that his mum and dad had shared, and thrust the phone back into Chris's hand.

Chris looked blankly at his clearly irate brother, waiting for a response, while Anthony was still spending time with their mum.

"YOU can deal with him from now on, brother, I'm SICK of his attitude and behaviour. I'll be round later, Mum." Paul went over to kiss his mother on the cheek, before heading back out of the house and towards home.

Paul was heading home; his mobile, sitting on the passenger seat, made him jump slightly as it began to ring.

He breathed a sigh of relief, hoping that it wasn't the drugs baron again; it was only his best mate, John.

He managed to find a pull-in in the road, and answered it, while keeping the engine running.

"You ok, Paul?" John sounded like he was out drinking, with the sound of clinking of glasses.

"I'm ok, where are you?"

"I'm out with the lads at our local, having a few, fancy joining us?"

"I can't, mate, I've got too much going on," Paul said, dejectedly. "Another time."

"Sure I can't tempt you?" teased John.

"I really can't, but hold that thought."

"What's going on? Is everything ok?" asked a concerned John, hoping that his best friend was ok.

"Yeah, everything is good. Listen, I've pulled in to take this call, so I'd better go." Paul didn't want to worry his best friend, though he sensed himself that John could feel that something might be wrong.

Paul sat contemplating in his car for a while.

Everything had hit him hard, all at once, but he decided that he was going to take back control.

He put his phone down on the passenger seat, and drove off.

He was heading to go and see his wayward brother, Dean.

He pulled up outside their house, feeling a bit calmer, despite knowing where he was.

He knocked on the door and it was immediately answered by him.

"If you've come to cause trouble…" Dean started to close the door on Paul.

"No, I've not," snapped Paul, "but, seeing that you owe me, there's something I want you to do for me."

Paul was in the house for around an hour, before getting ready to leave.

"Now, just remember what I've told you." Dean stood staring at his brother, watching Paul walk back to his car.

He was soon home, and pulled into his drive.

He got out of his car, before letting himself in the house.

The pressure was starting to mount on top of him, all at once.

He started to pace the floor, walking one way, then the other, stressing about what he was needing to do for the drugs baron, just to keep his family safe.

He sat down on the sofa, contemplating his next move.

'The money would come in handy,' he thought, 'but drugs are the one thing I hate the most, and he's such a slimeball.'

Paul got his mobile phone out of his pocket and put it on the sofa next to him.

He stared at it momentarily, before getting up and wandering into the kitchen area.

It was good that Sarah was away; that gave him time to decide what he was going to do about the offer from the drugs baron.

He got himself a glass from the glass rack, and poured himself a large glass of white wine.

He was not a big drinker, but he felt that he needed a drink, giving him time to decide what to do.

'If I do it,' he thought, 'what if I get caught? I was lucky last time.'

Thinking of the easy money he could make, he started to reluctantly think of the benefits.

He finished his wine, before quickly pouring himself another, picking the bottle up and carrying it back into the lounge, where he had been, before putting the bottle on the floor next to him.

He quickly gulped the next glass of wine down, almost with a sense of Dutch courage, grabbed his phone, and took it into the bedroom.

He decided to call the drugs baron, Mr Barnes.

The baron quickly and smugly answered the phone.

"Ah, Mr Arnold, what a PLEASANT surprise hearing from you. Have you thought any more about my proposal?"

"Yes, I have," he snapped. "I'll do it, but you've then got to leave my family alone. It's the only reason I'm agreeing to this."

"There's a good fellow, you knew that it was always going to make sense in the end, didn't you?"

"What about Dean? He owes you money. I want that written off, with me agreeing to this, and you not deal with him anymore, and no more threats towards the rest of my family either. That's the deal."

"Now, now, Mr Arnold, I run a business, I'm not going to turn business away, now, am I? As regards your family, I'm sure I can ease off, but, mark my words, FUCK WITH ME, or step out of line, one false move, and your family will be, shall we say, ripped apart," said the baron arrogantly, puffing away on his cigar.

"Ok, I'll come and see you tomorrow morning. I'll be there for eleven."

"You'll be properly rewarded, put you on my payroll, chuck you in a girl or two."

Mr Barnes then hung up.

Time passed, and Paul decided to call John, see if he was still out.

John answered, and Paul could still hear clinking of glasses, and his other friends laughing and joking.

"You free yet?" John asked, in a slurring voice.

"I am, and need a pint. You still at the Adlington Arms?"

"Yes, mate, we are, and we're all still here." John's speech was becoming more and more muffled. "Come and have a pint with us, or six if you fancy it," he joked.

"Think six is sounding very inviting right now, John. You've not mentioned anything to the others about what I've told you, have you?"

John got up from his chair and wandered over to a quieter place in the pub, away from the others.

"Now, what sort of mate would I be to you," he whispered, "if I told them what's going on? But SERIOUSLY, you NEED to get out of that shit, Paul, it isn't good."

"I'll think of something, but, for now, get the staff to get pouring me a beer, and I'll be there before you know it. I can taste it going down my neck already." Paul tried to make light of his situation.

He got in his car and made his way towards the pub.

He arrived in a short space of time, locked his car and walked in, where he was greeted by his friends.

He had a sullen look on his face, which Steve and the others picked up on, not knowing that John knew the reason why Paul wasn't looking himself.

"Everything ok with you, buddy?" asked Charlie.

"Yeah, just a lot going on at the minute with work, and things going on with Sarah. I'll be alright after a few of these bad boys." He was talking about his favourite beer, the Killer Whale, which had been poured and was sitting on the table in front of him.

John kept glancing across at Paul, as the men got chatting, and Paul also glanced over to John, in a way of saying not to let anything slip out that he knew.

"You sure you're ok, Paul? You don't seem yourself tonight." Although Steve wasn't as close to Paul as John was, he still noticed him a different light tonight.

"All is ok, yeah, just need to sort some shit out, that's all, I also need to get more of these down my neck."

The friends chatted for some hours, and it was getting late.

Paul had drunk far too much, and decided that it was time for him to go.

"Thanks for tonight, boys, just what I needed." Paul stumbled from his chair and almost fell to the floor.

"We really don... don't do this enough," murmured Gary, struggling to put his words together, he was so drunk.

"How you get… ting home?" John asked, with a glazed look in his eyes.

But Paul didn't seem to hear him, and made his way out of the pub door, drunkenly waving back to everyone as he did.

He fumbled around for his car keys, and opened the door of the car, before getting in.

'It's only a short journey, I'm sure it'll be ok,' he thought.

He carefully pulled out of the car park and, with no other cars around, started driving home slowly.

He wasn't too far from home and, being drunk, was swerving around the road erratically, but he was trying to be as careful as he could.

Suddenly, he caught a small pothole in the road, making him swerve, and ending up in a ditch.

Thankfully, there were no police cars around, and he was just around the corner from home.

He sat in his car for a few moments, slightly shaken, while still trying to clear his head from the alcohol he had consumed, and trying to visualise the road ahead, and with his head still spinning.

He sat in his car for a few more moments, the engine still running, before he pulled out of the ditch and finally pulled into his driveway, and home.

He clumsily got out of his car, almost falling onto the drive, before locking his car and finding his keys to make his way inside.

The house was eerily quiet, as he staggered towards the sofa, before collapsing onto it.

Just then, his phone rang; it was his mum, Joan.

"Where are you, son? I thought you were staying here tonight?"

"I've had a few too many to drink, Mum, I'll be round tomorrow."

"As long as I know what's happening," she said, feeling slightly lost on her own.

"I'll be round first thing, unless you want me to come now. I can grab a shower."

"No, son, that's ok, I'll see you in the morning instead. Love you."

"Love you too, Mum."

Paul started to hate himself that he'd forgotten that he was meant to be staying at his parents' house instead that night.

He started to ponder how his life might be about to change, now he was under the mercy of the drugs baron; there HAD to be a way out, but HOW?

GET OFF ME

Mr Yang and Sarah had been going over the fashion designs, as Alice sat quietly next to her.

"I've got to say, Sarah, I'm very impressed with these new designs, and I'll soon be putting in a large order for many of them. You've surpassed yourself again, as always," declared Mr Yang, who was Sarah's most important customer.

"Always a pleasure doing business with you, sir, glad that the designs please you, as much as we enjoy putting them together."

"And you've brought a beautiful assistant with you too. Any time you wish to let her join my company instead…" he chuckled.

Alice laughed.

"My assistant is priceless, Mr Yang," joked Sarah.

The meeting was over. They all shook hands, and the girls left the meeting, but not until they had finished the coffee that had been brought in during the discussions.

"Let's go and drop these bits off, and let's go for lunch," declared Sarah.

They went back to their room in the hotel, and dropped the drawings on their large bed that they were sharing later.

They left the hotel, and were soon ready to eat.

"I'm taking you to this lovely restaurant, call the Man Wah. I come here a lot when I come here."

"Lead the way, darling." Alice smiled.

They were soon at the restaurant and sat down to eat.

They both ordered the same thing: sweet-and-sour pork and rice, as Alice was going to attempt to use chopsticks for the first time, much to Sarah's amusement. They also ordered a cold bottle of wine.

"Mr Yang was nice."

"He's my most valued customer, puts in loads of orders, spends big, and keeps me accustomed to my lifestyle," joked Sarah.

"I've got a nice surprise for you," whispered Sarah, while tucking into a pork ball.

"Ooo, I'm intrigued now. What is it?"

"How do you fancy staying out here a bit longer, make a week of it, seeing that Paul's been in such a mood too."

"WOW, erm, really?" Alice was both shocked and excited at the thought of the two of them spending more time together. "What about the office, and the other girls?" Alice was puzzled how Sarah was going to be able to do it, being away for longer than planned. "Won't they need to know what designs need to be sorted out etc.?"

"I've had changes in my plans before, and they've just got on with it, they're an organised lot," explained Sarah. "It will just take a simple phone call but, if you don't want to…"

"Oh, I didn't say that." Alice winked in Sarah's direction. "Besides, it'd be nice to see more of this lovely country."

"That's it, it's sorted then, I'll obviously pay you at your usual rates," Sarah laughed, herself glad that they were both going to be able to spend more time together.

"Oh, hang on, I've only brought enough clothes for a few days." Alice panicked that she might have to wear the same outfit on more than one occasion.

"Don't worry about that," exclaimed Sarah. "I'm SURE I could treat us to a little shopping spree while we're here. I'm sorry it's not Paris or Milan but will Hong Kong clothing do?"

"As long as you treat me to Paris and Milan another time." Alice was now more relaxed, and loved joking around with Sarah, and was excited that she was going to be able to do more exploring.

"That's a given, you know that," chuckled Sarah.

They soon finished the wine and their meals, and Sarah paid the bill.

"Let's go back to the hotel room; maybe I could give you a massage," teased Alice.

"Mmm… I'm liking the sound of that."

They were soon back at the hotel room, which was airy and fresh, and the day was very warm.

As soon as the door was closed, Alice was pushing Sarah up against the wall by the bed.

"I want you, Sarah."

They started to passionately kiss each other, and were soon naked once more.

Their hands were all over each other's bodies, and Sarah pushed Alice onto the bed.

She got on top of Alice, and started to grind herself

between Alice's legs. She was thrusting herself onto her, and they both moaned with pleasure. She then lay on top of Alice, and they again kissed passionately.

Alice rolled Sarah onto her back, slowly kissing her neck, then licking her breasts and nipples, before moving her tongue down her body, and between her legs.

"Oh, baby, that feels so good, don't stop," moaned Sarah, thrusting herself onto Alice's tongue as it went deeper inside her.

Sarah hadn't felt this height of ecstasy for so long, and she wanted Alice just as much.

Alice was sliding her fingers in and out of Sarah's pussy, but Sarah wanted to return the favour before she came.

Sarah pulled at Alice's head, beckoning her to come back up, which she did, before she rolled Alice on her back and went to work on her body.

They were both in the height of passion as they entwined their legs, thrusting onto each other.

"Oh my God, I'm going to cum," sighed Alice passionately.

"God, baby, me too."

Almost in an instant, their legs quivered, and a burst of emotion engulfed them, before shuddering to a halt. They had both cum.

They untwined, bodies dripping with sweat, as Sarah leant over to kiss Alice, before lying down next to her, both trying to catch their breaths, and she put her arm under Alice's head.

"That felt so good. I have missed you, and this," stated Sarah.

"Plenty where that came from," Alice joked.

They rested for an hour, chatting away.

"Have you ever had a girlfriend, Sarah?"

"Why, are you offering?" she joked.

"I just wondered. I just want to know more about you, and any past girl experiences."

"I've had a few 'girlfriends', I guess you could call them, but nothing long term. Just for sex and company, really. Why do you ask?"

"Like I say, I just wondered."

"Paul doesn't really know too much about my past, and that's just the way I like it."

"Hmm, ok."

"Do you want to talk about Stacey, where you met etc.? It's ok if you don't. Do you miss her?"

"Is it ok if we skip that subject? It's still too painful."

"Yes, of course. I'm here if you ever want to talk about it, though."

"I know, thanks."

Once showered again and dressed, each put on a pair of light-blue jeans and trendy tops, and decided to finally go out sightseeing.

They took in the sights of the botanical gardens and museums, and travelled on the tram, taking in picturesque sights of their surroundings.

The week was soon upon them, and it was time to head home.

The flight was on time, twelve noon, but it was going to be around midnight before they got home.

Their flight landed without any delays, and they collected their luggage and were out of the airport.

There were taxis waiting, so they grabbed the nearest one, and headed first to Alice's.

"I've had an AMAZING time, thank you." Alice smiled.

"Me too," said Sarah.

"See you in the morning," said Alice, kissing Sarah sweetly goodnight.

Sarah smiled, as she waved Alice off.

Sarah was back home within minutes, paying the driver and stepping as quietly as she could towards the house, knowing Paul would be asleep.

She suddenly realised that she hadn't rung him on her arrival in Hong Kong, and she dreaded how that might have affected his mood.

She crept quietly into the house, locking it behind her.

She carefully placed her luggage on the floor, and drawings on the sofa, taking her shoes off as quietly as she could.

She walked upstairs to the bedroom; the bed lay empty.

The house felt very cold, un-lived-in, almost, as if he had not been there for a while.

"Paul, are you here?" she called.

Again, there was silence; he was not in the house.

"No doubt out drinking AGAIN!" she thought. "I'll give John a call, no doubt they'll be curled up in a corner together."

She suddenly took a sharp intake of breath, as she noticed a shadow of someone, before the lights came on.

It was Paul, seeming very disorientated, his shirt hanging out of his trousers, with a splattering of blood on it, from both his nose and mouth.

"Enjoy your TRIP?" he snarled, swaying and hanging onto the door, to stop himself falling over.

"Yes, I did, thank you. What the HELL has happened to you? Let me take a look at you." Sarah was showing signs of concern.

"You've been galivanting all over the place, in, your FANCY CLOTHES, flashing your cash, FUCKING whoever takes your fancy, not giving a SHIT about me..." he snapped, waving his arms around, in a ferocious manner.

"Just you hang on. How DARE YOU talk to me like that! I work hard. You had the chance to come with me, but you DIDN'T, and don't you DARE say that I don't give a shit about you. You've been like a bear with a sore head lately, and drunk AGAIN, no doubt, and probably been fighting too, by the looks of you."

He lunged towards her and – SMACK! – lashed out at her face, with an almighty slap, almost throwing her into the air, leaving her in a heap on the floor, sobbing.

Paul stumbled towards the front door and out, into the still of the night.

Sarah stayed on the floor for a moment, still sobbing, and shaking with fear, in case he returned.

She was soon on her feet, her face still sore from the slap, and ran to the front door, locking it quickly.

She texted Alice.

Are you still awake? He's hit me! Can I come and stay at yours?

Alice responded.

Oh my God! Are you ok? Get a taxi, grab some clothes and bits, and come here.

Sarah, still in a daze, rushed to the bedroom, to get more clothes. She ordered a taxi to Alice's, while frantically opening her suitcase, and practically throwing her clothes in.

The taxi arrived in prompt time outside.

Beep beep… the driver pips his horn.

She grabbed her suitcase and drawings once again and flung the house door open, before closing it behind her. She shakily delved into her bag, to find her keys to lock up. She didn't care if he came back; he was locked out, unless he had his keys.

She opened the back door of the taxi, flinging her luggage and drawings in, before getting in and slamming the door shut.

"Applewood Road, please, driver," still shaking after the ordeal.

The driver pulled away from the house, heading to Alice's.

No sooner had the taxi pulled up outside Alice's than her front door flung open.

Sarah opened the taxi door in a hurry, leaving it wide open, and straight into Alice's waiting arms.

"Go and sit down. I'll get the bits and pay the driver," Alice said, in a soothing voice.

Sarah, clearly still shaken by her ordeal at the hands of Paul, sat down, as Alice calmly walked towards the driver, money in hand, paid him, and grabbed Sarah's bits from the back seat.

She walked back to the house, pulling the bulky suitcase behind her, and the drawings in the other hand, and closed the front door with her foot.

"I've got a bag of ice in the freezer; let me give you that, get the swelling down."

Alice walked towards the kitchen, getting the ice from the freezer drawer, and passed it to Sarah.

"Are you cut? What the HELL happened?"

"He was drunk, and he erm… he… just… hit me." She stumbled, still shaken.

"Well, stay here as long as you want, you know that."

"I know, darling, thank you."

"It's late, Sarah, let's just go up to bed… to SLEEP!"

They walked up the stairs to the bedroom, undressed, Alice once again passing Sarah one of her nightshirts to sleep in.

They got into bed and fell asleep, with Sarah in Alice's arms.

Paul, meanwhile, had gone to stay at his mum's that night, still drunk, after the episode with Sarah.

He stumbled towards his mum's door, and knocked abruptly.

He could hear his mum approaching carefully, with it being late and, with no hesitation, let her know that it was him.

"Look at the state of you," a concerned Joan said. "What the hell has happened?"

"I've just had a fight with her, that's all," he mumbled.

He walked into his mum and dad's house, rudely brushing past her as he did.

"I'm going to go for a shower, then straight to bed," he slurred, not even giving her a second look, with his drunken glazed eyes.

"Haven't you got work…?" But he was too drunk to listen to her.

Joan looked on with worry, stopping mid-sentence, as he ventured up the stairs.

Paul sat on the spare bed, where he was going to sleep,

taking his shoes and socks off, as he swayed from side to side, almost as if he was about to tumble over, before taking the rest of his clothes off.

He got up from the bed, completely naked, and stumbled towards the bathroom, to take a shower.

He seemed to take an eternity in the big double shower, as the water sprayed into his face and down his muscly body, as he pressed his hand firmly onto the shower wall, taking in what had happened earlier.

After washing himself, he turned the shower off, stepped out, and wrapped a big towel around his waist.

Still feeling pretty drunk, he sat on the bed, staring into space, still swaying from side to side.

"Do you want anything to eat, son? I can rustle you something up."

"I'm ok, Mum, I just want to sleep," he shouted down the reply, and, sure enough, he dried himself off and climbed into bed.

It was early the next morning, six, and Joan was knocking on Paul's bedroom door.

"Are you awake, Paul? Haven't you got work?"

There was no answer to her tap on the door, so she knocked again.

Again, there was no reply.

She paused, before deciding to leave him to it; after all, he had come back in a real state the night before.

It got to eight-thirty, and Joan could hear Paul coming down the stairs.

He looked slightly dishevelled, as he strode towards the kitchen.

"Go and sit down; I'll do you a cooked breakfast," Joan

snapped at him, feeling a little angry. "Not at work today, then?"

"No… I erm… booked a few days off." He knew that he was lying to his mum. "Gives me a chance to spend a bit of time with you too."

Joan stared into the back of him as he spoke to her, Paul not daring to look at his mum, in case she could see him lying.

Suddenly, Paul's phone rang… it was Mr Barnes, the drugs baron.

"Ah, Mr Arnold, you've not forgotten our little arrangement, I hope."

Paul got quickly up from the table, grabbing a piece of toast, from the breakfast that his mum had just put in front of him, before sharply walking out the back of the house.

Paul had been round to see Mr Barnes and his bruising heavyweight bodyguards, and had done one or two deliveries, without any dramas.

"I have a few more deliveries for you to make for me; I want you here within the hour, there's a good boy," said the arrogant drugs lord, puffing away on his cigar, before hanging up.

"Sorry, Mum, I've got to run."

Joan looked at him leaving the house. "But your breakfast!"

Paul was already out of the house.

He ordered a taxi from his mum's, to take him back home, where his car was, having called for one the night he stormed out after hitting Sarah.

He soon arrived back at the house, grabbed his keys from his pocket, and got in his car, knowing full well that he was still over the limit, hoping that he wouldn't be pulled over.

He arrived at the house where Mr Barnes lived, and dreaded the thought of going in.

Again, youths were circling his car on their bikes, as he parked up.

"He's waiting for ya," said one of the youths, nodding in the house's direction.

Paul gave the youths a sharp stare as he walked towards the house.

He walked into the dark, dingy lounge, where he was greeted by the drugs baron, two bodyguards, and two scantily clad girls flanked either side of him.

"Ah, Mr Arnold, what a PLEASURE it is to see you again," said the drugs baron, arrogantly puffing away on his half-smoked fat cigar.

"Shame I can't say the same," came Paul's reply.

"Now, now, Mr Arnold, your next assignment has arrived for your delivery, and you may be needing THIS." One of Mr Barnes's bodyguards pulled out a Magnum .45 pistol from a drawer and held it out in Paul's direction.

"WHAT THE FUCK IS THIS? I'm not taking that. Who do you think I am?" He glanced at the stern-looking thug.

"It's for your protection, Mr Arnold, we don't want another episode like the last time, now, do we?" said the smug baron, leaning back in his dark-brown worn leather chair, the girls brushing his chubby cheeks with their hands.

"I'm not about to run into any of your dodgy customers, now, am I?"

"This is why you need to protect yourself, Mr Arnold." The drugs baron smirked at him as he nodded, gesturing for him to take the gun being handed to him. "I take it you've used a gun before?"

"Of course, but not like this."

"Then it will be child's play for you, then, won't it?"

Mr Barnes looked over to the other bodyguard and gestured for him to hand Paul over the bag of drugs, all ready for him to take.

Mr Barnes pulled open a drawer from the very large table that he was sitting behind, and tossed Paul a large bundle of bank notes, tied up with an elastic band.

"There's your payment, and remember, another large sum of money when you return, now, there's a good boy, run along, my customers are waiting for their meal." Mr Barnes was still sitting smug in his chair, chuckling in Paul's direction and waving for him to leave.

Paul took the bag, put the gun inside his jacket and, looking angrily at Mr Barnes, walked out of the room and towards his waiting car, closely followed by one of the bodyguards, heading towards his black 4×4.

The youths were still hanging around, a little further away this time, riding up and down the street, but rode towards Paul as he was putting the bag on his passenger seat, before closing the door.

The older of the youths, while chewing gum, gave Paul a smirk, before laughing in his direction as they turned around on their bikes and rode back up the street.

Paul got in his driver's side door, closed it and put his seatbelt on. He sat momentarily, staring at the bag; even though he'd done this drugs run a few times previously, so was getting used to the procedure, he still felt uncomfortable.

He then noticed some headlights flashing behind him, the thug in his 4×4, issuing Paul to drive off, to deliver the shipments.

Paul opened the bag beside him and pulled out the list of the addresses that he needed to deliver to.

There were twelve addresses on the list, two of them requiring money to be handed to him.

The first few drop-offs went without a hitch, as no money needed to be handed over.

He then got the third house, and a big burly man answered the door.

He was wearing a white string vest, very overweight, with a cigarette hanging from his mouth, unshaven for a few weeks.

"I've got your delivery from Mr Barnes," Paul whispered, opening the side of his jacket, where he was hiding the drugs packet.

"I don't have his money; tell him I'll pay him next week," the overweight man told Paul confidently, standing tall.

Just then, Paul pulled the other side of his jacket to one side, and, with it still inside his jacket, so as not to draw attention to anyone, pointed the gun directly at the man.

He suddenly felt a sense of power, almost enjoying putting the man under pressure to find the money that he had come for.

"I'll… I'll… just go and get it."

"Hurry up," summoned Paul to the man, again having a sense of enormous power.

He wasn't enjoying doing the drug baron's dirty work, but he enjoyed the brief moment of putting the man on the spot.

Paul looked back at the thug who had followed him, nodding in his direction, while waiting for the man to reappear with the money, gesturing that all was well and that the transaction was about to take place.

The man reappeared with the money soon after, and carefully handed it to Paul, while continuing to keep a close eye on the gun being pointed in his direction.

"Now, that wasn't so bad, was it?" A nervous, yet relieved Paul headed back to his car, before screeching off.

He still had a few more drops in the area to do, but was starting to feel more confident doing them, even though he wasn't enjoying it, and needed to find a way out.

Thankfully, his last few drug drops were in Austin.

He had no more issues with the last of the drops.

He took the empty bag back, with the money he had collected, and parked up back up outside Mr Barnes's house, closely followed by Mr Barnes's minder.

The youths, who were at the top of the road, decided not to ride down this time, but looked on as Paul got out of his car and walked towards the house, stepping inside.

The bodyguard followed closely behind him.

"GOOD JOB, Mr Arnold, you've done me proud." He again reached for his drawer and threw Paul another bundle of notes.

Suddenly, Paul remembered that he had a gun in his pocket, and pulled it out on the drug lord, while he shuffled across the room, so he also had view of Mr Barnes's bodyguards and the girls.

"Get over there, all of you… GO ON." He pointed to where he wanted them to go.

But none of them moved and instead looked at Paul, before laughing.

"What's funny?" said an agitated Paul.

"You didn't HONESTLY THINK I was going to give you a LOADED GUN, now, did you? How foolish would

I have been to do that?" said the drugs lord, puffing on his cigar and continuing to laugh at Paul.

Paul angrily started to pull the trigger of the gun, but it just clicked; it was EMPTY.

"You BASTARD, you gave me an empty gun, knowing full well that you were putting me in danger. What if one of your lowlives had pulled a gun on ME?"

Mr Barnes continued to laugh. "But they didn't, did they? So it was all good. You complain too much, you need to chill a little bit more." The baron smirked.

"Here's your STINKING MONEY." Paul tossed what he collected on his drops over to Mr Barnes.

"And here's a little something for you in return, TEN THOUSAND there." Mr Barnes threw another, larger bundle to him, as promised. "I've another few drops for you to do for me tomorrow, be here for ten, SHARPISH."

Paul made a sharp exit from the house, and into his waiting car, before speeding off back to his mum and dad's house in Churchfield.

After arriving at the house, he opened the door, before storming in and up the stairs, not even giving himself time to greet his mum on the way up.

"Is that you, son?" she called. "Paul?" Joan went to the bottom of the stairs and called up to him. "Did you want to eat? I've just made a stew, used to be one of your favourites."

He went into the room he was sleeping in and sat on the bed, before getting up and pacing the floor, before sitting back down on the bed again, clearly very agitated, burying his head in his hands, wondering how he was going to get out of the mess that he had got himself into.

Joan walked up the stairs and saw her son sitting on the bed, with his head still firmly buried in his hands.

"Whatever is the matter, son? Whatever it is, we can sort it out." Joan had not seen her son like this before, and felt real concern.

She'd not seen her son in such a state, and put her reassuring hand on his shoulder, before he shrugged it off.

"I don't want to talk about it, ok?" he snapped.

Joan turned around to walk away, feeling a bit upset with the way he had just spoken to her.

"Mum, I'm so sorry, just got some stuff I'm trying to sort out, but I will, that was un-called-for, the way I've just spoken to you, I'd LOVE some stew, it smells DELICIOUS, let's go and eat."

She smiled, and tucked her arm underneath Paul's as they left the room together.

After eating, they sat together in the lounge, with the television on in the background but neither of them watching it.

Joan kept looking over at her son, whose mind was clearly elsewhere.

"You've got your father's eyes," she muttered, trying to build a conversation.

Paul could just barely raise a grin in his mum's direction, but she could sense that he seemed troubled by something.

"Have you heard from Sarah? How is she?"

"She's away on business, Mum, and no, I've not heard from her, she's probably having too much of a good time anyway. I miss Dad, Mum, miss him so much." Tears started to well up in his eyes.

"We all miss him, son, you were always able to talk to your dad, but I'm here for you to talk to as well, you know." She tried to get her son to open up, with whatever was on his mind.

"I know, Mum, and I appreciate it, but it's something that I need to sort out alone, nothing to concern yourself with. Right, I'm off to bed, Mum, see you tomorrow."

Paul got up, and gave her a kiss on the forehead, before walking up the stairs and to his room.

He headed towards the shower room, before getting undressed, turning the power shower on and stepping into the large double shower.

Water gushed down on his toned body as he contemplated what tomorrow was going to bring.

He was deep in thought, as the shower rained down on him; he'd not even started to wash himself, he was so deep in thought.

After twenty minutes, he finally began to wash himself, before turning the shower off and wrapping a towel around him.

After drying himself off, and cleaning his teeth, he headed to his room, took the towel off and climbed into bed.

The next day, Paul awoke at eight, late for him, so he clambered out of bed and went for a shower.

After having his cooling wash, he could smell his mum's cooking downstairs: sausages, bacon, eggs, mushrooms and toast.

"Coming down for breakfast, Paul?"

"Down in a minute, Mum," he called, as he was still drying himself off.

He was down the stairs in a flash, obviously feeling very hungry.

"Come and sit down, son, tuck into what I've rustled up."

He sat down and started munching through what his mum had cooked.

"What are your plans today, son?"

"Oh, I have a few errands to run, so don't know when I'll be back." He knew that he'd probably have more drug runs to do for the evil drugs baron, but he did not want to tell his mum.

Paul finished his breakfast and thanked her.

"That was delicious; shall I load the dishwasher?"

"No, it's ok, it's only a few bits," Joan murmured.

Just then, his mobile rang; it was Mr Barnes.

"What do you want?" an agitated Paul said, whispering, as he walked away from his concerned mum. "Especially so early into the day?"

"I have another job for you, son, a BIG ONE, has the money ready at the house, so get yourself here soon," chuckled the drugs baron.

Paul really didn't like him, but knew that he had to do it, to protect his family, and himself.

"Ok, I'll be there soon," he continued to whisper, not wanting his mum to worry about who he might be talking to.

But Joan knew her son inside out, and, after he finished talking on the phone, she could see worry and concern in his face.

"Who was that, son? You're not in any trouble, are you?"

"No, Mum." He stumbled over his words, wondering what to tell her. "Erm… just an old colleague, wants me to help him move some things in his house. I may be some time, so don't wait up."

He didn't like lying to his mum, but he knew he had to, as he gave her a gentle kiss on the cheek, shuffling towards the front door before filing his way out of the house.

He glanced back at his concerned mum as she stared out of her large French window, giving her a brief smile and a half-hearted wave, pausing before getting in his car and driving away, not knowing what faced him, with this job that the baron had organised for him.

Paul soon pulled up outside the dirty, dingy house, where the baron was waiting.

As usual, the gang of youths were riding their bikes at the top of the road, all of them stopping to watch Paul begrudgingly get out of his car, and with a big sigh trudged towards the house.

Paul saw one of the girls, who constantly flanked him every time he went round, get off her knees and pull her thin blue dress straps back over her shoulders, covering her breasts as the baron did his trousers back up, before pulling up his zip, puffing away on his large, thick cigar.

"Ah, my boy, just in time." He ushered one of the bodyguards to go to the drawer, and get Paul his usual bundle of dirty money.

"I'm NOT your boy," snapped Paul, as he was chucked a larger than normal pack of money.

He looked down at the packet, frowning, wondering why it felt larger than normal.

"I've been impressed with you, lad, you've done some important drops for me, so I've decided to let you go it alone, but remember: we WILL still be watching you, so no funny moves. Remember what I said about your family," snarled the baron, giving Paul an evil stare.

"But, boss, we should still track him, I don't trust him," one of the bodyguards snapped at the baron, while also giving Paul an evil stare.

"QUIET!" snapped the baron. "I give the orders around here; let's see what he's made of."

The huge, muscly bodyguard walked across the dark, smoke-filled room, and grabbed a large brown holdall that Paul had handled many times before, before the stone-faced bodyguard thrust it to him.

"The instructions for the drop are in there, along with a large stash of goodies for him. Make sure the man pays you… off you go now." Mr Barnes smirked.

Paul walked towards the door and looked back at the baron, the scantily clad girls and the bodyguards.

The baron's hand gestured Paul towards the door, pushing the back of his fingers towards him, in a show of his authority.

Paul walked out, clutching the heavy bag, and went out the door, opened the front passenger door, and threw the bag onto the seat, the seat puffing down with the weight of the bag, before he slammed the door shut.

He opened up the well-worn back to reveal a huge quantity of drugs, and a note to say where it was to go: 44 GREENACRE ROAD, two hundred and fifty thousand pounds worth, the biggest quantity he's had to handle so far.

He kept staring at the note, but, as he had done so many drops now, it had almost become second nature to him now.

He put the postcode in his satnav and drove off.

He had only been driving for ten minutes, and he found the road.

He casually drove into the road, so as not to cause suspicion, and quickly found the house.

It looked a respectable road and house, nothing like the street where the baron was, with circling youths watching his every move.

'This should be nice and easy,' thought Paul.

He rattled the knocker of the blue door, and it was answered by a well-dressed, smart man, clean-shaven, six feet tall, with dark, well-kept, if a little oily, swept-back hair.

"I'm here with your delivery," an ashen-faced Paul said to the man.

The man smiled, and gestured for Paul to come in.

"It's ok, I'd sooner get the payment and go."

"Nonsense," said the man. "Besides, I need to try and remember where I've put the damn money. Please, come in, I shouldn't take too long."

Paul felt at ease with the man; he seemed a genuinely nice guy, and this made him feel more comfortable, so he stepped inside.

"Drink?" asked the man.

Even though he felt more comfortable that the man seemed a nice guy, he still felt slightly on his guard.

"One drink isn't going to hurt, now, is it?" He pushed a small tot of whisky into Paul's direction.

The man walked out of the lounge where Paul and the man were, and into another room.

Paul sat down to wait, as he drank his whisky quickly, as the man slowly wandered back towards the room.

"You don't look so good," smirked the man to Paul. Let me take your glass off you.

"I don't feel so good," slurred Paul. "What have you…" and in an instant he collapsed, and dropped to the floor, falling unconscious.

He came round to find himself gagged and bound to a chair, his hands tied behind him, while sitting in in a darkened room where there were no windows, just a tiny glint of light shining from underneath the door of the room, from what he could tell, as he had his back to it.

He hadn't a clue what was going on, or indeed why he was there.

He just felt that he was in a heap of trouble.

Paul began to shake, and his breathing became heavier, as beads of sweat began rolling down his forehead; he started to fret for his life.

He had entered a world that was unfamiliar to him, got mixed up with some unsavoury people, and this was all down to his brother Dean.

'What the HELL am I going to do?' he thought. 'No-one even knows that I'm here, wherever HERE is.'

He could hear a group of men talking on the other side of the door to the room; there sounded like there were at least two, maybe three of them.

Suddenly, with the creaking of the door opening, Paul saw a shadow of what appeared to be a large-built man, with two other men flanking him.

It felt like an eternity for the man to face him.

When Paul looked up, he saw what was indeed a chubby man, much like the evil Mr Barnes, but this man was much bulkier, dressed in a smart blue-striped suit, looking smartly pressed, and shiny light-blue shoes that went well with the suit.

"So glad to meet you, Paul, sorry the room isn't up to much but it'll have to do," said the stocky man, looking down at Paul with a show of authority.

"My name is Mr Franks; most of my associates call me Jerry. Now, I'm going to tell you WHY you're here. You see, I don't particularly get on very well with your boss, and I'm sure the feeling is mutual." He smiled. "But, here's the thing… I want YOU to tell me why he's covering my patch, where he gets his supplies from, and WHY one of his lowlife guards shot and killed one of our own." He grinned. "Once you've given me ALL of that information, you're free to go. Oh, forgive me." The stocky, bald Mr Franks gestured with a stern glance for one of his men to ungag Paul.

"I haven't a CLUE what it is you're asking for," he said, with a heavy breath, having been gagged for what appeared to be hours. "Besides, shouldn't you be taking it up with HIM, not ME?"

He thought back to the time in question, regarding the shooting, where the baron's bodyguard shot the man during the struggle, when he had gone to do a drugs drop.

"Now, now, you know better than to try and pull the wool over MY EYES," said the baron, in a slightly more agitated voice, "I don't think you're really listening to what I've just asked you. Have another think; I'm SURE it'll then all come flooding back to you."

Paul was unsure how to reply, not knowing what might happen to him if he gave a response that the man disliked.

"I REALLY DON'T KNOW what you want me to say. All I know is—"

And with that came an ALMIGHTY SLAP across Paul's face, from one of the other men in the room, knocking him onto the floor on his side, while still being tied to the chair.

The baron was clearly getting very upset that he wasn't getting the answers that he was wanting.

Again, he glanced across to the two heavies that he had brought into the room with him, to pull Paul back up, and sat back down in the chair, in an upright position.

"Now, I'm a patient man, but what I won't stand for is BULLSHIT, and I can smell it in abundance coming from you, so let's try that again, shall we?" said Mr Franks, now getting angry that Paul was not coming up with the answers to his questions.

Paul was now starting to get very upset, with some tears appearing in his eyes.

"I'm TELLING YOU, I know NOTHING about my boss's operations… scratch that, he's NOT my boss, I just do a bit of work for him, to protect my family from him, I SWEAR, that's all I know."

The baron looked up to one of his bodyguards, gesturing to go over to Paul. As he did, he grabbed one of his tied-up hands and started to squeeze it with force, using his own hands.

Paul winces in pain.

"I keep telling you, I know NOTHING of his operations, it really is all I know."

"Maybe we should leave you to have some reflection time; like I say, I'm a patient man," said the baron. "I'll get one of my men to get you some food and something to drink; you must be parched. Sorry we have no windows for you to look out of but, hopefully, you'll soon be out of here."

The baron took both of his men and walked out of the room, slamming the door shut.

"HELP… HELP!"

Paul felt helpless, and not knowing what he was going to do.

A short while later, the door burst back open, with one of the guards holding a plastic plate of food and a large plastic mug, containing what looked like tea.

The guard went and put the food and drink down in one of the corners of the room, behind where Paul sat.

"And how do you propose I eat and drink, if I'm going to be left tied up?"

The bodyguard, not saying a word, untied Paul's hands, so he could go and grab the plate of food and drink.

When he was untied, he felt his wrists, rubbing them, as if to get the blood circulating again.

The bodyguard walked backwards out of the room, keeping his eyes on Paul, in case he made any sudden movements, before locking the door behind him.

Paul got up from the chair, checking to see if the door was actually locked, twisting and turning the door handle and, unfortunately for him, it was.

He paced the floor, up and down, for a few moments, before going over to see what he had been brought in to eat.

There was chicken, lots of chicken, a bread roll, a few sandwiches, cheese and some pork pie, and a hot cup of tea.

He remembered that he hadn't really eaten or drunk for some time, and the thought suddenly made him feel both hungry and thirsty.

He stuffed the sandwiches down, almost making himself choke.

He gulped down the tea, as it was starting to cool anyway.

He'd got himself in a situation, and he was wondering how he could get himself out of it.

'Maybe I could thread them a little lie, maybe say that I'm willing to show them where that bastard Barnes gets his drugs, and see if I can make a getaway somehow, though I know what a dangerous move that could be,' he thought.

Meanwhile, Sarah's phone rang; she was still waking up next to Alice. It was Paul's older brother, Anthony.

"Hi, Anthony, is everything ok?" she asked, curious as to why he'd need to call her.

"Not really, Mum has been taken into hospital with a suspected heart attack; it's serious, and we cannot get hold of Paul. Have you seen or heard from him?"

"OH MY GOD, is she ok? I've not, no, I've only just come back from a business trip. He's not with you, then? Where is Joan? I'll come to the hospital, and try and get hold of him on the way. Have you tried calling his best friend, John?" she replied, with panic in her voice.

"He was my next port of call, as I've just got in the house and he isn't here either."

"We've not seen him for a while now, keeps himself to himself, you know what he's like. Besides, he's been very distracted of late, and I've not tried his friend; don't know his number, if I'm honest," Anthony replied. "You don't have to come but mum's been brought into Barnwood Hospital, would love some moral support, catch up too, Sarah; it's been too long, hasn't it, but I don't want to put you out."

"Yes, it has been too long, hasn't it? Just wish I could come and see you in nicer circumstances. Right, I'm on my way now, I'll try and get hold of Paul while I'm driving. I imagine he's in some hole somewhere, with his drinking buddies, probably doesn't know either where he is or who he is, he's probably that drunk," she responded, with a slight anger to her tone of voice, especially because his mum was seriously ill in hospital and all he could think of is drink.

She didn't want to mention to Anthony about her and Paul's fight, but he was surely going to notice the bruises on her face.

She got dressed, leaving a naked Alice in bed, gave Alice a kiss, and raced out of the house, before getting into her car.

She started to call Paul, see if he'd respond.

Ring… ring… ring… ring… went to voicemail. "Sorry, can't get to the phone but you know what to do…"

"I'll try John. BOUND to be with him."

Ring… ring… ring… ring. "Hello?" came a sober sounding voice.

"Hi, John, it's Sarah. Paul's with you, I guess?"

"No, not seen him for a while. I was going to call him, see if he fancied catching up. He's not with you, then?" John responded.

"No, he's not. Where the HELL is he, then?" she puzzled. "Not with any of the other crew, then, I take it?"

"No, because we always all get together at the same time. I'm sure he's about somewhere. Is everything ok?" John asked.

Sarah decided to tell John about Paul's mum, just in case he heard from him before she did.

"OH MY GOD! If I see or hear from him before you do, I'll get him to call you URGENTLY. Send her my love."

"Yes, I will," she replied.

She raced towards Barnwood Hospital, still trying to reach Paul, but got his answer machine each time.

'Where the HELL can he be?' she thought, feeling both angry and frustrated that she couldn't get hold of him, especially seeing that his mum was in hospital.

She soon arrived at Barnwood Hospital, and parked her car.

She went into the hospital reception area, where she was greeted by Paul's brother Anthony.

"Thanks for coming, Sarah; you really didn't have to," said a worried Anthony. "Oh my God, are you ok? He hasn't hit you, has he?"

"No, just me being clumsy, fell down the stairs, my own fault, I'll be alright. STILL can't get hold of your brother," she exclaimed. "I'll keep trying him but he's not with John. I haven't got a clue WHERE he is. How's your mum?"

"She's critical, but stable. I think it's all the stress brought on by things going on with Dean, and Paul being so up and down, then she's not coped too well since Dad passed away. It's all got a bit too much for her, I think." Anthony started to cry, and Sarah put her arms around him, in a show of comfort.

"I really should come and see your mum more, and I will, once she's out of hospital. I've always got on well with your mum and dad, and I'll make a conscious effort to come and see her," Sarah said, defiantly.

"Hang on, did you just say Harold has passed away; when?" More tears were starting to roll down her already puffed eyes, with all the crying.

Anthony went into detail with her, of his dad's passing just recently.

Sarah stopped hugging Anthony, as they both went and sat down in the waiting area of the cardiac department that he had taken her to.

"Are Chris and Dean here with you too?"

"Chris is; he's sitting in with Mum now. Haven't a clue where Dean is but, then, he's so wayward with his junkie of a girlfriend, they're probably shooting up now as we speak. I just let them get on with it, if they want to kill themselves, then that's up to them. We've done all we can with Dean but he doesn't seem to pay the slightest bit of notice, so we're done with him," Anthony said, feeling very disheartened that things were going so wrong since his dad died.

"I can't even imagine the pain you're all going through right now, Anthony, but once this ordeal is over we MUST get together, as a family. It'd be lovely to have some family time, wouldn't it?"

"That sounds like a plan," Anthony smiled, trying to raise his spirits.

"Won't be a second, Anthony, I just need to sort things regarding work in the morning, and I'll give Paul another call; he'll SURELY answer this time." Sarah smiled to him, trying to stay positive.

"You don't have to miss work, Sarah, I couldn't ask that of you. If things change here, I'll be sure to call you, please don't miss work, I know how busy you must be."

"No, Anthony, I insist, besides, I've just jetted in from Hong Kong on a business trip, and I'm the boss. I'll just go and make a few phone calls; I won't be a second." And, with that, Sarah walked down the corridor of the cardiac department, far enough away so Anthony couldn't hear her conversations with Alice, and to try to get hold of Paul again.

Sarah first decided to give Alice a call, seeing that she hadn't called her since they had arrived back from the airport.

Ring… ring… ring… ring. Alice answered almost straight away.

"Hi, my sexy boss. I'm lying here thinking about you, touching myself, why don't you come over, let's have some fun?" Alice was clearly in the mood for Sarah.

Sarah was not in the mood for fun right now.

"Darling, listen, something has come up. I'm at Barnwood Hospital. Don't worry, I'm ok, but Paul's mum has had a suspected heart attack, so I'm here with his brothers, with no sign of HIM," she whispered. "I'm going to stay here tonight, get some rest too if I can, so will you open up for me, make sure the girls are getting on with outstanding orders, and I'll call you when I get a chance, ok?"

Alice was suddenly very concerned.

"OH MY GOD, is she ok?"

"Not too sure, she's critical but stable, apparently. I've not had a chance to go in and see her yet but I will in a bit."

"And there's me lying here fantasising about you. I'm SO SORRY."

"That's ok, you weren't to know. Listen, I'm going to go but IF you hear from Paul, will you let him know, please? I can't seem to get hold of him, just keeps going to voicemail, and he's not with John so I'm at a loss as to where he is." Sarah was still feeling concerned about Joan, and Alice could tell in her voice just how worried she was.

"Yes, of course, IF I hear from him I'll make sure I call you straight away. Are you ok?"

"Yes, I'm ok, tired from the travelling but, apart from that, I'm ok, just a bit worried about Paul's mum, but I'll keep you posted. I love you."

"I love you too," Alice replied.

She didn't really have to tell Alice about Paul's dad, but she'd fill her in when she saw her.

Sarah hung up the line, and tried to call Paul again.

Ring… ring… ring… ring. "Sorry, can't get to the—" Sarah hung up, knowing it was again about to go to his voicemail.

'He REALLY doesn't give a SHIT about ANYONE but HIMSELF,' she angrily thought.

Sarah went back over to sit with Anthony, just as Chris was coming out of the room where his mum lay.

A nurse appeared who had been looking after the stricken Joan, and Anthony got up to speak to her.

"Do you have any updates to give us?"

"I'm sorry, you'll need to speak to the doctor; I'm not really best qualified to make that call," she replied.

The surgeon who had worked on their mum, and also on their dad, appeared through the doors that the nurse had come from.

"Any updates, doctor? We're worried sick," fretted Anthony, just as Chris was walking out of the room where his mum was, and up to his brother, to listen to what the doctor had to say. Chris put his arms around his older brother, himself feeling and looking very tired and visibly upset.

"Well, as you know, your mum suffered a massive stroke, and the next twenty-four to forty-eight hours are going to be critical," said the surgeon. "She's comfortable, we just need to keep an eye on her, and wait and see, but the operation went well. But I can't make any promises, I'm afraid, but she's in good hands, ok?" Just then, the surgeon walked away and gave what appeared to be a reassuring nod of the head.

"Is there anything I can go and get for you, Anthony?" asked Sarah, seeing that he was clearly not thinking about anything else.

"No, it's ok, I'll, erm… just stay here for a while," he mumbled.

"Why don't you get your head down, Anth? I'll keep an eye on Mum," said Chris, himself clearly in need of some rest.

"Maybe you should both go and get some rest. Look, I'm going to stay here for a while anyway; why don't you two go home, and I'll call you if there is any news." Sarah tried to reassure both of them.

"No, it's ok, I'd rather stay here tonight, just in case I'm needed, but you go home, Chris, maybe try and get hold of Dean again, not that he probably isn't spaced out with HER," Anthony snapped. "You've been here as long as me, and I'll call you if there is any news."

"If you're sure," Chris replied, safe in the knowledge that his mum was in the best place, and his older brother and Sarah were there anyway, to keep an eye on her.

Chris gave both his brother and Sarah a hug, before slowly making his way, looking a lonely figure, out of the hospital and home.

"Would you mind if I looked in on your mum, Anthony?"

"She's resting after surgery, but the doctors said we can

look in on her from time to time, so go ahead; she might like hearing the sound of your voice," Anthony replied, looking up at Sarah as he had slumped into a waiting chair for the night, with his coat acting like a pillow, trying to get as comfy as he could, knowing it was going to be a long night ahead.

Sarah gave Anthony a little grin, as his eyes began to close, and she quietly crept towards the room where Joan lay, though the ward was particularly noisy, so her creeping towards the room was forlorn.

She gently pushed the door open, as it was slightly ajar, and she made her way in.

There she saw Joan, lots of wires in her arms, wearing a breathing mask, her breaths as if everything were normal.

"What are you doing here?" Sarah whispered, giving a gentle grin, not that Joan could hear or see her, as she was in a deep sleep. "You need to get yourself better; I've promised your brothers that, as soon as you're better and out of here, we're going to arrange to meet up regularly, a few times a week. You'll be sick of the lot of us at the end of it; you'll be glad to get rid of us," Sarah joked, trying to raise a smile, realising how immortal we all are, and that her own parents were a lot older now too, and would need to be kept an eye on.

"You rest," she whispered. "I'm here with Anthony, and Chris has been in too to see you, but he's just popped home; he'll be back in a while."

Sarah went and planted a kiss on Joan's forehead, giving her a gentle smile, before creeping quietly out of the room, closing the door as she left.

It was two in the morning, and the hospital was awash with doctors and nurses wandering around, seeing to other patients.

Sarah had sat next to Anthony, who, by this time, was fast asleep.

She got her coat and, following Anthony's example, used it as a pillow, and got as comfy as she could, and laid her head down, to try to get some rest of her own.

Time ticked on, and it was seven-thirty; the morning had broken.

There appeared to be more doctors and nurses on the day shift, going about their work, lots of coming and going of medicines, clipboards and trolleys of the morning breakfast for other patients.

Sarah and Anthony woke at pretty much the same time, stretching as they did so.

"Well, I've had more comfortable nights," Anthony joked, looking at Sarah with a wry smile.

"Hmm, me too," declared Sarah, stretching and letting out a gentle yawn.

"I'm going to pop to the canteen; would you like something for breakfast, Sarah?"

"Don't be silly, you sit there, I'll get us something from the canteen; you need to be here, just in case the doctors need you."

"Yes, you're right. Will you grab me a bacon roll, please, and a latte coffee? I'll give you some money when you get back; let me know what I owe you."

"Breakfast is on me; I'll sort that. I won't be too long."

Sarah made her way down the corridor, and saw signs for the canteen, and made her way in.

There were just two other people in front of her, and she decided that she too was going to have a latte and a bacon roll.

It was soon ready.

She paid the canteen assistant, put breakfast on a small polystyrene tray that she was given, and made her way back down the corridor.

Anthony was still sitting in his chair, though Sarah had only been about twenty minutes anyway.

"Where the HELL can Paul be? Lying in a gutter somewhere, no doubt." Anthony felt angry that his brother wasn't there to support him, as well as Sarah. "Are things ok between the two of you?"

"We've been having a few problems, but don't we all?" Sarah was feeling very rejected by a once-happy Paul. "He definitely seems like he has something on his mind, but you know him: he doesn't let you in, tell you how he's feeling."

"He's always been the same, Sarah, don't worry, it's not just you. Does he tell you much about his days growing up?" asked Anthony.

"Not really, his life is all a bit of a mystery to me; he doesn't really tell me anything. It's all a bit of a secret."

"So, he's not told you about the time…" Anthony had a momentary pause. "Hmm, maybe I shouldn't say," he declared, not wanting Sarah to get concerned, or ask too many questions.

"What time?" she quizzed, with a slightly worried look on her face.

"You should speak to him; it's not really my place to say. This breakfast is lovely, Sarah, thank you." He tried to change the subject.

"No, come on, Anthony, we're family now, what time are you talking about? Should I be concerned?"

"It really is something you need to talk to him about;

I'm sorry I've concerned you." Anthony felt really bad that he'd even brought up the subject, especially that their mum was now his main concern, not his brother.

"You know, we used to be a close group of brothers, having the same group of friends, never out of each other's sights, even having the same girlfriends sometimes," Anthony joked, trying to raise both his and Sarah's spirits.

"Like I say, he doesn't really talk to me about his life growing up." Sarah felt quite sad that she lived with a man that, in reality, she barely knew. "Have the two of you always had a good relationship?" Sarah was inquisitive about what Paul had been like as a child.

"Generally, yeah, but, like most brothers, we had our fights, always got forgotten after, though." Anthony started reminiscing.

"What about Dean? Have you always been close with him?"

"He's always had a bit of a wild streak in him, always hung around the wrong crowd. It's also where he met his druggie girlfriend; he was hooked. We tried to get him away from the group, but he just drifted further and further away, and he just didn't really seem to care; he was too hooked on getting high. We couldn't talk him out of it."

"I'm really sorry, Anthony. I guess there is one in every family."

Sarah and Anthony sat up, as the doctor who'd been looking after Joan came out, strode down the corridor towards them, and started to talk to them.

"What news, doc?" asked Anthony.

"Can I see you in the relatives' room?"

"Can you just tell me here? It's ok, Sarah here is family, so you can tell us both."

"Ok, well, we've had to take your mum in for more surgery just now. She had a relapse. She appeared to be stable, and responding well, but her organs are failing, I'm afraid, and you may need to prepare for the worst. I'm really sorry."

"Can I see her?"

"Not really," replied the surgeon. "We've only just taken her in. We'll let you know when she comes out, ok?"

The doctor paused before leaving the room, to let Anthony gather his thoughts.

He sat down and started to cry. Sarah decided to put a consoling arm around him.

"Try and stay positive, Anthony, however hard it feels right now, we're all here for you, you know that."

Anthony pulled away slightly, his cheeks still wet with his tears for his mum, as he kissed Sarah full on the lips, in a sense of passion.

She suddenly pulled away from his kiss, in a slight sense of shock.

"I'm… I'm sorry, Sarah, I wasn't meant to do that, please forgive me."

"Erm, that's ok, you're just not thinking straight, that's all, forget it."

"I'll go and get us a drink," she continued.

She got up to head towards the canteen, as she saw Anthony bury his head in his hands.

"I don't know what I'll do if we lose mum; we've not long lost Dad," he cried.

Sarah paused, looking at him briefly, not knowing what

to say, knowing that, whatever she said, he probably wasn't going to hear. She just had to be as supportive as she could be for Paul's brother.

She came back with the drinks, and a bite to eat, a sandwich for them both.

"Here you go, get something down you; you need your strength."

"I'm not hungry," he replied. "I've just rung Chris; he's on his way here."

"That's good, at least you've got one of your brothers here. Have you tried Dean again, and Paul?"

"Dean's phone just went straight to voicemail, as I suspected. Paul? Huh, not a clue with him; I'm done with his behaviour and attitude."

Sometime later, Chris arrived, and was as shaken as Anthony, pacing up and down the corridor, biting his nails with worry.

"Will you SIT DOWN? Pacing up and down isn't helping either of us," Anthony snapped angrily.

Chris sat down hastily and buried his head in his hands, just as his brother had done earlier.

"I'm sorry, Chris, I didn't mean to snap; we just need to help get each other through this."

Both brothers, and Sarah to some extent, were clock-watching. Hours had passed since Joan had gone back into the operating theatre.

Doctors and nurses were busying themselves around the hospital corridors, looking after other patients, floating between one ward and another, making up beds, and passing notes and clipboards on to other scrubbed-up surgeons.

"What is taking so long?" Chris was still frantic with worry.

Anthony and Sarah looked at each other, remaining tight-lipped, but both equally anxious with worry.

"Excuse me, do you know what is happening with our mother? She went in for surgery some hours ago." Chris was becoming more and more anxious, and just wanted to reach out to any nurse who was willing to listen.

"I'm sorry, I'm assisting another patient, sorry," the nurse replied, walking off in an opposite direction.

Suddenly, the surgeon who had been operating on their mother appeared, looking sullen.

"Can I speak to you, please, in the relatives' room?"

Chris started to cry.

"Tell us here: is she gone?" Anthony asked, his eyes welling up with tears, and his cheeks going red with anguish.

"Please, it would be easier if I spoke with you all in private," replied the surgeon.

Both brothers burst out into unimaginable anguish and despair, almost accepting what the surgeon was about to tell them. Sarah too was starting to cry, having formed a good bond with their mum.

They all walked into the room, the surgeon being the last one to enter, and he carefully closed the door behind him.

Chris, Anthony and Sarah all sat on a large grey sofa, and the surgeon sat in a single grey chair opposite.

"As you know, your mum suffered a heart attack, we operated, and she remained comfortable. Joan then had a relapse, as you know, and it was decided that we needed to operate." The surgeon was trying to go through each step, bit by bit, so the brothers could try to digest what he was saying.

"She's gone, hasn't she? Just tell us." Anthony just wanted to be told, and not be messed around.

"I'm afraid so," replied the surgeon, with sorrow and sadness also showing in his face. "We did all we could, but your mum suffered another massive heart attack while in surgery, and we couldn't save her. I'm so sorry. Is there anything we can do?"

"Bring our mum back," Chris replied, his face all crumpled up with tears and sadness.

Anthony too was crying uncontrollably, Sarah giving Anthony a hug, as Chris came across to them both, and they joined in a group hug, tears and frantic emotion coming from the huddle.

"Can we go and see her?" asked Anthony, pulling away from the huddle.

"Give it an hour, we'll make her look comfortable, we'll move her to a private room and, yes, of course you can go and see her," said the surgeon, giving them time to take in the news he had just given them. "We'll come and let you know when we've moved her but, until then, you're welcome to take as long as you need in here, ok? I'm so sorry that it's not the news you want to hear, and really, if there is anything else you need, just come and let someone know, ok?"

The surgeon stood up and looked at the three of them briefly, still partly huddled together, before casually walking towards the door and out of the room.

"We'll need to organise her funeral, and, and, the house, and…" Anthony was trying to think straight, of all the things that would now need to be sorted, now his mum had gone.

"There's plenty of time to sort things like that, Anthony, but first you need to look out for each other, take time to take in what's happened. I can help you sort things out, you need to take time out for your mum first; you need to take time to grieve, but I'm here for you all, just remember that." Sarah was trying to help with calming and practicable words; it wasn't the time to think about funerals and other things yet.

"I guess you're right," Anthony sniffled. Chris was still too overcome with emotion to reply; it was Anthony who appeared to be a lot calmer, being the oldest, and almost accepting that their mum wasn't going to pull through.

Chris managed to pull himself together a short while later, and started talking about the happy times growing up with their mum.

"She used to read to us, even when we went into our teens." Chris smiled, trying to remember all the good times growing up. "We used to say, 'MUM, don't you think we're a bit too old for story-telling now?' but that was just her way; she'd say, 'I've done it all my life, why should I stop now?'"

Anthony too was starting to reminisce about the old times, growing up together, smiling as he told his story.

"I remember one time, just after Mum had cooked a lovely Sunday roast, Dad had been to the pub, though he was a lightweight when it came to his beer. Mum was a bit angry with him that he'd come back drunk. She decided to pour coffee onto his dinner, purposely, instead of gravy, see if he knew the difference. Do you know what? He ate the lot, saying how tasty the dinner was, and could she make it again like that the next time. We all sat laughing to each other. I remember mum raising a smile but Dad was too drunk to tell what was going on." Anthony was starting to feel a bit better, though they knew they still had the uncomfortable task of going to see their mum.

Suddenly, there was a knock on the relatives' room door. A Doctor Franklin appeared.

"Are you the relatives of Joan?"

"Yes, we are," replied Anthony.

"Would you like to come this way?" replied the doctor. "Your mum is in one of the side rooms. Take as long as you need; there's no rush."

Chris, Sarah and Anthony trudged out of the relatives' room and into a side-room of the ward, the doctor showing them the room where the brothers' mum lay.

They could see her through the glass in the door, peering through, as if not wanting to go in to her, before opening the door and going in, closing the door behind them.

Joan looked peaceful, in no more pain, no more stresses about them, as both Anthony and Chris hugged each other, as the emotion and tears once again appeared.

Sarah stood away from them a little; after all, she was their mum, but it made her realise just how immortal we all are, and also made her think of her own mum and dad.

"I'm just going to step out for a little while, give you some time alone with your mum. I'll just be out here." Sarah wanted to give her own mum and dad a call.

She spoke to her own parents often but seeing Joan just made her want to speak to them over the phone again.

"No, please stay with us. You've helped us get through all this. Besides, you're practically family now to us." Anthony wanted Sarah to be with them, help them grieve.

"I'll just be out here; I'll be back in in a short while. Spend some time with your mum; I won't be long," replied Sarah, before she glided gently out of the room, closing the door gently behind her.

She took her phone out of her pocket and called her mum.

Her mum, Jeanette, answered almost immediately.

"Hi, darling, are you ok?"

"Yes, Mum, I'm good," Sarah said quietly, not wanting to speak too loudly, in case Anthony and Chris overheard her talking. "Paul's mum, Joan, has sadly just passed away, and I'm just at Barnwood Hospital with Anthony and Chris. No sign of Paul or Dean but I'm giving them my support. They're both in a room with Joan, and I wanted to leave them to grieve, so I wanted to pop out of the room, and give you a call, to check in, and make sure that you're both alright."

"Oh my God, Sarah, I'm so sorry. I'll tell your dad. Please pass on our condolences to them, won't you? I know we never really got to know their mum but she sounded a truly wonderful mum to them. I'm so sorry, love. Tell them that, if they need anything, or just want to talk, then we're always here for them."

"I know, Mum, thank you. I'll let them know when I can. Are you both alright?"

"Yes, we're fine, God knows where your dad is, probably in his man cave, as he calls it, down the bottom of the garden; you know what he's like."

"I'll pop in a bit later if I can, have a cuppa and a chat."

"It's ok, love, you spend some time with them if you can. We'd love to see you, of course, but think they'll need you around a bit so we'll see you soon. We've got some friends coming round for dinner so we'll be entertaining most of the day; give us a call tomorrow."

"Ok, Mum, I'll do that. I love you. Give my love to Dad too."

"We love you too, darling. Where is Paul? You said you didn't know where he was."

"I honestly don't know, Mum. We've all been trying to get hold of him. He'll show up, just, with his mum passing away, and he probably doesn't know… he's going to be distraught but we cannot get hold of him. I'll give his friend John another call, see if he's heard from him. Love you, Mum."

"See you soon, love."

With that, Sarah hung up and paused outside for a little bit longer, not wanting to go back into the room just yet, wanting to give the brothers more time alone with their mum, to grieve.

Sarah peeped through the glass of the door, to see what was happening.

She could see both brothers sitting down, appearing to be talking, as she decided to give John a call to see if he'd heard from Paul.

Sarah's phone rang briefly, before John answered.

"Hi Sarah, is everything ok?" John had concern in his voice.

"Have you heard from Paul at all, John? Joan has just passed away, and he's not here."

"Oh my God, Sarah, no, I haven't, not since the last time. Oh my God, I'm so sorry, where are you?"

"I'm at Barnwood Hospital with his brothers but still no sign of him."

"Maybe you should call the police, just in case something has happened to him." John had some concern for his friend's welfare.

"He's been off for ages, John. I'll try and give him another call, tell him to call me urgently. If I don't hear anything, then I'll think about calling the police."

"When is the last time you heard from him?" John asked.

"I've not long come back from a business trip, and he was in a mood with me before I left, so he's probably gone off in a huff somewhere. Might he be with his other friends?"

"No, I keep in regular contact with the others, we've tried calling Paul too but it goes straight to voicemail."

"He'll turn up when we least expect it. I'll give him a call now." Sarah seemed convinced that she'd get hold of him this time.

"Ok, I'm SO SORRY to hear about Joan. I'll keep trying Paul too; speak soon."

John then hung up.

Sarah found Paul's number in her phone and started to dial.

"Sorry, can't get to the phone but you know what to do."

"Hi, it's me, I haven't a CLUE where you are but will you call me URGENTLY? It's your mum."

Sarah didn't want to go into the details of her passing away, so just decided to hang up and wait for him to call.

'GOD KNOWS where he is. I'll try him again later, but if he can't be bothered to get in contact…' she thought.

She decided to give Alice a call too, put her in the picture.

Again, she found Alice's number and it just rang a couple of times before Alice answered.

"Hey, darling, is everything ok? I've been thinking about you." Alice was concerned that she'd not heard much from Sarah, but knowing that things were going on with Paul's mum.

"Joan has passed away, Alice, and I'm at Barnwood Hospital with Paul's brothers right now. Everything ok at work?"

"OH MY GOD, BABY, I'm SO SORRY. Do you want me to come down to you?"

"No, it's ok, I need to be with Paul's brothers right now, but I'll come and see you later, maybe stay at yours."

"You know you can: cook us a nice meal, curl up and watch a movie too, maybe? Yes, everything at work is ok, everyone wondering where you are but getting on with work. There have been a few new orders come through so I have processed them, sent you an e-mail with the details, and filed them away; as usual, they're for about twelve months' time, so got a while yet."

"Thank you for holding the fort for me, darling, I'll pop over to yours later, ok?"

"Ok. I love you."

"I love you too, Alice, see you later," Sarah whispered, not wanting Chris and Anthony to hear her declaring her love for someone other than their brother.

Sarah peeped through the glass on the door again, and saw both brothers talking, yet sitting closer together this time, their arms around each other, both looking like they'd shed more tears.

She decided to walk in and join them.

She closed the door quietly behind her and stood looking at Joan, looking so peaceful and beautiful.

"Come and sit down, Sarah," Chris asked. "We've just been doing some more reminiscing." He smiled.

"That's good; it'll certainly help. Your mum looks so beautiful; she'll be dancing with your dad now, I bet." Sarah was trying to raise a little smile, to try to raise the brothers' spirits a little.

"Mum was a good dancer," Anthony replied. "Won a

few awards too down the years for it, at local halls, near to where they lived at the time. Dad would often get worn out with her quick feet: he was a rubbish dancer." He laughed. "He just couldn't keep up with her; she was a strong woman."

All three of them chuckled at the story.

"I guess we should go: we need to make arrangements, and let others know," said Anthony.

Chris nodded in agreement.

The brothers got up from their chairs and, in turn, walked over to their mum, each planting a kiss on her cheek.

Chris was the first one to go over to say his goodbyes.

"Thank you, Mum, for being the BEST MUM in the WHOLE WORLD." He gave her gentle squeeze, with fresh tears rolling down his cheeks.

He held her for what seemed like an eternity, before getting up, walking backwards to take a final look at her, trying to hold back more tears, sniffling as he did.

"You go now, Sarah," said Anthony.

"Are you sure? I mean…?"

"Yes, she liked you," he responded.

As asked, Sarah walked over to Joan and planted a kiss on her cheek, just as Chris had just done.

"Rest in peace, Joan. I'll never forget you." Sarah too was trying to wipe away tears, having got to know Joan. She was the perfect in-law to her.

Anthony was the final one to say his goodbyes.

With tears already rolling down his puffed-up eyes, fresh tears again appearing, he too went and gave his mum a gentle squeeze.

"I'll remember all the good times, Mum, the way you used to make me laugh, and told me off when I needed it.

You and Dad made me the man I am today, and I'll never forget you. You go and put Dad in his place up there; I'm sure you're doing that right now," he murmured, sniffling, as he also planted a kiss on her cheek, wet from all the tears of Chris and Sarah.

Anthony wiped her wet cheek with a handkerchief that he carried in his pocket.

They all took one last look at Joan, before walking backwards out of the room, and closing the door behind them, looking through the glass on the door one last time on their mum, before walking out towards the exit of the hospital.

Sarah said her goodbyes to both Anthony and Chris, and made her way back to where she was staying with Alice.

She arrived back, pulled her car into the driveway and stopped the car, before getting out and making her way towards the door.

Alice heard her pulling up and opened the front door, wearing jogging bottoms and a T-shirt, her ample breasts almost bursting the T-shirt open, and was braless.

"I've not long got out of the shower. If I'd known you were coming home, I'd have waited for you."

Sarah closed the front door, dropped her handbag on the floor beside her, and immediately flung her arms around Alice, before bursting into tears.

"Hey, hey, you're back here with me now, I'll ease your pain."

With tears still rolling down Sarah's cheeks, she started to passionately kiss Alice, and put her hands up her T-shirt, and fondled her breasts, making her nipples erect.

Alice started to passionately kiss Sarah too, and pushed

her against the wall in doing so, kissing her harder and harder.

The girls were in a deep sense of passion, as Alice started to unbutton Sarah's shirt before vigorously pulling it off and out of her skirt, before unclipping her bra.

Alice then pulled her own T-shirt off and carried on passionately kissing Sarah, licking her way around her ears and neck, before sliding her tongue down to Sarah's heaving breasts and hardening nipples.

Alice's tongue was going to work on Sarah's breasts, licking her nipples and sucking them hard, making them look hard and very red.

Alice came back up, rubbing her own breasts and nipples across Sarah's, before grabbing hold of Sarah's hand and leading her to the bedroom.

The girls walked towards the bedroom, as Alice pushed Sarah onto the bed.

She pulled her jogging bottoms down and slid her body onto Sarah's, and started to kiss Sarah again, as passionately as she had been doing just moments before.

Sarah rolled Alice onto her back, got up and off the bed, and slowly started to unzip her black pencil skirt, watching Alice slide her hand down her knickers, to touch herself, as she watched.

Sarah kicked her shoes off and laid her slender, toned body onto Alice, and again began to passionately kiss her as Alice grabbed Sarah's peachy arse cheeks, as Sarah kissed and licked her way around Alice's neck.

Alice started to pull Sarah's knickers down, Sarah helping her, wanting to forget everything that had happened that day.

Sarah was now completely naked, as Alice frantically began to try to tug at pulling her own knickers down and off, which she finally managed, the girls now lying across each other's beautiful naked bodies.

They carried on kissing each other, entwinned in sexual desire, wanting to make love to each other in the most ferocious way.

They begin to sweat, as the passion rises to a crescendo, writhing on each other, Alice kissing her way back down Sarah's body, past her navel, and was soon between Sarah's legs, licking every inch of her moist pussy.

Sarah was thrusting hard onto each lick and kiss from Alice, pulling her head harder between her slender legs, her thighs tensing up, as Alice went to work on her, Sarah's panting becoming deeper and faster, knowing that soon she'd be wanting to cum.

Sarah pulled at Alice's head, wanting her to come up to kiss her, so she too could go to work on Alice's body.

Alice obliged, and came up to kiss Sarah some more, their tongues dripping with saliva, and the very intenseness of the moment.

Sarah rolled Alice over, and she too started to kiss and lick her way down Alice's body, and felt the emotion in her lover's body as Alice also began to feel a sense of wanting to cum.

Sarah carried on kissing and licking her way around Alice's pussy, licking harder and faster, Alice panting and sighing, knowing that she wasn't going to last long before releasing her juices onto Sarah's waiting mouth.

Alice came, and Sarah could feel the moistness of Alice flow onto her waiting lips, as Alice's legs began to shudder, pulling Sarah's head harder between her toned thighs.

Alice pulled at Sarah's head, summoning her to come up to kiss her.

Sarah duly obliged, laying her moist sweaty body onto Alice's.

Sarah started to grind herself on Alice; she hadn't cum yet, but felt like she wanted to.

She started to thrust her pussy hard onto Alice's, still feeling really horny with their lovemaking, Alice again pushing Sarah's arse hard into her, so she could feel every inch of Sarah's pent-up sexual emotion.

Sarah thrust harder and harder, as Alice squeezed and licked Sarah's bulging breasts and nipples, as Sarah pressed herself on her lover's body.

Sarah's thighs quivered, as she too shuddered to a grinding halt, knowing that she had cum, releasing all the emotions of the day.

She rolled off Alice, and onto the now-sweat-soaked bed, as the two started to catch their breaths.

Sarah lay gazing up at the ceiling, almost not quite believing how the day's events had taken place, and where things were going to go from here.

"What you thinking, honey?" asked Alice, knowing that Sarah's mind was going to be fixed on what was going to happen, now Joan was no longer alive.

"Today has just been a roller-coaster of a day; I still can't quite take it all in." Sarah still seemed to be in a state of shock, but knew that she really wanted Alice, to be with her, and, by making love, it might try to release some of the day's tensions.

"Everything just seems to have happened all at once; my head is still spinning, and I don't quite know how I'm feeling about it all. One minute, Joan is ok, resting after her op, the next she is gone and I still cannot get hold of that ARSEHOLE of a man of mine," declared Sarah, still mystified by not hearing from him.

"What happens when you call his mobile?" asked Alice.

"It just rings, then goes to his voicemail. I'm going to call his work tomorrow; I still cannot believe that he's nowhere to be seen."

"Maybe he's just swamped with his work, perhaps; he works in the City, doesn't he?"

"Yes, a financial director, but I know how much he hates it there, maybe if he found something else he might start to chill a bit, and I might start seeing the old Paul again."

"He'll turn up at work, I'm sure, but, yeah, maybe give them a call tomorrow, then mystery solved," said Alice, trying to reassure Sarah that he was just working so hard.

Alice pulled the quilt over Sarah as they lay in bed together, now wrapped around each other, still cooling from their lovemaking.

"I love you, Sarah, I know, after today, everything that has happened, you must be all over the place with your emotions. I must admit, I wasn't expecting you to come back here and make love to me, I truly wasn't, however AMAZING it was, as usual. I just wanted you home here, with me, to hold you, to be here for you. I know how much I wanted you, how much I ALWAYS want you, but just didn't want you to think that I had sex on my mind, as soon as you came back. But I'm not complaining," Alice chuckled, hoping that it would stir Sarah into sharing one of her beautiful smiles back at her, but Sarah was still very lost in the moment of Joan's passing, and soon the tears started to roll down her face once again, just as they had done at the hospital.

"I don't know why I'm crying so much, Alice," a teary Sarah sobbed. "I mean, don't get me wrong, I did love Joan, I really did, she was like another mother to me, I even planned to go and see her soon, have a family party, get everyone together, smiles and laughter and the next moment, she's gone. Why am I feeling so emotional? I don't get it."

"Maybe it's the feeling that we're all vulnerable, that we're all immortal, it creeps up on me sometimes, especially when Stacey died," said a sombre Alice, thinking back herself to her ex-lover's passing.

"I'm so sorry, Alice, I didn't mean to drag up painful memories." Sarah felt bad that her feelings and emotions had surfaced for her too, and started to make her think about how things were for her, before she even met Sarah.

"It's ok. I do miss her but things have changed now; I'm a different woman now, and I've got you too." She smiled.

Alice started to kiss Sarah's cheek, and began to gently kiss her neck, and caress her legs under the covers, starting to feel a bit horny again, wanting Sarah all over again, but Sarah wasn't in the mood now.

"Can we just sleep now, Alice, do you mind? I'm just drained with everything that has happened today, as much as I want you too, but, we've LOTS of time for days like this, hey?" She smiled, as Alice pulled away from her gently, feeling slightly rejected.

"I'm sorry, of course, I'm just being selfish, but I cannot resist you, I should let you sleep. Come and rest your head in my arms; things will be clearer tomorrow, I'm sure." Alice again was trying to reassure Sarah that things would turn out ok: Paul would be at work, his head buried in paperwork.

Despite knowing that there'd be some dark days ahead, being supportive to Anthony and Chris, as well as spending time with Alice, both at her home and also focussing on work, Sarah knew that things would get better, and she felt a sense of calmness with what Alice had said, and that she was sure that she would hear tomorrow that Paul was at work, and that she could tell him about his mum, knowing just how upset he'd be.

The girls decided to chat for a little while, before going to sleep.

"How are Paul's brothers feeling? Stupid question, I know," asked Alice.

"They're pretty cut up, devastated, as you can imagine, and I need to be as supportive as I can for them; would you mind holding the fort again for me at work tomorrow, please, Alice?"

"No, of course I don't mind. Are you going to go and see Paul's brothers?"

"Yes, I think so. Might call in at Paul's work too, that's if he'll even talk to me." She knew how he had been towards her the last time she'd seen him.

Both Sarah and Alice slowly started to drift off to sleep, their arms wrapped around the other, as the night closed in, ready to start the new day.

Alice started to gradually awaken, wrapping her arm around Sarah, who was already awake.

"Mmm, good morning, how long have you been awake?"

"I've not really slept much. Thinking about yesterday. I might have got a few hours, I guess." Sarah was still clearly upset at how the day had gone yesterday, and knowing what faced her today.

The time was six-thirty, and it was time for them to rise.

"Fancy a shower?" asked Alice, as she leant across Sarah, to plant a kiss on her lips, before she pulled her perfectly formed naked body out of the bed.

"It's ok, I'll grab one in a while. You have yours, and I'll grab one after. Make sure everyone is aware of what orders they need to focus on this morning at work, and I'll pop in if I get a chance. Also, if any of them ask where I am, just tell them that I have a few personal issues that I need to sort out, ok?"

"Don't worry if you can't come in, honey, I'll hold the fort, and take any messages that need taking, and of course I'll be subtle. Just focus on sorting out what you need to, and give Paul's brothers my love, and deepest sympathies, and give that man of yours a roasting when you catch up with him at work."

"Oh, trust me… I WILL," declared Sarah, her face scrunching up with anger at the very thought of catching up with him.

"Sure I can't tempt you to join me in the shower?" Alice teased, trying to summon her lover to join her.

"No, because we know what happens when we shower together, don't we?" Sarah grinned in Alice's direction, finding it hard to raise a big smile for her, and she was not really in the mood to take having a shower with her, knowing that it normally ended up with them making love.

Alice strode towards the bathroom, as Sarah heard the shower being turned on.

Sarah sat up in bed, contemplating what was in store for her that day.

Sarah heard the shower being turned off, before seeing Alice appear semi-naked, the thick white soft towel just wrapped around her waist.

Sarah got out of bed and walked up to Alice, before embracing her.

"Thank you for being there for me, darling. I don't know how I'd have got through it without you; I wouldn't have known where to turn and who to turn to."

"It's ok; it's what you do, isn't it? Be there for each other." Alice was trying to be a calming influence for Sarah, as she knew that she needed to be, with yesterday's devastating news.

Sarah pulled away, and gave Alice the biggest kiss.

Alice undid her towel and it dropped to the floor, the two of them, once again, standing naked in the centre of the bedroom.

Sarah knew what Alice had in mind for them.

"I really can't, not this morning, Alice, I'm sorry."

"That's ok, just wanted to offer you the opportunity." Alice smiled, before Sarah walked off towards the bathroom herself, to have a shower, just as Alice went to her drawers to pull out some underwear, some stockings and lacy knickers.

Sarah was still feeling in a sombre mood, and wanted to take a quick shower and get dressed, wanting to go and see Anthony and Chris, and, of course, that no-show man of hers.

Sarah was soon out of the shower, water dripping down her bare breasts from her soaked blonde hair, her body glistening from the moisturiser cream she had lathered into herself, her hair smelling of fragrant flowers just picked from the garden, her skin looking so fresh and toned, even though she had been through hell of late.

Alice was practically dressed, looking radiant, in a one-piece pencil purple dress, and was sitting down at her dressing table, gazing at the mirror, to arrange her hair and make sure she was all primed and ready to go to the office.

"You look lovely, Alice, love that dress on you." Sarah smiled, feeling slightly guilty that she, too, wasn't going in, but knowing that she had to sort things out this morning.

"And OUT of it too, I hope?" Alice smiled, trying to raise Sarah's spirits, on what was going to be a tough day for her.

"But of course." Sarah smiled back, trying to think about other things, hoping to distract herself, if only for a moment.

Alice was as good as ready to leave, as Sarah was still rummaging through which was the best dress to wear for today, if she was going to wear a dress at all.

"Want a lift to work, Alice? I shouldn't be too long."

"Yes, please, get to spend a little longer with you." She smiled.

Sarah did decide that she was going to put a dress on; she wanted to look her best for Anthony and Chris, knowing that they had to start thinking about arranging their mum's funeral.

She chose a light-blue one-piece dress, just off the shoulder, yet still very elegant.

She too rummaged through the underwear drawer, and put on some tights and some white knickers, before slipping into her dress.

"Will you zip me up at the back, please, Alice?"

"Of course I will, darling, anything for you." She smiled.

Sarah opened the wardrobe drawer and pulled out some light-blue matching high-heeled shoes that were hidden away at the back. She didn't wear these shoes very often, but she remembered just how comfortable they were when she did put them on.

"You too look amazing, honey." Alice smiled. "I'll feel a little jealous, as when you go to see Paul, no-one will be able to take their eyes off you. Just wish I was coming with you."

"On another occasion, Alice, I would bring you with me but, you know…"

"It's ok, I understand, and I'll get to see you later, be it at work or here at home. I'll cook us something nice tonight." Alice was a good cook; she could turn her hand to anything.

Both girls were ready to leave out, Alice locking the door behind her before getting in Sarah's car.

Sarah was noticeably quiet, but Alice understood, with the magnitude of what faced her today.

Sarah pulled over before reaching work, wanted to give Alice a quick kiss, before driving her in, as she didn't want anyone to notice them kissing in the car.

Sarah soon pulled up to her business, before bidding Alice goodbye.

Alice got out and opened up, with the keys that she carried and that Sarah had given her, for situations like there was today.

Sarah waved, before pulling off.

She decided to drive straight to Paul's place of work, pulled into the car park, got out of the car and locked up.

'This will be an interesting conversation,' she thought. 'And he doesn't even know about his mum, I bet.'

She walked in and went straight up to the reception desk. The lady behind reception asked if she could help.

"Yes, I'm here to see Paul, Paul Arnold?"

"Who?" the receptionist replied.

"Paul Arnold, he's a financial director here." Sarah couldn't quite believe that the receptionist didn't know who Paul was, but assumed she might be new.

"Just one moment, please." The slender, small-framed receptionist, went onto the reception phone and called for someone to come down.

"There's a lady in reception to come and see Paul," the receptionist whispered, to whoever it was she was talking to on the phone, which Sarah found to be a little odd.

'Why the secrecy?' she thought.

"Is he here?" an agitated Sarah asked the receptionist.

"Erm, someone is coming down. If you'd like to wait here."

Sarah was getting more confused.

Mr McGee suddenly came strolling into the reception area, and greeted Sarah.

"Can I help you, madam?" he demanded, with a demeanour in his voice that certainly put Sarah's back up.

"Yes, I'm here to see Paul Arnold, I've got some personal information to share with him."

"Well, you'll be lucky," bellowed Mr McGee. "He hasn't worked here for a little while now, maybe a month, I think," he said confidently. "We had to make a few people redundant and, unfortunately, he was one of them. I'm sorry to waste your time, Miss…?"

"What? Doesn't work here?"

Sarah was in complete shock, didn't know what to think.

'WHERE THE HELL IS HE?' she thought.

"So, where has he gone?" she asked the slimy Mr McGee.

"That's something that you'll have to ask him. Look, I'm sorry you have wasted your time, Miss, but I really must be getting on."

Mr McGee turned around and walked his heavy frame back across the office, before disappearing around the corner.

Sarah glanced briefly at the receptionist, who gave Sarah a brief grin.

"Thank you," she said to the receptionist, as she walked slowly out of the building, still not quite believing what she'd just been told.

She walked slowly out of the building and headed towards her car.

'What the HELL is going on?' she thought.

Sarah decided to try to call Paul again, see if she could get through to him this time.

"Sorry, can't get to—" and she hung up.

She decided to call Alice and fill her in on the news.

"Hey, it's me. You're never going to believe what I'm about to tell you," she snapped. "He no longer works at the financial company, hasn't done for a little while, so where the HELL is he?"

"Oh my GOD! WHAT?" shrieked Alice, not quite believing herself what Sarah had just told her.

"Do you think it's time you rang the police?" Alice declared. "Because something isn't right, is it?"

"I will, Alice, but I've more pressing matters, like going and offering my support to Anthony and Chris, and Dean, if he decides to show up." Sarah was in no mood to think about

Paul at this time. She was sure that Paul was out drowning his sorrows somewhere, or sleeping with whoever.

"I'll call you when I get a chance. How are the girls getting on? Are they sorting those urgent orders?" Sarah wanted to make sure that the girls were all ok, and that they were keeping on top of the workload.

"Yes, they're all ok. They did ask about you when I walked in, but I told them that you had some personal matters to deal with, but that you would hopefully call in later."

"Thank you, darling. I knew I could rely on you. Talk to you later. Love you."

Sarah then hung up her phone, got in her car and drove off towards Greenwood Drive, where Joan and Harold resided, and where she knew that Anthony and Chris would be, sorting out their late mum's house and sitting down together to organise her funeral.

Paul, meanwhile, was still planning his escape route out of wherever he was.

He decided to wait for the security guard to come in with his food, see if he could speak to him, to get him on his side.

Paul banged on the door where he was being held, and shouted out, "WHEN AM I GOING TO GET MORE FOOD? AND I'M GETTING THIRSTY TOO IN HERE!"

"BE QUIET, YOU'LL GET MORE FOOD WHEN YOU START TO CO-OPERATE," came the shouted response from the security.

"MAYBE I'M READY TO TALK, BUT I WANT FOOD AND SOMETHING TO DRINK FIRST," he shouted.

"STAND BACK," came the shout from the other side of the door, as the bodyguard unlocked the thick, grey cast-iron door and flung it open, bustling his way inside, carrying food and drink for him.

"Did you hear what I said?" Paul snapped angrily. "I'm ready to TALK, GOD DAMN YOU."

The musclebound guard put Paul's food on the floor and, as the guard turned around to walk out, he noticed that the guard was carrying a gun in a side holster, but unfortunately Paul was not close enough to grab it out and use it as his possible escape, however dangerous a situation it would be.

The next day, Paul sat in his chair, untied; the baron felt comfortable enough to leave Paul free, so it was less hassle to untie him, so he could eat.

Paul heard a noise outside.

It was one of the bodyguards, coming with his food.

He decided to hide behind the door, and hopefully surprise the guard.

The door flung open and, sure enough, it was the guard with Paul's food and something to drink.

The guard walked inside, being taken aback that there was no sign of Paul.

Suddenly, he was immediately behind the guard, and quickly stooped down and pulled his legs from under him, the guard collapsing in a heap on the cold, stone floor.

This gave Paul the chance to grab the gun out of the guard's holster.

Suddenly, Paul felt in complete control.

"GET UP... GET UP NOW..." he demanded.

The guard felt powerless, and did as Paul said.

"Now, walk out there, and don't mutter a word, and don't try anything stupid."

The two men walked out of the room that Paul had been holed up in for however long it was. He had completely lost track of what day and time it was, as his watch and phone had been taken from him after he had been drugged.

There appeared to be a row of rooms in the house. 'God knows if there is anyone else in those rooms,' Paul thought as he walked by them, but right now he was only thinking of his own safety.

He suddenly came across a very large kitchen area, where the other guard and the baron were drinking and smoking cigars.

There were also appeared to be huge amounts of cocaine on the table.

Some had been opened, and clearly sniffed by the men, but it looked as if many hadn't been opened.

The baron and the other guard were startled by the other guard, and Paul walking behind, appearing in the kitchen.

The bodyguard left the room, with his hands in the air, and his arms were still raised as they wandered in.

Paul pushed the bodyguard into the kitchen, nearer the other men.

Paul angrily waved the gun towards the three men, gesturing for one of them to put the unused drugs into the holdall that Paul had brought with him initially with the drugs from Mr Barnes that he had for these men.

"You're not going to get away with this, Paul. Why don't you put the gun down, and let's talk?" said the baron. "I'm sure we can come to some kind of agreement."

"Oh, that classic line," chuckled Paul arrogantly. "You've been watching too many gangster movies. Now, do as I've just FUCKING TOLD YOU, bag the drugs up into that holdall there, and put the holdall on the floor next to you, and no-one will get hurt," he snapped angrily.

Paul was in no mood to be messed around with; besides, they had just locked him away in a room, and didn't have a clue what day it was, the time, or even WHERE he was.

"Do as he says," snapped the baron to one of his guards, while the baron still kept his eyes firmly fixed on Paul, and firmly fixed on the gun.

"Have you ever even used a gun before?" asked the baron, trying to put pressure on Paul.

The baron could see beads of sweat appearing on his forehead, and wanted to try to force Paul's hand a little bit.

The baron slowly started to walk towards him, gesturing for him to give the gun up.

At that point, Paul had lost sight of the guard putting the drugs in the bag, and suddenly… a bag of the cocaine was thrown in Paul's direction, just as the gun was going off.

BANG! BANG!

In a blink of an eye, Paul had shot and killed one of the guards, his body lying motionless on the floor, face down, blood pouring from this body.

He had also shot the baron, in the leg, and he too lay crumpled on the floor, holding the wound just below the knee.

"WHAT THE FUCK did you have to do that for? I told you all: NO FALSE MOVES, and look what's just happened."

"YOU BASTARD… YOU'RE GOING TO PAY FOR THIS… BIG TIME!" said the baron, blood still pouring from his leg wound. "I have friends in VERY HIGH PLACES, and your life isn't going to be worth living when they hear what has happened here."

The baron winced in pain once again, holding his leg and trying to stop the flow of blood pouring from his leg.

"Ah, you'll live." Paul smiled.

"You don't remember me, do you, you FUCKING WASTE OF SPACE?" Paul had suddenly remembered the drugs baron from before. "COME ON, YOU FUCKING ARSEHOLE, actually, haha, that's quite apt, remember back? COME ON… COME ON… I don't know why I don't just shoot you now, for what you did to me all those years ago."

"What the FUCK are you on about?" quizzed the baron, still trying to think back, to when he might have crossed paths with Paul before.

"A couple of your mates, in a pub car park, seeing a young, athletic lad cross your path, bet you thought, 'Oh LET'S HAVE HIM, bet he's game for a FUCK.'" Tears started to well up in Paul's eyes as he recollected when he was pinned against a wall and raped by three men, the main antagonist being the baron.

"Maybe, as a leaving gift, I should find something to shove up YOUR ARSE. Got any CARROTS IN THIS STINKING FUCKING HOUSE?"

"OH MY GOD, I thought I recognised you from somewhere. I was young, very drunk and I'd just come out, that was then, and this is NOW," said the baron, trying to justify the fact that this was a different time.

"Do you know what? You're not actually worth it so I'm going to leave you here, to FUCKING BLEED TO DEATH in this SHIT-HOLE OF SQUALOR, take the drugs and run, leave you to clear up your own SHIT." And, with that, Paul summoned the remaining guard outside, waving the gun in the direction of the front door, to go outside, as Paul grabbed the holdall full of cocaine and walked behind the bodyguard, the stocky man occasionally glancing back at Paul and seeing the gun pointed at his back.

The man held his hands in the air constantly, and, as they walked outside, there was no sign of vehicles.

Paul kept a safe distance from the bodyguard, just in case he decided to jump him and try to rescue the gun from Paul's grasp.

"HANG ON, where are all your FUCKING CARS?" asked Paul.

"We ditch them as soon as we kidnap people. There's no trace then," said the guard.

"Oh, that's FUCKING CONVENIENT, isn't it? Well, I suggest we go back to the house and get your boss to FUCKING ring one of his cronies and get a vehicle here NOW." Paul was in no mood to be messed with, and he wanted out as soon as possible, but he knew that it wasn't going to be easy.

They trudged back to the house, where they saw the baron still sitting where Paul left him, in the corner of the kitchen, leg still pouring with blood.

He appeared to be almost losing consciousness, using his now blood-soaked hand to try to stem the bleeding.

Paul walked over to the baron, kicking his wounded leg as he did so.

"Ahh," screamed the baron.

"Painful, isn't it?" chuckled Paul, still wafting the gun in the directions of both the baron and the bodyguard.

"Can you at least give me something for my leg?" The baron almost begged Paul for some kind of compassion.

"Here, use this." Paul found a piece of cloth on the side of the kitchen that was just long enough to be tied around his leg, and tossed it over in the direction of the baron.

"Why don't you go and sit with your boss, maybe sing him a lullaby?" Paul said to the bodyguard, and the guard did as Paul asked, and sat down next to the injured baron.

"Why are you back here, anyway? I thought you might have been long gone," said the baron, his leg now bandaged up and the blood now appearing to have stopped for now.

"I have a little job for YOU for a change. I bet you're FUCKING HATING this lack of power, aren't you? Knowing that someone else is giving out the orders for a change," Paul said smugly, knowing that he was now in charge of the situation.

"What do you want?" asked the baron. "Surely you've got everything you want now; you've got the drugs, you hold the cards, and I'm POWERLESS to stop you, one of my guards are dead, which you WILL PAY FOR, BY THE WAY. I don't know what else you want from me."

"How about some transport to get me out of here? You've fucking ditched it all, how convenient of you." Paul grinned, demanding some immediate answers from the injured baron.

"Yes, we do ditch them, saves us being tracked, but I can get one of my main men here to help you get away, but, REST ASSURED, I WILL FIND YOU, and I WILL KILL YOU."

"Haha, you're VERY SURE OF YOURSELF." Paul laughed. "I haven't decided what I'm going to do with you yet, so DON'T BANK ON IT." He smiled.

"Remember who 'holds the cards here', as you put it. I'm the one with a gun in my hand, fully loaded. I've used one before, so you're walking on VERY THIN ICE, DON'T PUSH ME."

"If you were going to kill me, you'd have done it by now. Pass me my phone, will you, Carl?" The bodyguard slowly got up and reached very carefully towards the drug baron's jacket pocket, watching the gun that Paul was holding, not taking his eyes off it.

"No funny business." Paul was still waving the gun in the direction of the bodyguard, letting him know that he could pull the trigger at any moment.

Carl, the guard, slowly pulled out the baron's phone from his left-side jacket pocket, before walking backwards and back towards the baron, before sitting back down next to him.

The baron held the phone close to his ear.

"It's me, come here quick, I need you to transport something for me." The baron then tossed his mobile phone on the floor.

"There you go, done, he should be here soon."

There was an eerie silence between the three men, as he waited for his getaway.

"So, what's your long-term plan? You can't run forever; we're going to catch up with you." The baron wanted to talk to Paul, try to break the silence.

"SHUT THE FUCK UP. That's NO CONCERN OF YOURS, is it?" Paul felt very agitated at the baron's questioning, and just wanted peace while he waited for the getaway driver to turn up.

Paul grabbed a chair from the kitchen table and sat down, waiting for man to turn up.

"Well, this is cosy, just the three of us. Are you REALLY

going to leave me here to die?" the baron asked, feeling weaker at each passing minute.

"DID YOU NOT HEAR WHAT I JUST SAID? SHUT THE FUCK UP!" Paul waved the gun in the direction of the baron once more. "Actually, I want more answers. How many more men have you raped? I'm sure I wasn't the first," Paul snapped.

"It was a one-off thing. I was curious, young and horny; you were just there, wrong place, wrong time, I guess." The baron tried to convince Paul that it was a mistake.

"Don't give me that FUCKING BULLSHIT. I can smell it a mile away."

"It REALLY WAS. You know what it's like growing up: you're all over the place. If I could take it back…"

"A BIT TOO LATE for that now, isn't it?" snapped Paul, not wanting to hear the baron talk any more.

"You didn't inform the pigs?" murmured the weak-sounding baron, his breath becoming more and more shallow, with the bullet still in his leg.

"Oh yeah," said Paul. "'Hello, I'd like to report a rape, I've just been raped outside a pub, by a group of men.' How do you think that would have gone down around here if it came out?"

The baron looked over to Paul, not quite knowing what to say.

The baron's mobile phone rang, and Carl slowly sat up and leant across the floor to grab it, still keeping an eye on Paul as he did.

Carl passed the phone to the baron, as the baron answered it.

"I'm nearby, boss, about a minute away. What is it you want me to take?"

"I'll tell you more when you get here." The baron slumped back into the position he was in after he'd been shot.

There was a sudden noise of a van or 4×4 pulling up outside, and the opening and slamming of the vehicle door shut.

The man walked through the front door of the house and headed towards the kitchen, where the three men were.

The man suddenly appeared for them all to see… it was Paul's best friend, JOHN.

John looked expressionless at the three of them, as Paul was glad to see his best friend.

"Ah, mate, THANK GOD you're here, but how did you know… hang on, WAIT A MINUTE, PLEASE DON'T SAY you are a part of all this."

John looked sorrowful in Paul's direction, not muttering a word.

"You FUCKING TRAITOR," scowled Paul, in John's direction.

"I'm sorry, mate, the money was just too good to turn down." John looked at Paul, again, showing no emotion towards his friend.

"Don't you FUCKING 'MATE' ME. HOW COULD YOU, after all we've been through?" Paul continued to scowl at his former friend's turning.

John turned to the baron, wanting to know what he wanted him to do.

"Are you ok, boss?" John asked, almost as concerned for the baron's welfare as he was of Paul's.

"You've been shot; we must get you to a hospital." John bent down to look at the baron's wound.

Paul seemed shell-shocked that someone he considered to be his best friend had actually got involved with drugs and was probably the baron's employee.

"Don't you FUCKING TOUCH HIM, my SO-CALLED FRIEND, and just how FUCKING LONG has this been going on? HOW THE FUCK COULD YOU? This isn't your scene at ALL, are you out of your FUCKING MIND? Do the others know: Gary, Charlie and Steve?" Paul was incensed that John, who he thought he knew inside out, would do such a thing.

"No, they don't know, and that's how it's going to remain, they don't need to find out, Paul, do they?"

"Oh, don't they?" fumed an incensed Paul. "Well, guess what? I've got news for you: they are GONNA FIND OUT just what a TREACHEROUS, CONNIVING, LYING BASTARD you REALLY ARE. I cannot BELIEVE you have betrayed me like this."

Paul continued to wave the gun in the direction of the injured baron, as his bodyguard looked on.

"What are you going to do, Paul?" John was concerned that he was waving a loaded gun around.

"We're not staying here… though HE can." Paul pointed in the direction of the baron. "Time to leave." He waved the gun in the direction of the door, signalling for both John and the bodyguard to leave.

"So, you REALLY ARE going to leave me here to die?" The baron was still bleeding heavily from his wound.

"I'd like to stay and chat but, yeah, I guess so." Paul was in no mood to be distracted; he knew that he had to get away, in case any of the baron's other henchman might decide to turn up.

John, Paul and the bodyguard Carl headed towards the black 4×4, no doubt given to John as some kind of getaway vehicle.

Paul had remembered to grab the holdall stashed full of drugs on the way out of the house; it was, after all, the loot that had been passed to him from Mr Barnes, and he was determined that he wasn't going to give it up.

Paul let Carl and John walk out in front first, as he kept a safe distance behind them, with the gun still pointing in their direction.

Both the bodyguard and John gingerly looked behind them, still seeing Paul holding the gun at them, and obeying Paul's orders.

"Now, FUCKING GET IN and drive." He ordered John to get in the driver's seat.

"YOU, you can get in the front too, but no funny business. I'll be sitting in the back watching you, and remember: I've got a loaded gun."

All three men got in the vehicle, as Paul asked, and were soon pulling off.

"Where are we going?" asked John, worried what Paul's plans were.

"I don't know yet. I've still not decided what I'm going to do with the two of you yet." Paul was still angry that his former best friend had betrayed him the way he had.

"Where the FUCK are we, anyway?"

John decided not to answer; the vehicle started to drive through a wooded area.

The drive was very bumpy, driving through trees and

hilly points in the woods, as John started to put his foot down harder on the accelerator.

"Why are you driving so hard?" Paul was vigorously rocking around in the back of the vehicle, as were the other two men, as speed had picked up.

"Slow the FUCK DOWN, we're going to cra—"

The vehicle was being driven at some speed when, all of a sudden, the vehicle drove over the top of a hill in the woods, and came crash-landing down an embankment, going down on its side uncontrollably, rolling down many times, hurtling towards a fast-flowing deep river, before grinding to a halt, hitting a tree on the way.

The men were all still in the vehicle, all of them bloodstained from the impact of the crash.

All men were unconscious, lying still for some time.

Paul's head was badly gashed, as were his ears, blood pouring from both, yet he remained unconscious.

John's head was also gashed, as was the bodyguard's, who was slumped down in his seat, motionless. None of the men had put their seatbelt on, and all three of them were badly hurt.

John slowly started to gradually open his eyes, unsure if the other men were still alive.

The vehicle was in a bad state, as John tried to come round.

He glanced in the back, to see Paul still appearing to lie unconscious.

John checked on the bodyguard, pulling his lifeless body back into his seat.

Again, there was no sign of life from him, but John was more concerned about trying to get out of the badly damaged vehicle.

He tried pushing at the driver's door to open it, vigorously pushing with as much energy as he could find, despite wincing in pain.

John was unsure if he had broken any bones, though his right arm was extremely painful, while he was pushing at the driver's door to try to open it.

John sat back in his seat, trying to catch his breath from the trauma.

He glanced back at Paul, but he still appeared unconscious, as was Carl.

"Paul, Paul, are you ok?" But there was nothing.

The vehicle started to budge from where it landed on the tree, and started to slide towards the fast-flowing river.

John knew that somehow he had to try to get out.

He again tried to force his door open, and finally it gave way, and opened.

John managed to pull himself out of the top, before he got out, sliding off and crumpling onto the embankment on his arm; again, wincing in pain, he felt that he had clearly done something to it.

It was fairly warm day, so at least he didn't have to battle against the cold.

John lay down, as he was still feeling the effects of the crash, but at least he was still alive.

The weight of the 4×4 was starting to come away from the tree that it hit, and was dangerously creaking slowly towards the river, and the river was deep.

John got to his feet and noticed that Paul had come round, in the back, still holding his gun.

Paul also gradually opened his eyes, and, with the gun held firmly tight, his head badly bruised and bloodied, managed to force his back door open, before he too pulled himself out, stumbling, pulling the full bag of drugs out with him, before crumpling onto the soft ground, still pointing the gun in John's direction, the heavy holdall lying beside him.

There was no sign of movement from the bodyguard, not that Paul cared; he too was glad to be alive.

Just as Paul got out, the vehicle suddenly gave way and slid towards the flowing river.

Neither man had the energy to stop it in any way, and, seeing no movement from the bodyguard, watched as it slid slowly into the river, before sinking down and out of view, with the bodyguard still inside.

Suddenly, it was just Paul and his former friend, John. Paul had managed to pull himself up against another tree, still badly hurt, but still able to point the gun in John's direction.

"So, what now? We can't stay here forever."

"Like I say, I've not FUCKING decided yet," Paul snarled. "I want to know WHY, and… DRUGS, JOHN? Are you out of your FUCKING MIND?"

"I needed the money, like I said; it was business, that's all."

"You've been part of this all along, haven't you? Bet you even knew I was trapped in that room, being tortured. What else do you know?"

"Look, like I say, it was business, I needed the money, and…" Just then, Paul flung himself in John's direction, and the two men started fighting.

Both men were exchanging blows, as much as they could muster, considering they were both injured from the crash.

The gun had been left over by the tree where Paul had left it, and, as both of them fought, one then the other tried to struggle to their feet to grab the gun.

Both men fought each other for some time, punches being traded, before Paul finally got the upper hand and managed to get to his feet before finally grabbing the gun.

Both men were out of breath, as Paul managed to get stumble back over to the tree, which he leant on after the car had come to a stand-still.

"I should just FUCKING SHOOT you, here and now, you FUCKING ARSEHOLE, doing what you've done, and getting involved in this shit. What else are you involved in?"

"Take a FUCKING GOOD LOOK AT YOURSELF, PAUL! You're a SHADOW of the man you used to be, so stuck up your own arse, thinking you're better than everyone else, strutting around with that woman of yours, thinking you're both something special, yet, all the time, your mother lies dead, and I bet you don't give a fuck."

Paul began to tremble, out of fear and anger.

"What are you talking about? My mother is home, getting on with her life after my dad. Don't you fucking DARE say that my mother is dead."

"She IS, you FUCKING WASTE OF SPACE, but then you only ever FUCKING cared about yourself anyway, didn't you? Then you decide to chuck your life away, getting wrapped up in drugs, and I bet you're LOVING IT."

Paul began to cry and shake with anger, shaking at the very thought that John might be right and that his mother might be dead.

"You're FUCKING LYING, my mother is not dead, you're just trying to wind me up."

"WAKE UP AND SMELL THE COFFEE, see, stuck up your own arse, like you always were, then, suddenly—" BANG! BANG!

Shots rang out from the gun that Paul was holding, and John was slumped down, with no movement from his lifeless body.

John was dead.

The sound of the gun seemed to echo through the woods, but there was no-one in sight.

Paul held the gun for a few moments, his eyes as wide as he could get them. He had shot his best friend, and he knew that he was probably dead.

Paul was motionless, not quite believing what had been happening, whether it was some kind of a dream, but it wasn't, and he realised that he had to try to get the hell away from wherever he was.

Paul was in shock, and shaking, and realised that he had to do something with the gun.

He got up and looked momentarily at John's lifeless body, before deciding to stuff the gun as far down into the holdall as he could, just in case he needed it along the way.

The day was starting to draw in, and he didn't seem to know where he was; he just knew that he was deep in woods, with no direction as to where to go.

'If I follow this river, it should lead me somewhere,' he thought.

Before he stumbled off to follow the river downstream, he walked over to John's dead body, and stood over him.

"Thanks for the memories, but you just went too far. You were a FOOL getting mixed up with all this; at least you're out of it now."

Paul gingerly kicked some leaves over his body, as much as he could, before walking back to the tree, picking up the holdall, and walking as best he could, following the direction of the river.

Paul was still quite badly hurt from the crash, and needed to take plenty of rests along the way.

He was still thinking back to the fight he'd had with John, before shooting him dead, and was starting to feel remorseful, but he was dead, and he couldn't do anything about it now.

He continued to trudge through the woods, taking regular breaks, but the night was drawing in, and it was starting to get dark and very cool, so he decided to try to find some shelter for the night.

He came across an old-looking hut that looked like it was ready to fall down, but it was somewhere to rest his head for the night.

He brushed away some leaves in the hut, and found a porn magazine. He put the holdall down, and went and sat down in the corner of the hut. The magazine was the other side of the hut, so he got back up, grabbed it and went and sat back down where he had set himself up.

He found an old, thin, brown blanket, and, despite the fact that it smelt of mould, and the stains on it that he didn't want to imagine what they might be, covered himself over with it, to try to keep himself as warm as he could.

The night drew in very quickly, but he had light coming from the glow of the moonlight shining through the woods.

Paul was feeling very cold and very alone. He picked up the magazine, knowing that it had probably been used a few times, and started to look through it.

There were lots of very grubby pictures of sexual

activity, between men and women, and other pictures, and this aroused him.

He was looking through the pictures, and started feeling very horny; his cock had become erect at the sight of the sexy pictures in the magazine.

Feeling alone, he slid his hand down the blanket and started to caress his hard erection.

He started to masturbate, though he knew how wrong it was, knowing everything that had happened that day. It seemed a strange thing to do but he was horny and he wanted a release.

He masturbated harder and harder, flicking through the pages as he did, getting turned on very quickly, before he exploded his cum all over himself, onto his stomach, having pulled his jeans down a little so he could hold his hard cock better.

He lay still for a moment, catching his breath after masturbating so hard, before rubbing his cum into his stomach and chest and pulling his jeans back up, as his limp cock started to rest.

He lay motionless, tossing the porn magazine away, as tears started to well up in his eyes.

Everything had seemed to happen in a flash, and he wasn't quite believing what had happened.

It was cold, but at least he had some warmth from the dirty, mouldy-smelling blanket. He decided to just get his head down, and get as much sleep as he could, before trying to find a way out of the woods, by following the river, as he had planned.

Morning broke, and he awoke to the sound of crows circling, probably seeing John's body, but he wasn't going to worry about that now; he just wanted to get away and find some forms of life.

His body was still in pain; he hadn't got much sleep with how much pain he was in from the crash.

He stood up, still feeling the effects of the previous day's events, and went over to grab the stash of drugs in the holdall. This was his meal ticket out.

He started to head back towards the river, where he had left John, and, as he approached, his body wasn't there.

Paul stood motionless once again, in shock. He was sure that John was dead but, if he was, where was his body? It was well away from the river, and the river hadn't risen overnight; there were no signs that it had, anyway. Had he dreamt that he'd shot him?

Paul went over to the tree that he had leant against the day before, and there were marks of where he had sat.

'Am I going mad?' he thought. 'I know I shot him, and he looked pretty dead.'

As he started to walk down to follow the river, he heard some noises, and, thinking that it might be more of the baron's henchmen, decided to duck down and take cover.

His breath started to quicken, thinking that he might need to make a run for it as best he could, just in case it was more of the baron's bodyguards.

He could definitely hear talking; there was more than one, he was sure of it.

He tried to be as quiet as he could, despite the pain to his body.

He winced as he tried to hide and get as comfy as he could, while trying not to make a sound.

The footsteps appeared to be getting closer, as Paul tried to manoeuvre around a big mound of mud that was covered by a layer of bright green grass.

As he continued to edge himself further around the mound, and away from whoever it was lurking nearby, he stepped on a twig, and it snapped as loud as a clap of thunder. Paul realised this, and spotted a tree that he was able to quickly crawl towards and hide behind, dragging the holdall as quickly as he could with him.

The men headed towards the mound, where they had heard the snap, to find nothing there.

One of the men did spot on the ground that something had been dragged towards the tree that Paul was standing behind, as the man started to gradually and carefully walk towards it.

As the man was approaching, Paul suddenly remembered that he had hidden the gun back in the bag, and he carefully slid his hand into the bag to grab it, making as little noise as he could.

Suddenly, the other man shouted towards him. As the man drew closer to the tree, Paul's breath once again quickened.

"Eddie, this way, I think I've spotted something or someone."

The man approaching the tree stopped and paused, turned around to walk away, before pausing once again, glancing back at the tree, before carrying on walking, then running, towards his partner.

Paul sighed with relief; he thought that he might have needed to shoot someone else, and it wasn't something that he was really used to doing.

He waited a while, gradually peering around the tree, to see if the men had gone.

Maybe they had moved John, but where? Maybe they had thrown John in the river.

There was very little noise now, so Paul decided to grab his things, along with the bag, and carefully work his way out of the woods.

He had to try to find a way out, and along some roads, so he could head back towards Barnwood, call in at the house, grab a few things, and give Dean a call.

He was still in no mood to call Sarah, but wanted to know what was happening with his mum.

He was gingerly walking through the woods, looking around him, in case any of the baron's bodyguards appeared.

He carefully trod on twigs and leaves, as he was still unsure if there was anyone around and also what had happened to John's body.

He managed to find the stream that he had passed on the way to the hideout, and started to walk along it.

All Paul could hear was the stream flowing, the slight wind blowing through the trees and birds singing and flapping their wings, but he realised that he still had to be cautious.

The stream seemed to go on for an eternity before he caught sight of a road.

He headed towards the road, still looking around him in case anyone turned up who he didn't want to see.

He walked along the lonely road for a good while, before a red car appeared in the distance.

Paul kept looking round as the car neared him, and he started to put his thumb out for a lift. But the car kept on going, sticking two fingers up as it whizzed past.

He carried on walking in one direction, not knowing where he was, not knowing if he was going in the right direction.

This clearly was in the middle of nowhere, as there hardly seemed to be any traffic, going in either direction; it seemed to be a pretty lonely road.

Paul walked on, before hearing the sound of another car on the horizon.

As the car got closer, Paul once again stuck his thumb out, hoping they would pull over and, sure enough, the blue BMW pulled up.

"Where are you heading?" said the rugged man.

Paul looked, and noticed that it wasn't any of the bodyguards of the drugs baron, so Paul replied to him.

"I'm heading towards Barnwood and Churchfield," replied Paul, with a slight hesitation in his voice, just in case it was one of the thugs that had been hovering around in the woods.

"Hop in; I'm heading that way myself," said the man.

Paul gingerly climbed into his car, with a slight nervousness, clinging tightly to his bag, which was still full of drugs.

Paul was keen not to really make any eye contact with the man, or as little as he had to.

The man could see that Paul was a little bedraggled, and blooded, looking like he hadn't washed for a while, and smelling like it too.

The man drove, while continually glancing over in Paul's direction, hoping that he'd start talking.

"You ok there? You've not said a word since you got in," said the man, giving a slight grin.

But Paul wasn't really in the mood for idle chat; he just wanted to get to where he was going, and not engage with a stranger.

"You're clinging onto your bag rather tight there, if you don't mind me saying," said the man, again hoping that Paul would engage in conversation, so the journey was less boring.

"I'm Neil, and you are?" But, again, Paul was having none of it; he just wanted to get back to an area that he knew, and didn't want to talk.

"You look like you've been through the mill a bit there, fella. You sure you don't want me to take you to—"

Paul interrupted him.

"If it's all the same to you, can you just drive me to Churchfield, please? I don't want to talk." He was just focussing on getting back to his mum's, to find out if she was ok.

Neil's car arrived in Churchfield, close to where Paul's mum and dad's house was.

"Here will be fine," a stone-faced Paul said to Neil, and upon opening the car door thanked Neil for the lift, before closing the door behind him, before watching Neil pull off.

He walked a few hundred yards to the house, before walking up the steps towards the front door, and it seemed eerily quiet, the curtains closed and the place in darkness.

He let himself in using the key that he had, and walked into the lounge, before dropping the bag on the floor.

"Mum? Mum?" he shouted. "Are you home?"

There was a deafening silence. It felt very cold, and something felt very wrong.

He found the burner phone that he had been given by Mr Barnes, and he was able to retrieve it when leaving the drugs den during his getaway, and decided to get on the phone to his brother Anthony.

Ring… ring… ring… ring…

"Hello, who's this?" came Anthony's voice.

"It's Paul." He knew that Anthony would be shocked to hear from him.

"Where the FUCK have YOU BEEN?" Anthony was clearly angry that his brother had gone missing all this time.

"Never mind where I've been. Where's Mum? Have you seen her?" Paul was totally unaware of sad news of his mother.

"Well, if YOU had been around, instead of swanning off to GOD FUCKING KNOWS WHERE, you'd have been around long enough to come and say goodbye to our mother at Barnwood Hospital, just as Chris and I did, as did your FUCKING AMAZING GIRLFRIEND, but WHERE WERE YOU? Probably in a gutter somewhere, holding a bottle, and there was me thinking that you had more about you, but, just like that other wayward brother Dean, you were NOWHERE to be seen."

"Wait, what the FUCK do you mean, say goodbye?" Paul was in a state of confusion, and his eyes started to well up with tears, and emotion started to run through his body.

"Are you DUMB? She's DEAD, and it's all YOUR FUCKING FAULT!" and at that point Anthony hung up the phone, still angry and confused with what he had just heard.

Paul crumpled up into a heap on the floor in the living room, as he burst into a loud and sorrowful cry of anguish.

'This CANNOT BE HAPPENING,' he thought, his head buried deep into his hands on the floor, where he had shared so many memories of growing up as a child, with many ups and downs as a family.

He decided to call Anthony back once again.

He answered almost immediately.

"WHAT DO YOU WANT NOW?" Anthony was still in no mood to talk to him.

"Where is Mum now?" Paul, even though he was still feeling very numb at the news he had been given, was trying to slowly compose himself.

"For YOUR INFORMATION, she's at Barnwood Hospital mortuary, but DON'T BOTHER trying to go down to see her. You HAD YOUR FUCKING CHANCE BEFORE, when you should have been a PROPER SON and been there for her, yourself and the rest of us. INSTEAD, you were represented by your AMAZING GIRLFRIEND, Sarah, who was a ROCK, for us all, including me, and even saw Mum during her last hours."

"Don't tell Sarah that I've called." Paul didn't want her knowing that he was around.

"Oh, DON'T YOU WORRY, I WON'T. Now, go back to your bottle, I'm SURE you're in need of a drink or two. I'll send you the details of when the funeral is but, in the meantime, FUCK OFF, and let me grieve alone with my family, you FUCKING WASTE OF SPACE," and, again, the phone disconnected.

Paul just continued to sit in a heap on the cold laminated floor, the house still in darkness, not knowing what to do, wiping tears from his eyes, his face puffy with the outburst of emotion that came from him.

He sat, almost motionless on the floor for what seemed like hours, and darkness had well and truly fallen in Churchfield.

He hadn't eaten for what seemed like days, but, after getting the devastating news of his mum, had no appetite to eat anyway.

He then picked himself up off the floor, and slowly started to walk around the eerily quiet house, slowly pulling open drawers of cupboards and chest of drawers around the house.

He found old pictures of them all as kids at the seaside, his mum and dad laughing, while they had been playing near the sea, finding pictures of his mum drying him off, during a frolic in the sea with his brothers.

There were hundreds of old photos.

He grabbed them out of the drawer, carefully sat down with them, and tried to hold back his emotions as he started to go through them, one by one.

He smiled, as he came across some that meant so much to him, as they all did over the years, but some were more special than others, meant more to him.

As he was going through them, smiling and crying almost at the same time, his mobile phone bleeped. It was Anthony.

Next Wednesday,
Barnwood Crematorium 2pm.
Paul paused for a moment to look at the text, knowing that his mum's passing was very real, and he had to get his head around the fact that she was gone.

At that point, he again started to burst out crying, and lay down on the photos, holding one or two in his hands as he began to wail with emotion once again; he felt lost and very angry.

The Wednesday of the funeral arrived, and everyone was at Barnwood Catholic Church, a church that Joan had often visited, along with her husband, Harold, and the church where they had married.

Joan and Harold had also taken the boys there as they were growing up, but none of them, except Anthony, kept going; indeed, he had even been taking his own children along, wanted his kids to have something to believe in, wanted them to have a faith, believe in a god, whichever god they wanted to believe in as they got older.

It was one in the afternoon, and everyone had turned up looking all dressed up for such a sorrowful occasion.

Anthony and Chris had arrived, both dressed in smart black suits and ties, and their boys stepped out of the car, looking very sad at the occasion of their grandma's passing, yet still looking smart in dark blue blazers and smart trousers, and gleaming black shoes.

Anthony's daughter Clarissa wore a dark purple dress, with dark purple shoes, again glistening in the bright sunshine.

It was a warm, clear-skied day, a few white fluffy clouds floating in the sky.

Joan used to love watching the clouds passing her window. She found them fascinating.

Harold used to ask her why she loved clouds so much.

But it was just her way of wondering how the world was.

Sarah also went to the service, and stepped out of her car, looking as elegant as ever.

She wore a dark blue one-piece dress, with matching shoes, a dress that clung to her hourglass figure, yet she hoped that it wasn't too much, and wouldn't turn too many heads, as she didn't want to take the focus away from Joan; after all, this was Joan's day.

She had previously asked Anthony, if he would mind, whether she could bring her assistant with her, Alice, to which Anthony had no objection.

Alice stepped out of Sarah's car, also looking very elegant, wearing a similar dress to Sarah's, a black dress and hat, with white buttons going up the back.

Alice wore some matching-coloured shoes, which also shone in the sunlight, when the sun gleamed over them.

Alice was conscious not to try grabbing Sarah's hand, as this would obviously cause some suspicion.

The Reverend Benedict Johnson stood at the entrance of the church, ready to welcome the congregation into his church.

Sarah scanned round, seeing so many people, some she didn't know but, with some looking so elderly, assumed that some of them may have been old friends, or indeed neighbours of Joan, people who may have known her and Harold down the years.

As she was looking round, she noticed a figure of a man standing at the back of the crowd.

It was Neil, whom she had not seen for a while.

She politely glided herself through the crowd, as they were slowly starting to make their way inside, and wandered up to him, with Alice following close behind.

"Hello, you," said a surprised Sarah. "Fancy seeing you here."

"Well, I kind of knew Joan and Harold, not much, and when I heard of her passing I thought I'd come and pay my respects."

Neil wore a very smart light-grey three-piece suit and matching sparkling shoes; he was clean-shaven and smelling like he'd stepped out of a beauty salon.

"You don't think anyone will mind me being here, do you?" he asked.

"Don't be silly," replied Sarah. "I'm sure they'll be grateful that you have come along to show your respects. How can anyone knock you for that? You've met my assistant, Alice, haven't you?"

"Yes, you introduced me to her in the pub that time, don't you remember?" He smiled.

Sarah allowed herself a little chuckle, as Alice grinned.

The hearse carrying Joan's coffin pulled up outside the church, and pallbearers had already been organised, as neither Chris nor Anthony could bring themselves to carry their mum's coffin inside; they were both worried that it might be all too much for them.

Both Anthony and Chris, both of their heads bowed, walked slowly behind the coffin as it made its way inside the church.

Most of the congregation had already made their way inside, as Reverend Johnson smiled at them, almost gesturing for them to make their way towards the entrance, allowing him to start the service on time.

"I guess we should start to think about making our way inside," grinned Sarah to both Neil and Alice, as they strode gently together towards the church door, before it was closed shut by the church warden.

The church was a pretty church that would comfortably hold around three hundred parishioners, with gleaming stained-glass windows that kept everyone inside warm, even though they were warm enough with it being such a lovely day, fitting for Joan.

Everyone had made their way to their pews, Anthony, Chris and their children all sitting at the front, with Sarah and Alice sitting just behind, and Neil just behind them.

There were lots of tears and sniffles among the congregation, but, of course, two noticeable absentees, in Paul and Dean, though Anthony had promised that he wouldn't tell Sarah that he had spoken to him, as much as he wanted to; besides, he was too angry and upset for his mum to even think about Paul and his other wayward brother, Dean.

"Let us all stand, and sing the first hymn in the order of service, that you will have found on your seats before you sat down, 'The Lord Is My Shepherd," said the Reverend Johnson to the congregation, and, almost in unison, everyone stood up as the organ music started to play.

In front of the congregation lay Joan, in her oak-finished coffin that looked very polished with the sun shining on it, just as everyone would have wanted, as Joan was everyone's shining light.

The service was beautiful, and elder brother Anthony had composed a few words for their mum that he wanted to read, though he was going to do so through the stinging tears that streamed from his eyes, wiping them away with his ever-dampening handkerchief, through almost every moment that the service went on.

After the hymn, the reverend spoke.

"Our dearly departed Joan's son Anthony has written a few words that he'd like to read to you. Anthony, if you'd like to make your way up to the altar," and, as the reverend stepped aside and went and sat back down on his chair nearby, Anthony gingerly and slowly rose to his feet and walked slowly towards the front of the church, and to face the congregation, so many that he didn't know, so he could read some words that he had composed.

"Our mum," he sniffled, "she was the best mum anyone could have wished for. I remember once, on a holiday somewhere in England, I can't remember exactly where it was, she pretended to be asleep in her deckchair, with a straw hat covering her eyes and face, protecting it from the glare of the sun, and our dad had sneaked some beer bottles into one of the picnic bags. Mum was never really a fan of Dad drinking while we were away as a family but, if Dad could try and get away with it, he would." Anthony smiled, with tears still streaming from his eyes, his handkerchief clasped tight, as if to try to strain some of the tears that had already built up inside it, with wanting to wipe away some more of the tears that he had, with still feeling the pain of their loss. "I watched him and, as quiet as he could, as not to disturb my mum from her sleep, would carefully try and open the bottle top. He managed to get it open, and started to drink it, but it wasn't beer he was drinking." He raised a smile again while remembering, trying to think happy thoughts on such a sad day. "I remember seeing my dad's face grimacing, and looking at what he thought was beer." Anthony chuckled to himself slightly, almost not giving any eye contact to the congregation of his sadness yet, as if he was almost starting to forget that it was a sad day, and more of a day of refection, and thinking of all the good times, and remembering what happened next.

"'How's your lemon squash?' Mum said to him, without moving a muscle. It was as if she had X-ray vision, having the straw hat on, covering her eyes from the sun, but you couldn't see through it, it was impossible." Anthony smiled. "'Do you really think you were going to sneak that beer past me, mister? Do you think I was born yesterday?' Dad saw the funny side, and we all laughed; funnily enough, Dad never tried to repeat that trick ever again. He knew he'd met his match in Mum, I guess, but they did love each other, and I feel SO PROUD to be able to call myself their son." Anthony went from feeling happier with the fun story that he shared with everyone, raising smiles and a few chuckles, to one filled with incredible sadness, and, once again, had to hold the damp handkerchief to his eyes, as streams of tears again engulfed him, his face looking puffy and blotchy with the emotion running through him.

He stood for a moment at the altar, not quite knowing what to do with himself, before glancing over at his mum's coffin, which was just to the left of him.

He carefully walked over to it, before giving it a loving kiss and wrapping his arms around it, wanting to say his final goodbyes.

A few more hymns were sung before it was time for the service to come to an end.

The pallbearers went to pick the coffin up, and carefully made their way out, and headed towards the waiting hearse; one of the pallbearers opened the back of the hearse, before the others slid the coffin inside and slowly started to make its way to where Joan was to be buried, next to her beloved Harold, who had been buried in Barnwood Cemetery not long before.

Anthony and Chris slowly walked behind, following their mum's coffin out, towards her final resting place.

As the brothers were near the entrance of the church, they noticed a smartly dressed, lonely figure of a man to their right, standing, head bowed, his arms crossed straight in front of him, sniffling away to himself, droplets of tears falling to the floor of the church, before looking up at both Anthony and Chris.

It was Dean.

The three of them gazed at each other momentarily, before Dean stepped away from his pew, flinging his arms, and sobbing uncontrollably, around his two brothers, forming a tight huddle, knowing that, despite their differences, this was all about their mum, and that they were there for her, and they needed to be strong for each other.

On a day full of emotion, bad feeling had to be put aside, though there was still no sign of Paul.

But at least there were three of them there to say their goodbyes to her.

The brothers all stood outside of the entrance, along with the priest, as the rest of the congregation made their way out, to be greeted by both the priest and the brothers.

"Thank you so much, Father, what a truly lovely service," sniffled Chris, trying to be strong and raise a smile for him.

"You're welcome. I didn't know your mum overly well, met her when she came to church, met your father too, what a lovely man; they always came across as being a truly wonderful human beings. You were so blessed to have them."

"Please join us at the wake, Father, after Mum has been buried; she would have loved that. We're having it at my house, if you're not otherwise engaged," asked Anthony.

"Oh, I don't want to be any bother to you," said the reverend.

"You really wouldn't be any bother, Father, and it would be lovely if you could be there, as long as you don't mind too many children running around you." Anthony was accommodating towards anything and everyone to do with the church, especially the one where his mum and dad had been married, and also attended. "It'll be around three-thirty this afternoon, after Mum's... you know, after Mum has been..." Anthony was still finding it hard to get his head around the fact that his mum was no longer around, but he knew that, though his feelings were still very raw, things would get better.

"As long as I wouldn't be in the way!"

"It would be an honour to have you there, Father. Here's the address; see you in a while." Anthony always carried business cards with him, showing his address and contact details, yet he didn't pass it out to everyone, just mainly in meetings and other important events.

Sarah and Alice made their way out of the church, both their heads bowed in respect.

"Thank you for coming, Sarah," said Anthony. "You've been such a rock to me; don't know how I'd have got through this without you." Anthony gave Sarah a gentle hug, Sarah returning the hug, wrapping her arms around Anthony as Alice stepped gently away, giving the two of them room, with a slight hint of jealousy.

Anthony pulled away from Sarah, hugging her for what seemed like an eternity.

"Ah, you must be Alice." He smiled in her direction. "Heard so much about you."

"All bad, I hope." Alice smiled awkwardly, wanting to relieve the tension as much as possible.

Anthony smiled politely in Alice's direction, not being able to raise a smile for anyone, being so overcome with grief for his late mum.

"I guess, then, we should go and do this; can't prolong it much longer." Chris was trying to rally everyone to head off towards Barnwood Cemetery, so they could lay their mum to rest.

"Need a lift, girls?" Chris asked.

"No, it's ok, we've come in my car; we'll meet you there." Sarah was looking out for Neil, but could not see any sign of him. "We'll just go, Alice. I'm sure Neil knows how to get to the cemetery, if he decides to come."

Everyone made their way out of the church car park, slowly following the hearse, slowly making its way towards the cemetery, which was near her home village of Churchfield, on the borders of Barnwood.

"I'm sorry I've neglected you a bit, Alice, but I will make it up to you, once all this has calmed down a bit. I have had to be there for Anthony and Chris, and for Joan too, of course." Sarah put her hand on Alice's leg in reassurance, squeezing it gently.

"I know, its ok, I know the situation but, rest assured, I will hold you to that." Alice grinned in Sarah's direction.

The time was fast approaching two in the afternoon, and the hearse had finally reached its destination, followed by a swarm of cars, with Anthony, Chris and Dean following the hearse in, with Sarah and Alice a car or two further back.

All the vehicles managed to find a space in the cemetery

car park, as the pallbearers got out to get the coffin carrying Joan out of the back of the hearse.

Anthony, Chris and Dean sat motionless, watching their mum being carried towards the graveyard, and the plot where Harold lay.

Tears once again engulfed the brothers, but, knowing it was something that they had to do, got out of the car, the three of them puffy and red-faced, with the crying that they had been doing, and slowly followed the coffin once again, followed by the rest of the congregation.

Alice was struggling with wanting to hold Sarah's hand, but Sarah gave her a meaningful glance.

"We'll have time for all this, just not today, ok?"

"I'm sorry, just wanting to hold you so much, Sarah."

"Me too," Sarah whispered back, "but we'll have plenty of time for each other, ok?"

Loud but slow bells started to chime out, as Reverend Johnson had made his way to the cemetery almost without being seen by anyone.

The Reverend walked slowly in front of the coffin, as he and the rest of the congregation headed towards the burial plot.

The pallbearers laid the coffin down just outside the plot, as the rest of the congregation gathered round.

"We gather here today to mark this sad occasion, of the burial of Joan Margaret Arnold. May the Lord bless you and watch over you always. May the Lord make his face shine upon you and be gracious to you in the Kingdom of Heaven. May he guide your soul, giving you eternal life in the resurrection of life itself. May he surround you, your brothers and sisters of Heaven, and may the Lord look kindly on you, giving you eternal peace, in the name of the Father, and of the Son, and of the Holy Spirit, amen."

"Amen," replied the gathering.

The reverend's words brought a tear to everyone who had gathered to say their final goodbyes to Joan, as they bowed their heads in respect, as the pallbearers, pulled up the ribbons to lower the coffin down, as cries of emotion came from everyone.

Sarah was stood next to Anthony, as he had had an outpouring of grief, and he rested his head on her shoulder, crying uncontrollably.

Sarah pressed her hand on his now-wet cheek, as Alice also cosied up to her, resting her head on her lover's shoulder.

When Joan's coffin had finally come to rest, Chris, Anthony and Dean all threw mounds of dirt on top of the coffin.

Anthony had brought some sunflowers, which were Joan's favourite, and he also thew these in.

The gravediggers, who stood back from the gathering, picked up their spades, as the crowd had started to disperse.

The brothers, along with Sarah and Alice, stood around for a while, as the others in the gathering all swept past, again offering their condolences to them.

Sarah rested her head on Anthony's shoulder, feeling the same anguish that the brothers were feeling, as he ran his fingers through Sarah's hair, her tears falling onto his suit jacket, as Alice stroked her arm, trying to show her support.

She suddenly shot up off his shoulder and spun round, as she could sense someone's eyes boring a hole into the back of her head.

"Paul?" she shouted. "Is that you there?"

There were rows of trees further up from the crematorium, and she could have sworn she had seen him, standing and watching.

"I think I must be dreaming, but where the HELL is he?"

"Come on, let these guys do their work," said Chris. "I'm sure they have other things to do, apart from waiting for us to move," and, just as Chris had finished speaking, they all gradually walked off towards the car park, to head back to Anthony's and to the wake, while Sarah kept looking back towards the trees, where she thought she had seen the figure of Paul.

As the congregation had disappeared, and had all driven off, Paul walked slowly towards the plot where his mum had just been buried.

Tears started to roll down his cheeks, followed by an outpouring of grief, not quite believing that he wasn't going to see his mum anymore.

The gravediggers had finished digging, and had gone off to work on a different plot, with another grieving family.

Paul continued to sob uncontrollably, as he fell into a heap by his mum's grave.

"What have we done, Mum?" he sobbed. 'I should have been there for you, but I'm going to sort this out, mark my words, people will pay for this,' he chillingly thought.

He sat by her grave for a few hours, and it was starting to get dark before he lifted himself up off the floor.

He wiped away what tears were left, giving her one last look before turning around and walking away.

He had booked himself a taxi to get there, and rang the same firm to take him back, back to his mother's house, knowing that he had things to sort out of hers, not knowing if anyone else was going to do it.

The taxi pulled him up outside the house, paid the driver, and slowly made his way inside.

The house was all dark, and it was just how he wanted it, not wanting anyone to know that he was there.

He pulled the curtains closed, but there was sufficient light coming from a full moon shining through the back window, so he decided to use that for light.

He mooched around in the lounge, picking up from the sideboard old pictures of his mum and dad on their wedding day, grinning to himself slightly as he did so.

It was eerily quiet in the house, not something that he was used to.

He reminisced back to the time when he would run around, playing with his toys, playing hide-and-seek with his other brothers, and playing with his dad, while Mum cooked in the kitchen.

It was a warm and happy place to be back then; not now everything had changed, and he was not in the mood to be messed with.

He found some old photos stuffed in a cupboard in the lounge, hundreds of them, so he decided to pull them all out at once, as they fell to the floor, almost covering the whole of the floor space.

He sat on the floor, before deciding to lie on his front as he went through what must have been thousands of photos of them all growing up.

So many of them had faded, caught by sunlight, but he could still make out many of them.

He sifted them all out all over the floor, lying on many,

crying as he looked through so many memories, before drifting off to sleep, still clutching some of the photos in his hand.

His eyes opened, with some of the photos stuck to his face, and day had broken; light was shining from outside: he'd been lying there all night.

He heard some traffic outside and peered out of the window to see what was happening.

Two of Mr Barnes's bodyguards had turned up.

He quickly pulled himself down and, as out of sight as he could get, grabbed the bag containing the drugs and went into the kitchen, to grab as many knives and damaging instruments as he could find.

As much as he had the gun in the bag, there was no silencer on it, so he knew it would make a noise if he was to use it, but, if he had to use it, he would.

He quickly and quietly made his way up the stairs, to choose which of the bedrooms to go into, one where he knew wardrobes would be, somewhere where he could hide; hopefully they wouldn't find him.

He quickly darted into the bedroom that he used to share with his brothers growing up, quietly opened the wardrobe door, and pulled himself inside, closing the door as quietly and quickly as he could.

His breath quickened, as he could hear voices and footsteps from outside the house.

He could hear talking outside.

"You take the front door, I'll take the back, but be discreet: don't want to arouse any suspicion," Paul managed to hear.

"If he's not here, we'll try his house, but I've heard he's

been here a lot, so we need to fucking find him and kill him, grab the drugs and get back to Mr Barnes."

Paul heard one of the doors cranked open, wasn't sure which one, but both men were clearly inside.

"He's clearly fucking been here, there's all these out on the floor, look, must be him," one of the bodyguards said to the other. "I knew we couldn't trust him with the deliveries out on his own."

Paul's breath quickened, as he could hear footsteps coming up the stairs, but he knew that he had to be as quiet as he could be, otherwise he'd be an easy find.

He could hear the floorboards creak as he heard footsteps come into the bedroom that he was in.

The bodyguard looked around the room and checked under the bed, before seeing the wardrobe and heading towards it.

"Mike, come and see this," the other bodyguard called.

Mike paused, looking at the wardrobe before turning round, and headed out of the room.

Paul saw this as an opportunity to quietly come out of the wardrobe, pulling the bags of drugs with him, before closing it shut, as quietly as he could.

He slowly started to make his way towards the bedroom door.

He peered around it to see both bodyguards engrossed in something in another of the rooms, before quietly trying to leave the room, totally forgetting that the floorboards creaked, especially the one in the bedroom that he slept in.

"There he is, let's get him!"

Paul raced down the stairs as fast as his legs could carry him, especially with carrying the bag of drugs too.

Paul was nearly down the bottom of the stairs, but one of the bodyguards caught him up and grabbed his legs, before they both tumbled to the bottom, throwing punches in each other's direction.

One of the bodyguards, Mike, was soon on top of Paul, punching him, but Paul managed to use his weight to push him off, as both men grappled on the floor, continually throwing punches towards one another.

The other bodyguard was also down the stairs, and a three-way fight erupted.

Both bodyguards were the throwing punches at Paul, falling over furniture along the way.

Chairs and tables were hurling into the air, as the bag of drugs were flung over to one side.

The bodyguards were taking turns to throw punches in Paul's direction, but he was giving as good as he was getting, but was finding it hard to fight off one well-built man, let alone two.

Mike had managed to get Paul into a headlock, but Paul was able to free himself by throwing his elbow into his face, almost knocking the heavy bruiser unconscious. Paul raced towards the bag, where he had earlier put all of the knives, and where the gun had been hidden.

He had almost got to the bag, before the other bodyguard grabbed him from behind, pulling Paul back down to the floor.

Just as he was grabbed, he managed to fight the bodyguard off; he grabbed the bag and was just able to undo the zip and pulled out a knife. Just as the bodyguard was about to pounce back onto him, he managed to turn himself around, having been lying on his front after the struggles, and plunge the carving knife deep into the chest of the bodyguard, killing him.

He pulled the knife out of his chest, and headed towards the other bodyguard, Mike.

As Paul approached him, Mike still appeared to be lying down after Paul had elbowed him into the head.

As Paul was about to plunge the knife into Mike, the bodyguard managed to stretch across and grab Paul's legs, pulling him to the floor once again.

Another fight ensued, and both men were trading blows.

As Paul's legs were pulled from him, the blood-soaked knife was flung in another direction, and away from both of them.

"You're going to die, you piece of shit," said Mike, as he was sitting on Paul, punching him hard to the face. "I KNEW the boss should never have trusted you from the beginning."

Paul was almost out cold from the barrage of punches that had been aimed in his direction.

"Now to fucking finish you off, once and for all."

Paul lay pretty motionless on the floor near the kitchen, exhausted from the energy he had used from the fighting of two big men.

Suddenly, Mike reappeared, this time with the knife in hand, and was about to plunge it into Paul, before Paul managed to pull himself away, and the knife plunged into the floor instead, missing Paul by inches.

He managed to summon up enough energy to punch Mike in the face once again, hurtling him to the floor.

This time, the knife had not gone too far, but was now out of the grasp of both men.

Another fight entailed, as both men grappled on the floor, trading blows once again.

The fighting went on for a little while, punching and pulling at each other, trying to gain some initiative.

As they grappled, Mike managed to climb on top of Paul, and was beginning to strangle him.

Paul was trying all he could to feel around the floor; surely the knife wasn't too far away.

Just as Paul was starting to lose consciousness, he felt the knife, and managed to plunge it straight into Mike's neck, again killing him stone dead.

Mike's dead body collapsed on top of Paul, who then had to push him off.

Both bodyguards were now dead.

Paul sat exhausted on the floor, but realised that he couldn't leave their bodies where they were, as he knew that, at some point, his brothers were going to come round to the house to sort things out.

'I've got to move them, but where?' he thought. 'Got to get myself cleaned up too, wash all this blood off me.'

Paul managed to find a few black bin liners, and managed to put the bodies in them.

It was a struggle, as both men were so heavy, but he knew that he had to do it.

He managed to get three layers of bin bags on them, before opening the back door, and pulling one of them out, and into the garden, being wary that there wouldn't be any more blood from the house to the garden.

The body thumped to the floor as it was dragged outside.

Harold and Joan had a particularly large garden, and at

the very top was a large, ungrassed, muddy patch, and this is where Paul decided to dump them.

He pulled the first of the bodies to the top, and pushed it as far into the corner as he could, out of sight of prying neighbours.

He trudged back to the house, feeling quite exhausted with the fighting and dragging of the first body up to the mount.

He grabbed the other bag and, once again, pulled it into the garden, thudding onto the floor with the weight of the man inside.

Again, he pulled the bag up to where he had laid the other body, and pushed them together as close as he could.

He grabbed some dead leaves and old tree branches, and threw them over the bags, to try to cover them up as much as he could.

He made his way back to the house and looked around for something to clean the blood up from the floor.

Thankfully, most of the house was laminated, so at least there was no carpet to stain.

He closed and locked the back door behind him and found some floor cleaner and an old blue cloth.

There were quite large pools of blood that he had to clean up first.

He used the cloth, and soaked up as much of the blood as he could, before rinsing the cloth under the tap in the kitchen.

He did this on the first pool of blood first, before spraying the floor with the floor cleaner, and wiping up the rest of the blood with it.

He repeated this on the second pool of blood, where

he had managed to kill the other man, and started to spray floor cleaner onto the area where the pool of blood was.

He stood back, to look and see if he had managed to get all of the blood off the floor, and he had.

'THE KNIFE,' he thought.

He grabbed it from the floor, took it into the kitchen and began to wash it.

He scrubbed it as hard as he could, wanting to wash both the blood off it and the memory of what had just happened.

He put the knife away, along with the rest of the knives that were still in the bag that he had grabbed before they broke in, and decided to go and take a shower, put some fresh clothes on, and chuck his blood-soaked clothes in another bin bag and throw them in the bin outside.

He headed towards the shower room, stripped off his bloody clothes, turned on the shower, and made his way inside, blood dripping from his still-toned body, and into the shower floor.

He pressed his hand onto the shower wall, just taking in what had occurred moments before, the shower water bounding from his wet hair, and deciding on his next move.

He quickly freshened up, went to the bedroom to get some fresh clothes, spray his deodorant, and feel fresh again, something he hadn't felt for what seemed like ages.

'Time for stage two,' he thought.

He made his way downstairs, gathered up all of the photos that he had looked at the night before, and managed to now put them all away, as best he could.

He pushed the cupboard door closed, looked for something quick to eat, and knew that he was needing to make a phone call to someone.

He managed to find an unopened, yet slightly out-of-date large chocolate bar in the cupboard in the kitchen, and unwrapped it, before sitting down on the sofa.

He grabbed his phone and started to make a phone call.

Ring… ring… ring… ring.

The line connected.

"Hi, it's me, you owe me a favour, remember? Now, listen up, I'm going to tell you EXACTLY what I want you to do, and when."

A few moments later, and the conversation finished.

It was time for Paul to make his way back to the house that he shared with Sarah.

A few weeks had passed, with no word from Paul, and the girls went straight back to work the next day, Sarah sporting a now-disappearing purple bruise on her face that her employees had all noticed but decided not to say anything, despite Sarah's best efforts to cover it up with make-up.

"I'm going to go back to the house tonight, Alice; he's not going to drive me out."

"Don't you think it's too soon?"

"I'll go back tonight, and I'll text you as soon as I'm there."

"Promise?"

"Yes, I promise." Sarah calmed Alice's uncertainty.

The day passed, and Mr Yang's orders were nearly complete, ready for shipping.

The employees left for the day, bidding the girls goodbye, as they always did, before closing the door behind them.

"Are you SURE you want to go back there tonight?"

"Yes, or I never will, as lovely as it has been staying at yours."

The two embraced, and kissed in the office, as they always had, having closed their laptops and putting their files away.

They closed the office up, before leaving the building, Sarah locking up behind her, as she always had.

They said their goodbyes to each other, as Sarah pulled away, after getting in her car, watching Alice walking home in her mirror.

Sarah did wonder if she was doing the right thing, but decided to stay strong.

She got home, with the house plunged into darkness.

She nervously got out of her car, grabbing her bag and phone along the way, and gingerly walked towards the front door, before carefully letting herself in.

It was eerie.

There was no sign of him; it was spookily quiet.

Suddenly, her phone beeped, making her jump.

I'm staying at John's for a while.

She was still a bit on edge, knowing how he'd reacted before, and she didn't know if he was at John's or not.

She carefully opened each door, and it did appear that she was alone.

She decided to text Alice, as she promised.

I'm home, and he's not here. He's just texted, saying that he's staying at a friend's for a while.

Alice replied.

Do you want me to come over?

Not tonight. Tomorrow night maybe, perhaps have some fun?

You're on. See you in the morning. Might bring something kinky with me.

Sarah smiled to herself.

She grabbed herself something to eat, and, while it was heating, went to make sure that the front door was locked, so he could not come in.

The night passed without incident.

The next day arrived, and Alice was in work.

She had brought Sarah's suitcase in with her, along with the drawings, something that the other employees found a bit strange.

Why did Alice have them?

Sarah got into work, and the day went as smoothly as any other.

Mr Yang's order had been processed, and despatched that day, and Sarah rang him to inform him of the impending order.

Mr Yang thanked her and paid her accordingly, via a wired transfer, as he always had.

"We still on for tonight, Sarah?" whispered Alice. "Got something special in mind for you," she teased, raising her eyebrows, and biting her bottom lip.

"Mmm… have you now?" said Sarah, licking her lips. "Looking forward to that."

The day drew to a close, and both Sarah and Alice were feeling very turned on, and wet, at what was in store later.

They said their goodbyes in the office, as usual, anticipating the nights events.

"GOD, I WANT YOU," Sarah purred.

She raced home, after locking up the building, showered, and put on her sexiest see-through lingerie.

She was feeling so excited at the thought of seeing Alice.

Suddenly, she thought she heard something, or someone, come in the back door; it freaked her out.

She crept over towards the door, feeling a little edgy, and noticed that it was slightly ajar, so, not seeing anyone around, closed it gently behind her.

'Maybe it was a slight gust that blew it open,' she thought.

She was too excited at the thought of seeing Alice, so she tidied her hair up and made sure she looked her best for her.

They had arranged around seven o'clock, and, sure enough, the doorbell rang almost spot on the hour.

'Right on time,' Sarah thought.

She opened the door and saw Alice standing in the doorway, clutching a bag and some bubbly.

Alice had never looked so good, or smelt so good.

"You waiting for ME?" Alice teased, with a sexy smile.

She walked in, brushing her hand across Sarah's breasts, her nipples even more erect at the sight of Alice.

Alice closed the door with her foot, and, putting down on the floor the bits she was clasping, Sarah started to passionately kiss her, while removing her coat.

"I'll grab some glasses for that bubbly, maybe take it into the bedroom," teased Sarah.

Alice stroked Sarah's bum as she walked by, as she headed to the kitchen for the glasses.

"I've got something special for you." Alice smiled sexily.

Sarah smiled back with anticipation.

Sarah put the glasses on her bedside table, and grabbed the champagne from Alice.

She grabbed Alice's hand and led her to the bedroom.

As Sarah unpopped the cork to start pouring, she watched Alice slowly unzip her dress from the side, and wiggle out of it, revealing a lacy see-through bra, with matching stockings and suspenders.

Sarah was starting to touch herself, feeling very turned on and wet, just watching her.

"WOW, you look SO HOT, Alice."

"Close your eyes," Alice asked.

Sarah obliged, excited at the thought of what was going to happen.

Alice strode over to Sarah and put a blindfold on her. Sarah was shaking with anticipation.

She went back over to Sarah, lying on the bed, removing her lingerie, leaving Sarah totally naked.

She then went into her bag that she had brought with her and, Sarah hearing a jangle, pulled out a few sets of handcuffs.

She locked Sarah's hand in one, and the other to the bedframe. She then did the same to the other hand, with the other set, followed by more handcuffs for both of her ankles.

Sarah was totally at the mercy of Alice, but it made her very wet.

Sarah thought she could hear Alice removing her own lingerie, and suddenly felt her climb on Sarah and grind herself between Sarah's legs.

She then felt Alice feel her breasts, while wearing gloves. This felt strange, yet very erotic.

Suddenly, Alice's hands were around Sarah's throat, as

she ground herself harder on Sarah, while pressing harder onto Sarah's neck.

Sarah was struggling to breathe, and was trying to fight Alice off as best as she could.

"Aaa… GET OFF ME… GET OFF ME."

Sarah cried out but she was powerless to stop her, and, as she continued to struggle, Alice pressed harder on her neck.

Sarah was soon motionless as the front door was flung open.

"Is it done?" called Paul.

"Yes, it's done." Alice smiled.

"Thank you, my AMAZING WIFE, you're SO CLEVER to have dreamt this idea up."

"Well, you did the same for me, my DARLING HUSBAND, getting rid of Stacey for me." Alice smirked.

"Ok, my beautiful angel, get dressed, and let's get the HELL OUT OF HERE. It's a shame John didn't run her off a CLIFF the day he ran her off the road."

Alice left Sarah's lifeless body where she lay, and was dressed in an instant.

They ran out of the door, closing it behind them, and into Paul's waiting car, before speeding off into the ever-darkening, yet full-mooned night.